THE
WANDERING HILL

Also by Larry McMurtry
in Large Print:

Terms of Endearment
Anything for Billy
Some Can Whistle
Buffalo Girls
Streets of Laredo
Comanche Moon
Crazy Horse
The Last Picture Show
Texasville
Duane's Depressed
Walter Benjamin at the Dairy Queen
Roads
Boone's Lick
Sin Killer

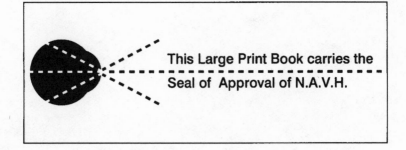

This Large Print Book carries the
Seal of Approval of N.A.V.H.

LARRY McMURTRY

THE
WANDERING HILL

THE BERRYBENDER NARRATIVES, BOOK 2

WHEELER
PUBLISHING

Published in 2003 by arrangement with Simon & Schuster, Inc.

Wheeler Large Print Hardcover Series.

The text of this Large Print edition is unabridged.
Other aspects of the book may vary from the original edition.

Set in 16 pt. Plantin by Liana Walker.

Printed in the United States on permanent paper.

Library of Congress Cataloging-in-Publication Data

McMurtry, Larry.
   The wandering hill : a novel / Larry McMurtry.
      p. cm.
   ISBN 1-58724-437-3 (lg. print : hc : alk. paper)
   1. British — West (U.S.) — Fiction.   2. Eccentrics and eccentricities — Fiction.   3. Yellowstone River — Fiction.
4. Women immigrants — Fiction.   5. Young women — Fiction.   6. Large type books.   I. Title.
PS3563.A319W36 2003b
813'.54—dc21   2003045063

The Berrybender Narratives *are dedicated to the secondhand booksellers of the Western world, who have done so much, over a fifty-year stretch, to help me to an education.*

As the Founder/CEO of NAVH, the only national health agency solely devoted to those who, although not totally blind, have an eye disease which could lead to serious visual impairment, I am pleased to recognize Thorndike Press* as one of the leading publishers in the large print field.

Founded in 1954 in San Francisco to prepare large print textbooks for partially seeing children, NAVH became the pioneer and standard setting agency in the preparation of large type.

Today, those publishers who meet our standards carry the prestigious "Seal of Approval" indicating high quality large print. We are delighted that Thorndike Press is one of the publishers whose titles meet these standards. We are also pleased to recognize the significant contribution Thorndike Press is making in this important and growing field.

Lorraine H. Marchi, L.H.D.
Founder/CEO
NAVH

* Thorndike Press encompasses the following imprints: Thorndike, Wheeler, Walker and Large Print Press.

Book 2

Abandoning the steamer *Rocky Mount*, which is stuck in the ice near the Knife River, the Berrybender expedition makes its way overland to the confluence of the Missouri and the Yellowstone, where we find them snugly ensconced at the trading post of Pierre Boisdeffre.

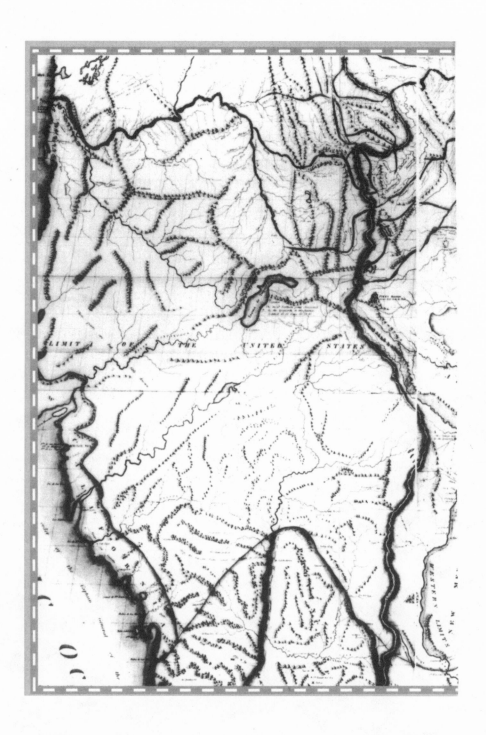

But while none, save these, of men living, had done, or could have done, such things, there was much here which — whether either could have done it or not — neither had done . . .

GEORGE SAINTSBURY

CONTENTS

Characters

CHARACTERS

MOUNTAIN MEN

Hugh Glass
Tom Fitzpatrick (The Broken Hand)
Jim Bridger
Kit Carson
Eulalie Bonneville
Joe Walker
Milt Sublette
Bill Sublette
Zeke Williams

FROM *Sin Killer*

Lord Berrybender
Tasmin
Bess (Buffum)
Bobbety
Mary
Sister Ten (*later*, Kate)

Gladwyn, *valet, gun bearer*
Cook
Eliza, *kitchen maid*
Millicent, *laundress*
Venetia Kennet, *cellist*
Señor Yanez, *gunsmith*

Signor Claricia, *carriage maker*
Piet Van Wely, *naturalist*
Tim, *stable boy*
Father Geoffrin, *Jesuit*
Jim Snow (The Raven Brave; Sin Killer)
Toussaint Charbonneau, *interpreter-guide*
Coal, *his wife*
George Catlin
John Skraeling
Malgres

NEW

Pierre Boisdeffre, *trader*
Pomp Charbonneau
William Drummond Stewart
Prince Maximilian zu Wied-Neuwied
Karl Bodmer, *his painter*
William Ashley, *trader*
Herr Hanfstaengl, *Pomp's old tutor*
David Dreidoppel,
    Prince Maximilian's hunter

INDIANS

The Hairy Horn, *Oglala Sioux*
Little Onion, *Jim's Ute wife*
Otter Woman, *Minataree*
Weedy Boy, *Minataree*
Squirrel, *Minataree*
Blue Thunder, *Piegan Blackfoot*
Climbs Up, *Minataree*

Skunk, *Assiniboine*
Bad Head, *Assiniboine*
Red Crow, *Assiniboine*
Old Moose, *Piegan Blackfoot*
Antelope, *Piegan Blackfoot*
Two Ribs Broken, *Piegan Blackfoot*
The Partezon, *Sioux*
Limping Wolf, *Piegan Blackfoot*
Quiet Calf, *Piegan Blackfoot*
Red Weasel, *Piegan Blackfoot*
Bull, *Piegan Blackfoot*
Red Rabbit, *Piegan Blackfoot*
Wing, *Piegan Blackfoot*
Three Geese, *Sans Arc*
Grasshopper, *Sans Arc*
Cat Head, *Sans Arc*
Big Stealer, *Sans Arc*
Little Stealer, *Sans Arc*
Greasy Lake, *shaman*
Walkura, *Ute*
No Teeth, *Ute*
Na-Ta-Ha, *Ute*
High Shoulders, *Ute*
Skinny Foot, *Ute*

1

. . . tall, gaunt, furious, snow in his hair and beard, and murder in his eyes . . .

The old mountain man — tall, gaunt, furious, snow in his hair and beard, and murder in his eyes — burst into the big room of Pierre Boisdeffre's trading post just as the English party was sitting down to table — the table being only a long trestle of rough planks near the big fireplace, where a great haunch of elk dripped on its spit. Cook had just begun to slice off generous cuts when out of the winter night the wild man stormed. Tom Fitzpatrick, called the Broken Hand, had just been filling a pipe. Before he could fully turn, the tall intruder dealt him a blow that sent him spinning into a barrel of traps — man and barrel fell over with a loud clatter.

"Good Lord, it's old Hugh Glass," Pomp Charbonneau said, turning, Tasmin thought, rather white, a surprising thing to see. Pomp Charbonneau, educated in Germany, as correct with knife and fork as any European, was a man not easily discommoded.

"Hugh Glass he may be, but why has he

struck down the Broken Hand?" Mary Berrybender piped, in excited surprise.

Before Pomp could answer, the furious stranger rushed past Tom Fitzpatrick and leapt at young Jim Bridger, who, with his partner, Kit Carson, had been nodding on a pile of blankets — both youngsters, tired from a day of trapping, came unwillingly awake.

"Why, Hugh!" Jim Bridger said — he leapt up just in time to keep the invader from grabbing him by his throat. Pomp Charbonneau half rose from his chair, but then settled back. Several of the mountain men — bald Eulalie Bonneville, Bill Sublette and his brother, Milt, Joe Walker, all of them as shaggy in their tattered buckskins as bears — stumbled hastily out of the way of the combatants. Kit Carson, who managed with difficulty to get his eyes open, soon opened them wider when he saw that his friend Jim Bridger was locked in mortal combat with Hugh Glass.

Kit immediately jumped into the fray, as did Tom Fitzpatrick, once he got free of the traps. Soon several mountain men were clinging to old Hugh's back; they smashed into a shelf, pots fell, crockery broke, and the old parrot Prince Talleyrand, a great favorite with the mountain men, flew up into the rafters to escape the commotion. Pierre Boisdeffre, the proprietor and landlord, rushed out of a storeroom and began to declaim indignantly in French; he surveyed the spreading carnage with dismay. For a moment it seemed to the startled spectators that the old man, in his terrible anger, might defeat them all. Five mountain men clung to his back; soon all of them crashed to the floor and rolled around in confusion, scratching, biting, kicking, as Monsieur Boisdeffre continued his futile protests.

"Hugh Glass is supposed to be dead, killed by a grizzly bear," Pomp explained. Several mountain men now contented themselves with sitting on the old fellow, waiting for his fury to subside.

"If that disputatious gentleman's dead, then he's pretty active for a ghost," Tasmin remarked, indicating to Cook that it was time to serve the cabbage — cabbage was the only thing in the way of a vegetable that the Berrybenders had been able to bring with them on their hard trek overland from the steamer *Rocky Mount*, though a happy consequence of unloading the cabbages was the discovery of their missing sister, Ten, aged four years; little Ten had evidently been living happily amid the cabbages for some weeks, missed by no one.

Some vittles, of course, had to be left with stout Captain Aitken, who had stayed behind to defend his icebound vessel during the chill months ahead. Marooned with him were seven *engagés,* the old Hairy Horn, Toussaint Charbonneau and his young wife, Coal, Master Jeremy Thaw — too damaged from his clubbing at the hands of the late Fraulein Pfretzskaner to survive a hard trek in deep chill — and the Danish painter Holger Sten, who argued that if he came ashore his paints would surely freeze, a consideration that had not deterred the American painter George Catlin from disembarking with the English party. Throughout the lengthy packing and departing the Hairy Horn, half naked, had annoyed them all by repeatedly singing his death song, though everyone had long since stopped expecting the old chieftain to die.

"Tell us, Pomp — why is Mr. Glass so very angry with Jim Bridger and the Broken Hand?" the ever-curious Mary piped.

Pomp was about to attempt an answer, but Tasmin, out of patience with her inquisitive sister, picked up her fork and warned him off.

"We're eating, Mary — no interrogations," Tasmin said. "It's hardly to be considered surprising when mountain men fight — I can think of one I wouldn't mind fighting with myself, if only he'd show himself."

She meant her husband, Jim Snow, known to some as the Sin Killer, who refused absolutely to take his meals at the trading post, or to sleep under its roof, either; a life spent almost entirely outdoors on the raw Western frontier had unfitted Jim Snow for life of an indoor, or civilized, sort. Walls and roofs made him feel so close that he got head-aches; he quite refused, despite Tasmin's pregnancy, to contemplate an indoor life, a fact that Tasmin found decidely vexing. Jim cooked his meals at their modest camp over-looking the Yellowstone River, more than a mile away from Pierre Boisdeffre's well-chinked log trading post. Though Tasmin would have preferred to dine with her hus-band, she was not about to forgo Cook's ex-cellent victuals when she could get them; nonetheless, the fact that her husband re-fused even to consider coming up the snowy slope to dine with her put Tasmin in a testy mood — a fact of which everyone in the post was by then well aware.

At the far end of the great table the other members of the party — George Catlin, Lord Berrybender, Bobbety, Buffum, Father Geoffrin, Señor Yanez, Signor Claricia, Venetia Kennet, and their nominal host, the tall Scotsman William Drummond Stewart, watched the ongoing struggle of mountain men against mountain man with varying de-grees of interest. Lord Berrybender, sitting just across the table from Drum Stewart — as the tall sportsman preferred to be called — took only a momentary interest in the fight, though he did take care to keep his one leg and his good hand under the table, in case knives were drawn. Lord B. had lately become wary of knives — fortunately the struggle seemed to be moderating with no one having recourse to edged weapons as yet. The several trappers now sitting on Hugh Glass were talking to him soothingly, as if to reassure him of their friendship. Even Pierre Boisdeffre had managed to rise above the loss of his crockery — he too spoke to the fallen warrior in mild tones.

"Glad there's no slicing tonight," Lord B. remarked pleasantly. "Every time there's slicing I seem to lose an appendage — how many is it now, Vicky?"

"One leg, seven toes, three fingers," Venetia Kennet reported, without enthusiasm. Venetia had not adjusted well to her young pregnancy; the trip across the frozen wastes had been, for her, a horror. Her cheeks were hollow, her eyes dark-rimmed, her smile now only the mockery of a smile. And yet Lord Berrybender casually assumed that she would be pleased to keep up with his ever-diminishing number of fingers and toes.

"Hear that, Stewart?" His Lordship asked. "I find myself rather whittled down, although fortunately there's been no threat to the principal — perhaps I should say the indispensable — appendage."

"Which would that be, Papa?" Tasmin inquired. In her testy mood she saw no reason to spare her tablemates whatever grossness her father chose to come forth with.

"Why, the organ of generation — you know what I mean, Tasmin," Lord Berrybender insisted. "My favorite appendage by a long shot, I can tell you that."

"I hardly see why you should be so proud of a mere prick," Tasmin told him coolly. "All it's got you is a collection of violent brats and bitches. I'm sure you know how our sainted mother used to refer to it, within the confines of the nursery, of course."

"Er . . . no . . . why would my dear Constance call it anything?" Lord B. inquired, growing rather red in the face. Tasmin's shocking impertinence often took him by surprise.

" 'Papa's big nasty,' that's what she called it!" Mary yelled, before her sister Buffum could drive her off with a few sharp slaps.

"Thank you, Mary — you're precise for once," Tasmin said.

"I don't thank her," Buffum said. "How painful to hear obscenity out of the mouth of a child, here on the Yellowstone in the year of our Lord 1833," she intoned.

"My daughter Tasmin has a tongue like an asp," Lord B. observed, under his breath, to Drum Stewart. "Don't argue with her, Stewart — just slap her if she annoys."

Drum Stewart made no reply — he was happy, at such time, to take refuge in Scots taciturnity. Though he was soon to be the seventh baronet of Murthly, the vast family seat in Perthshire, Drum walked with the trappers, slept with the trappers, waded in icy streams with the trappers, ate what the trappers ate, and starved when the trappers starved. He did nothing to set himself apart from the hardy group of mountain men — Bridger, Carson, Fitzpatrick, Bonneville, Walker, and the Sublettes — with whom he had traveled north. Most of them were now sitting on Hugh Glass, trying to persuade him to let bygones be bygones where Jim Bridger and the Broken Hand were concerned. His own understanding was that Hugh Glass — oldest and, by some accounts, wildest of the mountain trappers — had been killed by an enraged mother grizzly some years before, while trapping with Major Henry's men; clearly this was a misjudgment, since the man was alive and kicking — literally kicking, whenever he could get a leg free. Neither Bridger nor Fitzpatrick was any longer engaged in the struggle — both stood by a table, looking somewhat stunned, as would only be natural in the light of the violent return of a man they had supposed to be dead.

"You know, Stewart, it's a goddamned nuisance, having to drink whiskey with my meals," Lord Berrybender complained. "I miss my leg, of course, but the plain fact is that I miss my claret more. Never thought I'd be reduced to a life without claret — when we fought together on the Peninsula I distinctly remember that you were a man who drank claret — no small amount of claret, either. You wouldn't have a few bottles hidden away, now, would you? For your private use? Come on, man, confess. . . ."

"Oh, do shut up about that claret, Papa," Tasmin said sharply. "It's gone, and good riddance. You've drunk more than enough claret for one lifetime, in any case — overconsumption explains why you're such a gouty old brute."

"Didn't ask you, asked Drum Stewart," Lord Berrybender insisted. "A man who's fond of claret doesn't change. I expect you've got a few bottles secreted away here somewhere . . . now haven't you, Drum?"

"I *walked* here, Albany," Drum said bluntly. "We had a few ponies, but we needed them to bring out the pelts. Can't clatter around with a lot of bottles, in country like this."

Drum Stewart did warm to the way Lady Tasmin's color rose when she heaped abuse on old Albany Berrybender; and he was hardly the only man in the post who liked to hear her heap it. When Lady Tasmin spoke in her spirited and witty way, all the mountain men fell silent and became shy. The purity of her diction, the flash of her wit, the bite of her scorn all fell so naturally from her lips that no one would have dared interrupt, particularly since her fulminations were often accompanied by a heaving of her young bosom. Young Carson, young Bridger, and the Sublette brothers were so smitten that they scarcely dared breathe, when Lady Tasmin spoke.

Despite his admiration for Lady Tasmin's looks, and those of Vicky Kennet's as well, Drum Stewart could not but be vexed that the English party was there. When he came to the Yellowstone valley with the Sublettes and the other trappers, he had supposed himself to be in a wilderness so remote that it would be years before the English rich arrived — getting clear of the English rich was one reason he plunged so eagerly into the Western wild. But then, before he had been at the post even ten days, who should arrive but Albany Berrybender himself, a man whose high title alone had kept him from being cashiered in Portugal for grand disregard of even the most elemental military discipline. No sooner had he settled in at the trading post than here the Berrybenders came, with Lady Tasmin herself driving a wagonful of servants and attendants. Old Albany — his left leg having been recently removed — bounced up in a buggy driven by an Italian of some sort. To Drum Stewart's dismay a Little England was immediately established at Pierre Boisdeffre's trading post, where, to the astonishment of the mountain men, a callow American named Catlin set up his easel and began to paint the various Indians who wandered in to trade; lordly Piegans, squat Minatarees, wild Assiniboines from the northland, all virtually jostling for positions in line in order to allow the American to render their likenesses.

It seemed to Drum that everything he had traveled six thousand miles to escape had caught up with him before he could even draw his breath in the high West. Far though he had traveled, he had only beaten the English by little more than a week — already the one-footed old lord had taken to racing across the prairies in his buggy, with the Italian applying the whip to two fine mares. Albany, of course — in the normal way of English sportsmen — shot at everything that moved. Already the buffalo and elk had learned to avoid the vicinity of the post; the pot hunters had to forage farther afield every day, in order to find game.

That Lady Tasmin had already managed to locate and marry a frontiersman judged to be wild and untamable even by the loose standards that prevailed among mountain trappers did not greatly surprise the worldly Scot. English ladies could always be counted on to seek out wild meat; there was little left in the East that could qualify, when it came to wildness. He had to admit that he *did* still admire the white throats and long legs of the Englishwomen, two of whom, graceful as swans, sat at that very table: the voluble Lady Tasmin and the somber cellist, Venetia Kennet. In Drum Stewart's view there was no escaping a certain moral equation: with beauty came difficulty, and with great beauty came great difficulty. Thus he looked aside from Lady Tasmin and let his gaze linger now and then on the admirably long-legged cellist — she was said to be with child but hardly showed it yet. Lady Tasmin *would* keep talking, whereas the silent cellist spoke only when required to. Drum Stewart was, after all, a Scot of the Scots, taciturn by nature. Ten minutes of Albany Berrybender's selfish ramblings made him want to cut the old brute's throat.

"Are you fond of cabbage, Miss Kennet?" Drum asked politely.

Not the least of the woman's attractions was a soft, full lower lip — on the long trek north from Kansas, Drum had largely held aloof from native women, put off by their short stature and the grease with which they liked to anoint themselves. To a man not naturally celibate, Vicky Kennet's full lower lip suggested the possibility of quickening passions and tangled bedclothes.

"She better like it, it's the only vegetable we're likely to have through this long winter," Tasmin said — she was quite aware of how frequently the tall Scot's gaze sought out Vicky.

"It'll do, sir, when there's naught else," Vicky said, allowing, just for a moment, her full lips to curve in a smile.

"Well, if there's no claret we'll have to make do with brandy, I suppose, Drum," Lord Berrybender said.

2

. . . a wife, wanted — simply a wife, wanted.

Pomp Charbonneau had formed the pleasant
habit of walking Tasmin back to her camp at
night, a courtesy Tasmin found both reassuring and yet obscurely irritating.

"Pomp, you needn't — Pomp, it's quite un-
necessary — Pomp, don't bother," she protested, though never with much force. Not
once did she strictly forbid this polished,
friendly, very polite young man to take this
trouble on her behalf. Tasmin liked Pomp
very much, and yet why was it Pomp, rather
than her husband, Jim Snow, who felt she
needed protection on the easy walk from the
trading post to the modest camp by the Yellowstone? Why — besides that — were she
and Jim, in the coldest months of a northern
winter, living in a tent on a riverbank? Because Jim found indoor lodgings "close"?

"You've now bewitched our good Pomp,
Tasmin," Buffum said, once the elk and cabbage had been consumed. Pomp himself had
hurried over to join the conclave of mountain
men around Jim Bridger, Tom Fitzpatrick,
and Hugh Glass — evidently some long-held

grudge on the part of the latter was being adjudicated by a kind of trappers' jury.

"Shut up, Buffum, I've done nothing of the kind," Tasmin retorted. "Why would it matter to you if I have? Last I heard you were entering a nunnery, as I recall."

The fact was that, with the passage of time, Bess Berrybender had begun to feel considerably less nunlike; she would happily have allowed Pomp to pay *her* a good deal more attention, and Tasmin a good deal less.

"That's right, Tasmin — not fair to hog Pomp," Bobbety said. "When spring comes he has promised to take Father Geoff and me to some excellent fossil beds."

Bobbety and Father Geoffrin had become an inseparable pair, constantly babbling on about geology, vestments, or licentious French literature, over which they were prone to giggle and smirk.

Tasmin found the two of them increasingly hard to tolerate, though the rest of the company was not much more to her liking — always excepting Cook, who followed the progress of Tasmin's pregnancy with the attentiveness of the seasoned midwife that she was.

Tasmin had spoken sharply to George Catlin so many times that the disappointed painter seldom uttered a word while in her presence — why give the woman a target?

Mary Berrybender, her young breasts just

budding, was not so easily squelched.

"I fear you may commit adultery with Pomp, if you aren't careful, Tassie," Mary said. "Indeed, I fear it very much."

"Hush, you minx!" Tasmin said. "I have no improper feelings for Pomp."

Mary turned aside and began to kiss and stroke the gloomy botanist, Piet Van Wely, her special friend. Numbed by the cold and depressed by the short winter days, the Dutchman had fallen into a deep melancholy. Now and then Mary could coax a sentence or two out of the sad fellow, but no one else could persuade him to speak a word.

Seeing that Pomp Charbonneau was deep in conversation with Eulalie Bonneville and Tom Fitzpatrick, Tasmin left the table and strode briskly out of the trading post into the cold Montana night — she had scarcely passed beyond the gates of the stockade when the ever-watchful Pomp appeared at her elbow, which irritated her. She liked the young man very much; but she didn't like him coddling her. Coddling was her husband's job, though one he entirely refused to do.

"What was all that stir?" she asked.

"Hugh had a grudge against Jimmy Bridger and Tom Fitzpatrick," Pomp informed her. "It was Jim and Tom who left him for dead, after the bear clawed him. His whole chest was ripped open — the boys thought he *was* dead, and the Sioux were close, so they took his gun and left, hoping to save their hair."

"Aha, but he lived to chase them down," Tasmin replied — Hugh Glass's survival did not seem all that surprising. Even in her own short time in the West she had observed the sort of things human beings could survive, provided they had sufficient vigor. Her own father had roared like a bull while his leg was being sawed off, and yet, scarcely a week later, he was hobbling around on his crutch with considerable agility, shooting unwary buffalo from the boat and assailing Vicky Kennet, who was plenty wary but had no place to run. Vigor did seem to be the necessary factor. Tim, the stable boy, only lost two fingers and a toe to the bitter frost, and yet came near to dying, and even now looked like a haunt of some kind, a man not sure whether he belonged to life or death.

"Yes, Hugh chased them down," Pomp said. "It's lucky there was a bunch of the boys handy to jump on him — otherwise there might have been blood spilled. Jim and Tom convinced him they did their best — it's not always easy to say when a man's alive, not when the Sioux are in the neighborhood."

They walked on. The winter stars were tiny pinpoints in the dark sky. Their feet crunched the crust of a light snow. Pomp Charbonneau's manners were so easy, so nearly infallible, so European, that Tasmin found herself rather resenting them; it seemed to her that those manners masked a certain neutrality, a preference for standing apart, a trait she could not but disdain. Pomp had been educated in a castle near Stuttgart; perhaps the castle was the trouble, Tasmin reflected — when had she *not* disdained men raised in castles? Drum Stewart had also been raised in a castle; he too was eligible for her rich scorn. She had not liked the cool way the Scot had skipped past her in order to focus his charms on Vicky Kennet. Glances were not neutral acts, where grown men and women were concerned.

"Pomp, have you never lusted!" Tasmin burst out suddenly. She could not tolerate neutrality and was determined to smash Pomp's, if she could.

"Not strongly, I suppose," Pomp said, with a quick smile. The question did not seem to surprise him, a fact irritating in itself.

"Oh, hell — why not?" Tasmin asked. "Inconvenient as men's lusts frequently are, there's not much else a woman can trust about them."

Tasmin picked up the pace of their walk, stung by Pomp's refusal to be ruffled by her pique.

"I don't mean I want you lusting for *me*," she said. "But I'd like you better if you lusted for *someone* — perhaps a wild Ute, of the sort my Jimmy once found so appealing."

"I did once care for an Italian girl, but she died on the Brenner Pass," Pomp said, a little sadly.

"Not good enough — you're young and handsome — there are native beauties aplenty," she told him. "Besides, it's no good loving a dead woman — indeed, it's quite unfair to those of us who remain alive. We might need you."

"You're just annoyed that it's me that's walking you home," Pomp said. "I expect you'd rather it was Jim."

"You've hit it!" Tasmin exclaimed. "Only I'm more than annoyed — I'm furious. Why isn't it Jimmy? After all, you *are* a very good-looking man. Unlikely as it seems, a sudden lust might overwhelm you — overwhelm us for that matter. I'm flesh and blood, after all: nothing I respect more than sudden lusts. Yet this possibility never occurs to Jim — does the fool believe he's the only one subject to sudden lusts?"

"Jimmy and I have roamed together — I expect he just trusts me," Pomp said — whereupon Tasmin felt her fury burn even hotter.

"You, certainly — he can quite clearly trust *you*," she said. "But it's *me* he's married to, and I'm rather a more volatile animal! I won't be taken for granted, not by Jimmy Snow or anyone else. He can't just entertain

35

me with a little conjugal sweat and assume I'll be docile forever. Others are quite capable of working up similar sweats — wouldn't a good husband know that?"

Pomp gave a polite chuckle.

"Jim, he's different," he said. "I expect he'll walk you home himself, once it warms up a little."

"Why would the weather matter — cold doesn't affect him," Tasmin said.

"No, but the grizzly bears will be coming out — Jimmy's careful about bears — so am I," Pomp told her.

Tasmin was in no mood to receive such vague assurances. That her husband would prefer that she not be eaten by a grizzly bear hardly checked her fury; Jim had always been alert in protecting her from Indian abduction and other local dangers — she granted him that normalcy, at least. But the notion that she might need to be protected from her own strong feelings was a notion her husband simply didn't grasp. She was his wife — it was settled — and they would live where he chose. At the moment that meant a drafty tent by a frozen river. If Pomp chose to walk her home, that was fine — so there she was, being walked home, every night by a neutral, amiable chaperone, in this wintry wilderness.

It made Tasmin furious, and yet, when they reached the camp and Jim turned his mild eyes up to her, and moved so as to make a place for her on the robe beside him, Tasmin failed, as she usually failed, to sustain her hot feelings, and quickly forgot all the things she had meant to thrash out with Jim once Pomp was gone.

"Hugh Glass came by," Jim said. "That bear didn't kill him after all — he's mighty hot about the boys that left him, though."

"Oh, we noticed that," Tasmin said.

"He busted Tom in the jaw and tried to strangle Jimmy Bridger," Pomp said. "It took about all of us to get him calm."

Pomp chatted only a few more minutes, and then slipped off into the night. Tasmin sat on the robe her husband offered, her anger melting away like snow in a teapot. It was easy enough to be mad at her husband when she was away from him and could examine his actions coolly — and yet she could rarely manage to sustain her hot angers once she was with him. Instead of bursting out in fury, she leaned her head against his shoulder and all too meekly subsided, worn out from the turbulence of feeling she had just experienced.

At the trading post it was easy enough to feel like a woman rather undervalued, or misunderstood, or not taken seriously. She might complain to Cook about the drafty tent or various other aspects of their domestic arrangements, and yet once Pomp was gone and she and Jim crept into the tent and turned to one another, beneath their warm robes, Tasmin forgot her complaints. In the tent, amid the furs, with her husband, she felt like a wife, wanted — simply a wife, wanted. In the nighttime, at least, that was enough.

3

Otter Woman was old now, cranky and almost blind . . .

In the still night, once he had delivered Tasmin to her husband, Pomp could already hear sounds of the coming carouse at the trading post — naturally the trappers would want to welcome old Hugh Glass back to the land of the living. Pomp, not much of a carouser, did not immediately return, though he liked Hugh, a man who had seen much and was not loath to share his information. Hugh Glass had fought with William Ashley and Jedediah Smith in their great defeat at the Arikara villages a decade earlier — it had been that defeat that drove the trappers off the Missouri River and forced them to seek out beaver streams deep in the Rockies. It was at one such stream that the enraged mother grizzly left Hugh so torn and broken that Jim Bridger and Tom Fitzpatrick left him for dead.

Even now, at the fort, Hugh was trying to convince the skeptical trappers that he had crawled and hobbled some two hundred miles before being rescued by friendly Cheyenne. Already, before Pomp left with Tasmin, he had seen Joe Walker and Eulalie Bonneville rolling their eyes and shaking their heads at old Hugh's claim of a two-hundred-mile crawl. Some of the boys were so glad to see the old man that they pretended to believe him, while privately regarding the story as just another tall tale. No doubt the story of Hugh Glass, the bear, and the two-hundred-mile crawl would be told around Western campfires for years to come: the bear, the desertion, the crawl, and the search for revenge seemed to Pomp to have the makings of a play, or an opera even — he had seen plenty of the latter in Germany.

Though glad, of course, that Hugh Glass was alive, Pomp felt no inclination to join in the party. Tasmin, in her annoyance, had stated an awkward truth about him: he was not often lustful, and he had rarely been able to join in the spirit of any group celebration. The English girl stated clearly what he himself had never quite articulated: he stood apart, not hostile or critical of the lusts or greeds of others; his gaze contained no stiff judgments, as her husband the Sin Killer's fierce look was apt to do. Pomp would have liked to love a woman, feel a brother to a man, and yet he never had — or at least, he hadn't since the death of Sacagawea, his mother; and that had occurred when he was only a boy.

Down the Missouri, a few miles from the post, a small band of Minatarees were camped; one of them was his old aunt, Otter Woman, his mother's sister, who had also, for a time, been married to Pomp's father. Pomp thought he might just visit the Minataree camp and talk with his aunt a little. The cold was sharp, but Pomp didn't mind it. Otter Woman was old now, cranky and almost blind, but she had been at Manuel Lisa's fort the day the sudden fever had carried Pomp's mother away. Pomp was in Saint Louis, living with Captain Clark at that time; his father, Toussaint, had been there as well. When the trapper John Luttig came in with the news of Sacagawea's death, Pomp's father wept, and then Captain Clark wept too. The two men drank much whiskey that night; more than once they wept, a thing that surprised Pomp — he knew that Captain Clark was a very great man, and yet he wept for the death of an Indian woman. Seeing the two men, both drunk, so bereaved, caused a kind of breaking in Pomp — after that he saw his mother only in dreams; she became a woman of the shadows, a phantom he could never see clearly; though he could remember the warmth he had felt when she carried him close to her body in his first years.

Later, looking back, it seemed to Pomp that it was on that night in Saint Louis, when he had realized his mother would hold

41

him close no more, that he had begun to live at a distance from other men, the distance that Tasmin Berrybender noticed and complained about. In Germany his kindly old tutor, Herr Hanfstaengl, had cared for Pomp deeply; and though he liked Herr Hanfstaengl and the jolly cooks in the castle of the prince of Württemberg, who, with William Clark's consent, had taken Pomp to educate, he could not really close the distance between them. The cooks all wanted to hug him, but Pomp would rarely let them.

Now, a grown man, he was back on the river of his birth, the great Missouri. Much had changed since his mother and father had brought him to Saint Louis so that Captain Clark could see to his education. The whites were in the West now, exploring every stream and trail. In his office in Saint Louis, Captain Clark, old but still alert, kept a great map of the West tacked to his wall; this map he amended constantly, as reports came in from trappers, priests, military men, merchants, informing him about a river or a pass that had escaped his attention. The old captain, tied down by his duties as commissioner of Indian Affairs, talked longingly of going out again, making one last, great trek, perhaps this time to California; it made Pomp sad to hear the great captain talk so — for it was only an old man's dreaming.

It was in Captain Clark's office that Pomp

had met Drummond Stewart — Pomp had just been helping Captain Clark amend his great map again, putting in one or two of the tributaries of the Green River, where he had gone trapping with Jim Snow and Kit Carson only the year before. At once the tall Scot had asked Pomp to guide him on a hunting trip, a great expedition meant to last three years. The Scotsman didn't just want to kill the great beasts of the West, the bears and the bison; he wanted to capture specimens of all the Western animals — elk and antelope, cougars and wolves, mountain sheep, hares, and porcupines, even — and take them back to Perthshire, where he planned to establish a great game park on his broad northern estates. Of course, they would hunt for the table as they traveled but Drum Stewart was a man who had no interest in slaughter for the sake of slaughter — his enthusiasm for the West was so keen that Pomp happily agreed to go with him as a guide. Drum Stewart's questing spirit had so far never faltered, though here they were, more than two thousand miles from Saint Louis, at Pierre Boisdeffre's new trading post where the two waters joined, the brown Missouri and the green Yellowstone.

Only ten days before, as Pomp was just starting off on a hunt, who should surprise him but Jim Snow, trudging along the Missouri at the head of a shivering party of English, trailing behind him in a wagon and a buggy.

Jim Snow took to groups even less readily than Pomp, which is why the sight of him at the head of such a party was such a surprise. Word had reached them from some wandering Hidatsa that a big boat was stuck in the ice somewhere downriver; two or three of the trappers had been vaguely planning to investigate this wonder — but here the whole party came, with Jimmy Snow well in advance of the others. Kit Carson and Jim Bridger had been playing a game of kick ball with some Assiniboines when the Sin Killer suddenly appeared, carrying only his rifle and bow.

The sight of Pomp, his old friend, seemed to cheer Jim Snow up.

"Are you hired?" Jimmy asked at once. "If you ain't I want to turn this bunch over to you — all except my wife."

"So, Jimmy — got a fresh wife? What tribe would she belong to?" Eulalie Bonneville asked — he assumed, of course, that Jim would have taken a native woman — he himself had several native wives.

"The English tribe — that'll be her driving the wagon," Jim admitted. The statement quite flabbergasted all the trappers. To see such a beauty as Tasmin on the Yellowstone was miracle enough; but then to hear that Jimmy Snow, a man who never bothered much with women, was married to her at once set the fort abuzz.

There were more than a dozen people in the wagon this English beauty drove; in the buggy was a tall woman, a short Italian, and the old lord himself, his left leg now a heavily bandaged stump.

"Jimmy, I *am* hired," Pomp admitted. "I've been engaged by a Scot — we mean to be out here three years, catching critters for his zoo."

Jim Snow felt a little disappointed — Pomp had lived in Europe and would no doubt be the best man to deal with a lot of Europeans.

"Well, there's Kit — I might try him," he said. "Kit's polite, at least."

Before the wagon even reached the stockade Jim Snow had shaken hands with the boys, said a few words to Kit Carson, privately, and left, headed, evidently, for the nearby Yellowstone.

"Dern, Jimmy left before he even got here," Eulalie said.

"That's our Jimmy — he don't linger," Milt Sublette remarked.

"Jim's married — I expect he just intends to make a separate camp," Pomp said. "He's shy — not like you, Bonney."

"He could have told us the news, at least," Jim Bridger said, rather annoyed. He always liked to get the news.

"At least he brought us a circus, though —

let's watch it," Tom Fitzpatrick observed. "I wonder who that old one-legged fellow could be."

Then, as they all watched, the sprightly English girl stopped the wagon, jumped down, and sprinted off after her husband, Jim Snow, by then nearly to the frozen Yellowstone.

"Why, look at her go — she's a regular antelope," Billy Sublette allowed.

"She don't mean to let Jimmy skip out, does she?" Joe Walker observed.

Kit Carson was astonished — he had never seen a woman run as fast as the English girl.

"Why's she chasing after Jimmy so hard?" Kit wondered. "I expect he'll come back and get her, if she'd just wait."

"You'll learn this soon enough, so I'll tell you for your own good, Kit," Tom Fitzpatrick said. "There are some girls who won't be made to wait."

4

In fact, the mouse was sleepy too . . .

When Pomp walked up to the campfire, three young Minataree braves were playing a game with a mouse. They had three leather cups and were shuffling them rapidly, singing a kind of mouse song to distract the boy who was trying to guess which cup the mouse was under. It was an old game. The boy who was supposed to guess which cup the mouse was under proved to be a very bad guesser. He was wrong three times in a run — the quick boy who shuffled the cups laughed at such ineptitude.

"You try," he said to Pomp. "This one will never beat me."

"I'm sleepy, or I could beat you," the first boy said. His name was Climbs Up.

Pomp sat down and immediately won three games, merely by keeping his eye on the place the mouse had been. In fact, the mouse was sleepy too — or bored. The mouse ignored the cups and stayed in the same place. The cup shuffler, whose name was Weedy Boy, soon grew irritated at the lethargic mouse whose idleness had cost him victory.

He picked the mouse up by the tail and flung it off into the snow.

"You put a spell on our mouse, so you could win three times," Weedy Boy said to Pomp.

Pomp just smiled. He liked the three gangly Minataree boys and sometimes took them hunting when they were camped nearby. Some of the Minataree braves considered Pomp a Shoshone — his mother's tribe — and were rude to him accordingly, but the three boys accepted him and badgered him to let them shoot his gun, a fine rifle Drum Stewart bought him while they were in Saint Louis. The Minataree band owned only a few guns, and they were just old muskets, in bad repair.

"There are too many Assiniboines around here," Weedy Boy commented. "They have been stealing our horses."

"We want to go to war with them, but we don't have very good guns," Climbs Up complained.

There were several bands of Assiniboines north of the post, most of them far better equipped than the Minatarees — a war was unlikely to turn out well for this little band. Pomp was careful not to say as much to the three boys, who would have regarded his apprehension as an insult.

"The old woman will be up pretty soon," Weedy Boy said, referring to Pomp's aunt.

"She never sleeps very long."

Two of the boys retired to a lodge, but Weedy merely took a blanket and curled up by the fire.

Pomp seldom slept much, either. Some nights he merely rested, neither fully awake nor sound asleep. The pure silence of the winter night, broken only by the sighing of the wind over the snowfields, was a restful thing in itself. In summer the nights were never silent: insects buzzed, night birds called, and the buffalo bulls, in their rut, set up a roaring that could be heard for many miles.

Weedy Boy had been right about Otter Woman. Long before dawn she crept out of her lodge and shuffled up to the fire. It irritated her that Sacagawea's boy had shown up again, smelling of white man's soap, an unpleasant thing to smell so early in the morning. He looked like his mother, her sister, and that annoyed Otter Woman too. Though she and Sacagawea had been married to the same man, they had never been close. Sacagawea was not a bad person, but she was cunning and could always get her way with men, a skill Otter Woman did not possess. Though Sacagawea had had only one husband, this smelly boy's father, and Otter Woman had had several, it still annoyed her that Sacagawea had always been able to get her way.

"If you are going to come around here and burn up our firewood you should at least bring me a new blanket," Otter Woman said. "There were too many mice last summer — some of them nibbled holes in my blanket."

"I'll buy you one, Aunty," Pomp said. "If you want to come to the trading post you can take any blanket you want."

"Too far," Otter Woman said. In the cold weather her knees didn't seem to want to bend. Let this boy of her sister's choose a nice blanket and bring it to her. As long as it was warm and had blue in it, it would do very well. She had a fine buffalo robe, which she had tanned and worked herself, but it was too heavy to sleep under, except on the coldest nights. A nice blue blanket would be a comfort on days when the wind blew sleet or fine snow through the camp.

Pomp knew his aunt didn't particularly like seeing him — his father claimed she had never liked seeing much of anyone; she was often rude to guests and, besides that, was slipshod about her chores. Now her face was as wrinkled as a dried apple and she rarely had two words to say, unless they were words of complaint. Also, she was greedy — the last words she spoke to Pomp, as he got up to leave, were to hurry up and bring her the new blanket he had promised. Minataree braves were in and out of the post — any one of them would have been glad to bring her the blanket if Pomp asked them to, but that wouldn't do, either. Otter Woman didn't trust the Minatarees, even though she lived with them. She felt her nephew should hurry up and make the delivery, although she still resented the fact that his mother had been so clever about getting her way with men.

"Bring it today, and don't lose it, either," she warned.

"Why would I lose a blanket?" Pomp asked, a little taken aback by his aunt's stridency.

"Your father was a big gambler, he was always losing everything," Otter Woman said. "It's going to be cold tonight and I'm tired of this old blanket the mice have nibbled."

Pomp was almost back to the stockade when the very thing Weedy Boy predicted happened right before his eyes. From just inside the stockade, war cries suddenly rent the morning silence. A musket went off, and there was the snarling of dogs, the neighing of a frightened horse, another gunshot, and loud sounds of battle. Pomp raced in, expecting to see a party of besieged mountain men under attack, but in fact not a mountain man was to be seen — only the painter George Catlin, cowering under his easel, his paints spilled everywhere, as six or seven Minataree braves chopped and stabbed at as many Assiniboines. One man, an Assiniboine, had already fallen; a stout Minataree was just taking his scalp. One horse, a bay, had taken an arrow in the neck, its split vein spewing blood over the nearest combatants, as if they stood under a fountain. As Pomp watched, an Assiniboine boy no older than twelve picked up the fallen warrior's musket and shot a Minataree right in the stomach, blowing the man backward. The man screamed so loudly that combat froze, allowing Pomp to rush in and drag George Catlin out of the fray.

The man whose portrait he had been working on, a vividly painted Piegan, stood calmly over by the posts of the stockade, evidently not much interested in the sudden conflict between Assiniboine and Minataree.

"Thank God you came, Pomp, I thought I was lost," George Catlin said in a shaky voice. "Hadn't we better get inside, before they start up again?"

"I don't know what it was about, but I think it's over — for now, anyway," Pomp said. Indeed, the two bands had stepped back from each other, though they still brandished hatchets and knives. The wounded horse continued to bleed, and the skinny dogs to snarl. Two men lay dead, but the urge to fight seemed to have left the warriors as rapidly as it had come. Both groups retreated warily. An Assiniboine went to the wounded horse, jerked the arrow out, and stuffed a rag into the wound. The dead warriors were picked up; no more threats were made. A retreat took place, by silent and mutual consent.

The Piegan who was waiting to have his portrait painted suddenly voiced a raucous curse.

"Better get your paints, Mr. Catlin," Pomp said. "It's safe now, but that customer of yours doesn't look like a patient man."

"None of them are patient — they all rush me," George Catlin said, before picking up his scattered paints and motioning the Piegan to stand in front of his easel again.

5

"Boys, do you see an angel over there?"

Hugh Glass got so drunk that he began to
have visions of heaven — he looked up and
saw an angel making sweet music over by the
English table. She was tall and fair, this
angel, with long auburn hair hanging down
her back; the sweet music came from a big
instrument, rather like a swollen fiddle. Hugh
Glass watched, entranced; it was warm in
heaven, and there was plenty of grog, as
there should be.

Drum Stewart had persuaded Vicky Kennet
to bring out her cello and favor them with a
little Haydn, a development which vexed
Lord Berrybender considerably. He was impatient for bed, and perhaps a spot of copulation just beforehand; but he held his tongue
for once, mainly because he was still convinced that the Scotsman had a few bottles
of claret tucked away somewhere; he didn't
want to offend the man until the question
was firmly settled.

"Boys, do you see an angel over there?"
Hugh asked the company, some of whom
were nearly as drunk as himself.

"What would an angel be doing up here on the Yellowstone, in the dead of winter?" Eulalie Bonneville wondered.

"Why, playing the harp, I guess — ain't that a sort of harp she's got?" Hugh inquired.

"That's no angel, that's an Englishwoman," Tom Fitzpatrick informed him. "I expect she's the old lord's whore."

Hugh looked at the Englishwoman again, his head lolling slightly to one side. Now it seemed to him that he saw two female angels — one slid out of the other and then slid back in again, as his vision wavered.

"No, it's an angel — maybe two," Hugh declared. "The reason you can't see 'em is because none of you have been dead. I'm the only man here that's been dead."

This claim made Jim Bridger indignant.

"Dern, Hugh — you come bustin' in here and tried to strangle me because you claimed me and Tom left you for dead when you was alive all the while."

"Jim's right, Hugh — which was it?" Tom Fitzpatrick said, with a smile — he was well aware that Hugh Glass was far too drunk to make good sense. He was so drunk he was even seeing double. He himself, while on a carouse near the Tongue River, had once shot at a careless elk and missed entirely because he had shot at the double and not the real animal.

"You were right, boys! Here I've been hot after you for months when at the time you left me I was dead," Hugh declared, more humbly. "I was floating up to heaven, only an angel with feathers like a prairie chicken came and lowered me back to earth."

Jim Bridger and Kit Carson — the only trappers who weren't drunk — looked at each other in amazement. Why would Hugh make up such a wild lie? After all his hot accusations about being deserted, now he was trying to claim he had been dead after all.

"No, you're off, Hugh — angels don't have wings like prairie chickens," Joe Walker said. "Prairie chickens can hardly fly at all — angels have wings like them big white swans."

"Who's seen one, you or me, Joe?" Hugh said, his temper flaring.

"I agree with Joe," Bill Sublette said. "There's plenty of books with pictures of angels in them, and they all have them big white wings, like swans."

"Yes, and the damn fools that drew the pictures had probably never been killed by a grizzly bear, like I was," Hugh protested.

"You're a mouthy old fool, Hugh," Jim Bridger said — he was getting hotter at the thought of the injustice of the old man's claim.

"Don't bait me now, Jimmy," Hugh said threateningly. "It ain't easy to remember being dead. I'd forgotten it until I seen that angel over at the English table, playing that big fiddle."

"If you were dead why didn't you stay dead, like most people do?" Milt Sublette said, a little spooked. If old Hugh *had* been dead, then maybe they were all talking to a ghost.

"Heaven didn't want me, I guess — nor the other place either — so that prairie chicken angel just lowered me back down, and that's when I started my crawl," Hugh said. He sensed a rather uneasy skepticism among his listeners, one of whom, little Mary Berrybender, had just joined the crowd.

"Oh, Mr. Glass, that's transubstantiation you're referring to," Mary said. "Few among us have been granted such an interesting experience."

Mary's long word stopped the conversation dead.

"Young miss, could you say that again?" Eulalie requested. "I reckon that's the longest word any of us has ever heard spoke."

"Transubstantiation," Mary repeated. "The soul departs the body, but decides to return. Only the very holy experience it."

"That leaves Hugh out, then," the Broken Hand said. "I doubt he's got a holy bone in his dern old body."

"Point of order, Mary — point of order!"

Bobbety cried out. "Many Hindus experience transubstantiation on a regular basis."

Both Sublettes looked pale, took their guns, and prepared to leave.

"If you're a ghost, then, Hugh, I believe I'd rather sleep outside," Bill Sublette declared.

"Now, Bill, there's no need to worry — I've settled back into myself now," Hugh assured him — though in a slurred voice. He saw that everyone was looking at him strangely. The room seemed to be rocking slightly. The English angel had put away her big fiddle and was leaving the company, with the old one-legged lord stumping along behind her on his crutches. Hugh was hoping to see the auburn-haired angel fly up toward the ceiling, where the parrot was — instead, after a moment, his head hit the table.

"Hugh didn't see no angel — the liquor got him," Tom concluded. "In my own opinion, a man that's dead stays dead."

"Exceptions do exist, Mr. Fitzpatrick," Mary said politely. "There's Lazarus, for one — gospel of John, chapter eleven, verse seventeen."

All the trappers had been staring at Hugh Glass — now they turned and began staring at Mary, whose face wore an unearthly but — in Kit Carson's opinion — very unholy expression.

"Things are sure changing around this

trading post," Kit Carson said, in bemusement, when Mary had gone back to the English table.

None of the trappers disagreed.

6

... a hand went immediately and accurately under her gown ...

"Damn it, a most unsatisfactory copulation," Lord Berrybender complained. "Came off before I even got inside. We mustn't let this get to be a habit, Vicky."

Venetia Kennet kept silent. What was there to say? Lord Berrybender's effusions, though copious, were mostly now premature, one inconvenience of which was that the sheets were permanently sticky, a fact the laundress, Millicent, could hardly fail to notice.

"Do try your bow, just a bit," Lord B. requested. "Accustomed to far lengthier pleasures, as you know. Don't relish these goddamn foreshortenings."

Vicky tried her bow — tried and tried; she could have managed a concerto in less time. In this instance, though, flaccidity prevailed. Much tickling of His Lordship's balls only produced a slight lumpiness — nothing that was likely to result in penetration.

"Effect of that whiskey, I'm sure," Lord B. said. "Never spunked in such a hurry when I was well primed with good red claret. I'll just sleep a bit now, I suppose — expect we can go at it well enough first thing in the morning."

Finding no water in the basin — it would never have stood empty had Mademoiselle Pellenc still been in charge of the rooms — Vicky pulled on a flannel robe and stepped into the corridor, meaning to refill the basin from little Mary's room, which was just next door. But she had scarcely put her foot out the door when lips found hers, lips with a stiff red beard below them — and a hand went immediately and accurately under her gown, while another squeezed a breast.

"Chilly here, Miss Kennet — my room's not far," Drum Steward whispered, his hand still squeezing and probing.

"I imagine old Albany takes a bit of pumping these days, as drunk as he gets," the Scot suggested.

"Oh yes, pump pump, that's all I do, sir," Vicky Kennet agreed.

7

Jim's slap came quick as a snake's strike . . .

"God damn this weather — now I'm stuck!" Tasmin said, without thinking. Jim's slap came quick as a snake's strike, before she could even close her lips; one of them split slightly, a dribble of blood ran down her chin, but Tasmin was too stunned even to dab at it. She had just been leaving for the post when the wind rose to a howl and snow began to swirl around their tent, blotting out the river and, indeed, the world. The trading post, only a mile away, might have been a hundred — in such a whiteout she could never find her way to it. This was vexing; Cook had been going to make her a kind of porridge bath, thought to be beneficial to women in her condition. Angry at having to miss her porridge bath, she had let slip a casual curse and been slapped for it.

And yet, only the moment before, they had been happy; they had been singing, in fact. Jim had a fine tenor voice. Tasmin was teaching him "Barbara Allen" and one or two other old ballads. Song one minute and then the slap, harder even than the first one she had received, for transgressing his powerful but, to Tasmin, mysterious religious beliefs.

Tasmin sat stock-still, her eyes wide, staring. Through the flap of the tent she could see only white — the snow enclosed them like a cocoon. The night before, when they were amid their robes, being a wife, wanted, seemed a fine thing; but in the howling blizzard, being a wife slapped was a very different article. Jim Snow watched her with the flinty eyes of the Sin Killer — Tasmin had the sense that if she misspoke he would at once strike her again. With many men — even some stronger than herself — her fighting nature might have caused her to fling herself into battle — but not with Jim Snow, the stranger with whom she was mated. If she deliberately provoked him she could not guess where it would end. She sat, staring, leaking a tear or two of embarrassment and shock, struggling to regain her composure.

"You ain't to cuss — you've been told," Jim said, gently wiping the blood off Tasmin's lip with a finger.

Tasmin, still struggling with her emotions, didn't speak. She didn't yet dare. Her bosom heaved; she held back tears — were it not for the blizzard she would have immediately run out of the tent, but now she feared to. If she ran into the whiteness, would her husband find her? Would anyone?

After a bit she calmed and reached into her bag for a tiny mirror. Her lower lip was puffy, but the bleeding had stopped.

"You ain't to cuss — you was told," Jim said again.

"I'm a mere human being, Jim," Tasmin said unsteadily. "Like most humans, when I'm frustrated I sometimes slip and utter words I shouldn't say. Your friends the trappers curse constantly and rather colorfully. I myself was brought up in a family that cursed a great deal — it's only natural that, now and then, a bad word escapes me."

"There's vanity in you too," Jim said, ignoring her comment about the trappers.

He reached for the mirror, meaning to smash it and end her preening, but Tasmin jerked the small glass away.

"This is my mirror — I'm prepared to be beaten rather than surrender it," Tasmin said. "Of course there's vanity in me — and in you, too. You're rather vain about the way your beard is trimmed."

"I wasn't until I met you," Jim replied.

"I see — so your vanity is my fault too," Tasmin said. "You seem to think everything is my fault."

Jim Snow didn't answer. There was still hostility in his look, so much hostility that Tasmin felt rather despairing; and yet she was determined, now that the die was cast, to speak her mind.

"I'm human, I'm fallible, I admit it," she said, staring straight ahead. "I *will* slip in my language — now and then I may even commit worse sins. There is, I believe, a Christian virtue called forgiveness — I guess it isn't in the part of the Holy Book you possess — perhaps you tore the forgiveness pages out to make our campfires."

Jim said nothing. As usual, he felt at a terrible disadvantage. He could not possibly speak as well as his wife. He had slapped her hard and yet it had not knocked the vanity out of her, or curbed her rebellious spirit. The Book said a wife should be submissive, and yet Tasmin, *his* wife, was defiant.

"There's forgiveness, I guess, but there's punishment too," he said, without confidence.

"I see," Tasmin said. "You like the punishment parts best — I suppose that's why you're called the Sin Killer."

Jim's eyes were softening a little, and yet the prospect of a return to their easy union still seemed distant and bleak.

"I don't want to get slapped every time I'm vexed and speak out," she said. "Somehow you've become convinced that it's your duty to punish sinners — which can make it hard on a wife — though I do think mostly I make a decent wife."

Jim didn't answer. He wished Tasmin could just be silent, and not always be spilling words out of her mouth at such a rate. Lengthy talk just made it harder for him to hold the simple articles of faith in his mind, the faith that Preacher Cockerell had beaten into him at an early age. Preacher Cockerell never hesitated: he took the horsehide whip to his own wife and children as readily as he took it to Jim. Sin was to be driven out and violence was the way to drive it. Sin was also constant; violence had to be constant too. Preacher Cockerell whipped in the morning, whipped in the noontide, whipped at night; when members of his congregation sent their unruly young to him, he whipped them too. Jim grew up fearing the whip but not doubting the justice. Before the morning meal and the evening, Preacher Cockerell read from the Holy Book, terrible passages about punishment, sin, hell, Lot's wife, the whore of Babylon, wars and floods and banishment, all the punishments that man deserved because of his sinful nature. Preacher Cockerell even whipped himself, for he had fallen into adultery with the wife of Deacon Sylvester. For such a sin even the whippings had not been enough, so Jehovah sent the lightning bolt that fried Preacher Cockerell and turned him black; the same lightning bolt threw Maudey Cockerell and Jim Snow aside as if they were chaff from the grain. For three days Jim lay unmoving; he seemed to float in red water, though there was no water where he was. Even the

Kaw was low that year. Maudey Cockerell lived, but her mind died, destroyed by the heavenly flash. From that time on Jim had felt it was his duty to punish sin, whenever he met it in the violent men of the West, red or white; the Indians feared him because of the ferocity of his attacks. He was particularly feared by the medicine men, because it was the heresy of their spells and potions that angered him most.

But he was not in battle with heathen savages now; he was with Tasmin, his wife, a woman who had just carelessly taken the Lord's name in vain. Her quarrelsome words had not really been checked, not even by the sharp blow he had struck her. His Ute wives, receiving such a blow, would have immediately ceased their disputes; they would have known to be quiet. But Tasmin was no Ute — she could outtalk him, make him feel a fool if he even tried to justify his behavior by reference to the Holy Book. Both slaps had shocked her; but not enough. He had no whip; he couldn't lash her as Preacher Cockerell had lashed his Maudey. Even then Tasmin was looking at him boldly, a little scared perhaps but not compliant, as a chastised wife should be. Jim made a fist, but then held back. He didn't strike her.

Tasmin saw the fist — she watched, rather numb, as battle raged within Jim Snow. His face had darkened. She could only wait, she couldn't run; if she ran into the blizzard the best she could hope for was to lose a toe or two. If there was to be a beating, better to stay and take it. All the same she felt herself trembling as she watched fury darken her husband's face. She didn't look at Jim; she looked at nothing, said nothing. She hoped that if she held a strict neutrality the crisis might pass — and it did. Jim Snow relaxed his fist — his face slowly cleared. He seemed as numb as she was; he started. When his knee accidently brushed hers he jerked back, as if burned.

When Tasmin thought it safe to speak she did so as gently as possible. An element of real danger had suddenly come into her union; she had become afraid of her husband, afraid that in him were angers she couldn't anticipate or soothe. These angers might have little enough to do with her; still, she was the wife who was there to meet them. She didn't like being fearful, and yet she was not sure that she understood Jim well enough to avoid setting him off.

"You've just made me scared of you, Jim — that's the most honest thing I can say," Tasmin began. "I accept that you don't like cursing, and that you disapprove of vanity."

"No, it's that I don't like you to *talk!*" Jim said — why would the woman keep on? "It's prideful, the way you talk. The Utes don't let their women babble like you do — a Ute man would likely cut your tongue out."

"I'm lucky I haven't married a Ute man, then," Tasmin said quietly. "I'm afraid speech is a habit I'm unlikely to be able to break. I was brought up in a talky family — I've been babbling, as you put it, from an early age. In England I was much admired for my wit, which I must say I enjoy employing. Silent is one thing I can't honestly promise to be."

His fist came quicker than his palm; it struck Tasmin squarely in the temple and knocked her partway out of the lodge. She did not entirely lose consciousness, but her vision blurred for a moment — she scraped her knee on the frozen snow as she struggled back into the tent. The world had become gray, like a thick soup; Tasmin's only thought was to crawl back under the robes and rest. The one thing that was clear was that her husband didn't like her to talk; his tolerance in that regard had abruptly ended, leaving her with a split lip and a lump forming on her temple. The injustice of it overwhelmed her: she had only been trying to understand Jim's feelings, so as to be a better wife! Tasmin began to sob — she could not stop the warm tears from flowing, although she knew Jim couldn't be expected to like her crying, either. She longed so for

Jim to comfort her, to talk to her normally — just that morning, they had been singing together! But then, as her vision cleared, she saw that this hope of comfort was in vain. Except for herself, their tent was empty. Blizzard or no blizzard, Jim Snow was gone — his gun, his bow, and his quiver were gone too.

8

Who but a haunt would come visiting...

"Uh-oh, who is it, Kit?" Jim Bridger asked — in the dim blue light of the storm, the man all white with snow who suddenly pushed into their lodge seemed ghostlike, at least from what Jim knew of ghosts. Who but a haunt would come visiting in such a blizzard?

Kit Carson was startled too — since old Hugh Glass's return from the bounds of death all the trappers had become a little jumpy. Now a man all icicles and snow came pushing in out of a blizzard so severe that no normal man would attempt to travel in it; he and Jim Bridger had taken one look at the storm and decided to make do with jerky for another day.

"Oh, wait — it's Jimmy Snow — I recognize his gun," Kit said.

"Well, Jimmy — I'd say you picked a bad day to get restless," Jim Bridger allowed to the guest.

Jim Snow courteously tried to shake all the snow off himself without sending too much of it into the small campfire. Carson and Bridger, the youngest and the soberest of the

71

trappers, prided themselves on their ability to live rough. The lodge was small and make-shift, and they seldom bothered to lay in extra firewood.

"I ain't restless," Jim Snow said. "I just thought I'd visit."

Jim Bridger received this news skeptically. Jim Snow, the Sin Killer, was by far the least sociable trapper in the Rockies. No one could ever predict where he might turn up, though it would usually be somewhere west and north of Saint Louis.

"You're smart about directions, Jimmy," Kit said. "I *might* could find your camp in a blow like this — but if I wasn't lucky I'd miss it."

"How is that pretty wife of yours? She is a treat for the eyes," Jim Bridger inquired. He distrusted his own grasp of manners, where married folk were concerned, but thought he might be permitted a polite inquiry.

"I just hit her a good stout lick, to stop her chatter," Jim Snow admitted.

Bridger and Carson received this information in silence. The world of marriage was a world they knew not. That husbands and wives sometimes came to blows was a cir-cumstance they had heard rumored. Among the native tribes, of course, women were fre-quently beaten; whether excessive chatter was a principal cause of these beatings they were not sure. Their own experience, not extensive, had so far been solely with native women; no beating had as yet been necessary.

Privately, both Kit Carson and Jim Bridger admired Tasmin beyond all women — in both their daydreams and their night dreams she made frequent appearances. They considered her to be quite likely the fairest woman on earth. Now her husband, the Sin Killer, had walked out of a blizzard to inform them that he had just silenced his wife with a good stout lick. What could the man expect them to make of such startling information?

"Silence is a comely thing, in a woman," Jim Snow informed them. "Silence before the Lord. It's in the Book."

Neither Carson nor Bridger could read — what was in the Book came to them in scraps here and there, at second hand.

"My wife don't know when to shut up," Jim Snow continued — clearly Tasmin's proclivity for talk was bothering Jimmy a good deal, but their roles in this matter left them feeling increasingly embarrassed. On a day of blizzard, when no man could see two feet in front of his face, Jim Snow had made his way to their lodge mainly in order to complain about his lovely wife.

"Tasmin talks all the time," he went on. "I had to crack her just to get a little peace.

"Knocked her out of the tent — didn't mean to," he added.

The two young trappers considered this information somberly. Neither man could imagine hitting Tasmin, much less knocking her all the way out of a tent. It was clear that Jim Snow was not entirely comfortable with what he had done — he had plunged into a blizzard in order to tell them about it, and now was looking at them expectantly, as if waiting for them to assure him that knocking a talky wife out of a tent was perfectly proper behavior in a husband, a judgment neither felt qualified to make.

"I expect she'll have a pretty fair lump on her noggin," Jim Snow went on — he seemed unable to get his mind off the fact that he had struck his wife.

"What is it she talks about, Jimmy?" Kit inquired cautiously. Excessive talk on Tasmin's part seemed to be the heart of the problem; Kit felt it might be appropriate to inquire about the subjects she dealt with in her chatter.

"Stuff — I can't remember much," Jim Snow confessed. In fact what Tasmin talked about was usually beyond his powers of description.

"Sometimes she cusses," he added. "That's what started it today."

"A woman shouldn't cuss," Jim Bridger agreed.

"Nope, it wouldn't be good etiquette," Kit Carson agreed. He had recently learned the

74

word "etiquette" from Tasmin's sister Bess, who had objected to his habit of spitting out gristle or other unsatisfactory foods while at the common table.

Outside, the blizzard was moderating somewhat. The snow still swirled, but the wind blew less fiercely.

"The blow's about over," Jim said. "If you see my wife tell her I'll be gone for a while. I promised George Aitken I'd check on him and the boat once I got the folks safe at the post."

"You're headed back to the Knife River *now?*" Jim Bridger asked, surprised. Both he and Kit felt that they had received a heavy commission. Neither trusted themselves to utter a word in Lady Tasmin's presence.

"Yes — I told George I'd come check on him when I got a chance," Jim Snow said. "If the wrong bunch of Indians was to show up, it might go hard with George and the others."

"It might," Kit Carson agreed.

"Don't forget to tell my wife where I'm going," Jim Snow insisted. Then he slid out of the lodge and disappeared.

"You go tell his wife, Kit," Jim Bridger said at once.

"No sir, not me," Kit said. "You go — you're far smoother with the womenfolks. I might spit in the wrong direction or do some other bad etiquette. You go."

After wrangling for an hour, during which the debate grew heated, they decided to draw straws, which they did later that day, at the trading post. Joe Walker held the straws.

"Short straw tells her," Kit said — the words were hardly out of his mouth before he drew the short straw.

"That wasn't a fair draw," he protested. "Joe was jerky."

Jim Bridger, however, refused to redraw.

Though oppressed by fears about his own shortcomings in the area of etiquette, there was nothing Kit could do but plod down to the Yellowstone and give Lady Tasmin the bad news.

9

The wind had become inconsistent . . .

Tasmin sat in the chilly tent all day, well swaddled in robes, nursing her hurt. Though her lower lip was puffy and her head ached, the deeper hurts were inside. Her feelings swung back and forth, regularly as a pendulum. One minute she longed for her husband's return — the next minute she feared that very event, for he might very well hit her again. The wind had become inconsistent as the blizzard lost its force. Several times, in moments of quiet, Tasmin convinced herself she heard footsteps. Twice she crawled out of the tent, hoping to spot Jim.

In the afternoon the wind stopped blowing, the sky cleared, and the sun shone with unusual brilliance on the snowfields. Tasmin could have walked on to the fort and asked Cook for her porridge bath, but she didn't — a lethargy seemed to take her; she merely sat, now and then putting a few sticks on the fire. At least Jimmy had left her plenty of firewood. Ordinarily she would have been ravenously hungry by that hour, but she didn't feel hungry. She made little snowballs and applied them to her puffy lip and lumpy temple. When she did go to the fort she didn't want any of her relatives to notice evidence of violence.

Even when the sun began to sink, Tasmin continued to wait. She felt that to leave her tent just then might mean leaving her marriage, which, despite the day's trouble, was a thing not wholly to be despised. There was little accounting for men's tempers, it seemed. Her own father, unprovoked, often fell to slapping and whacking. Perhaps it was merely a flaw in the male temperament — perhaps Jim Snow had awakened to some obscure anxiety having to do with sin which, unwittingly, her profane chatter had exacerbated.

It might be that enduring such unjust attacks was merely a part of women's lot — her mother had sported many a black eye over the years, and yet, somehow, it had never occurred to Tasmin that a man would hit *her*. Now that one *had* she felt that her best bet was to achieve a better understanding of her man — perhaps if she could penetrate to the cave of her husband's angers she would learn what set him off.

It was nearly dusk when next Tasmin heard footsteps approaching the camp. They seemed rather timid footsteps — perhaps Cook had sent Eliza to see about her. But when Tasmin cautiously peeked out she saw

Kit Carson standing nearby, evidently in deep perplexity of spirit. He wore a little rag cap, such as a shop boy might wear. Tasmin felt immediate relief. Kit was her favorite of the trappers; such a polite boy he was. Already Buffum, no longer nunlike, had conceived a passion for him.

"Why, hello, Kit," Tasmin said. "Were you looking for Jim?"

"No," Kit admitted. As usual Lady Tasmin's beauty caused a paralyzing shyness to seize him. He knew exactly what he was supposed to say — he had rehearsed it many times in his walk from the post, but he could not bring himself, bumbler that he was, to launch into speech.

Tasmin saw this — standing just by her tent, as the cold shadows of evening stretched over the snowfields, the young man seemed incapable of either speech or action.

It occurred to Tasmin that if she could just get him moving again he might make a useful escort. She no longer felt that leaving the tent meant leaving her marriage — that view was too dramatic. If she could persuade Kit to walk her to the post she might enjoy that porridge bath after all.

"It's a great convenience to me that you've been so thoughtful as to stop by," Tasmin said. "Jimmy's off somewhere and I was just heading for the post. I wonder if you would be so kind as to escort me — I'll just get my little bag."

"Went to the boat," Kit managed to say, as they started along the path.

"What's that?" she asked. "What about the boat?"

"Jim, he gone to the boat — said to tell you not to worry," Kit managed to bring out. "Said he had to go to the boat to see that George Aitken was all right."

Tasmin felt a flash of warmth — she had not been entirely forgotten, after all.

"Jim came by our camp and told us — he didn't want you to worry," Kit added, his tongue loosening, rather to his surprise.

"How nice of you to bring me this reassurance — he mentioned nothing of the sort to me," she admitted.

"Gone to the boat," Kit said again — he clung to this simple piece of information as a drowning man might cling to a spar.

"Marriage is not always a smooth path, Kit," Tasmin said — she now felt quite confident of her power over young Kit, and inasmuch as he had become putty in her hands, she felt a devilish need to twist him just a bit.

"Not always a smooth path at all," she repeated. "I confess that my husband and I had a tiny quarrel this morning — what you might call a spat."

"I know," Kit said — the comment popped

80

out before he could think.

"Pardon me — how can you have known about our quarrel?" she asked.

"Jimmy told us," Kit said, startled by his own volubility — his tongue, like a skittish horse, now threatened to run away with him.

"Well, goodness me," Tasmin said, watching Kit with surprise. Her devilish mood had not passed — she wanted to discommode this polite young fellow in some minor way — perhaps snatch his ridiculous rag of a cap, or even ruffle his hair.

"You mean my husband came to see you, in a howling blizzard, just to tell you about our quarrel?" she asked.

"Yep," Kit said. "Jimmy Snow can find his way around better than most. Mainly he came because he didn't want you to get all worried."

Having delivered the longest speech he had ever made to a female, Kit felt rather proud of himself.

"He said he knocked you out of the tent," he added, having just remembered that detail.

"Yes, I have a fine lump on my head and scraped my knee besides," Tasmin said. "Since he seems to have been so forthcoming, did he happen to mention what the quarrel was about?"

"Didn't like your chatter," Kit said nervously. "Hit you to keep you quiet."

"And yet, you see, I'm not really quiet, am I, Kit?" Tasmin said, favoring him with a brilliant smile.

"I am not quiet and I doubt I ever shall be," she went on. "You've heard my father roaring and my sister Bess, who's taken rather a fancy to you, complaining. We Berrybenders just happen to be a noisy lot — forthright in our appetites too. It wouldn't surprise me at all if my sister Bess attempted to become familiar with you soon."

"Familiar?" Kit said dubiously; he had no idea what sort of behavior Tasmin was predicting.

Kit's solemnity was so comical that Tasmin felt an irresistible urge to tease him. Just as they entered the stockade, with several trappers watching, she suddenly linked her arm in Kit's and strode boldly toward the post. Kit was too stunned to protest. Eulalie Bonneville, who had been sharpening his skinning knife on a whirling grindstone, stopped his sharpening and just let the grindstone whirl. Tom Fitzpatrick was so surprised he dropped his pipe. Hugh Glass, who had been bent over, trimming a corn on his toe, forgot about his toe.

Kit didn't dare withdraw his arm; but his gaze became unseeing as he contemplated the disgrace that had overtaken him — walking arm in arm with Jim Snow's wife, with everybody watching.

Happy with the consternation she had wrought in the breast of this too solemn young man, Tasmin released his arm just as Kit, still unseeing, tripped over a wagon tongue — it was half hidden in the snow — and fell absolutely flat on his face.

No comedian could have achieved a cleaner pratfall. The sight was so funny that Tasmin could not hold in a hearty peal of laughter — various trappers whooped and chortled too. Bess Berrybender, chatting with Father Geoffrin about the exciting levels of depravity in the dark Gothic fictions of Ann Radcliffe, saw Kit fall and felt very vexed with her sister. Here again Tasmin was misbehaving, teasing a nice young man she had no business teasing, the result being this sudden ignominy. Bess immediately rushed to Kit's side — ignominy, after all, sometimes led to opportunity — retrieved his shop boy cap, and tried to help him staunch the flow of crimson that was pouring copiously from his smashed nose.

"Bend over, bend over — no need to bleed on yourself, Mr. Carson," Bess said. "We'll just apply a bit of this handy snow and have the bleeding stopped in no time."

"It's broke, I guess," Kit said, wiggling his nose and bending over as instructed — soon a considerable patch of snow was stained with his blood.

"My God, Kit," Joe Walker allowed, "I've

kilt buffalo that didn't have that much blood in them."

"I'm so sorry, Kit," Tasmin put in. "I thought for sure you saw that wagon tongue."

"You are so wicked, Tasmin," Bess said hotly. "That's what our bad Tasmin does, in the main, Kit — she causes people to smash."

"What nonsense, anyone can trip on a wagon tongue," Tasmin replied coolly, before going in to see about her porridge bath.

10

"I'd call that a bad dream, all right."

Jim Snow tramped east, through the fading, thinning storm, very uneasy in his mind. He strode past herds of buffalo and elk but shot nothing, although it would soon be dark and he was hungry. He intended to walk on through the night until he felt calm again in spirit. He felt he had been right to slap Tasmin for her cursing — it was the other blow that troubled him. The Sin Killer had failed to heal sin in himself, in this case the sin of anger. Preacher Cockerell had strode through life angry, whipping, roaring, condemning — Preacher Cockerell believed his angers were righteous but Jim wasn't so sure, though he himself could always summon a just anger against the wild old native medicine men, with their snakes and bats and poisons.

But hitting Tasmin to stop her chatter was not the act of a holy man who was battling some great sin. There was no great sin in Tasmin — a mild shaking, to persuade her just to keep quiet, would have been enough. But he had made a fist and used it, and

85

now could not get the memory of her shocked face out of his thoughts. It was, of course, true that Tasmin found it difficult to be meekly obedient — she was not at all like his Ute wives, who said little and obeyed him without question. The difference perplexed him. Some adjustment to a new mate was normal, but he and Tasmin had now been together for several months and she didn't seem to be changing. Worse yet, she was always trying to get *him* to change, to let her cut his hair a certain a way, to be more sociable, unbend a little with her family. Nor was she a match for his Ute wives, Sun Girl and Little Onion, when it came to getting the chores done efficiently. Tasmin skinned game sloppily at best; she could barely get a fire going, and was no good at working hides. When it came to the daily practicalities of wifehood she failed every test; and her chatter and frequent defiance had to be put in the scales against her. In the nighttime, though, things were different. In the darkness, amid their robes, Tasmin pleased him far more than the two Ute girls, neither of whom were enthusiastic wives in the nighttime sense. Sometimes, in the deep night, Jim would come half awake to realize that Tasmin was beneath him, the two of them in the midst of an embrace whose beginnings were lost in sleep and whose long rapture carried them back into sleep again. Jim was not sure about such powerful and frequent lustings. Preacher Cockerell would have said that such strong lusts were sinful, even though sanctioned by the bonds of matrimony. It was all perplexing, and Jim did not enjoy perplexity. In the main he had lived alone because he liked things simple, but from the moment he had first seen Tasmin, naked in the Missouri's waters, nothing had been simple at all. His mind had become clouded, his actions confused; if only Tasmin would recognize her place and improve in her duties, the confusion in his breast might subside.

Lately, though, confusion had only been increasing. That morning it had reached an intolerable intensity; he had struck his wife and left, and yet, with him still were the very feelings that had caused him to strike out. Such tension was not what he wanted; there must be change, and yet where Tasmin was concerned he had no idea how it could be effected.

Just as the morning star appeared, Jim suddenly tired. He felt he must have walked nearly forty miles; he stopped, built a small fire near a frozen creek, curled up beside it, and slept. He had not slept long, though, when a throb in his ear brought him awake. Someone was coming, on horseback; the throb he had registered was the hoofbeats of a loping horse. It was puzzling. He was far from any camp. Why would the horse be loping?

Then the horse — it was Joe Walker's short-legged mare — became visible, with Pomp Charbonneau on its back. The mare's breath steamed white in the frozen air.

"You are a walker, Jimmy," Pomp said, sliding off the mare. "I knew I'd never catch you on foot, so I borrowed Joe's best mare."

Jim Snow would not have been prepared to welcome any of the other trappers — they were too garrulous and quarrelsome for his taste. But he was always glad to see Pomp; he was able and he knew when to keep quiet. Besides, Pomp had been reared in the old country, where there must be other women like Tasmin. Though not a womanizer himself, perhaps Pomp would have some advice on how to live with an old country wife.

"Why'd you want to catch me?" Jim asked. "I'm just on my way to the boat."

"That's why — Pa's on the boat," Pomp reminded him. "At least I hope he is."

"Oh, I expect he's there — he was guarding the Hairy Horn when we left," Jim assured him. "His wife was with him and we left them plenty of vittles. Why be worried?"

"Bad dreams," Pomp said. "Bad dreams for two nights. I dreamt of the Partezon."

"I'd call that a bad dream, all right," Jim said. The Partezon was the leader of the most aggressive band of the Brulé Sioux. His only pleasure was war, and his dislike of whites was well known. There had been talk of him on the boat, but the Hidatsa scouts all claimed that he was far out on the prairies, in the midst of many buffalo. Why would Pomp be dreaming of him, just now? It was deep winter — the tribes seldom raided then.

"I wouldn't expect him to show up now," Jim said — and yet he knew that dreams were not to be carelessly disregarded. Preacher Cockerell had dreamed of the lightning bolt, and not three weeks later it killed him.

"A raid may not be likely, but when I heard you were headed for the boat I thought I'd just come with you," Pomp said. "Sometimes people do what you don't expect them to."

"Particularly if they're Sioux Indians — that's right," Jim agreed.

11

"Shut up, you wretched little catamite!"

Tasmin's hope that the evidence of Jim Snow's violence toward her would go unnoticed at the dinner table was soon dashed — no one, it seemed, could talk of anything else, the exception being her father, who habitually took not the slightest notice of any wounds except his own. Indeed, when Mary, with her usual malice, pointed out that Tasmin had a puffy lip and a lump on her temple, Lord B. merely chuckled.

"Well and good," he said. "High time some fine fellow got the best of Tasmin. Might knock some of the willfulness out of her — a very sensible thing to do."

"No one got the best of me, Father — I merely slipped on some ice and fell into a ravine," Tasmin replied haughtily.

"Liar — black liar!" Buffum cried. "Your husband beat you — all the trappers are quite unanimous on that point."

"Dear Buffum, your grammar continues to erode," Bobbety said. " 'Quite unanimous' is, of course, redundant. A judgment is either unanimous or it isn't."

"Hear, hear, good point," Father Geoffrin cried. He and Bobbety had drawn even closer — they frequently applauded each other's modest flashes of wit.

Tasmin regarded them coolly.

"Very likely both of you, and Bess too, will fall into a ravine someday," she replied. "Let us hope it is a deep one. In fact, I'll go further — let us hope the earth swallows you up, so those of us at table will no longer have to listen to your idiotic chirpings."

"Oh, don't say it, Lady Tasmin," Vicky Kennet pleaded. She had long had a morbid fear of earthquakes, and could not bear the thought of the earth swallowing people up.

Father Geoffrin had long since exhausted his early fascination with Lady Tasmin Berrybender. He now saw her as the very embodiment of English arrogance and lasciviousness.

"What would a fellow such as our Mr. Snow know to do with such a one as Lady Tasmin *except* beat her?" he asked in his whispery voice — though he directed his remarks to Bobbety, Tasmin overheard.

She studied the priest silently for a moment, hoping her malevolent stare would wither him, a hope that was disappointed. Aided by Bobbety's flattery, Father Geoff had convinced himself that his own rhetorical powers were equal to those of an Aquinas or an Augustine.

91

"Your Mr. Snow," he went on, "accomplished though he undoubtedly is in the ways of the wilderness, has never read a book, seen a picture — if we except George Catlin's poor daubings — listened to an opera, heard a fine symphony, worshiped in a great cathedral, or visited a dress shop. If I may be permitted a little mot, his fists are his paintbrushes — as we can all see, he has sketched a rather vivid bruise on Lady Tasmin's temple. To which I say, tut, tut . . . it's what she gets for marrying an unlettered American."

"Shut up, you wretched little catamite!" Tasmin yelled. "If you insult my husband again, I'll come around there and smother you in your own filthy vestments."

Father Geoff merely gave one of his whinnying laughs, but Lord Berrybender came abruptly awake at the mention of the word "catamite," the practices it suggested bringing to mind certain brutish experiences he had suffered while away at school.

"What? Catamite? Surely he's not *that*, Tasmin!" Lord Berrybender said — the brutish experiences had occurred long ago, but had by no means been forgotten.

"Of course he's *that*, Father," Tasmin insisted sternly. "Surely you must have noticed that this little French whelp has enticed our Bobbety into the ranks of sodomites."

"Not Bobbety . . . not possible!" Lord B.

92

bleated. "Not my son and heir!"

"Now, Papa, pay her no mind," Bobbety said. "Father Geoffrin has merely been introducing me to subtleties of Jesuitical doctrine — things it can't hurt to know."

Bobbety smirked at Tasmin and then leaned over to whisper some piece of naughtiness into the smiling priest's ear, a bit of defiance, or dalliance, whose consequences were immediate and terrible.

Lord Berrybender, enraged that, under his very nose, his son might have been subjected to the same foul practices that he himself so much abhorred, grabbed up the long fork that Cook had been using to turn the goose and, leaning across the table, thrust it like an épée, his intention being to jab the fork right into Father Geoffrin's jugular vein. Instead, because of Bobbety's ill-timed whisper, the tines struck him — not the priest — full in the right eye. It was no gentle thrust, either — when Lord Berrybender withdrew the fork, Bobbety's eye came with it. Venetia Kennet screamed and fainted, as did Buffum. Father Geoffrin, fearing that Lord Berrybender might thrust again, slid out of his chair and fled. Piet Van Wely turned very pale and George Catlin looked 'round for Cook, who was always reliable in emergencies.

"Egad . . . 'scuse me . . . what's this now?" Lord B. asked, rather unclear in his mind as to what he had just done. Bobbety emitted a single piercing shriek; before it had ceased echoing, Drum Stewart had rushed over and covered his empty eye socket with a napkin.

Tasmin herself felt the room swirl for a moment, but she didn't faint.

"Be damned, what have I done?" Lord Berrybender cried. His son, one-eyed now, sat sobbing.

"You've made Bobbety a cyclops, Papa," Mary said coolly — "only his one eye is not quite in the middle of his head, as it should be in a proper cyclops."

"Loss of an eye is only an inconvenience — many men have borne it," Drum Stewart said, resolving, privately, to take his meals with the mountain men from then on, their tempers being somewhat more reliable than that of the Berrybenders. All the same, he liked the way Tasmin had threatened to smother the priest.

The mountain men, alerted by the shrieking, watched the proceedings from a respectful distance. No strangers to sudden mutilations themselves, they were nonetheless rather shaken by what Lord Berrybender had just done.

"Somebody needs to shoot that old fool," Tom Fitzpatrick observed.

"Good thought," Eulalie Bonneville agreed. "If he's left loose he's likely to do for us all before he's through."

"They're worse than the Blackfeet, them English," Joe Walker commented.

"*Blitzschnell! Blitzschnell!*" Prince Talleyrand croaked, startling the trappers.

"I've always been against forks," Jim Bridger remarked.

"Seeing a thing like that makes me wish I'd stayed dead," Hugh Glass observed. "The thought of getting an eye poked out gives me the shivers."

"I wonder if we could procure some smelling salts?" Drum Stewart asked. "Venetia Kennet's unconscious and so is Lady Bess."

Tasmin went to the kitchen and secured Cook, who came and surveyed Bobbety's injury as calmly as if she were making soup. Towels, soft rags, and warm water were soon supplied in abundance, though no smelling salts could be located.

"Mademoiselle took it," Tasmin said. "I believe she intended on doing a lot of fainting, up in Canada."

Bobbety was whimpering quietly. "I need Geoff, where's Geoff?" he kept asking.

"Hiding like the coward he is, I've no doubt," Tasmin said.

She soaked a rag in vinegar and managed to get Vicky Kennet awake, but vinegar had no effect on Buffum, or on Eliza, the plate breaker, who had managed to faint while no one was looking.

All through the crisis, as she dealt as best she could with the situation, Tasmin felt Drummond Stewart's hot eyes upon her, a fact which annoyed her considerably. The man had the look of a rank seducer — she was hardly in the mood for such attentions.

Cook made an excellent bandage for Bobbety's empty socket; soon he was led away, still calling plaintively for his Geoff.

To Tasmin's great annoyance her father, after pounding the table a few times, began to sob.

"Buggery, nether parts, buggery — there's a curse upon our blood, I'm afraid!" he cried. "Between Constance and Gladwyn I believe I miss Gladwyn the most — impossible to find a valet with his qualifications in these parts."

Tasmin had just noticed that Pomp Charbonneau was missing. Irritated only last evening by his determination to walk her home, she now found that she wanted him back. She didn't mean to allow the hot-eyed Scot to catch her alone, and Pomp could have been some help in that regard.

"Let me see that nose, Kit," she said, walking over to the mountain men.

"It's stopped bleeding — wiggles funny, though," Kit admitted.

"If I promise not to wiggle it, will you walk me home?" Tasmin asked.

"What an odd place your country is,"

96

Tasmin said, as they neared her camp. "I was struck, you broke your nose, and my brother lost an eye. Makes one feel lucky to be alive at all."

Kit Carson, silent and shy, merely tipped his cap when he left Tasmin at her tent.

12

... naked, mutilated, frozen, scalped ...

They found the first two *engagés* — naked, mutilated, frozen, scalped, eyes gone, genitals gone, leg bones split — more than ten miles from the river.

"These two made a good run for it," Jim observed.

"Not good enough," Pomp said — he was worried about his father.

"Your pa's got along with the Sioux for thirty years," Jim reminded him. "They wouldn't be this hard on your pa."

"When someone like the Partezon gets in a killing mood, thirty years may not mean much," Pomp said.

Tasmin's staghound, Tintamarre, they found not far from the river, speared and frozen stiff.

"That dog was bad to run off," Jim said.

The steamer *Rocky Mount* was now just a few piles of charred planks, scattered over the river ice. Master Jeremy Thaw had had his skull split open with an axe. George Aitken and Holger Sten were both scalped, burned, and cut.

"I liked George Aitken," Jim remarked. "He ought not to have traveled so slow."

"Probably the old lord's fault," Pomp said. "He kept George waiting so he could hunt."

None of the other *engagés* could be found, nor was there any sign of Toussaint Charbonneau and his wife, Coal. The Hairy Horn was missing as well.

"I expect your pa left," Jim reasoned. "Maybe the Hairy Horn finally decided he wanted to go home."

"That's the hopeful view," Pomp said. Most of the plainsmen he knew considered his father an old fool who could barely find his way from one river to the next; and yet his father had survived when many a better-equipped man had fallen. Some lucky instinct seemed, at the last moment, to propel him out of harm's way. Perhaps it would be so this time, as well.

They wrapped the corpses of George Aitken, Holger Sten, and Jeremy Thaw in a few scraps of blankets, hasty and imperfect shrouds, but all they had. Since the ground was frozen hard, burial presented a problem.

"George was a waterman," Jim said. "Maybe we can cut through the ice."

They carried the corpses far out on the ice, hacked holes with their hatchets, and shoved the bodies through. Neither felt quite right about it but there was no better option.

Jim Snow noticed another thing. The victims had been hacked and burned and stuck with arrows, but no one had been shot.

"That's the Partezon's way," Pomp reminded him. "I expect he may have a few guns but he don't use 'em much, and he won't let his people take nothing from the whites. His womenfolk still use bone needles. I think he may trade for a little corn with the Mandans, but otherwise he lives way off in the center of the plains. He tries to keep his people true to the old ways."

"Probably that's why he came all this way to burn a steamboat," Jim suggested. "Once steamers start coming up this river there won't be any Indians left to keep to the old ways — or any ways."

Jim had never met the Partezon — he had just heard tales. Though not a large man, he was said to be able to shoot an arrow clean through a running buffalo, which suggested a powerful arm. He himself had tried the trick a number of times but with no success — he could only get the arrow to go in to the haft. A chief powerful enough to keep his people from trading their independence for the cheap baubles of the whites was a man to be reckoned with. That he killed with a vengeance was evident from the bodies they had found. Plenty of Indians would kill their enemies in a painful manner, but the Partezon had brought his warriors several hundred miles for a purpose — to keep the steamboats out. He had come with at least a hundred warriors, too, judging from the tracks. Few chiefs could boast of full control over their warriors — the young ones, particularly, were apt to bolt and spoil a good ambush. But the Partezon had kept control. Just knowing he was there gave the plains a menacing feel.

"Let's follow the Partezon a ways, and see where he's headed," Pomp suggested; but then he recalled that Jim Snow had a wife to think about.

"I suppose you might be needing to get back to Tasmin," Pomp said. "I can track the Partezon for a day or two and then go look for my pa."

At the mere mention of Tasmin, Jim felt filled with confusion again. He wasn't yet clear in his mind or his feelings, when it came to Tasmin — he felt in no hurry to go back.

"I guess I'll stay with you," he said, a little awkwardly — but Pomp seemed not to mind the awkwardness. He was staring at a small, conical hill about half a mile away. The hill was mostly bare, but had a gnarled tree — cedar, probably — on top, a single tree with a dusting of snow.

Pomp looked troubled.

"That hill looks familiar," he said — "but it ought to be farther south. There's a hill just like that down by Manuel Lisa's old fort,

101

where my mother is buried."

Jim looked at the tree — it seemed to him that he had seen a hill remarkably similar to this one — hadn't it been near the South Platte?

"Maybe it's the wandering hill — they say you usually find it where there's been killings," Pomp said.

Jim had heard of the wandering hill several times — it was a heathenish legend that many tribes seemed to believe. The hill was said to be inhabited with short, fierce devils with large heads, who killed travelers with deadly arrows made of grass blades, which they could shoot great distances.

"If that's the hill with the devils in it they'd have a hard time finding grass blades to shoot at us, with all this snow," Jim said.

Pomp was still staring at the strange, bare little hill.

"My mother believed in the wandering hill," he said. "She claimed to have seen it way off over the mountains somewhere — near the Snake River, I think."

"Well, I thought I saw it once myself — on the South Platte," Jim admitted. "What do you think?"

Pomp shook his head.

"I don't know," he said. "I just don't remember that particular hill being here the last time I came this way."

They had not gone a mile more before

they found the other *engagés*. They had tried to make a stand in a thicket of tall reeds but had been burned out by the Indians and treated as the other *engagés* had been. Wolves had been at the corpses.

"I hate to leave men just laying dead on the ground," Jim said. "It feels unholy."

"I agree," Pomp said — he was still troubled in his thinking about that odd little hill.

They covered the dead *engagés* with driftwood and rocks. The wolves would eventually dig through to them, but it would take them a while.

That night, from a ridge, they saw the Partezon's campfires, red glows far ahead.

"Look at those fires," Pomp said. "That could be two hundred Sioux. The Partezon sure wasn't taking any chances."

"Nope — why would he?" Jim said.

13

Gladwyn felt a prickle of apprehension...

Gladwyn felt a prickle of apprehension when
the old warrior on the white horse rode into
the Sans Arc camp. Many warriors, from
many bands, visited the Sans Arc to look at
the Buffalo Man — women came, and small
children were brought here for him to bless.
When visitors stared at him Gladwyn spoke
loudly in Gaelic to impress upon everyone
that he was a god, a holy fool, born of a buffalo cow.

Always, when there were visitors, Three
Geese, his discoverer, and Grasshopper, his
protector, kept up a constant chatter, de-
scribing the miraculous birth which they both
now claimed to have witnessed. With White
Hawk dead of fever there was no one to con-
tradict them, yet skeptics remained, old Cat
Head in particular. Cat Head often proclaimed his disbelief, but he was not a pop-
ular man; the council of elders refused to
listen to him.

But it was Cat Head who, losing patience
with his gullible tribesmen, went off into the
prairies and returned with the old warrior on

the white horse, an old man who looked at Gladwyn with unflinching hatred. The old one had brought only a few young warriors with him, but Gladwyn felt frightened anyway. The wild newcomers looked as if they could easily wipe out the whole Sans Arc village, should they choose. Gladwyn didn't even bother with his Gaelic — these were not men to be impressed with a little babbling.

"You see, I told you," Cat Head said to the Partezon. "As you can see he is just an ordinary white man, and yet these fools believe he came out of a buffalo."

Three Geese was horrified at the situation he found himself in. Cat Head, without asking anyone, had gone off and persuaded the Partezon to come look at the Buffalo Man. Long ago Cat Head had ridden with the Partezon's band, but then he had hurt his back during a hunt and ever since had been leading an easy life in the Sans Arc village, with three wives to see to his needs. Cat Head was vain and sharp spoken — he was always causing trouble, but rarely this much trouble.

"What is this foolishness?" the Partezon asked Three Geese. "This is just a white man."

"He is a white man, but he came out of a buffalo cow. I saw it and so did Grasshopper," Three Geese said.

"If he came out of a buffalo cow once then he ought to be able to do it again," the Partezon declared. He spoke sharply to his young warriors, who immediately wheeled their horses and raced off into the prairie.

Gladwyn could not understand what was being said, but one thing was clear enough: the old man on the white horse didn't like him. In fact his dislike was so strong that the Sans Arc themselves began to dislike him as well. The whole tribe stopped whatever they were doing and waited idly to see what would happen. His own wives, Big Stealer and Little Stealer, always so eager to get him whatever he wanted, now backed away, waiting, with the other Sans Arc, for the old man's verdict.

The old chief did not bother to dismount and take a close look. He waited, his cold gaze unchanged.

Three Geese began to feel very uncomfortable. It seemed to him that people were turning against him — even Grasshopper had left his position behind the white man. Three Geese, who had found the white man and witnessed the miracle of his arrival, was losing status by the minute. The Partezon was the most respected of all living Sioux. No one challenged him. Thanks to the meddling Cat Head, the Partezon was now there, in the Sans Arc village. Three Geese felt like leaving — he thought he might go live with his brother in the Miniconjou band. Only, for now, it was too late. Whatever test the Partezon intended to make would have to be waited out.

Soon, from the prairies to the north, came the ti-yiing of the hunters. A great cloud of dry snow was being kicked up by the racing horses. The young warriors the Partezon had sent away were now coming back, running a large buffalo cow between them. Three warriors raced on each side of the big cow, driving her straight into the Sans Arc camp. People fell back in astonishment, but the Partezon's young warriors knew what they were doing. As the big cow, almost exhausted, lumbered into the camp, the lead hunter leaned over so close that he was almost touching the buffalo and loosed an arrow, then another.

The buffalo cow ran a few more yards, then stumbled and went to her knees. For a moment she knelt, her breath steaming, coughing blood onto the snow, and then she fell over. The Partezon made a gesture — the six young warriors jumped off their horses and rolled the cow onto her back, at which point the Partezon dismounted and walked over to the buffalo, now spread wide as the young warriors pulled back her legs.

"I need a sharp knife," the Partezon said. "Mine is dull from cutting up those Frenchmen we caught."

He looked at the Sans Arc women — his tone was mild. In a short while, to Gladwyn's horror, his own wife Big Stealer emerged from their lodge and gave the old man a sharp butcher knife, a blade he inspected critically.

"I can make a better knife than this, but right now we have to make a good womb for your Buffalo Man," he said.

Gladwyn felt terror seize him — he didn't know what the old man was saying, but he knew that his days as a holy fool for the Sans Arc were over. He wanted to leap to his feet and flee, but the whole band was close around him now — he would not get ten yards. All he could do was sit, numb with fear, waiting.

The Partezon, working hard with what he considered an inadequate knife, slit the buffalo cow up her whole length, from anus to nose. He made the cut as deep as he could, and then instructed his young men to lift out the guts, armful after steaming armful. The warriors were soon bloody to their shoulders. The Partezon had them string out the guts in long lines and coils — he waved, and the hungry Sans Arc children rushed on them. Those who had knives cut themselves sections — others gnawed at the slippery coils with their teeth.

While the children of the Sans Arc feasted on gut, the Partezon had the buffalo cow —

which was still breathing — cleaned out as completely as possible, opening the rib cage wide, making a large red cavity. When the cow died the old warrior borrowed an axe and broke off most of her ribs — then he turned to the Sans Arc and pointed at Gladwyn.

"Sew him in the buffalo," he said. "If he is a Buffalo Man, like Three Geese believes, then he will soon slip out again. Then I will know that I have been wrong and that he is indeed a god."

It seemed to Gladwyn that a thousand eyes were on him — all he saw were the eyes, as he began to scream. All the eyes were hard now, like the old warrior's eyes. Though he screamed and screamed, the warriors stripped him naked, removed the nice skins his young wives had sewed for him, and then shoved and squeezed until they had pushed him into the red carcass of the ripped-open buffalo cow. The same blood that had once warmed him and kept him alive now filled his eyes, his mouth, his nostrils — he gasped in blood when he tried to breathe.

"He is too large — he won't fit in this buffalo," one of the Partezon's warriors complained.

"Then cut his feet off — if he is a god he can grow more feet when he comes out," the Partezon instructed, handing the warrior the axe. The chopping was soon done, but even when Gladwyn had been crammed into the cavity of the dead buffalo, sewing him in did not prove easy. He struggled far longer than anyone had expected him to. His own blood now flowed into the buffalo, whose warm blood had once saved him. Even when the women pulled the sinews tighter Gladwyn somehow managed to gasp in air. When the sewing was nearly finished he managed to thrust a hand out — but this was a last effort; with the loss of blood Gladwyn slowly weakened; his staring eyes did not close, but he slowly ceased to see.

"I want that hand — I have never had the hand of a Buffalo Man before," the Partezon said. "Perhaps it will help us in the hunt."

The hand was easily cut off, but the young warrior who removed it began to have uneasy feelings about the whole business.

"He hasn't been in there long — I think he might come out when we leave," the young warrior said. "His eyes are still open — I don't like it."

"If you think that, then you are as big a fool as Three Geese," the Partezon said. He cleaned the butcher knife in the snow before giving it back to Big Stealer. Then he mounted his white horse and left the camp.

Later that same day Three Geese and his wives also left the Sans Arc camp and went to live with his brother, among the Miniconjous. In the eyes of the Sans Arc his disgrace was complete. If he stayed with the Sans Arc old Cat Head would never let him forget that he had been foolish enough to suppose that a man had been born of a buffalo.

Three Geese and his wives were not the only Sans Arc to relocate. The dead buffalo lay right in the middle of the Sans Arc camp, with the dead man inside it. The stump of his arm still protruded and his eyes were still open, staring at nothing.

"This is a pretty bad thing to look at," Cat Head concluded. "I don't want to get up every morning and see that buffalo, with that arm sticking out of it and those eyes staring."

For once, Cat Head expressed a sentiment shared by the whole tribe. In two hours' time all the Sans Arc tepees had been folded, goods were packed on travois, and the tribe was on the move. As they left their camp it began to snow heavily. By the time Cat Head himself was ready to leave the old camp, the dead buffalo was only a mound in the snow. Leaving it behind made Cat Head feel so good that he decided to make Big Stealer and Little Stealer his wives. After all, they were competent girls, and they had no husband now.

14

. . . a Hidatsa boy had just come running up with news . . .

"The Partezon is my half brother, but he doesn't like me," the Hairy Horn informed them. They were in the trader John Skraeling's camp — a Hidatsa boy had just come running up with news that the steamer *Rocky Mount* had been attacked and burned. Toussaint Charbonneau shook his head sadly; it was just as he had feared, from the moment they heard that the Partezon was on the move. He and Coal and the Hairy Horn had left the boat just in time.

"Why don't he like you?" the trader, Skraeling, asked. He too had taken precautions when he heard of the Partezon's advance, camping near the Mandan villages in what he hoped was a neutral zone.

"He didn't like it that I went to see the president," the Hairy Horn replied. "He thinks he is better than the president. He doesn't bargain with the white men, or make treaties with them, or smoke the peace pipe."

"He sounds like he needs to be taken down a notch or two," Malgres said. "I expect he's just an old bluffer."

Both Skraeling and Charbonneau looked hard at Malgres, a killer, but a man of little judgment.

"If you think he's a bluffer, why don't you pay him a visit?" Skraeling suggested. "If you're hot to kill somebody, go kill the Partezon."

Malgres didn't answer. John Skraeling was yellowish and thin. No doubt he would die soon. Malgres and the Ponca had discussed killing Skraeling and taking his money and the two young Hidatsa girls he had acquired; but the Ponca advised caution. Even sick, Skraeling was still quick with gun and knife. Besides, all the tribes trusted him and brought him furs. Let him get a little sicker and a little richer: then they could kill him.

Toussaint was not at ease in Skraeling's camp, but he had to stop somewhere until the threat from the Partezon passed. In a day or two, when it was safe, he meant to take Coal and rejoin the English party on the Yellowstone; the only impediment to that plan was the Hairy Horn, who was still officially Charbonneau's charge. There were plenty of Sioux around; the old man could have easily made it back to his band, but now the old fool was resisting all efforts to send him home. Captain Clark, safe in his office in Saint Louis, had specifically instructed Charbonneau to take the old chief

113

home — but it was not easy to make an Indian go home if the Indian didn't want to.

"My people chase around too much," the Hairy Horn said, when pressed on the matter. "I might just stay here, near the river, where there is no danger of thirst. There is some pretty dry country out where my people live."

"If you need a wife I'll sell you one," Skraeling suggested. "I've got one to spare."

This offer annoyed Malgres — if Skraeling was going to dispose of one of his girls, Malgres felt his own wishes should have been considered.

The Hairy Horn didn't want either of the skinny Hidatsa girls. The best woman around, in his view, was Sharbo's plump little wife. For some reason it didn't occur to Sharbo that he ought to share her, and this despite the fact that the Hairy Horn had made his interest plain enough. White men were often obtuse when it came to the common business of sharing women.

"I hope the Partezon wasn't too hard on George Aitken," Charbonneau said — he had a guilty conscience on that score. If he had just been a little more persuasive, George and the other two white men might have left the boat and come with him to safety. George's concern had been for the boat, but after all, his employers were rich men and could always build another boat.

"If the Partezon caught any white men he probably burned them," the Hairy Horn said. "He doesn't like to parley with white men, but he doesn't mind burning them."

"Well, at least George is dead — past suffering," Skraeling remarked. It had begun to snow a little. They all stood around outside the lodge, idle but anxious. Whatever business they might pretend to be conducting, what they were really doing was watching for any sign of the marauding Sioux. No one wanted to be caught snoozing in a lodge if the Sioux riders came flying through the snow.

Suddenly they all saw the Ponca, running as if for his life from the direction of the river — his leggings were loose, evidently he had just been with a woman and had to pull his pants up in a hurry. They all thought of the Partezon, but surely the Sioux would be coming from the prairies, not from the river.

The Ponca, out of breath, babbled his news, and Charbonneau relaxed.

"It ain't the Partezon," he said. "It's Pomp. My boy's coming."

Tears started in the old man's eyes, at the thought of seeing Pomp, his dancing little Baptiste, as Captain Clark had called him when Pomp was an infant. The thought of Pomp reminded him of Sacagawea, and of the fine family life they had had, so long ago.

"Why, that's good news, Sharbo," Skraeling

said. "I like Pomp. We'll kill a buffalo, if we can, and have a fine family reunion."

The Ponca grabbed Skraeling's arm — he was not through reporting, evidently.

"Oh, Jim's with him," Charbonneau said. "I guess that's why this fellow's upset."

"Jim Bridger — I thought he was over at the Yellowstone," Skraeling said. He knew that Jim Bridger and Pomp Charbonneau were good friends — it was merely surprising that the lanky young Bridger would be at the Mandans' instead of deep in the mountains where the rich beaver streams were.

To Skraeling's surprise the Hairy Horn, after chattering for a minute, suddenly launched into his death song, a tiresome chant that none of them wanted to hear.

"No, not Jim Bridger — it's Jimmy Snow that's with him," Charbonneau said.

"Well, well — this will be interesting," Skraeling said. "We don't get a visit from the Sin Killer every day."

15

Far in the distance, now and then, they saw a few brown specks . . .

The buffalo, so plentiful for the past weeks, had suddenly become scarce, Jim observed. Perhaps the fact of the Partezon and his two hundred warriors scared them off. On the trek over to the Knife River the two of them had seldom been out of sight of the great herds; but now, as he and Pomp moved cautiously downriver, toward the Mandan camps, they saw no buffalo — or at least none close. Far in the distance, now and then, they saw a few brown specks, many miles away. Other game was scarce also — scarce enough that when they saw a strange mound in the snow and discovered that it was a dead buffalo, their first thought was food. Cold as it had been, the meat would likely not be spoiled.

Pomp got out his knife and kicked at the carcass, to knock some of the snow off, when he got a bad surprise. The stump of a man's hand protruded several inches from the dead cow's belly.

"Jimmy, look here," he said.

Jim Snow looked — they poked tentatively at the frozen carcass a time or two. Though it was plain enough that the man inside the buffalo would have to be dead, they still moved cautiously. Both had seen numerous instances of decapitation and dismemberment; but neither of them had ever seen a man sewn into a buffalo before. It was impossible to say how long the man and the dead cow had been there, but thanks to the deep chill, they were now frozen together.

"Do you want to try and hack him out?" Pomp asked.

"What would be the point?" Jim said. "We've got no way to bury him. It must be that little fellow from the boat, the one who carried the guns for Tasmin's pa. He was lost in the storm and never found."

"Someone found him, I guess," Pomp said. "Didn't there used to be a good-sized Sans Arc camp around here somewhere?"

"I think so," Jim said. "I wonder where *they* went."

The two of them wandered around the area for a while, hoping some clue to the mystery might turn up. But they found nothing, and it began to snow. Soon the buffalo, with the small man sewn into it, was once more just a mound on the snowy plain.

When they left, drifting south with the snow on their backs, both felt that somehow things were drifting out of kilter. They had not managed to save Captain Aitken or anyone else from the boat, or even managed to bury them properly. The fate of Pomp's father and his young wife remained to be determined. The best place to start a search seemed to be the Mandan villages, and yet, as they went south, Jim Snow seemed so uneasy with the proceedings that Pomp stopped to consider what best to do.

"You don't have to come with me, Jimmy," he said. "Pa's probably at the Mandans' — I imagine he's safe, otherwise we'd have found him. You've got a wife and all. If you want to head back for the Yellowstone, suit yourself."

"No, we better stick together for a while yet," Jim said. "There could still be some of the wild men on the loose."

In fact he didn't believe his own answer — he just didn't want to go back to Tasmin yet. When he tried to think about what to do with Tasmin he felt tired — the complications of marriage took the spring out of his step, a thing that didn't happen when he thought of his Ute wives; but then he almost never thought of his Ute wives. They didn't fill his mind in the way that Tasmin did.

As things stood Jim was glad to have an errand to help Pomp with. It allowed him to put off, for a while, having to deal with the forceful English girl he had married, a woman who didn't understand that the duty of a wife was to be silent before the Lord. What if she never accepted that duty? What if she never obeyed? It was a problem Jim didn't want to think about too much, and yet he couldn't get it out of his mind as he plodded along behind Pomp.

To Pomp the fact that Jim Snow and Tasmin Berrybender had somehow proceeded into a marriage was one of those perplexing facts that no amount of reasoning could explain. That such incongruous matings happened, and happened often, was obvious, though. In Europe great princes were always confounding their subjects by marrying Gypsy dancers or Turkish slave girls — even, now and then, a French whore. If well-born princes couldn't manage to align their fancies with dynastic needs, there was no reason that a frontier boy such as Jim would be any more likely to choose a wife suitable to the circumstances of a mountain trapper or Santa Fe trail guide — professions that were sure to entail long absences from the domestic hearth. Of course, Jim had two Indian wives, but he seldom saw them and they were very likely much easier to deal with than Tasmin Berrybender.

It was a puzzle — on the whole Pomp felt glad that it wasn't his puzzle.

The snow, after a last intense flurry, suddenly stopped falling. The sky cleared, the sun cast down a thin winter light, and to the south, a dog barked.

"Hear that?" Jim said.

"Yep, a Mandan dog, I suppose," Pomp said.

Just then an Indian who had evidently been copulating with a woman jumped up from behind a snowbank, pulling at his leggings — the woman, short and almost square, scurried off like an outraged prairie chicken.

"Why, there's Pa," Pomp said. His father stood a head taller than many prairie travelers and was usually easy to spot in a crowd. He was standing with an old Indian and three or four other men near a Mandan earth lodge, but the bright sun on the new snow made it hard to see exactly the people they were approaching. A thin, high chant reached them, and the dog continued to bark.

"That's the Hairy Horn singing," Jim said. "At least your pa managed to keep up with one of the three chiefs."

"I believe I see John Skraeling," Pomp said, squinting against the glare.

"Be watchful of the little Spanish fellow who's with him," Jim cautioned. "He's the one who punctured Big White's liver."

"Skraeling don't usually run with killers," Pomp observed.

"He probably picked this one up by accident and ain't figured out how to get rid of him," Jim said.

16

"I shall never look noble now," Bobbety complained . . .

Since Jim Snow was gone, and Pomp Charbonneau too, Kit Carson quietly appointed himself Tasmin's guardian; he stuck to her like a burr on her walks from tent to trading post. Most days he waited with her while Cook dressed Bobbety's socket, a task Cook performed imperturbably, while Tasmin distracted her deeply depressed brother by reading him long passages from Pope or Prior.

Father Geoffrin soon made a cautious reappearance, in the main keeping well clear of Tasmin. Once he ventured to suggest that Bobbety might enjoy a snatch of Rousseau, but Tasmin greeted the comment with a look of such chill that the little priest retreated. He began to spend more time with George Catlin, who, despite the bitter cold, seldom passed a day without doing three or four Indian portraits. Some of the sitters had traveled long distances to be painted by the likeness maker.

"I shall never look noble now," Bobbety

complained, though in fact the kitchen girl, Eliza, clumsy with plates but skilled with the needle, had made Bobbety a very practical eye patch out of the soft leather on one of Lady Berrybender's old purses.

"You never did look noble, Bobbety," Tasmin told him frankly. "At best you looked silly."

"Quite right," Buffum agreed. "If anything, Eliza's eye patch lends you a particle of dignity."

"Something sorely lacking up to now," Mary remarked. "Now you look like an evil pirate — one of a sodomitical bent."

"You are all cruel, too cruel," Bobbety complained, though without force. "I wish Father would come and lash you with his horsewhip."

"Not likely — he is off lashing his horses with it, in hopes of catching up to some wild beast he wants to shoot," Tasmin told him.

"Ha ha, perhaps he'll run off a cliff, in which case the title will be mine and I'll make you all pay for your cruelty," Bobbety said. "I'll immediately parcel you out to minor curates and vicars. All frivolities will immediately cease — from then on you will be expected to walk the modest path of piety."

Kit Carson could only stand in wonder when the English spoke to one another in such fashion. What it meant he had no idea, though he did think it likely that Lord Berrybender might someday run his buggy off a cliff. Even the mountain men, well accustomed to the dangers of the wild, looked sharp when in close company with Lord Berrybender. A man who could casually poke out his own son's eye was to be allowed a certain space.

Kit did not understand the business about vicars and curates, but he didn't think that Bobbety stood much of a chance against three such forceful sisters. It was odd how the English could keep on insulting one another hour after hour — insult feeding on insult, rising now and then to an occasional slap or pinch. Among the mountain men ten minutes of such slanderous talk would have led, at the very least, to fisticuffs, and knife fighting or gunplay would not have been out of the question; but with the English it seemed to go no further than words. One thing Kit saw clearly was that Tasmin could easily outtalk anyone in her family — even the old lord grew tongue-tied and red in the face when he tried to match words with Tasmin, the woman with whom Kit was now so deeply in love that he spent most of his nights and days thinking about her. He was not so disloyal as to wish Jim Snow dead, but he did allow himself to hope that

124

Jim would be a while getting back. Perhaps a desire to trap the southern Rockies would come over him — some task that would occupy him for several months. Kit knew that this was unlikely — Tasmin, after all, was with child — but he couldn't help hoping. The mere fact that several of the mountain men had begun to exchange pleasantries with Lady Tasmin had begun to annoy him, a fact not lost on his friends and colleagues. Jim Bridger was huffy about it — not only did Kit no longer have time for *him*, but he had also begun to ignore the camp chores the two of them had been sharing.

"Kit wouldn't bring in a stick of firewood unless he stumped his toe on it," Jim observed to Eulalie Bonneville.

"Men in love need no firewood," Eulalie reminded him. "Their nuts keep them warm."

"Yes, but what keeps their *compañeros* warm?" Jim Bridger asked — though he himself had begun to think rather warmly of the pert Eliza, Cook's brown-eyed helper, who frequently allowed plates and platters to slip through her grasp. She had twice managed to spill gravy in Jim Bridger's lap, a sure sign of ripening affection, in Bonneville's view. Both times Eliza had made a great flutter and tried to daub Jim dry, attentions that embarrassed him and provoked caustic comment from the other mountain men.

"She's wanting pokes, I expect," Tom Fitzpatrick allowed, as the old parrot wandered up and down the long table, seeking scraps. "I suppose she thinks that if she spills enough gravy in Jimmy's lap he'll rise to the task."

"Anybody can spill gravy," Jim replied — he did not like the imputation of coarse motives to his Eliza, although it had to be admitted that his own thoughts often took a coarse turn when Eliza was about.

Tasmin knew, of course, that young Kit was deeply smitten — she had only to let her eyes meet his for a moment to bring a deep blush to his cheeks — even his ears turned a fiery red. When once she gave way to an irresistible impulse, grabbed his silly cap, and flung it onto the snow, Kit was so astonished that it seemed he might pass out.

Of course, in such a place, with the winter deep and the company limited, it was only to be expected that attractions would form and affections flourish or even rage. Tasmin saw with amusement that Drum Stewart, the overheated Scot, had unleashed a tigress in Venetia Kennet. Cook confided the colorful truth to Tasmin: Vicky had obtained some potent sleeping drafts from Monsieur Boisdeffre; these she stirred liberally into the old lord's brandy each night, putting him deeply under and leaving Vicky free to pursue strenuous nightlong tourneys of carnality with the highborn hunter — so strenuous were these tourneys that Drum Stewart only now and then had energy left for the hunt.

For the first week or so after Jim Snow's departure, Tasmin took an amused and lofty attitude toward what she observed at the post. After all, whatever her immediate differences with her husband, she was a satisfied woman, one who did not have to seek casual heats. But as the weeks passed she began to feel less amused, and also less serene — where *was* he, Jim Snow? News had reached them through native runners of the destruction of the steamer. Though too late, Jim had done his duty by Captain Aitken — why didn't he come back and take up his duties to his wife?

For three weeks she went every night to the tent, escorted by the faithful Kit. She knew that when Jim returned he would expect to find her there. It was their home; he had chosen the campsite; so she waited through more than twenty nights, never feeling quite safe, not sleeping very deeply, always half on guard against whatever threats might arise.

But Jim didn't come. Every night, walking out with Kit, Tasmin's spirits sunk a little lower. Why didn't he come? How could he leave her in such uncertain circumstances? That old raunch Hugh Glass had begun to follow her boldly with his eyes. Her noble blood did not impress old Hugh, nor did the fact that she was the Sin Killer's wife. To a man who had survived a bear, Jim Snow may have seemed like small beer. Tasmin did not want to make too much of what, after all, were only looks — but she didn't want to make too little of them, either. In one respect Hugh Glass was like her father: he was all appetite.

"I don't quite like that Mr. Glass," she said to Kit. "He has the look of a criminal, that man."

"Hugh's a rough cob," Kit agreed. "It's all three of us can do to whip him, when he's drunk."

"What about my Jimmy?" she asked. "Do you think my Jim could whip him?"

"Not in a wrestle, no — Hugh's a biter and a gouger," Kit said. "Jim might kill him, though — with a knife maybe. Killing him might be the only way to stop him."

Tasmin thought of the wild old man, watching her. What if he came, caught her before she could even wake up?

"I've made you walk all this distance for nothing, Kit," she said one night. "I'm going back to the fort — after all, I need to be careful. I have a baby coming."

On their way back, their feet crunching in

the snow, Kit imagined himself killing Hugh Glass in a savage fight over Tasmin. Once imagined, the vision wouldn't leave him — he dreamt it by night and dreamt it by day. Sometimes he shot Hugh, sometimes he stabbed him. In one vision Tasmin even gave him a warm hug, as he stood over the corpse of her attacker.

In the next weeks, as winter edged toward its end and the snows began to melt, Kit nourished his fantasy of rescue. Only in battle, he felt, could he show Lady Tasmin that he was worthy of her. With Tasmin living at the post and old Hugh often about, Kit felt that he did not dare relax his vigilance.

"Why's that Carson boy so itchy, when he's around me?" Hugh asked the Broken Hand. "He comes in puffed up like a rooster, ready to peck. Why would he think I'd need to fight a pup like him?"

"Oh, young men are like dogs — they go round snarling, half the time."

"Blitzschnell! Blitzschnell!" the old parrot said.

"It ain't you he's itchy about, Hugh," Tom Fitzpatrick replied. "It's Jimmy Snow's pretty wife he's itchy about. I expect Kit thinks you've got the randies for her."

"No, it's Kit's got the randies for her," Jim Bridger said. "He follows her around like a puppy. Won't hardly even speak to me, and I'm his partner."

"All the same, she is a fair beauty," Milt Sublette declared.

"Jimmy Snow got lucky," his brother said.

"Maybe he's lucky and maybe he ain't — maybe he's just got trouble," Hugh allowed. "If he's so lucky, why'd he run off?"

No one had an answer for that question.

"Jimmy Snow leads his own life," Joe Walker said. "Always has. Holy matrimony may not suit him particularly. It never suited me."

Across the room Tasmin was having an animated dispute with George Catlin — the two of them could hardly discuss any subject without quarreling, it seemed, a fact the mountain men took note of.

"I hope I've got better sense than to take up with a quarrelsome woman — and that one's quarrelsome," Hugh Glass declared. "In the dark one woman's as good as another, I expect, provided the hole ain't plugged."

This sentiment required considerable thinking over. The mountain men gave it seasoned consideration, thinking back over their experiences with women, quarrelsome or docile. Most of these experiences had been so brief that a clear statement of principles was hard to arrive at.

"Hugh may be right," Bill Sublette allowed.

"Hasn't Jimmy Snow got some Ute wives

130

somewhere?" Joe Walker asked.

"That's right — I believe they're down on the Green River," the Broken Hand said. "They're sisters, I believe."

"Probably went back to them," Hugh Glass concluded. "Probably got tired of listening to that English girl yap."

17

"That would be the missing valet."

Jim Snow and John Skraeling were startled by the warmth of the reunion between Pomp Charbonneau and his father, Toussaint. The old man hugged Pomp tightly, as he wept, his tears wetting Pomp's hair and dripping onto his shoulder. The old man was too choked up to speak, and Pomp, usually so shy and reserved, wasn't shy at all about his father's teary welcome. He held the old man close, patted him, whispered to him.

This long embrace of father and son, and the delight they took in being together again, was a wonder to Jim Snow, whose own parents had been killed when he was four. As a captive child, with the Osage, he had had to fight the camp dogs for scraps of food; when the Cockerells ransomed him from the Osage he had become an indentured boy, fed and worked but not loved. He saw in the Charbonneaus' sudden happiness something he had never known — perhaps the lack of it accounted for the fact that he had always felt a man apart. The trader Skraeling must have felt something of the same surprise — he

132

turned away from the Charbonneaus and questioned Jim closely about conditions upriver, the movements of the Partezon in particular.

"He's gone back out onto the plains," Jim said. "We followed him and saw his fires. Coming down here we saw about the derndest thing I've ever seen — a man sewed into a buffalo. Frozen hard, over by where that Sans Arc camp used to be."

As he talked he noticed that the Spaniard, Malgres, was following him with his eyes.

"That would be the missing valet," Skraeling said. "I heard of him from Draga. The Sans Arc — or some of them — believed he was born of a buffalo. I guess the Partezon decided to test the story."

"I guess," Jim said. He wanted to leave, though he wasn't entirely sure where he wanted to go. The sight of Pomp, so happy to be with his father, made Jim restless. While he was trying to make a plan the old Hairy Horn walked over.

"The Partezon is my brother," he said. "How many warriors did he come with?"

"Plenty of warriors," Jim said. "Could have been two hundred."

"He's mean, my brother," the Hairy Horn said. "So is that Spaniard who's with the Twisted Hair."

"You're right about him," Jim said. "He's the man who killed Big White."

"He's a bad one but he won't kill me — it's you he wants to kill," the Hairy Horn said. "You're more important. I am just an old man who will soon die anyway."

Jim glanced at Malgres again — the old Hairy Horn was probably right. Many men killed in battle, but only a few for reputation. Perhaps Malgres was one of that sort — he himself wasn't worried about the Spaniard but he thought it might be well to warn Pomp about him — Pomp, after all, was a highly respected guide, someone who, in Malgres's eyes, might be a reputable target.

Jim said as much to Pomp but Pomp dismissed the threat.

"He won't bother us while we're at the Mandans'," Pomp said. "I want to stay with my father a few weeks — we may go down and visit my mother's grave. If you're expecting to see the boys anytime soon I wish you'd take Joe Walker back his mare. Pa and I and Coal, we'll walk along and take our time."

He didn't mention Tasmin — Pomp tried his best to be tactful, where Jimmy Snow's domestic arrangements were concerned. His tact was appreciated, too. Jim didn't know what he was going to do about Tasmin. Sometimes he felt that Pomp should have married her — after all, he had been raised in Europe and could talk about all sorts of things of which he himself knew nothing; but Pomp, for all his education, didn't seem to be the marrying kind.

"Joe Walker's particular about horseflesh," Toussaint Charbonneau commented, when Pomp handed over the mare. "If that's a Joe Walker horse she'll carry you a good long way."

"Guess I'll find out," Jim said.

"Tell Mr. Stewart I'll meet him on the Yellowstone somewhere, when it's warm enough to start gathering up his zoo," Pomp said. Father and son stood watching as Jim rode away.

He soon learned that old Charbonneau had been right to applaud Joe Walker's judgment where horses were concerned. The little mare had an easy gait which she seemed able to hold indefinitely. Jim had never been able to afford the luxury of a horse of his own, though he had occasionally been given a mule or a burro to ride, when he was with one of the Santa Fe expeditions. In trapping, workhorses were used mainly for packing out furs — the trappers themselves usually walked, which meant that twenty miles was about as far as they could expect to get in a day.

The mare's name was Janey — the day after he left the Charbonneaus, Jim calculated that she carried him a good fifty miles. Such a pace would bring him back to the

Yellowstone in only a few days — but was he ready to go back to the Yellowstone? The weather was warm, the skies absolutely clear. Being alone in such a great space brought Jim a sense of calm that he knew he would soon lose once back in the small tent with his talkative wife. If only Tasmin could learn to behave like Sun Girl and Little Onion, his Ute wives, behaved.

That evening, while spitting a prairie chicken he had managed to knock over with a rock, a new thought struck Jim Snow. The little mare was hobbled some fifty feet away, grazing avidly on the brown prairie grass. Now and then she pawed away a patch of snow, to get at a few more stems. The thought that occurred to Jim was that, with the mare to carry him, the whole West was open to him. Why not cut south and west to the Green River and join his Ute wives? In fact, the best plan of all might be to take them with him down the Yellowstone to where Tasmin waited. Tasmin was no slow-witted girl — no doubt she would quickly learn by example how a good wife should be-have. Also, of course, the child was coming — his Ute wives could be a help with the birthing if they could all get there in time.

It seemed such a perfect plan that Jim was at a loss to know why it hadn't occurred to him earlier. His Ute wives could train his

English wife, not only in how to work skins or sew leggings, but in how to behave with modesty in relation to her husband as well.

Well before dawn Jim slid onto Janey and was off to the southwest, down through the Sioux country toward South Pass and the regions below the Great Salt Lake, where Sun Girl and Little Onion lived. The steady little mare carried him almost twenty miles before the morning freshness faded. The weather was warm, spring not far off. The Utes would soon be planting their little plots of corn. Jim felt a sudden, deep relief. Thanks to the energies of Joe Walker's little mare he had seen a way out of his dilemma. For the moment all he had to do was be watchful and let Janey cover the ground.

18

"At the moment he is devoting himself to lichen . . ."

"Piet is very gloomy still," Mary Berrybender confided to her sister Tasmin. "He only smiles now if I fondle him under the lap robe, which frequently produces some spunk."

"That's a detail you might have spared us," Tasmin replied. "It's hardly wise to provide casual services of that sort."

"Of course it isn't — and why, may I ask, is he gloomy?" Buffum said. "There's plenty of botany around here, let him study it. That's why Papa brought him, after all."

"But he *is* studying it," Mary assured her. "At the moment he is devoting himself to lichen — fortunately there's an abundance of lichen quite near the fort. He won't go farther afield for fear of the great yellow bears."

The fact was that, despite the warming weather, all the Europeans wore gloomy looks. They all lingered at table as long as possible, a much-smudged and diminished company, in Tasmin's view. Señor Yanez, Signor Claricia, and Piet Van Wely were nowadays mostly silent and sad.

"I see no reason why I shouldn't do Piet these little favors, since nothing else makes him smile," Mary said, annoyed, as usual, by her sisters' unyielding attitudes.

"Come to that, it is not only males who are frustrated in this lonely place," Buffum remarked. Unable to arouse much interest in the younger mountain men — Kit Carson was in love with Tasmin, Jim Bridger with Eliza, and young Milt Sublette with Millicent, the laundress — Buffum had been forced to have recourse to Tim, the stable boy; a mostly unsatisfactory recourse, as it happened. Tim had not yet recovered from the forced removal of his frozen digits — he no longer cared to grab Buffum's hand and hold it against his groin. When she herself attempted to remind him of that useful technique, he burst into tears and thrust her away, a rejection that did not improve her temper.

"I can't think why they're all so gloomy," Tasmin said. "The post is snug and the winter's nearly over. Cook, of course, sees that we're well fed."

"Material comforts are not enough, Tasmin," Bobbety said. "I expect they all despair of seeing good old Europe again — I myself will only be seeing it with one eye next time, if I'm fortunate enough to see it at all."

"The fact is, none of them expect to see Europe again, ever," Mary said. "They think Papa will succeed in getting every one of them killed on these harsh prairies, somehow."

"Well, we all have our troubles, in this year of our Lord 1833," Buffum declared. "Even our fortunate Tasmin at last can be said to have troubles."

"Oh, and what might those be, Bess?" Tasmin asked. "I'm aware of no troubles — certainly none worth complaining about."

"Really? It matters so little to you that your husband has deserted you while you are heavy with child?" Bess asked. "I consider it most unlikely that we will ever see the handsome Sin Killer again."

"Of course we'll see him — he's only off trapping somewhere," Tasmin said lightly. "Americans can hardly be expected to live strictly by the calendar, as we Europeans are apt to do."

Her remarks were met with looks of skepticism from her siblings, none of whom appeared to believe a word she said.

"Besides, I am hardly one to tie a man to my apron strings," she went on. "Jimmy and I agreed at once to keep certain freedoms for ourselves. It would be foolish to marry a mountain man and expect him never to roam."

Such statements — not the first Tasmin

had made on the subject of Jim Snow's absence — were served up mainly for the sake of defiance; privately she was furious with Jim for leaving her in such an embarrassing situation. Of course, in the literal sense her statements were true enough: freedom to roam was what defined a mountain man — in fact, most of the other trappers were now leaving too. Only two, Kit Carson and Tom Fitzpatrick, remained at the post. Hugh Glass, Eulalie Bonneville, Jim Bridger, the Sublette brothers, and Joe Walker had all drifted off, up the Yellowstone or along the Milk River, or the Tongue — anywhere they could expect to find beaver. Jim Snow's absence was merely a normal part of the spring exodus, though that didn't keep it from rankling, and rankling deeply, with Tasmin herself. Inwardly she raged one moment, despaired the next. The fact that the two of them had quarreled on the morning Jim left to do his duty by Captain Aitken no longer seemed to have much bearing on the matter. She had known, in fact, that he meant to check on the steamer soon. But almost a month had passed without news of Jimmy, though news did frequently trickle into the trading post through various natives. Only the day before, one of the Minatarees who was related to old Otter Woman had brought news to Drum Stewart: Pomp Charbonneau and his father were waiting for him near the headwaters of the Yellowstone, ready to begin trapping animals for the Scotsman's zoo.

No news could have been more welcome to the red-bearded Scot — to Tasmin's amusement he was packed and gone from the post within three hours, leading two pack animals. His fervor for Vicky Kennet's embraces had long since abated — it weakened even as Vicky's determination to become, someday, Lady Stewart grew stronger. In a fairly short time, though large with child now herself, Vicky had worn Drummond Stewart out — he could hardly wait to escape to the peace of the prairies.

Of course, Tasmin also was great with child. She and Vicky strode about the trading post, heavy and majestic, like two goddesses of the corn, overawing the skittish mountain men by their vast fecundities. Lord Berrybender, offended by the sight, had even attempted to ban the two of them from the common table.

"Takes my appetite, looking at you two great cows," he complained. "I always sent Constance to Dorset until the brats were birthed."

"It's rather a long way to Dorset, Father," Tasmin said.

"Perhaps I'll have Boisdeffre set up a tent — confine you until you've given birth," Lord Berrybender said, ignoring Tasmin's point. "Most unappealing sight, pregnant women. They look like melons with heads."

"Yes, and sometimes the heads even presume to speak, as I myself frequently do," Tasmin said crossly. "Vicky and I intend to stay where we are — *you* move into the tent if you don't like looking at us."

"I'll do better than that, you insolent hussy," Lord B. told her, turning rather red in the face. "Drum Stewart left and so will I. I'll go on a hunt, while the weather's nice and cool. You'll soon have brats at the teat, a sight I don't want to see. Of course, I'll take Millicent with me, to see to the laundry."

Due to her swollen state Vicky Kennet, it seemed, had ceased to appeal to Lord B.; he had abruptly transferred his attentions to the black-haired Millicent, a sturdy, solid girl with no pretentions to wit.

"And of course I'll need Cook," Lord B. went on. "And Señor Yanez and Signor Claricia, in case something goes wrong with the buggy or the guns."

"Cook's not going," Tasmin informed him. "I'll keep Cook."

"What's that? Of course she's going — whose cook do you suppose she is, anyway?" Lord B. thundered, half rising in his chair.

Kit Carson, watching the scene from a distance, felt sure there would be violence; he edged closer — for a moment it seemed it might be her father that he would have to save Tasmin from. But before Lord B. could whack her — which he showed every intention of wanting to do — Tasmin grabbed the same fork that had half blinded her brother and thrust it to within an inch of Lord Berrybender's nose. When he tried to grab it Tasmin drew back, only to lunge again, this time marking Lord B. slightly on the cheek.

Lord Berrybender, in disbelief, sank back into his chair. He touched his cheek, then regarded his bloody finger with surprise.

"You will do well to let be, Father," Tasmin said, still holding the fork. "I am with child, Vicky is with child. We shall each be needing a competent midwife in the not too distant future, and Cook is our best hope. You shan't have her."

Lord Berrybender stared at Tasmin in shock. The tines of the fork seemed to be pointed straight at his eyes.

"Signor Claricia is an accomplished Italian," Tasmin said. "We have all profited from his lectures on garlic buds and olive oil. I'm sure he can cook your bears or your stags or whatever varmints you kill. Cook — I repeat for emphasis — will not be going."

"Insolent Tasmin, so disloyal to our pater," Mary cried, hurrying over to wipe Lord Berrybender's bloody cheek with a napkin.

"Do smite her, Father — smite her hip and thigh," she added.

"God damn you, miss," Lord B. said, looking at Tasmin. "Take my cook, will you?

Next I suppose you'll be telling me I have to do my own laundry."

"I am hardly a miss, Father," Tasmin said. "You've heard the long and the short of it. Cook stays with us."

"And so will my good Piet," Mary said, giving the gloomy Dutchman a peck.

Lord Berrybender rose from the table, took his crutch, and stumped away. He said not another word. That his own daughter would threaten him with a turning fork was such an appalling thing that it put him off for the night. Of course, he meant to have Cook anyway — no child of his was going to tell him what to do with his own servants — it had merely seemed best to leave the field until all the cutlery had been gathered up. Napoleon, he recalled, had been reluctant to leave the field, when circumstances called for retreat.

When Millicent, in due course, presented herself for amorous service in Lord Berrybender's room, she found the old lord deep in thought. Millicent's way was to accept all duties placidly, whether that meant lying beneath Lord Berrybender while he groaned and grunted a bit, or else gathering up the soiled bedclothes. Duties were best done without fuss, but this evening, she had scarcely lifted her skirt when Lord B. waved her away.

"Go along with you, Milly — I've had

enough of girls for one night," Lord Berrybender said. "We're off hunting to-morrow — you'll pack for me, won't you?"

"Yes, if you'd like me to, sir," Milly said.

"That's what I like, Milly . . . a good girl like you, no fuss, no airs," Lord B. said. "We'll have some fine tupping, we will, once we're well out of this fetid hole. Prairie breezes, that's what I need — I'll stir up a bit, I assure you, once I'm out where the wind blows free."

"I dare say you will, sir," Millicent agreed.

19

. . . *a few vagrant flakes of snow* . . .

"Lady Tasmin and Miss Vicky, they'll be needing me once the little ones come," Cook said firmly. The hunting party was set to depart the trading post.

Lord Berrybender was stunned — a servant of his had just refused a direct order. A brisk north wind was blowing, carrying a few vagrant flakes of snow.

Tasmin, also firm, stood on one side of Cook; Venetia Kennet stood on the other. Pierre Boisdeffre, who had developed warm feelings for Cook, lurked in the background.

A wagon piled high with guns and blankets and other kit stood near. A great keg of brandy, acquired at great cost from Monsieur Boisdeffre, was lashed securely in the wagon. Señor Yanez and Signor Claricia, neither of them happy men, waited in the buggy. Both were convinced that their deaths awaited them somewhere on the plains to the south.

Tim, the stable boy, utterly miserable, sat on the wagon seat, grasping the reins as best he could with his damaged hands. Beside Tim, entirely sheathed in an all-enveloping fur coat, sat Bobbety, a Russian cap pulled down so far that his features were scarcely visible. He had been forced from his warm quarters by Lord Berrybender, who was determined that his son and heir should give up foppish ways and test his manhood in pursuit of buffalo and bear. Bobbety's protests and Father Geoffrin's horrified remonstrances were ignored.

"You'll come or I'll disinherit you — doubt you'd like being penniless," Lord Berrybender told his son.

"But, Father, I am accustomed to aiming with my right eye and now I don't have a right eye," Bobbety protested.

"No excuses now, we're off," Lord B. said. Millicent, like the good girl she was, had installed herself meekly in the wagon, next to the brandy keg. All was in readiness, until Cook, to Lord B.'s amazement, informed him that she wouldn't come.

"I'll just stay with Lady Tasmin," Cook said again. "And besides that, sir, Mr. Boisdeffre has been kind enough to offer me a position here at the post."

"A position?" Lord Berrybender said. "I don't give a fig for positions. "You're *my* cook, and so was your mother before you."

"I'm sure Millicent will do well enough, sir," Cook said. "Were it Eliza I might be worried, she's such a tendency to drop the plates."

"This is all your doing, Tasmin," Lord Berrybender shouted. "Cook has always done what I told her to — or what your sainted mother told her to. She is *our* cook — quite irrelevant what you want or what Boisdeffre offers. No more of this nonsense — it's time to be off. Cook, please get in this wagon now."

"Do remember, Milly, just to turn the kidneys a time or two — that's how His Lordship likes them," Cook said, and then, to Lord Berrybender's bafflement, she turned and walked back into the post.

"Here now, none of that!" Lord B. thundered. But Cook, a person of unusual firmness, merely kept walking.

"She can't do that! I forbid it! I won't have you stealing my cook," Lord Berrybender repeated to Tasmin, but his voice lost conviction once the sturdy little figure disappeared into the trading post.

"You will just have to get used to the inconveniences, Papa," Tasmin told him. "You've strayed into a democracy — a great mistake from your point of view, I'm sure. The citizens around here are rather determined to do as they please."

Lord B. didn't answer. He was remembering a great rich pudding, filled with plums and cherries that he had eaten once in his great house. Had it been a victory pudding? Trafalgar, perhaps — or Waterloo or something even earlier? His Lordship could not remember who had cooked this pudding — had it been Cook, or her mother, or, even, her grandmother? There had been some victory — or was it only a wedding . . . perhaps it had even been for his own marriage with . . . with . . . ? He could not, for the moment, recall the name of his fine wife. It was as if the brisk wind of the prairies were blowing away his memories, one by one. Constance it had been; he felt sure that *that* much was right. About the victory . . . if it had been a victory . . . he was not now sure . . . only sure, in the end, that the pudding had been wonderful, filled with cherries and plums . . . sugary and juicy it had been . . . never had he had such a pudding . . . and now Cook had left, and Constance had died, and such puddings as that, with their plums and cherries, would not be for him to eat again.

"Look out! The old boy's crying . . . now what?" Tasmin said. She was wondering what more they would have to endure before her father finally went on his hunt.

Lord B. stood by the buggy, indifferent to Señor Yanez and Signor Claricia. Tears streamed down his face — memories light as thistles seemed to be blowing 'round his head, memories of damsels blithe and jolly whores long dead, or puddings perfectly baked and kidneys correctly turned, of fine, velvety rich claret, of the duke . . . Some duke! . . . Which duke? Had it really been Trafalgar when Cook . . . some cook. . . . baked that great pudding, or was it merely a wedding, perhaps even his own?

The gunsmith and the carriage maker were horrified — were they fated to journey into the country of the great bears at the whim of this old man who couldn't stop crying?

Tasmin was merely disgusted. It was hardly the first such maudlin display she had witnessed of late — once Lord B. found some slight excuse to feel sorry for himself, buckets of tears were sure to flow.

Meek Millicent saw at once that it was her duty to put His Lordship in order.

"Here, sir . . . come on now, just sit by Milly," she said encouragingly. "There's plenty of room here on the blanket."

Grateful for a kind voice, Lord Berrybender did as he was told. He crutched his way over to the wagon and sat on the blanket Milly offered.

"Stop crying now, don't wet your shirt, please, sir," the girl continued. "Might miss your target if you catch cold."

"Let's be going now, Tim . . . snap to!" Milly ordered. Like Cook, she believed in speaking with authority when it came to lax young men such as Timothy.

Tim was not quite so broken in spirit that he enjoyed taking orders from a laundress, even though it was clear that she was His Lordship's new favorite. The old wild head was even then resting itself comfortably on Millicent's substantial shoulder. Tim popped the reins on the horses' rumps.

"Alas, I go! Au revoir, Geoff!" Bobbety cried.

Señor Yanez and Signor Claricia looked at each other and shrugged. It seemed that, for better or worse, the hunt was on; neither of them doubted that it would be for worse.

"Now, there's a turn. Papa's got a new bawd," Tasmin said to her sisters, as the wagon bounced off into the prairies.

"That's right, our wicked laundress," Buffum agreed. "Now who do you suppose will fold our clothes?"

20

. . . quietness and calm were at last to be met with . . .

With the departure of the mountain men, and then of Drummond Stewart, and finally of Lord Berrybender and his attendants, quietness and calm were at last to be met with in the nearly empty rooms of Pierre Boisdeffre's trading post; the calm would have been complete but for the fact that the early spring winds blew fiercely over the northern lands, sighing and roaring through the nights so violently that Tasmin was sometimes kept awake. Deep sleep, indeed, was not easily obtained; if it was not the winds that awakened her it was apt to be the baby, turning and stirring in her womb.

Venetia Kennet, almost as far along as Tasmin, experienced similar disquiet. Often the two of them found themselves in the kitchen in the early morning, letting Cook make them tea as dawn reddened the windows. Sometimes trader Boisdeffre, who had taken a great fancy to Cook, would play melancholy tunes on his Jew's harp. Buffum might appear, pale in her gown, then Mary,

153

then George Catlin; and last, invariably, would be Father Geoffrin, who would immediately announce that he hadn't slept a wink due to his anxieties about Bobbety.

Often Tasmin would suggest cards. Buffum would usually drift off with Boisdeffre; she was helping him organize his stores — so far rather scrambled — in return for which Monsieur Boisdeffre taught her songs of the *voyageurs* who paddled the northern streams in search of furs. Frequently, once the cards were brought out, Tasmin teamed with Vicky Kennet against the painter and the priest. Vicky, freed of the necessity of losing endlessly to Lord Berrybender, proved a skilled and savage competitor. As Tasmin herself was no mean hand at whist, the two women generally routed the men. With many of the Indians now gone away to hunt, George had little to paint except the landscape. Sometimes the card play went on all morning and well into the afternoon, entailing much lively banter. Even when Mary sided with the men, as a kind of coach, the women usually won. Occasionally George would let Mary play his hand; then he took out his sketch pad and did the scene in a few strokes.

"There, how's that?" he asked, handing the sketch around. "I shall call it *Three Ladies and a Jesuit at Whist*."

"Don't call it anything until you fix my

chin," Tasmin told him. "I'm sure my chin isn't *that* sharp."

"Nor is my bosom that *heavy*," Vicky Kennet protested.

George smiled, but held his ground. "I am sketching now not only the present but also the future," he told them. "I see you not only as you are but as you will be. That, after all, is the portraitist's gift — even his duty, I'd say."

"And you practically didn't put me in at all," Father Geoff complained. "You've made me so mere, you know . . . I'm only a wisp."

"Your spirit is particularly elusive, Father," George admitted. "Developments there will no doubt be in your life — they're not likely to make you markedly heavier, though."

Mary alone seemed happy with her likeness — so happy in fact that George Catlin gave her the little sketch, an act that annoyed all three of the other sitters, who would have liked to have it.

In the days round the card table, near the big fireplace, Tasmin found herself feeling more friendly toward her three companions, whom, previously, she had dealt with rather cavalierly. On the boat and in the trading post, crammed in with so many musky males, Tasmin had had little patience with Vicky, George, and Geoff; but with the musky males removed — the mountain men had been, of course, the muskiest — the talents and personalities of her companions could be better appreciated. Vicky Kennet, freed from amatory pressures long enough to get in some practice, was a more than decent cellist; and George Catlin, of course, though sometimes too hasty, was a more than decent painter. Father Geoffrin, though vain as the day was long, *did* have a subtle French mind, and *had* read many books. Though the little priest coveted Tasmin's attention all the time, and was filled with malice and spite when she denied him, he was not, on the whole, a bad companion.

On occasions when conversation bogged down, Tasmin and Vicky had their rapidly advancing pregnancies to fall back on, the uncertainties of which provided much grist for talk.

"The absence of wet nurses is rather shocking," Vicky observed one day. George Catlin's hasty pencil had not much exaggerated her bosom, which every day grew heavier still as it filled with milk.

Tasmin was experiencing the same phenomenon.

"There aren't any, if that's what you mean," she said. "I suppose we'll just have to let the little brutes suckle."

"Of course you should let them suckle," George said. "Why else do you think you *have* bosoms?"

"It wouldn't do in France — no lady

would think of such a thing," Father Geoffrin mentioned. "The better bosoms *there* are strictly reserved for amatory play."

"As you may have observed, we ain't in France, Father," Tasmin replied. "Vicky and I will simply have to risk scandal and give suck ourselves."

"It might even make a nice picture, George," she suggested. "The two of us nursing our young."

"Why, it might," George said, brightening a little. The fact was, he was growing weary of painting Indians. Necessary as it was to secure a vivid record of these vanishing Americans, the daily anxiety, as he waited to see if his wild subjects would approve of their likenesses, had begun to wear on his nerves.

Of course, he had long wanted to paint Lady Tasmin, and would have no objection to having Vicky sit too — either or both would be a nice change from chiefs and warriors, many of whom were at least as vain as any English lady. Now that both ladies had become better disposed toward him, perhaps something could be achieved.

"I suppose we might call it *Madonnas of the Missouri*," he suggested. "What would you think of having the parrot in it? People do like to look at birds."

"Tush, why not?" Tasmin said. She had come, over the last weeks, rather to like George Catlin. At first his stiffness and pomposity had irritated her so frequently that she delivered some sharp rebuffs — rebuffs that annoyed George so much that he sometimes jumped up and left her company. But she hadn't cowed him; the man defended his opinions, and his resistance earned her respect. With her husband gone and the company thin, having someone to argue with was not a thing to be despised.

"George, if you intend to do us as proper madonnas, you'll have to wait till our brats appear," Tasmin said. "Why not do us now — you could call it *Pregnant Cows of the Missouri*."

At this Vicky burst out laughing, Tasmin giggled, and even George could not resist a laugh.

"I demur, I demur," Father Geoffrin said, with a look of delicate disdain. "No sane person could enjoy looking at those vast bellies. I believe I speak for the civilized public when I say that."

Piet Van Wely, who had all but given up speech, suddenly perked up.

"It is nonsense this Jesuit speaks," he said, a gleam of life in his eye — the first in weeks. "*I* would like to look at this picture you talk about."

"Oh well, listen to our botanist," Father Geoffrin said. "A Dutch botanist, I might add — hardly an opinion we need consider."

Mary Berrybender, fierce in defense of her

Piet, flew at the priest and tried to scratch his cheeks with her sharp nails, but Father Geoff, no stranger to Mary's furies, fended her off with a large ladle.

"Hold your tongue, you sickly pederast, or it will be the worse for you," Mary hissed.

"Well, what about it, George?" Tasmin asked. "I've seen a good many pictures, here and there in our country houses, but I don't believe I've ever seen a picture of pregnant women. Why would that be?"

"Goodness, I think you're right," George said. "I've never seen one either — perhaps I have a chance to break new ground."

"Looking at pregnant hussies like these would be rather like looking at a dugong or a manatee," Father Geoff said, with a superior smile. "Who would want to hang a picture of a dugong on their walls?"

"I would — they are gentle creatures," Piet assured him. He had not spoken in so long that the sound of his own voice came as a pleasant surprise.

Tasmin and Venetia, their lovers absent, had lately been experimenting with hairstyles. It was something to do. Tasmin had been trying to persuade Vicky to cut her long hair. In frontier circumstances, why keep such a mane?

"You'll never have time to brush it properly, once the baby comes," she pointed out. Vicky, who regarded her long auburn hair as one of her chief glories, had resisted the notion so far, but seemed to Tasmin to be weakening.

"George, you must do us at once, before Vicky cuts her hair," Tasmin insisted. "In my opinion such a study will fill a niche: the harsh effects of procreation revealed for all to see."

"Without pregnant women there would soon be no human race," Vicky intoned — a sentiment that Father Geoff considered heavily obvious.

"No human race, exactly," Piet agreed.

"I'm not sure that Vicky and I should disrobe entirely," Tasmin went on, planning the sitting in her mind. "Perhaps we should just drape a shawl here and there, so as not to be absolutely stark naked."

Kit Carson, listening in quiet astonishment, felt his ears turn red with embarrassment. It seemed that Lady Tasmin and Miss Kennet were proposing to undress and allow the painter to draw them, an intention that would surely shock Jim Snow, or any of the mountain men.

"Why couldn't Buffum and I be naked too?" Mary asked. "We could be handmaidens of desire, could we not?"

"Personally I only desire to be my normal shape again," Tasmin said. "If George at some point wishes to draw your scrawny body, that's fine with me."

160

George Catlin had been racking his brain to see if he could remember a picture that showed a female in the heavily pregnant state. He could not think of one. A noble subject had suddenly been presented him — a subject not only noble but also universal. All mothers, at some point, looked rather as Tasmin and Vicky looked. His own mother must have looked so, though of course he could not remember it.

"I shall just call it *Motherhood*," he said, overcome for the moment by the solemnity of the undertaking.

"Oh tush, George, that's so boring," Tasmin said. "Can't you think of something a little spicier?"

"Why yes, he could draw a prick and call it *Fatherhood*," Father Geoffrin suggested, with a wicked smile.

Titillated, as always, by his own wit, the priest had failed to notice the stealthy approach of Mary, who had snuck into the kitchen and secured a large tureen of gravy, which she promptly dumped over Father Geoffrin's head, leaving the drenched priest too stunned to speak.

"You vile child!" he gasped, before running off to his room to change his dripping vestments.

George Catlin scarcely noticed the incident, so absorbed was he in planning the composition; though idly suggested by Tasmin, it had now quite taken hold of his imagination. *Motherhood*, if delicately yet boldly executed, might be the canvas that would make his name. Perhaps it should be hung in some great building in Washington — the Capitol, perhaps. The more he thought about it, the more excited he became. The allegorical dimension should not, in his view, be ignored. Were not these two Englishwomen, after all, giving birth to Americans — and, by extension, to the new America itself? Would not they represent the newer, the grander America even then being born in the West?

A grand canvas it must be, George decided — in the background there should be a winding river, the broad Missouri that they had just ascended. Forget the parrot, a bird of other lands. There should be nothing less than an eagle, hovering near, and with luck, rather with skill — he might even get in a buffalo.

21

. . . nude except for two long purplish shawls . . .

Venetia Kennet, clad mainly in her own long auburn hair, lounged on a velvet coverlet in the canoe, which was firmly anchored in the Missouri's shallows. Tasmin Berrybender — the Old World bringing its fecundity to the New, or, alternatively, the New World about to offer up its bounty — nude except for two long purplish shawls which she had looted from her mother's wardrobe, was just stepping ashore, behind her the great dun prairies of the West. Tasmin's problem wasn't George Catlin's ambitious concept, it was the shawls. A stiff prairie wind was blowing, frustrating Tasmin's efforts to drape the shawls around herself in a becoming fashion — now and then the two shawls unwound completely, leaving her naked, an obviously pregnant woman, clutching two purple sails — a spectacle so ridiculous that neither Tasmin nor Vicky could contain their mirth. The fact that a great and grave precedent was being set — pregnancy celebrated on canvas for the first time — did not make the proceedings seem less absurd — not, at least, from the models' point of view.

"We're quitting for the day, George — it's too goddamned windy," Tasmin declared.

George had to agree. Though he felt sure the allegory would be powerful, once captured, it was rather too breezy for accurate work. Vicky's hair was always blowing, or Tasmin's shawls.

"Perhaps tomorrow we should try this inside the post," he suggested. "I can always come out and get background — it's the two of you I haven't yet got quite right."

"What if you never get us quite right, George?" Tasmin asked wickedly, pulling on the skins the Oto woman had made for her back downriver. Somehow the woman had correctly estimated just what her pregnant dimensions would be.

"Why shouldn't I get you right?" George inquired. "It's only a spatial problem — Venetia is so long-legged that she takes up most of the canoe, putting you too far to the right. It just needs adjusting. Perhaps you should be lounging and Vicky standing up."

"No thank you, I prefer to lounge, otherwise my hair would blow," Vicky said. "It's even worse than Tasmin's shawls."

"I doubt the problem is spatial, George," Tasmin said — she was in a mood to tease.

"Of course it's spatial, what else could it be?" George asked.

"Oh, merely that you don't understand women," Tasmin said. "It's why I was such a long time liking you. You're only comfortable with us if you can allegorize us — have me stand for Vanity and Vicky for Lust, or vice versa. The fact that we are many things, not *one* thing, has confused better men than you."

George Catlin was unruffled.

"Be that as it may, I still need to do a little more work on the two of you in this canoe," he said.

"*Do* you, in your pride, suppose that you do understand women, George?" Tasmin persisted. She had no intention of letting the man wiggle off into the technicalities — she didn't care a fig about spatiality.

"Perhaps I don't quite understand them, but I *like* them," George insisted. "I hope you might at least give me credit for that."

"Do *you* think he likes us, Vicky?" Tasmin asked.

"He certainly likes to *look* at us," Vicky said. She had no desire to persecute nice Mr. Catlin, whose many sketches of her seemed to catch a fair likeness. Why Tasmin was so determined to be mean to the man was a mystery — Tasmin just sometimes displayed an inclination to be mean.

"There you have it — likes to look,"

Tasmin remarked. "I consider that quite a damning comment — likes to look."

"But it isn't at all damning, my dear," George replied. "I'm a painter. If I *didn't* like to look I'd be in a fine pickle. Painters like what their eyes like — or, to put it more strongly, they love what their eyes love. Why should that be wrong?"

"Myself, I'd want more than looking," Tasmin assured him. "Don't mind looking for a bit, but then I'd want a tumble. Your approach is much too pallid, George."

George was studying his rough attempt — Tasmin's badinage did not offend him. So far what he had was a fair study of the glorious curves of womanhood — belly, breasts, shoulders, thighs, derrieres.

"Regard," he said, handing the sketch to Tasmin.

"Regard what?" she said. "It's just a lot of curves."

"Yes, but that's the beauty of women — curves, and generous curves, in the case of you two," he said. "If I can get the curves right, then I've got the woman right. When the curves make a harmony, the spirit will have been caught — insofar as the spirit of woman can ever be caught, of course."

"Surely you can't suppose there's much harmony in *my* spirit, George," Tasmin said. "Vicky is a fine cellist, perhaps replete with harmony, but I'm all kettledrums and cym-

166

bals myself — so is my husband. The cymbals clashed so loudly that he ran off, as you know."

She *did* like the balance of the opposing curves, though — hers and Vicky's.

"What about it, Venetia — is it better to be painted, or to be courted?" Tasmin asked her companion.

"Why, I can hardly say, Tasmin," Vicky replied. "I don't think I've ever been courted — I've merely been assumed. That's the way it is, I fear, for women of my station."

Tasmin was startled. Vicky had not spoken in sorrow, particularly, and yet, if her remark was true, sorrow there must be.

Vicky Kennet stepped out of the canoe and wrapped herself warmly in a velvet coverlet.

"Tasmin, I've just decided — I want to cut my hair. I want to cut it all off! All! Will you help me?"

Tasmin was shocked, not because Vicky had decided to be sensible and rid herself of such a burdensome mane, but by her tone — a tone of bitter resignation, the resignation of one who would always be not courted, just assumed.

"Of course, Vicky — I'll help," Tasmin said, but George Catlin, in a panic, broke in.

"Cut off your hair — but you can't," he protested. "I mean, you can cut it, of course, but couldn't you just wait until I've finished my picture? I'm sure with one more sitting I can get it right. You've such splendid hair, my dear — far better than any drapery we could find. Couldn't you just allow me one more day?"

"Perhaps, but I'm not sure, we shall have to see," Vicky said, in sudden bitterness.

"But please — just one more sitting?" George pleaded, but Tasmin took his arm and led him away.

"Don't pester her, George. Let be for now," she advised. As they watched, Vicky Kennet, wrapped in the coverlet, hurried back to the post, her long hair dangling down.

22

"How grotesque pregnant women seem."

Buffum, Mary, Piet, Kit, Father Geoff, and Pierre Boisdeffre had been allowed to watch the painter painting the two women in the canoe, but they had been warned not to come too close, lest their idle commentary distract the artist — in his case the models themselves were sure to supply sufficient distraction.

Near the group from the fort were several Assiniboines, who had ridden in from the north to do a little trading. Being in no hurry, they stopped to watch the strange proceedings on the Missouri River's shore.

"How grotesque pregnant women seem," Mary declaimed. "I shall remain a virgin all my life in order to avoid that awkward state."

"I doubt your resolve will hold if you keep encouraging Piet," Buffum warned. "Males not infrequently misinterpret our good intentions."

"No, no . . . not the little one — she merely eases my anxieties," Piet protested, though not with much force.

"I don't yield the point, Mary," Buffum

said. "There's Tasmin, there's Vicky, proof positive. No doubt a great number of anxieties were eased while they were getting themselves in that state."

Kit Carson felt that his ears might burst into flame, so hot were they with embarrassment. Tasmin was some distance away, but, unable to handle the shawls, she now and then stood quite naked, and so, more or less, was Miss Kennet. If Jim Snow were to return at such a moment, murder would no doubt occur — perhaps more than one murder. He himself, entrusted with Tasmin's care, might come under attack, and he felt that he deserved to be attacked, for allowing Lady Tasmin to display herself so shamelessly — but how to stop her? None of the people watching seemed to be disapproving, a thing that puzzled Kit. Apparently if a painter like Mr. Catlin wanted to make a picture of women with their clothes off, then women simply took their clothes off and let him, with no embarrassment even.

More and more often Kit was troubled by the suspicion that the English were not really sane. Mountain men were thought to be wild, and they did get drunk and spit and fight, but no mountain man would simply take his clothes off and allow a painter to draw him in his nakedness. Kit had seen a good many of George's Indian paintings, and in those the opposite approach prevailed: the

Indians piled on all the finery they could get their hands on, bear claw necklaces, eagle feather headdresses, fine buckskin robes, and lots of paint. He would have suspected the English ladies to do more or less the same thing, don their best gowns and finest gems, not scamper around naked on the muddy banks of the Missouri River. The whole business was quite disturbing. Every few minutes Kit scanned the plains to the south, half expecting to see Jim Snow arriving, murder in his eyes.

The Assiniboines, for their part, were divided in their opinions about the strange activities in and about the canoe. A young warrior named Skunk claimed to have once used that very canoe, which he said was an ill-balanced bark of the utmost impracticality.

"That canoe will capsize if they're not careful," Skunk declared.

Bad Head, who had had more experience with whites than the boy Skunk, doubted that the pregnant women meant to go anywhere in the canoe.

"They're not trying to go anywhere," he pointed out. "I think they're just playing some game."

Red Crow, the leader of the little group, had recently had his portrait painted by the likeness maker. It was obvious to him that the painter had persuaded the women to take their clothes off so he could look at their big bellies, a desire that was beyond Red Crow's comprehension. He had never liked to look at his wives when their bellies were big.

"Maybe they want to have their babies in the canoe," Bad Head suggested — it was not reasonable, but then nothing the whites did struck him as particularly reasonable.

"It could be religious," Red Crow said. "They could be offering themselves to the river spirits, to make their babies come easier."

"I don't think so," Bad Head countered. "The river spirits like virgins — at least that's what I was taught."

In his view the river spirits, which were quite powerful, had a right to unsullied females. The two white women were English — perhaps the English didn't understand that the spirits were finicky in such matters.

As they watched, the painter and the women and the other white people began to walk toward the post. The two large women who had been naked had finally covered themselves, a relief to Red Crow, who didn't like seeing large white bellies.

Then the painter said something to Kit Carson and old Boisdeffre and the two of them picked up the canoe and began to carry it toward the trading post, an action that made no sense at all. A canoe belonged in the water.

"Maybe it has a hole in it," Skunk said.

"They probably want to patch the hole."

Bad Head rode over to the river, hoping he might hear the river spirits the whites had been attempting to entice, but all he heard was the low murmur of the Missouri River, flowing over some rocks.

23

. . . *light and graceful Molière* . . .

"I only supposed it to be a deer of some kind," Bobbety explained, looking at the dead horse. "I didn't want to come on this hunt, or shoot at beasts. I far prefer to collect fossils, or even rocks. You're the one who insisted I shoot, Papa. I merely shot to please you."

Lord Berrybender was shocked almost beyond speech. His horse, the great Thoroughbred Royal Andrew, descended in a direct line from the Byerly Turk, a horse that had been carrying him swiftly among the buffalo all day — he had knocked over at least forty of the great beasts — now lay dead, shot by his own son.

Lord B. had come in, as was proper, and given Royal Andrew to Tim, who rubbed him down. Then they allowed the horse just a bit of a scamper — it was while he was scampering, not far from camp, that they heard the report of a gun.

"My Lord . . . the savages . . . where are they?" Lord B. cried. He felt certain that they must be under attack, but Señor Yanez shook his head. He knew exactly which of His Lordship's rifles had just been fired.

"It's Master Bobbety," the Spaniard said. "He's only got the one eye now."

Bobbety had spent much of the day hiding in a small hummock of grass, near the camp. He remembered that the vast American plain had swallowed up Gladwyn, Fraulein, Tintamarre, a boatman, and at least two Indian chiefs. His one ambition was to avoid being swallowed up. From his hummock of grass he could clearly see the wagon and the buggy — at least he could see them when his one eye didn't water. Of course, various animals ambled by his post during the day — buffalo, elk, and antelope, plus several scurrying creatures. It was only as the day wore on toward evening that Bobbety decided to shoot a large beast — then he would have been "blooded," as his father put it, and, once blooded, perhaps he would be allowed to return to the trading post, whose comforts he sorely missed.

So, when a large brownish beast rather like an elk scampered within easy range, Bobbety, myopic from birth, shot it — only to realize, from a whinny the dying beast gave, that it hadn't, after all, *been* an elk or a deer, but only a horse. Not until confronted with his father's shocked face did Bobbety realize that he had killed Royal Andrew, the finest horse in his father's famous stud. There before them the great horse lay, dead as any of the forty buffalo that had fallen that day.

Lord Berrybender turned ash white — he attempted speech.

"My horse — my best horse," he said — of all the losses suffered by the Berrybenders since their arrival on the Missouri River, none struck home like this one.

Lord Berrybender stared at Bobbety, but had not the strength even to curse. He wavered, he wobbled, then he dropped the glass of brandy in his hand and slowly sank down across the still-warm rump of Royal Andrew, in a dead faint.

"Smelling salts, smelling salts," Signor Claricia demanded, snapping his fingers at Tim — the stable boy, fervently hoping that Lord B. was as dead as his horse, sauntered over toward the campfire, where Milly, the laundress, was attempting to cook a kind of hash which Lord Berrybender favored and which Cook had taught her to make, only Cook had not had to make it over an open fire with a strong wind blowing.

"The old boy's fainted — got any smelling salts, Milly?" he asked. Now that he was out of the chilly stables his own spirits had improved so much that he was not above attempting familiarities with the buxom Millicent. Seeing her bent over the campfire, he sidled up and rubbed himself briefly against her ample backside, only to receive a stinging slap for his efforts.

"None of that now — I ain't your whore, Tim," Milly said. "Just stir the hash like a good boy while I see to His Lordship."

"Oughtn't to be so high and mighty with me, Mill," Tim said. "Wasn't it I that carried water for you, and helped you all these years?"

Milly ignored that plaintive cry and hurried over to the dejected little group standing around the dead horse and the fallen lord.

"It *did* look rather like an elk," Bobbety insisted, to Signor Claricia. The carriage maker had been kicked or nipped several times by the dead Thoroughbred — his passing caused Signor Claricia no grief at all.

To everyone's surprise the forthright Milly bent over Lord Berrybender and administered a number of vigorous slaps, first to one cheek and then the other.

"Gets the blood moving, a smart slap or two," Milly said, continuing with the smart slapping until His Lordship began to stir. His cheeks were soon red, rather than white. With a little heaving and tugging Milly and Señor Yanez soon had him on his feet.

"There now, sir, you're fine — I'd best get back to the hash," Milly said. Tim, sulking from his rejection, attempted to make a grab for her as she went by, but Milly shrugged him off without breaking stride.

"Come now, no languishing, men — you've

got a good deal of work to do," Lord Berrybender said, once he had picked up his brandy cup.

None of the company knew what Lord Berrybender meant. The day was over, the bold big sun just sinking, in flaming glory, into the green plains to the west. Earlier Signor Claricia had gone 'round and taken the tongues from a number of fallen buffalo — Lord B., tired of kidneys, now preferred to breakfast mainly on tongue. The guns were cleaned — Señor Yanez had promptly seen to that. What work could His Lordship possibly mean?

"What do you mean, Papa — it's rather near the dinner hour," Bobbety inquired.

"No dinner for you, you myopic whelp!" Lord B. thundered, suddenly livid with anger at the thought that his own son had put an end to the life of Royal Andrew, the finest prize in his stud.

"No dinner for any of you, not till my fine boy is buried," Lord Berrybender decreed. "Get the spades, Tim — and the picks."

"Bury a horse?" Bobbety asked, very surprised. "Why would one bury a horse?"

"Of course you'll bury him — all of you get to work — you'll not have a bite until you finish. You don't suppose I'd leave Royal Andrew just lying out, do you? He must be buried honorably and promptly — so get to it."

"But, Father, it will soon be dark," Bobbety pointed out. "Couldn't we bury him in the morning? I'm sure we'd all be fresher."

"Didn't ask your opinion and don't give a damn how fresh you are," Lord Berrybender declared. "Bury my horse — bury him now."

"Good-bye, I leave now," Señor Yanez said in decisive tones.

Lord B. had been just about to hurry off and enjoy a good plate of Milly's hash when the small Spaniard made his announcement.

"I leave too," Signor Claricia said, no less firmly.

"My work is with carriages," he added. "I don't want to cut out buffalo tongues no more, or bury horses."

"Oh damn, now you're both acting like Cook," Lord B. said. "You think you can just leave me at your whim, I suppose. You'll mutiny when the task displeases you. Hardly reflects credit on your countries, I might say! Come back here! You're my servants — knuckle under now and do as you're told. Otherwise you won't get a cent."

"What good is cents if you're dead?" Signor Claricia asked, but he made the comment to Señor Yanez, as the two of them were strolling off toward the wagon, to secure their kit. Without addressing a word to Milly they took their blankets, a fowling piece, and old Gorska's fine Belgian gun and strolled away into the deepening dusk.

"Fools!" Tim said. "They won't get far — where is there to go?"

"I'm afraid I can't answer precisely," Bobbety said. "I don't know where there might be to go — but I rather believe Señor and Signor are going anyway. There has indeed been a small mutiny, and Papa has failed to quell it."

When they strolled over to get shovels, Lord B. was tucking heartily into Millicent's hash. He viewed the departure of the gunsmith and the carriage maker as a very temporary thing.

"Too excitable, these Mediterraneans," he declared. "Likely to flare up at the slightest provocation. Of course, they're both gifted craftsmen — I suppose one has to expect a bit of temperament, now and then, else one has to make do with indifferent guns and rickety carriages — never able to tolerate either, myself. Must have my guns cared for properly, and my carriages too. Those two will soon be back, I assure you — got their backs up merely because I asked them to dig a bit of a hole for fine old Andrew . . . a direct descendant of the Byerly Turk, finest bloodline in England, though I suppose the Godolphin Arab may have had his points."

Bobbety and Tim took advantage of Lord Berrybender's indignation at the gunsmith and the carriage maker to gulp down as much hash as possible, lest they had to dig all night, but their worries were unfounded. After another brandy or two Lord B. began to fumble with Milly. Thus the night ended as most nights ended, with Milly and Lord B. tussling in the tent, making, to Bobbety's taste, much too much racket with their rough copulation.

The prudent Tim took a blanket and rolled himself up in it, near the carcass of Royal Andrew. The fact that Lord Berrybender had found temporary distraction with Millicent did not mean that Royal Andrew would be forgotten. Tim's prudence proved wise — several wolves had to be discouraged during the night, and Lord Berrybender was out at dawn, ready to direct burial operations. These, in Bobbety's view, proved laborious in the extreme. Fortunately for all of them the energetic Milly was as handy with a spade as she was with a skillet or a laundry basket.

She and Tim dug all morning, while the old lord sat around, shooting at anything that came in sight. Bobbety attempted to throw out a spade or two of dirt, an effort that caused large blisters to form on both his hands. To Lord Berrybender's intense annoyance there was no sign of either the Spanish gunsmith or the Italian carriage maker. It was becoming apparent that their mutiny had not been a bluff.

"Can't think where those fellows can have got to," Lord B. complained. "Expected them back by now. Don't like work, that's their problem."

"I'm afraid I don't like it either, Papa," Bobbety declared.

A final embarrassment awaited Royal Andrew. The hole, once dug, was ten feet from his noble carcass, around which a good many flies had begun to buzz. When Tim, Milly, and Bobbety attempted to drag the carcass over to the hole, they found that they couldn't budge it.

"Timmy, you dolt, why didn't you put the hole closer to the horse?" Milly inquired: inexpert work always infuriated her.

"Don't know," Tim admitted — he had just started digging at Lord B.'s insistence. It had not occurred to him that a dead horse would be so hard to move.

Bobbety thought the hole looked rather comfortable. The strain of such close relations with the servants had set his nerves on edge. Were it not for the finality of the matter, he would not have minded resting in the hole himself.

"What, not buried yet? My great steed will begin to rot pretty soon," Lord Berrybender announced. He had stumped over in a state of considerable annoyance: one of his rifles was misfiring, and there was no Señor Yanez to fix it.

Millicent was of the opinion that there were few problems that could not be solved if a smart laundress addressed herself to them with a clear head. Royal Andrew was not the only horse in the company. It was only necessary to hitch one of the geldings to the carcass and Royal Andrew could at once be plopped into his grave. This was done with dispatch, after which all the dirt that had been shoveled out had to be shoveled back in, an effort that still left something wanting, in Lord Berrybender's view. The prairie 'round the grave looked very level, very bare, a fact which troubled him considerably.

"He ought to have a stone — never find this place again unless there's a marker of some sort," he complained.

"Why would you want to find it again, Papa? There's nothing here," Bobbety observed.

"I'm rather attached to my horses, always have been," Lord B. admitted, his eyes not entirely dry. "I might want to stop and pay my respects to Royal Andrew someday — take a moment out of the hunt, you know?

"Loved my horse," he added, as the tears began to course down. "Hate to leave him in this lonely place — so unlike England, you know."

His tears flowed swiftly, and yet more swiftly, until Lord Berrybender was racked with sobs; he began to pull at his hair and rip at his clothes. Bobbety watched it all, appalled: his own father was going berserk, right before his eyes, and all because of a horse that had too much resembled an elk. Lord Berrybender's despair seemed very nearly Shakespearean, though the latter was an author with whom Bobbety was not deeply familiar. He and Father Geoffrin were of the opinion that the light and graceful Molière or even the somewhat heavier Racine was an author with considerably more wit than the bard of Avon.

Bobbety's concern did not lessen. Lord Berrybender had begun to cry to the heavens, cursing his fate — in his frenzy it might not be long before he began to curse his children, starting, very probably, with the child who had shot his favorite horse.

Fortunately Milly, who had been carrying a bucket of water up from the Yellowstone River, heard the commotion and came striding over.

"Here now, silly boy, stop that!" Milly said to Lord B. "Come along now with your Milly — we'll just slip into the tent and see what we can find to do."

"I believe I'll just go in search of a suitable stone now, Father," Bobbety said, strolling quietly off. More rough copulations he did not care to hear.

24

. . . they could not afford to strike out wildly . . .

Señor Yanez and Signor Claricia, having abruptly decided to cast their lot together in the New World, decided it was time to dispense with the strict formality which each had felt compelled to maintain while with the English.

The two men, once out of the Berrybender camp, made haste over to the Yellowstone River and hurried south along its banks for a few miles, enough to discourage the old lord if he should miss his prized Belgian rifle and attempt to chase them down. One thing they knew with certainty was that they could not afford to strike out wildly, into the empty land. As long as they kept close to the riverbank and followed it upstream, they had a chance of running into some of the trappers who had set out in that direction.

"Now that we are not with those English we don't have to be so stiff," Señor Yanez said.

"You may call me Aldo," Signor Claricia replied. "With all that riffraff on the boat it was better to be formal."

"Yes — that Pole, the German woman, the Dane — I didn't like any of them," Señor Yanez replied. "You may call me Pedro."

"Pedro, okay," Aldo said. "That's not so different from Aldo. We might get our selves mixed up." He meant it as a joke, but the solemn Pedro Yanez didn't laugh.

"I have always been Pedro, and Pedro I will always be," he declared firmly, looking sternly at the Italian, in the event that he had objections.

Aldo Claricia had none. Pedro, Aldo, Aldo, Pedro — at least they were both Europeans, and from the south. Though night had come and it was very dark, he felt that the two of them ought not to stop until they were well out of range of His Lordship's wrath.

"Do you want to walk awhile?" he asked Pedro. "It might be better to get farther away before we stop."

Hardly had he said it before a terrible roar was sounded, directly in front of them. A huge dark shape suddenly loomed up so close that they could have touched it — but it was a moonless night and neither of them could see the beast that roared. Terrified, both fired their guns, though Aldo Claricia had only a fowling piece, a weapon hardly likely to save them from this leviathan of the prairies — Pedro Yanez thought he saw a flash of great teeth. Though both wanted to flee, they stood as if paralyzed — what if they fled right into the maw of the beast? Though wide awake, they thought themselves to be in the sort of dream where flight offers the only hope — and yet their limbs refused to move.

"Pedro, why don't you reload your gun?" Aldo requested.

"Be still, don't blab your mouth," Pedro said. "We may have killed it."

Pedro didn't believe that they had killed the great beast, though. In shock, expecting death, he had fired both barrels of his gun straight up into the air. Unless the creature with the great roar was a bird, it had survived unharmed.

The prairie had become totally silent. Aldo could hear Pedro breathing, and Pedro, likewise, Aldo.

"Are we alive?" Aldo asked. He was so frightened that it seemed to him that death might have stolen over them imperceptibly, as he had always hoped it would, when it came.

Pedro Yanez was annoyed by the question. Only Italians could be so slipshod as to doubt their own existence. The important question was not whether they were alive, but where the great beast had gone who made the roar — it was, he felt sure, one of the great grizzly bears: even the mountain men feared them. But the two of them were in unknown land — it wouldn't do to draw hasty conclusions. In Spain there were plenty

187

of bears — the Gypsies had them — but they were small bears, nothing like the size of the beast that had made the roar. On the other hand it wouldn't do to guess wrong: what was it, if *not* a grizzly?

"What if it was something *worse* than a grizzly bear?" he asked.

"Don't be silly — nothing could be worse than a grizzly bear," Aldo assured him.

"Well, *el tigre* could be worse, or elephants," Pedro replied.

"Not elephants — there are no elephants here," Aldo assured him.

"How do you know?"

"Because Lord Berrybender never spoke of them. He didn't bring a gun for elephants."

Pedro made no comment — his silence suggested that he was unconvinced.

"The mountain men didn't mention elephants," Pedro said, less confidently. It seemed to him that the great shape that had risen in front of him had been as large as an elephant — but did elephants roar? He didn't know.

The two of them had been standing stock-still since the great fearsome beast had roared at them.

"Where do you want to go?" Aldo asked. After all, the great beast hadn't killed them. Maybe they should move on.

"I think we should stay here till daylight,"

188

Pedro said. "If we move we might disturb it again."

"I mean tomorrow," Aldo said. "Where do you want to go when the sun comes up?"

"Let's go to Santa Fe," Pedro said. The name just popped out. Many people on the boat had spoken of Santa Fe — there would be plenty of Spanish there.

"I don't know about Santa Fe — think of another place," Aldo asked.

"Well, we could go to California — lots of Spaniards there too."

That was just what Aldo Claricia didn't want to hear. Though he had thrown in his lot with a Spaniard and was prepared to travel with him on equal terms, he was not at all eager to go to a place filled with Spaniards — after all, a race of thieves, in his considered view. He would have been far happier to travel to a place where there was an abundance of Italians — only where would that be, in the New World? What if he were the only Italian in all of the West? It was a sobering thought.

"Let's just sleep here and decide in the morning," he said. "Maybe then we can see the beast that made that roar."

"I don't want to see it," Pedro said. "I just want it to go away."

They sat down back to back, feeling that it was important to keep watch in both directions, though it was now so dark that neither could see a foot in any direction. Both vowed to remain alert through the perilous night.

"Vigilance, amigo — vigilance! It is our only hope," Pedro said. Then he fell sound asleep — Aldo Claricia soon slept too, just as soundly.

Bright sunlight woke them up.

"I only nodded for a moment," Pedro claimed, chagrined. "I'm glad you were able to stay alert."

Aldo saw no reason to mention that he had slept soundly for several hours.

Only a yard or two from where they had spent the night the spring grass bore the imprint of a great body. The beast had been resting. Another step and they would have stumbled over it — but now, fortunately, there was no great beast in sight. The plain around them, from horizon to horizon, was entirely empty. They seemed to be the only two living things in the world. There was not even a bird in the sky.

"A beast that large must have made a track," Aldo said. "You Spaniards are such good trackers. Perhaps you can find its track."

"No, amigo, I am only a gunsmith," Pedro admitted. "I have never tracked a thing in my life. *You* track it, if you know so much."

"I'll certainly know if it was an elephant we woke up," Aldo told him, confidently. He peered at the ground in a careful, studious manner.

"I don't see even one track," he was forced to admit. "Perhaps this beast made a great jump, just to fool us."

"It was too big to jump much," Pedro assured him. "Who knows where it went?"

"If it comes at us, shoot good, amigo," Aldo said. "Don't miss next time."

"For that matter, you missed too," Pedro reminded him.

25

. . . Little Onion came walking demurely . . .

When Little Onion came walking demurely up from the birthing hut to tell old Charbonneau that his wife, Coal, had at last been delivered of a healthy baby boy, Charbonneau wept in relief, somewhat to the astonishment of Jim Snow. The labor had taken two days and a night — perhaps Charbonneau was so glad to have the long wait over that he was crying in relief.

"Hard to get into this world and easy to get out," Joe Walker observed. Only Jim and Joe and Toussaint Charbonneau were left in camp — Pomp and the rest of the boys had gone south with Drummond Stewart, into the high Rockies, in search of bighorn sheep.

"It ain't always easy to get out, Joe," Charbonneau said, once he had calmed down. "If you was tied to a Comanche torture stake I guess you'd think getting out was about as hard as getting in."

"I grant the point, that's why I never go anywhere where there could be a Comanche," Joe replied. "What will you name your boy?"

Charbonneau had given the matter no thought. Coal's labor had been so long that he half expected a death — the baby's or the mother's or both — such was not uncommon. Fortunately there had been two experienced Shoshone women in the camp, and their skills had at last prevailed. Jimmy Snow's demure Ute maiden Little Onion was too young to have much experience as a midwife. Now that the matter had been resolved happily there was plenty of time to think of a name.

"Don't know," he admitted. "What are you planning to name yours, Jimmy, if it comes out a boy?"

Jim pretended not to hear the question — he had given no thought to naming, and in any case, it was none of Charbonneau's business. To hide his annoyance he wandered over to the creek to try his luck with a little fish spear he had made.

"Jimmy's a touchy boy," Joe Walker said. "I ought to charge him a hundred dollars for riding my mare halfway around the world."

The little mare, looking as fit as ever, grazed not far from the birthing hut. All the mountain men had been astonished that Jim had passed so quickly from the Knife River to the Green, skirting winter, skirting the Rockies, skirting the Sioux. Joe Walker found that, thanks to Jim, his mare was famous. Several of the trappers tried to buy her from him, but Joe made it clear that she was not for sale.

Jim Snow thought highly of the mare, but he didn't regard the ride as anything unusual. Mountain men tended to amble when they traveled — good hunting, an untrapped stream, native women, or general laziness might slow them down. They moved in fits and starts, capable of hurry when they needed to hurry, but otherwise taking their time and picking their way. They rarely held a steady pace, which is what Jim had done on his ride. He had known exactly where he was going and had no reason to linger along the way. Also, he had been lucky: the weather had been unusually warm, and he had not seen a single Indian in his crossing from the Mandan villages to the Ute country. The little mare liked to go, and go they did, straight across South Pass and into the Ute country, where, upon arriving, he discovered to his dismay that he only had one Ute wife, not two. Sun Girl had died the previous winter, only a few days after he had visited her for the last time; neither Little Onion nor anyone else in the camp could say exactly what it was that carried Sun Girl off. She was well one day, a little shaky the next day, and gone the second night.

Jim was disappointed by this news — disappointed and a little disturbed. It was Sun Girl, mainly, whom he had ridden across the

West to rejoin. She had been his first woman, and had always exerted herself vigorously to make him a good wife. Her sister, Little Onion, he scarcely knew; a plan had been afoot to sell the girl to an old man of another tribe; Jim had agreed to the marriage at Sun Girl's request. Little Onion had been his wife for less than a week when he and Kit and Jim Bridger had trekked out of the mountains. It was Sun Girl he had counted on to give Tasmin instructions; Little Onion was very young, not more than fifteen, and very shy, something Tasmin wasn't. Mortality had destroyed his whole plan. Uncertainly and a little reluctantly he had been traveling north with Little Onion when they ran into Drummond Stewart's party. The tall Scot immediately offered Jim a place in his company, but Jim declined.

Now old Charbonneau, relieved that his own wife had narrowly survived childbirth, had reminded Jim that his other wife, his English wife, would soon face a similar ordeal. He had told Tasmin he would be with her when their child came — then she had been freshly pregnant, and such a promise easy to make. Now he had come a long way south, and the wife he had hoped would help Tasmin learn proper behavior was dead. Her little sister, though polite and obedient, was not as experienced as Sun Girl had been.

It was all vexing — deeply vexing. Jim

stabbed with the little spear at several trout, but missed them all. Life had seldom presented him with situations that were so unclear. Usually, if it was a matter of guiding some company, he either took the job or didn't. Weather conditions might affect his choice, or the makeup of the group, or something he had heard about Indian hostilities along the way; the choices were seldom hard to make. But here he was now with two wives, neither of whom he knew well. One morning, by the Missouri, he had seen a girl bathing; she had seen him at the same time. He had not found her particularly likable — she talked too much, and often acted foolishly — but they had come together in pleasure — come together often, for a period — and a child was coming, his child. Now that he had been away from Tasmin for some weeks, what had occurred between them seemed almost like a dream. His place, to the extent that he had one, was with the overland guides, or the mountain trappers, categories that frequently overlapped. He belonged with Kit and Pomp and Jim Bridger and the rest. What business did he have being married to an English girl? It was not that he didn't like Tasmin. For all her boldness, he liked her; when she took him into her arms he felt feelings he had never felt before. But what was he to *do* with her? Should he bring her and the child with him on his treks? Would she live in whatever shelters he could throw up, with Little Onion? And what would Little Onion think of a woman who blabbed so much and yet could do little of a practical nature? There was such confusion in his thoughts that he missed and missed with the fish spear — and yet there had been many times when he fed himself with no more equipment than a fish spear and a flint.

"Jimmy's a strange lad," Joe Walker observed to Charbonneau. The latter was trying to whittle himself a whistle out of a section of reed.

"Maybe it was the lightning done it," Charbonneau suggested. "I guess being struck by lightning would make a fellow a little strange.

"That's what the Hairy Horn thought, anyway," he added.

"Oh, that old fool!" Joe burst out. "His opinion is bound to be wrong.

"Jimmy had a hard raising," he added, after some thought. "That old preacher was a rough one — put Jimmy off people, I guess."

"Mostly," Charbonneau said. "But it didn't put him off that English girl. That's his problem now."

26

Often she walked out beyond the stockade . . .

In the last month of her pregnancy, with the weather warming daily, Tasmin slowly withdrew from the chatty group at the trading post. She ceased teasing George Catlin, ceased insulting Father Geoffrin, ceased responding to anything that Buffum or Mary said. In the main, she waited, a dual waiting: for Jim Snow to come back, for the baby to come out. Often she walked out beyond the stockade and sat with her back to the poles, watching for her husband. She didn't doubt that one day he would appear — rumors had already reached the post that he was on his way north, with old Charbonneau and his Hidatsa wife, Coal, who had borne her child.

"Coal was first — I wonder which of us will be next, Vicky?" Tasmin asked. The two of them often sat together, saying little, glad to have a chair to support their increasingly substantial weight. To Tasmin it seemed extraordinary that women could *be* so stretched and not burst open — it was only with difficulty that she could see her own feet.

198

"Perhaps they'll come at the same time," Vicky said. "The madonnas of the Missouri bringing forth their young in tandem."

"Yes, accompanied by a good deal of screeching, I fear," Tasmin replied.

Mary Berrybender, hearing that prediction, smiled in her sinister way.

"Papa won't like that, now that he's back," she said. "Papa is not one to tolerate undue noise."

"Then let him leave again, the old brute," Tasmin said. "I intend to holler as loudly as I can — it's said to help."

"Señor Yanez and Signor Claricia seem to have made good their escape," Mary said. "Now Papa has no one to load his guns or harness his buggy horses. You shouldn't have sent Kit Carson away — he might have helped Papa in this hour of distress."

"Kit was left here by my husband to be helpful to *me*," Tasmin reminded her. "I sent him off to locate Jim and make him hurry back. This child is not going to be willing to remain unborn much longer."

"Perhaps Millicent can learn to load His Lordship's guns for him," Vicky remarked. "At least she's become proficient at *unloading* a certain gun, if you take my meaning."

"I take it," Tasmin said. "I suppose you're happy to have been relieved of that chore, Vicky."

Venetia Kennet *was* relieved — it *had* been

tedious to have to always be copulating with Lord Berrybender, at best, in recent months, an uncertain stud; nonetheless she could not but feel rather moody when she observed the stout laundress cooing over him, murmuring endearments, and even making so bold as to sit on His Lordship's lap. Drummond Stewart had made, for a time, a fine copulator, but the Scot had then left abruptly, with no promises made; it might be that she would never see him again, in which case, once the baby came, she would have to bestir herself and recapture Lord Berrybender's interest. She had no doubt that she *could* reclaim the old lord — after all, there was her skill with the bow — but a general sense of vexation, of the order of things not being quite right, beset her anyway.

In idle moments — and most of their moments *were* idle — Tasmin and Vicky addressed themselves to the problem of names.

"I doubt I shall bring forth a girl," Tasmin said. "I've always rather fancied myself as the mother of sons. I think 'Edward' might do. He would, of course, be called Eddie until he attains his growth."

"I too rather expect a son," Vicky replied. "I was thinking 'Gustavus' would be nice."

Father Geoffrin happened to overhear her remark.

"No, no — that's an odious name, reminiscent of the northern emperors," he objected.

"No one invited you to vote," Tasmin reminded him. "I guess we can name our babies without any help from you, Geoff."

"Venetia can, she's a commoner," Father Geoff said. "You, however, have dynastic obligations to consider — at least you will once you get back to England."

"Who says I plan to go back to England?" Tasmin asked. "I married an American — for all you know I'm here to stay."

Father Geoffrin merely smiled wickedly and drifted off to find Bobbety, who was trying to explain to some Piegans what fossils were — he was hoping they'd bring him some.

As usual, the catty Jesuit had managed to upset Tasmin in ways that caused discontent long after he himself had left the scene. Normal musings about what to name her baby now gave rise to a growing anxiety about what, in fact, the future *did* hold for herself and the child soon to come. When Jim Snow was actually with her she rarely worried. Even if he insisted on an inconvenient life in a tent she didn't feel seriously troubled. Physically she had complete confidence in Jim — he would handle whatever came along. The slap and the sock he had given her the day he left had almost been forgotten — after all, *everyone* told her she was intolerable — Jim Snow had just made that point physically rather than verbally.

Spats between husband and wife would occur — that one hadn't dampened her enthusiasm where Jim was concerned at all.

And yet, once he returned, then what? Lord Berrybender's plan was to hunt in a generally southern direction through the summer and fall, going up the Yellowstone and across the Platte.

Where would she and Jim and the baby be, while that progress was occurring? And after it occurred? Her father seemed to be planning to pass through Santa Fe and then hunt on down the plains and the southern forests until they came to New Orleans, where a ship could be procured to take such survivors as remained back to Portsmouth.

Just thinking about the future — Platte River, Santa Fe, New Orleans, England — left Tasmin feeling low and confused. Jim Snow had once seemed willing to take her to Santa Fe. Would he still want to? Would he agree to stay with the Berrybender party, or did he mean for them to strike out on their own?

The more Tasmin thought about these vague prospects, the gloomier she became. After all, it was only a rumor that Jim was on his way back. Perhaps he wasn't. Perhaps her cursing and chattering had driven him off for good. What if he had decided that he preferred the simpler women of the Utes? — if they *were* simpler?

George Catlin observed Tasmin, sunk in her low mood, sitting alone by the fireplace. There was melancholy in her gaze. It was in such low moments that he found Tasmin most appealing; with her brash self-confidence momentarily subdued she seemed vulnerable to any kindness.

After watching her for a moment, George attempted to sneak out, but Tasmin sensed the movement and beckoned him with a lift of her chin.

"Don't be sneaking out, George — I need you," Tasmin said.

"You need *me?*" he asked, surprised.

"Yes. I feel as though there's a crowd inside me. I am extremely stretched. Could you just rub my back?"

"Rub your back? Of course," George agreed. But when he did put his hands on Tasmin's back his pressure was very tentative.

"No good — can't you do anything right at all, George?" Tasmin chided. "Rub harder — much harder."

George rubbed harder, but still not hard enough.

"Hard, George, really hard!" Tasmin insisted; she gave a sigh of pleasure when George complied, pressing his fingers into her back as hard as he could.

"That's good, keep it up," Tasmin said, her eyes half closed.

George Catlin was in the process of

keeping it up, digging his fingers as hard as he could into Tasmin's bent back, when he looked around and saw a young man step into the trading post, a stout young Indian woman just beside him. The young man said something to Pierre Boisdeffre. Tasmin, her eyes in a half doze, didn't notice. George did another push or two and then looked at the young man a second time; then he at once jerked his hands away. The young man was Jim Snow.

"I think you better wake up, Tasmin," George said. "Your husband just came home."

27

But then Tasmin, overjoyed . . .

Jim Snow stepped out of bright sunlight into the dim trading post and almost bumped into Pierre Boisdeffre, who was trying to untangle a heap of beaver traps. Once his eyes adjusted Jim saw George Catlin, over by the fireplace, but he didn't immediately see Tasmin, who was bent over. Jim was, for the moment, most concerned to ease Little Onion's intense anxiety. Shy anyway, Little Onion had never before been inside a trading post. For a minute Jim feared she might bolt back outside, but Little Onion, though extremely frightened, just managed to control herself.

But then Tasmin, overjoyed to see him, came hurrying toward them, as fast as she could move in her heavy state.

"Oh, Jimmy . . . it's been such a wait!" she said, opening her arms to him. She saw a young Indian girl standing just inside the door but didn't connect her with Jim Snow — Indian girls often showed up at the trading post.

Just as Tasmin was about to fall into a

long-awaited, long-imagined embrace, Little
Onion, seeing a large white woman coming
toward her husband, did just what Jim had
been afraid she would do — she bolted back
out the door, to the safety of the plains and
sky.

Tasmin's surge carried her close to Jim —
though he grasped her arms, he did not embrace her.

"Oh now, you've run her off," he said.
"Maybe Kit will slow her down."

"Run who off? Can't I even kiss you?"
Tasmin said in frustration, managing only the
briefest peck.

"Little Onion," Jim told her. "She's skittish.
Quick too. If Kit don't stop her there's no
telling where she'll get to."

"I don't understand," Tasmin admitted. "Is
she a friend of Kit's? I don't understand why
he should stop her."

Jim felt awkward — he thought he must at
some point have mentioned Little Onion's
name; he must have told Tasmin that she
was one of his Ute wives — but perhaps he
had not actually said her name. Even if he
had said it, long ago in the Oto village, it
would be natural enough for Tasmin to
forget it.

"She's my Ute wife," he said. "My only
one. Her sister was the other one, but she
died."

Tasmin started to press forward, determined to kiss her husband, when what he said struck home.

"Your wife? That young girl is your *wife?*" she asked.

"Yes, Little Onion," Jim said again, calmly. It seemed he considered it no news at all, that he should show up with an Indian wife.

"I thought you'd be down at the tent — the mice have about et it up," Jim said; in his tone was a mild hint of censure, just enough that Tasmin heard it and felt annoyed.

"I left to be closer to Cook," Tasmin said. "Did you really expect me to walk a mile once my labor starts?"

There it was already — Tasmin's contentiousness. And meanwhile, there was no telling where Little Onion was getting to.

"Boisdeffre could have stored the tent," Jim said mildly — now a good enough tent had been virtually ruined by neglect.

"You left rather abruptly, Jim," Tasmin reminded him. "I received no instructions about the tent. Am I supposed to read your mind? If so, I fear this whole adventure is a failure. I *can't* read your mind, especially not when you take it hundreds of miles away.

"And now, without a word of warning, you just show up with another wife!" Tasmin said with some vehemence; but just as she said it, the room began to swirl. The walls seemed to be turning and turning around her, like a carousel. Tasmin swirled with the walls for a moment and then fell forward, in a dead faint. Jim Snow and Pierre Boisdeffre just managed to catch her.

"Oh dear, more smelling salts needed, and we have none," said George Catlin. "I'll go ask Cook for a wet rag."

Jim left Tasmin with Catlin, Cook, and Boisdeffre — he wanted to run Little Onion down before she got too far away. To his annoyance not a soul had seen her leave the fort — both Kit Carson and Toussaint Charbonneau were mystified when told that she had left. Kit ran down toward the Yellowstone, Jim toward the Missouri, but Charbonneau soon waved them both back — Little Onion had been sitting quietly behind the stables.

Jim hurried back inside the trading post to see about Tasmin — he felt that he might have been too stern about the matter of the tent. But when he got inside Tasmin was gone.

"Now, where'd *she* go?" Jim asked, exasperated by his wives' tendency to disappear.

"Just into her quarters, with Cook," George said. "It seems her labor has begun. I guess you'll soon be a father, Mr. Snow."

28

Jim Snow crept in shyly . . .

Tasmin's labor was no easier than Coal's had been. Jim Snow crept in shyly and received one kiss before he was firmly banished by Cook, who needed all her skills and didn't propose to tolerate any husbands underfoot.

More than thirty hours passed — Tasmin had long since screamed herself hoarse; the screams left Venetia Kennet atremble, well aware that the same agonies soon awaited her.

Little Onion felt sure she knew what to do — the old Shoshone women who had delivered Coal's child had taught her a few things — but at first she could get no one to understand her. She spoke no Hidatsa, Coal no Ute. So when Little Onion first showed up with a rattlesnake rattle, Cook was baffled. Tasmin was weak, half uncaring; she had come to doubt that she was going to live. But Little Onion was insistent that the rattlesnake rattle could resolve the situation, and Toussaint Charbonneau finally understood. He remembered that that very substance, ground-up rattlesnake rattle, had been given to Sacagawea when she was being delivered of Pomp.

"Won't hurt to try it," he told Cook. She put no faith in such remedies, but, aware that Tasmin was slowly losing ground, agreed to grind up a little and give it to Tasmin in water.

"It isn't poison, is it?" Tasmin asked, too weak to care very much. To her astonishment and Cook's, only a few minutes later, Tasmin's pains sharpened again and then ended. The child was a boy — in only a few minutes Little Onion herself had cleaned him up, wrapped him in a soft bit of flannel, and laid him on Tasmin's breast.

Tasmin, exhausted but triumphant, thought it passing strange that she should be receiving her newborn son from her husband's other wife — the baby itself gave out a cry scarcely louder than the squeakings of a mouse.

"I saved just a wee bit of that rattle," Cook said. "It might be that Miss Vicky will need it, rather soon."

The baby — Tasmin had decided to call him Montague, or Monty for short — was for a time reluctant to take the nipple, and again, it was little Little Onion who proved most helpful, teasing the baby with a tiny bit of milk squeezed on a rag. At last he took hold of the nipple and they were all rewarded with the sight of some greedy suckling. Jim

210

Snow was allowed — and seemed to want — only the briefest of peeks.

Cook, of course, still had the company to feed; it at once developed that Tasmin's main helper, as she slowly got back on her feet, was Little Onion. Shocked as she had been that Jim would show up with another wife just as she was about to deliver their child, Tasmin soon found that she could not regard Little Onion with the hard eye that she would normally have turned on a rival. Partly it was the girl's youth, but even more, it was the gentle and loyal attention that she paid to Monty that deflected any jealousy that Tasmin might feel. Tasmin could not get enough of her baby, nor could she be unkindly disposed to a girl who paid him attentions that were as keen as — and, perhaps, a little more expert than — her own. Though the two women had no language in common, they muddled through together, as Monty surmounted his first small crises. He had not an easy stomach, and would sometimes spit up almost as much milk as he took in; also he had a tendency to colic in the night.

Jim had had to go away on a hunt — Tasmin did not quite understand why — and there were nights when Tasmin still felt so weak from her labor that she could scarcely deal with the crying baby. At these times Little Onion walked the baby for her, and cleaned him when he fouled himself. Jim's

Ute wife became Tasmin's nursemaid — and, for Little Onion's part, it was only when she was with Tasmin and the baby that she felt at all relaxed. She slept in a corner of Tasmin's room, ate little, and did her best to avoid everyone else in the fort. She could not for the life of her understand why people chose to live crowded up in such a place, when it would have been so much healthier to be outside, on the airy plains.

Jim had been gone for almost a week when Mary revealed to Tasmin that he had been sent on a moose hunt by Monsieur Boisdeffre. The horns of the moose were thought to contain broad medicinal properties, when ground up; Monsieur Boisdeffre foresaw immense profits if only he could obtain a few good racks.

"You mean Jimmy left me for a moose?" Tasmin exclaimed, her mood alternating between anger and amusement. In fact she and Little Onion had all they could do to keep young Monty on an even keel — at this particular time the absence of a husband was not of much concern. Cook even expressed the opinion that it was best thus.

"The menfolk, they've no interest in bairns," Cook told Tasmin cheerfully. "Once the little one is big enough to work I expect Master Snow will find a use for him."

This attitude was shared by Lord Berrybender, who had bestowed upon his grandson only the most casual glance.

"Bring him to me when he's ready to get on with his Latin," Lord B. said. "Can't be much use until then, that I can see."

If the males in the family were more or less indifferent to Monty's arrival, the females were anything but. Buffum was intensely jealous — now Tasmin had acquired a tiny plaything, while she herself had neither infant nor lover.

"How like you to have produced such a greedy brat, Tasmin," Mary said, watching Monty attack a nipple. "No doubt he will become a great criminal and be hung at Tyburn. People will pelt him with ordure."

"That's rather stretching things, even for you, Mary," Tasmin replied. "I should think you yourself are the main criminal in the Berrybender family. In a wiser age you would have been burnt as a witch for your habit of talking with serpents, if nothing else."

George Catlin, at Tasmin's request, came and did a few hasty sketches of Monty at the breast, but the nursery was so thick with females that he felt rather smothered, what with the two Indian women and Mary and Buffum and Cook and the immensely pregnant Vicky Kennet: the place smelled of milk and baby shit and so much femaleness that he could scarcely draw a clean masculine breath.

When, a little later, he attempted to describe the scene to Bobbety and Father Geoffrin, they both rolled their eyes at the thought.

"Why, it's a regular gynocracy," Bobbety exclaimed.

"Females — so *fecund*," Father Geoffrin complained. "They exude — they *drip!*"

"Yes, excessively fecund it sounds," Bobbety went on. "A moderate fecundity must be maintained to secure the continuance of the race, but trust my good sister Tasmin to take things rather too far."

"Now, now . . . it's only one baby," George reminded them — he felt he must come to Tasmin's defense.

"For now," Bobbety said. "But Vicky will soon bring forth, and there's that tiny brat of Coal's. Civilized discourse will soon have to compete with the squallings of several infants."

Bobbety's prediction about the imminence of Venetia Kennet's delivery was very soon borne out. That very night, after a labor that, to Tasmin's envy, lasted a mere eight hours, Vicky brought forth a fine son, whose little head was already covered with fine auburn hair. He was thought, by the ladies who examined him, to have, distinctly, the Berrybender nose.

"No necessity for resorting to the rattlesnake rattle," Cook said. "Miss Vicky was so quick. I suppose I had best save it for the next one."

"Yes, whose ever that may be," Tasmin said, with little Monty snuggled at her breast.

29

"Don't you see how the light's too thin . . . ?"

"Don't you see how the light's too thin, up here in Canada?" Kit Carson asked. "The air's not very thick either. Makes it hard to breathe."

"Why'd you come, then?" Jim asked. "You knew we were headed north, to the moose country. If you don't like north as a direction why didn't you go south, with the boys?"

Jim Snow liked and respected Kit Carson, but he had forgotten how picky and hypochondriacal he could be. Last night black ants had gotten into Kit's clothes — they had had to waste half the morning applying mud poultices to Kit's various bites.

"I came because I don't have any money and I need a new gun," Kit explained. "I can't shoot a bow and arrow, the way you can. My old musket misfires half the time. If I don't get a better gun a grizzly bear will eat me — or else I'll lose my scalp."

"You could learn to shoot a bow and arrow if you'd just practice," Jim told him. "Thousands of Indians learn to shoot bows and arrows. I don't know why you couldn't learn."

It was a conversation the two had had before, so Kit didn't answer. He didn't exactly disagree. Skill with the bow would be useful. Jim had just killed three good-sized moose with arrows. But when Kit picked up a bow he just felt silly. When he shot at targets arrows flew every which way. If he had to be dependent on such a weapon, he felt sure he would starve.

"It's hard to see good, in light this thin," he said, returning to his original complaint.

Jim ignored him — if offered a sympathetic ear he might never stop complaining. They had three moose down, all bulls with good racks; except for one small catch, their commission was as good as fulfilled. The catch was that each of them had thought the other was packing a saw — now they had no saw.

"We'll just have to chop them out," Jim said, picking up an axe.

"I can't chop, you'll have to chop," Kit said. Ever since his bad nosebleed at the fort he had been leery of large quantities of blood, such as would surely result if some moose racks were being chopped out.

Jim was exasperated. First Kit failed to pack the saw, then he complained about the light, and now he refused to chop.

"You're a dead loss then, I guess," he said.

Kit, ever sensitive to criticism, wanted to remind Jim that he had looked after Tasmin pretty well while Jim was off meandering, but before Kit could speak in his own defense Jim began to chop. Within a minute or two blood seemed to cover an acre. Kit retreated, so as to stay clear of the blood and bits of flying bone.

"Are you sure my little boy didn't have any hair?" Jim asked, once he had the racks detached. Kit had reported that fact as the two of them were traveling north — he had caught just a glimpse of the baby as Little Onion was greasing its navel.

"Nope, no hair — I didn't see none," Kit repeated.

"That can't be right," Jim said. He walked over to a trickle of a creek and washed the blood off his axe.

"I've seen plenty of Indian babies and they all had hair," he said. He had had a quick look at the baby but Monty had been swaddled in flannel at the time and his head scarcely showed. Now he was disturbed by the news that he and Tasmin had somehow produced a hairless infant.

"Oh, my Lord!" Kit said, in a tone of deep apprehension.

Jim turned, expecting to see Indians, but instead saw two bears — grizzlies, a mother and a sizable yearling with a yellowish coat. The bears were about forty yards away.

"I knew we'd get killed if we came up here where the light's so thin," Kit lamented.

"We're not killed — those bears want the

moose, not us," Jim pointed out. "Let's pack up these horns and let them have the moose meat. These old stringy bulls ain't fit to eat anyway."

The bears advanced another ten yards and stopped. Kit was trying to tie the moose horns to their pack animal, but in his haste was making a sloppy job of it.

"Take your time with those knots," Jim cautioned. "I don't want to lose these horns if we have to run for it."

Once the horns were secure the two mounted their skittish horses and rode away. The bears didn't follow.

"I ain't coming up into this thin air no more," Kit said. "We're lucky to be alive."

"You can say that any day," Jim reminded him. "How big was that boy of mine?"

Though happy to have escaped the grizzly bears, Kit was irked by Jim's attitude. Why would the man question him about a matter he should have investigated for himself?

"He wasn't big at all," he replied. "He just got borned. I suppose he weighed about twelve pounds."

"I hope he's stout," Jim said.

What annoyed Kit most was that Jim showed so little concern for Tasmin, who, after all, might have died in childbirth, as many women did; nor did Jim express much gratitude for his own sacrifices in staying by Tasmin's side. The boys had gone south; they were probably trapping beaver by the hundreds. He, Kit, by choosing to stay with Tasmin, was losing money — lots of money. But Jim Snow lived in his own world. He didn't seem to realize that Kit had done him a whopping big favor.

"I expect that baby of mine will grow quick," Jim said. "Tasmin eats hearty — she's probably got plenty of milk."

Jim Snow had always been the most pessimistic of mountain men. He always expected the water holes to be dry, the Indians hostile, the beavers absent. Yet here he was predicting that his baby would be fine. And when two grizzlies showed up with hungry looks on their faces he hadn't turned a hair.

"Do you think you're such a good shot with the bow and arrow that you could have killed those two grizzlies, if they'd come at us?" Kit asked.

"Why no, Kit — I don't think nothing of the sort," Jim said. Kit seemed in a pouty mood, not uncommon with him. Such moods were best ignored.

"I think you might have got that young bear with an arrow — I don't know about the mother," Kit said.

"The fact is, when it comes to bears, I prefer the rifle," Jim replied.

30

... three fresh infants ... hung from pegs ...

It took Jim only a moment to discover, with relief, that Kit had been wrong about Monty's hair. The three fresh infants, each in its own pouch and cradle board, hung from pegs on the wall of the nursery — one of Boisdeffre's half-empty storerooms had been hastily converted. His little Monty had only the lightest hair on his head, it was true, but it was hair — brown like his own, rather than black like Tasmin's. It seemed to him that a totally hairless infant could not have been expected to last long.

The three babies were all sound asleep, hanging from their pegs and watched closely by Little Onion, who had brought her blankets into the nursery. She considered the infants her charges, whisking them off to their respective mothers when the time came to nurse. Even Cook, a stern judge of nursemaids, approved of Little Onion, a mere girl but with an expert eye for the problems of her young charges.

"Vicky's has got the most hair," Jim pointed out to Tasmin.

"Yes, that's Talley," Tasmin said. "His mother's got the most hair too."

Venetia Kennet had not cut her hair after all. With the birth of her child her mood of resignation passed. She sometimes brought her cello into the nursery and played Haydn for the babies.

Tasmin, though glad that Jim appeared to take an interest in their child, found herself unaccountably awkward in his company. Partly this was because Jim could not really be at ease indoors — not even for an hour. Only under the open sky did he seem himself, the assured plainsman who had won her heart. The smell of the wild was on him, and the need for the wild in him. Indoors, he seemed diminished — seemed a shaggy awkward boy whose hair and beard had grown long since Tasmin had last had an opportunity to trim them.

"I suppose you just aren't meant to be inside four walls, Jimmy," Tasmin said, noting his restlessness. "Would you prefer that we move back to the tent? Coal and Little Onion have done a good job of patching those holes."

Jim was staring at their son — he was shocked by his tininess. For a moment Tasmin had to struggle to choke back tears. The thing she had hoped for had happened; her husband had come back to his family, and yet somehow she still felt disappointed.

Cook had explained that women who had just given birth were prone to sudden weepings; she didn't want to cry just then, in front of Jim. He would take it wrong, and why not? What did she have to cry about now? Little Monty was a healthy baby — indeed, all three infants were fit as fiddles, a thing which Cook assured her was quite exceptional. And Jim himself seemed in a mild mood, diffident in relation to his son — so diffident that, so far, he had not dared touch him. And yet, the disorder within Tasmin's breast persisted. Somehow the birth of Monty had made Jim Snow seem younger — perhaps weaker, also. She was now a mother, heir to responsibilities both great and grave. Her child must be kept well nurtured, protected, taught: all things Tasmin felt confident she could do, given an even chance. But would her Jimmy, whom she kept wanting to kiss, whose hair she still wanted to trim, really be a helpmate in this long endeavor? Would he stay with them, or would there be more casual departures after spats or quarrels, or in response, merely, to trapping opportunities or other vicissitudes of the plainsman's life?

It was only two weeks since Tasmin had given birth — a little kissing she would have welcomed, some touching, some tenderness, but, for the moment, not more. Still torn from her long birthing struggle, she felt none of the swelling passion that had linked her so tightly to Jim Snow. Of course, she would soon heal; their ruts, as he called them, might bind them again; but, as they stood together looking at the three infants hanging from their pegs, Tasmin felt a great tumult of feeling, and yet contented herself with holding her husband's hand, while his other wife, Little Onion, watched cheerfully from her corner of the room. Tasmin wanted to ask Jim how things could have gotten so complicated, yet she didn't speak because she knew it was a question he would have no way to answer, and no interest in anyway.

Tasmin had become a woman — little Montague Snow was evidence of that — but her Jimmy, though formidably skilled, was still mainly a boy. How would it end? What would they ever do?

31

. . . Tasmin had lifted little Monty from her purplish nipple . . .

Jim Snow, though relieved that his son, Monty, had at least the beginnings of a normal head of hair, tried not to show his own perplexity as he stood in the improvised nursery with his two wives. That he even *had* two wives, both of them in the same room of a trading post on the Yellowstone River, was a fair enough mystery in itself. Tasmin, his English wife, was slow of movement, not yet solidly back on her feet after her long labor — he had heard that it was often so with white women. Indian women were supposed to recover from childbirth more quickly, and yet Coal hadn't. One reason they had been so long getting back to the post was because of Coal's weariness. Joe Walker had been kind enough to lend the Charbonneaus a mule, otherwise Coal and her infant would have had to be left behind.

Now Tasmin had modestly offered to go back to the tent with him, since she knew he would be more at ease there himself, but of course he couldn't take one wife and leave the other. When he first came into the nursery after the moose hunt all three women were giving their babies suck, Coal sitting on the floor and Tasmin and Vicky sitting in chairs. It was Little Onion who handled the babies after their milky meal, expertly causing each to belch before returning them to their cradle boards. He had felt uncomfortable in the nursery and was about to leave but Tasmin had lifted little Monty from her purplish nipple so Jim could see his face, the wrinkled apple face of a small baby.

"So, should we pack up?" Tasmin asked, a few days later. Jim didn't know what to say. He was annoyed with himself for having drifted into such a morass of responsibility — it was all the result of having taken Sun Girl to wife in his first hard winter on the Green River. The snows had been heavy, the trapping hard. Having an energetic young Ute woman to do the camp chores was a big help — but then the situation with Little Onion had cropped up, just before Jim left the valley. Thanks to his effort to be courteous to Sun Girl he now had two wives, neither of whom he knew well, and he didn't have Sun Girl, the most competent of the three. What made matters even more sticky was the Berrybender party itself — or what remained of it. Lord Berrybender was determined to set off on a big summer hunt up the Yellowstone valley, linking up with Drummond Stewart at some point; and Kit Carson, like a fool, had agreed to guide the Berrybenders all the way to Santa Fe, although he knew well that to go overland to Santa Fe meant passing through the lands of several tribes of Indians who were likely to be full of fight. None of it made sense to Jim. The old lord had already killed many buffalo, and every other game animal except the grizzly bear and the mountain sheep. In Jim's view he would do well to avoid grizzlies, build a pirogue or two, and float his party back downriver to one of the normal disembarkment points for Santa Fe. Why strike out into the wildness of the West along one of the most dangerous routes of all? But when he said as much to Tasmin she merely shrugged.

"I doubt Papa will turn back," she said. "I think he's keen to go shoot some woolly sheep, or whatever else he can find."

"Death's what he'll find, most likely," Jim told her, but Tasmin shook her head.

"No, but that's what the rest of us will find," she said. "Our help has dropped like flies already, but what is that to Papa? He'll just hire more help."

As they stood before the drowsing infants Jim could feel Tasmin waiting, though not in the snappish way she had waited before the baby came — now, temporarily weakened, she was waiting for him to decide what to do.

"We don't need to put up the tent," he said. "It's warm enough — just bring a blanket or two and come outside with me."

"But, Jim, what about Monty? When he wakes up he'll be hungry," Tasmin reminded him. "He's very young — he doesn't sleep long."

She watched her husband closely, hoping to see that he was really happy to be a father. For a few minutes it seemed that he was. When told that Monty had weighed just seven pounds at birth, he was startled.

"Seven pounds? Why, Kit thought he weighed at least twelve," Jim said.

"Nope, and if he had weighed twelve I doubt I would have lived," Tasmin told him. Jim, so practical in most matters, clearly had no very clear notion of what babies weighed, or what the weight meant for the mother.

They strolled out of the nursery, leaving the cheerful Little Onion in charge of the babies, and walked out of the post for a few minutes. Tasmin was still nervous, still diffident, only a little troubled by Jim's evident indecisiveness where their future was concerned. They had not even settled where to sleep, much less any of the larger questions. When they were alone Tasmin did press a few mild kisses on him; Jim accepted these with an air of distraction, but he shook his head abruptly when she suggested that his hair and beard could use a trim.

"Hush about my dern beard," he said. "It's just now growing good again."

Although rebuffed on that score, Tasmin was relieved to see that, outside the fort, under the bluish skies so high and wide, Jim did seem to be his full self again — not a talker, not easy, but not just a boy, either.

"We ought to bring Monty out," he said. "It's too stuffy in there — he needs to get a good breath of this breeze."

Tasmin's heart lifted. Jim wanted their baby to breathe the air that he had breathed all his life — the fine, windy air of the plains.

"I'll go get him — or do *you* want to?" she asked. At the question Jim looked dismayed.

"You get him — he'll recognize you," he told her.

32

"Seven pounds ain't enough to weigh."

Moving faster than she had moved since her lying-in, Tasmin hurried to fetch the baby before Jim's fatherly mood passed.

Once back outside, she took Monty out of his pouch and cradled him in her arms. He awoke and uttered a few of his little mouse cries — protests that stopped instantly when Tasmin opened her shirt and gave him the breast.

"He's greedy, this boy of ours," she said.

Jim watched as Monty's little mouth attacked Tasmin's swollen nipple.

"Seven pounds ain't enough to weigh," he said.

"No, but he's growing fast — I expect he's already put on a pound or two," Tasmin said. "When we go back in we can weigh him on Monsieur Boisdeffre's scales."

She was not, though, in a hurry to go back in. It was a fair day, the long afternoon just beginning to wane. High white clouds spread shadows across the wavy plains, which were yellowish in places with the first wildflowers. Jim allowed Tasmin to rest her back against

230

his chest — for a few minutes she dozed in unaccustomed peace. For the first time the two men in her life were in the same place. Monty's mouth slipped off the nipple, he had gas, he wiggled and squirmed; Tasmin woke and patted him until he belched; but he still fretted, he was still hungry. When she lowered him to her bosom he eagerly attacked her other breast. So tiny, her little boy was, she thought, and yet a will was there — a young will, of course, but a will all the same. And Jim had a will too. She herself had been called willful many times in her life; now she wondered if she would ever again have the freedom to be willful in her own interest. In passion she had mated with Jim Snow and given birth to Monty; now, sitting in the waning sunlight of evening, looking south to the place where the Yellowstone River lost itself in the brown Missouri, she felt that her own always sharp identity was no longer either sharp or distinct. Like the waters, she was now a kind of junction, a place of merging, the channel through whom Jim and Monty had become part of each other — or at least she hoped they would. Rather as the two rivers constantly caved in their banks and ate whole acres of prairie, now these two males were doing as much with her. Their needs would soon cave her in, sweep through her, suck her away as Monty was sucking even now. Of course, it was peaceful and right that Monty would put on the weight that his father wanted him to have. It was right, too, that Jim would want to bring her out of the fort, under the vast sky — it was being outdoors, attentive to all that there was to attend to in nature, that made Jim Snow whole. And yet, beneath the peace and the feeling of rightness, Tasmin felt a bubble of apprehension forming in her — a small bubble, like the little milk bubbles Monty sometimes blew for an instant with his young breath. What chance did she have, in the circumstances she faced, to remain herself, Lady Tasmin Berrybender, mother but more than mother, wife but more than wife, a woman whole but also a woman separate from the needs of men?

"Ho, now! Tom's coming," Jim said, suddenly alert.

Tasmin looked where he pointed. Sure enough there was a kind of bobbing dot on the prairie — in her opinion it might just be a buffalo. She was reluctant to have their rare idyll interrupted by a bobbing dot — and yet it already had been, for Jim's attention had shifted away from herself and the baby.

"That's Tom Fitzpatrick — I recognize the limp," Jim said. "A mule kicked him when he was young and the leg never healed properly. It don't slow him much, but it's a limp."

Tasmin did her best to suppress her irritation. She had been enjoying her first moments with her young family, and now the mood was lost.

"He's hurrying along, Tom — that's odd," Jim told her. "Tom don't usually hurry."

"I can't help wishing Mr. Fitzpatrick would just leave us alone," Tasmin said, with a touch of her old asperity. "You were gone such a long time, Jimmy. I was enjoying having you back, and I'm sure Monty feels the same way."

If her husband heard her, he gave no sign. His eyes were focused on the moving dot — lost from time to time in the dips of the prairie, but now clearly a man.

"If Tom's in such a dern hurry, it probably means bad news," Jim said.

Tasmin's irritation soon faded into a kind of listlessness. The sight of Tom Fitzpatrick had caused Jim to forget her and the baby completely.

"If you want, we'll sleep out with you tonight," she said. "Monty's such a regular feeder — I have to keep him close."

Jim Snow leapt up suddenly — aquiver, as a hound might be, with some new scent the wind had borne him.

"Tom's running for his life," he said. "We have to run too. Hold the baby tight."

"But why?" Tasmin asked — she could only just see Tom Fitzpatrick across the plain of waving grass and yellow wildflowers. She didn't argue, though. Monty was hastily stuffed into his pouch — as soon as he was secured to the cradle board, Jim pressed her into a run. They were more than one hundred yards from the post; Tasmin feared her strength would give out before they reached safety. But she held out, half supported by her husband. She was gasping for breath — her legs trembled. Monty peered around him in puzzlement. They just made it inside the open gate of the stockade.

"Go find Kit . . . find Boisdeffre, find Charbonneau," Jim instructed. "Tell anybody who can shoot to get their guns."

Then he left her. As Tasmin stumbled on, meaning to do as he instructed, Jim raced across the wagon yard to the stables, where a laggardly Tim was in the process of shoeing Lord Berrybender's fine mare Augusta. Buffum stood nearby, occasionally delivering a tart criticism.

"I'd like to see you drive a horseshoe nail if you'd lost half your fingers," Tim was saying, when, to his astonishment, Tasmin's shaggy husband came racing over. Tim had been just about to lift the mare's foreleg, but before he could, Jim Snow grabbed the dangling halter and swung onto the filly's back. Her nostrils flared in surprise, but in a moment Jim was racing through the gates of the stockade, the filly running flat out.

"What can it mean, Tassie?" Buffum asked, running over to her sister. Tasmin, quite out of breath, couldn't answer, and, in any case, didn't know.

Lord Berrybender stumbled out of the trading post on his crutches just in time to see his filly racing as if for the prize at Ascot, his American son-in-law clinging to her bare back.

"What ho! Look at her run!" he said, rather pleased by the sight in spite of his disapproval of the son-in-law.

"There are few things in life better than watching a good horse run," he said. "But where's he going, Tasmin? What's he up to?"

"A rescue," Tasmin said. "Mr. Fitzpatrick is endangered. Jim says you should all get guns."

"Get guns — damn it, where *are* my guns? Call for Milly, she'll know," Lord B. said. "That traitor Señor Yanez *would* leave just when I need a gun in a hurry."

Mary, the quick sprite, raced up to the lookout tower in the corner of the stockade, and was rewarded with a fine view of the impending conflict.

"Hey up there, you brat! What do you see? Tell us!" Tasmin demanded.

"I see a fine sight!" Mary cried, making no effort to suppress her flair for histrionics. "The Sin Killer races to save the Broken Hand, who appears to be near the end of his strength. Many painted savages are in close pursuit."

Kit Carson ran out of the trading post carrying his musket. Pierre Boisdeffre and Toussaint Charbonneau were close behind. The latter two were both clearly in their cups. At the same moment Tasmin heard ululating war cries, high and chilling, suggesting that indeed many Indians were not far away.

"Go hide — go hide! They're Blackfeet," Kit Carson urged, but Tasmin shook him off and ran to the gate, determined to see her husband as he raced into battle. Just as Tasmin reached the gate George Catlin came stumbling up, nearly exhausted. He had been painting a prairie landscape and happened to look up just as Jim Snow came racing out of the post. Though George could not see the Indians, one look at Jim was enough; abandoning easel, canvas, and paints, George ran for the fort as fast as he could go.

"Too late!" Mary cried. "The Broken Hand will soon be speared by the fleet Piegan."

Tasmin, losing sight of her husband in the prairie's dip, pulled herself up the steps to the tower where Mary was. Below her the men were all fumbling with their rifles while Tim, Buffum, Bobbety, and Father Geoffrin watched apprehensively.

Once high in the lookout tower, Tasmin finally saw the scene which had caused her husband to jump up in excitement: thirty or more Indians, still producing the ululating

236

war cries, were closing in on the old Broken Hand. There was a long gap in the pursuit. One warrior, especially fleet, was many yards ahead of his fellows. He held a long lance and was almost close enough to touch Tom Fitzpatrick with it. The Broken Hand still ran grimly, though not very fast.

Then Jim Snow flashed out of a dip and was on them just as the Piegan drew back his arm for the thrust. Startled in the extreme, the Piegan not only stopped, he dropped his lance. Jim Snow set the mare on her heels, jumped off, picked up the lance, and ran the fleet Piegan through with his own weapon, leaving him still standing and very surprised — the shaft of his own lance protruded from his chest.

The other Blackfeet, though, were closing rapidly — this time, Tasmin thought, there were no stick-figure gods scratched in the rock to turn them. Jim remounted, swept up Tom Fitzpatrick with one arm, and held him across the filly's back as they raced for the fort. Arrows began to fly, several of which hit the riders, but Jim didn't slow and neither did the horse.

Tasmin had reckoned for a moment that her husband's startling rescue would take the fight out of the Indians — after all, one of their own was staggering around mortally wounded, his lance stuck through his innards. But the Indians showed no sign of slowing, even though they were charging a well-fortified stockade where several riflemen were arming themselves for battle.

"Shoot, Papa, why don't you shoot?" Tasmin cried, wishing she had had the forethought to take the baby inside to safety.

"Can't yet — your husband and my horse are in the way," Lord B. told her. "Can't risk hitting my filly — already lost Royal Andrew, after all."

"Ravishment awaits, as I have long predicted," Mary said.

Tasmin thought that Mary might be right, for once. The Indians were not slowing.

Jim Snow flashed through the gate, still holding grimly to Tom Fitzpatrick, and, at once, the riflemen fired, but with puny — indeed, counterproductive — results. Lord Berrybender's rifle exploded, causing him to fall backward with a great yell, his face black with gunpowder. Kit, Boisdeffre, and Charbonneau all fired but no Indians fell, though one did brush at his sleeve, as if brushing off a wasp.

Tasmin went running down. She had seen the arrows hit her husband and thought he might need immediate succor — but the arrows, it appeared, had merely stuck in Jim's buckskins — he and the other men bent themselves to closing the large log gate — and none too soon. The Indians were not more than one hundred yards away.

"Shut it, let's make 'em climb!" Jim said. He seemed startled to see Tasmin coming down from the tower, but closing and barring the large gate was a task that couldn't wait.

"I'm blinded, I'm blistered. Where's my Milly?" Lord B. yelled.

"You better go hide our baby — and hide them others too," Jim said in a businesslike tone. Before Tasmin could get inside, Little Onion came, took Monty, and at once scurried back into the post. An old bin that had once held corn had been chosen as a hiding place.

Jim, Tom Fitzpatrick, and the rest all hurried up to the lookout tower, fully expecting the Blackfeet to press the conflict. The Broken Hand, having caught his breath, seemed eager to go on with the fight.

Then, to everyone's surprise, the attacking warriors stopped, all of them waiting in a group just out of rifle range. They were watching the lanced man, who was walking slowly toward them, the two ends of the lance protruding from either side of his body.

"Now, there's a sight," Charbonneau said. "Stuck clear through and still walking. Ever see anything like that, Tom?"

"No, but my brother was shot clean through with a bullet — that occurred in a barroom in Cincinnati, Ohio, and my brother is as active today as any man you'd want to know," Tom said. "The bullet missed his heart, missed his lungs . . . and there you are. I suppose a lance like that could go through and miss the vitals — that's what it looks like happened."

"No it couldn't — no it *couldn't*," Kit Carson said. He did not like the sight of a man who must obviously be dead walking around on the prairie.

"They do say the Blackfeet are tough as bears," Charbonneau announced.

Jim Snow, though not apprehensive, was as startled as Kit Carson at the sight of a lanced man walking. The Blackfeet warriors seemed startled too — who could blame them?

"Perhaps that wicked Piegan is filled with such a power of sin that even the Sin Killer cannot subdue him," Mary Berrybender suggested, with her usual, slightly insane smile.

"Shut up, that's nonsense," Tasmin insisted — but Jim refused to second her objection. He just looked hard at Mary, a girl he had been suspicious of ever since he came upon her talking to a snake. He knew that he had been very lucky in his race to save the Broken Hand. It was not often that a warrior dropped a lance — surprise had caused it. Luck, not skill particularly, had decided that struggle. And here the man came, walking slowly — but walking.

"I'm in a hurry for that man to die," Kit Carson said. "It's way past time for him to die."

"I guess Piegans don't feel like they have to die just because you want them to, Kit," the Broken Hand said. "I would have died this afternoon myself, if Jimmy hadn't come on that fast mare."

The Indians were talking to the wounded man, who seemed to be delivering a firm opinion. Then one of the older Indians came walking slowly toward the post. The other Blackfeet watched. The fighting urge seemed to have left them, for a time.

"Well, I'll swear, they want to parley, after chasing me five miles," Tom said. "Do you want to go talk to them, Sharbo?"

"I can't talk much Blackfoot — just a few words," Charbonneau admitted. "What about yourself?"

"I'm no better at it," Tom said. "The Blackfeet don't have many whites as guests. There's not much opportunity to learn their lingo."

"I can talk a little," Pierre Boisdeffre said. He was a trader — his job depended on getting along with Indians; otherwise they might burn his trading post down.

"All three of you go, then," Jim said. "Just don't wander out far enough that they can cut you off."

"I suppose we all know better than that,

Jimmy," the Broken Hand said, with a touch of impatience.

Charbonneau, Boisdeffre, and the Broken Hand all walked out of the stockade. After a few minutes of conversation in sign, they all came slowly back.

"They want a horse," Boisdeffre said. "That fellow with the lance stuck through him wants to go home to die — I guess he don't think he can make it if he has to walk."

"They're not having my mare Augusta — or the carriage horses either," Lord Berrybender announced. Though severely blistered, his face peppered with gunpowder, he was not blinded — though he did have gunpowder on his eyelids, a circumstance that did not improve his temper.

"No need — give them Joe Walker's mule," Boisdeffre suggested. "I'll pay Joe for her myself." What was the price of a mule compared to the distress of watching his trading post burn?

Tasmin, Jim, and all the rest went up to the lookout to watch Pierre Boisdeffre deliver the mule. The animal was duly turned over, and the wounded man carefully lifted onto its back.

"I doubt we'll ever see a thing like that again," Charbonneau said, as they watched the party of Blackfeet move slowly off to the west.

"I hope not," Kit Carson said. "Once is enough to have to look at a dead man who won't die."

33

The wounded man was called Antelope . . .

Old Moose, the leader of the little band of Blackfeet who had been trying to chase down the trapper known as the Broken Hand, led the small mule that the wounded warrior rode. The wounded man was called Antelope, because he could outrun anyone in the tribe — or anyone in any tribe, for that matter. Antelope was a very fast runner, though it was not likely that he had much more fast running to do. How fast could a man run with a long stob stuck through him? That he was still alive was wonder enough. Old Moose and everyone else in the band expected Antelope to fall over dead at any moment. Old Moose tried to pick a smooth route, so as not to jostle Antelope too much — a man with a lance through his breast would not enjoy being jostled.

In fact, though, to everyone's surprise, Antelope did not seem to be feeling too bad.

"Let's go a long way before we camp, otherwise the Sin Killer might come and stick spears in all of you," he suggested.

"I'm not sure that was the Sin Killer," Old

Moose said. "He was moving so fast I didn't get a good look at him."

"Of course it was him," Two Ribs Broken said. "He killed a bunch of moose up north — the Assiniboines told me. They call him the Raven Brave. They were mad because they wanted all those moose for themselves."

"Don't be in a hurry to camp," Antelope repeated.

There was a bright moon, so the Blackfeet traveled deep into the night. Even if the Sin Killer wasn't following them, someone might sneak up on them and try to steal their mule. Everyone still expected Antelope to give up his ghost any minute, but he didn't — instead, he began to eat jerky — tough jerky from an old mountain goat Two Ribs Broken had killed.

Antelope's main problem was that he now had to sleep on his side — the protruding lance made it impossible for him to turn on his back.

"I don't like sleeping on my side," he complained, and yet he was up at dawn and walked over to a nearby creek, where he drank plenty of water.

The band began to face the fact that they were likely to have Antelope on their hands for at least another day. He was not particularly well liked. Thanks to his speed of foot he got a lot of attention from the women, including the wives of several members of the party. In general the man was aloof, but there he was, with a lance stuck through him, just as difficult as he had always been.

"I think we could pull that lance out of you if several of us pull," Old Moose suggested. Antelope's state of health struck him as ridiculous. Was he really going to have to walk along leading a mule all day because Antelope was too stubborn to die?

"No, if you did that my soul might fly out," Antelope said. "I don't want my soul to get away."

Antelope's comment provoked much debate — when it came to the tricky business of souls, opinions differed. Who knew what might prompt a soul to leave? Two Ribs Broken sided with Antelope this time, though he had never cared for the man much.

"He's right — it would be risky," he said.

The band traveled all that day, shot a doe, and wounded a buffalo; at night, though he complained about having to sleep on his side, Antelope was still very much alive.

Some of the warriors were of the opinion that Antelope wasn't really a human being, since a human being would undoubtedly have died of such a wound. A small warrior named Red Weasel was now firmly convinced that Antelope was some kind of witch. Red Weasel thought the best thing to do was to cut the witch's throat, a plan he had to abandon because no one would agree to help him.

"If we had a saw we could saw off this lance right where it goes into my body — then I wouldn't have to sleep on my side," Antelope remarked.

"There are saws at the camp," Old Moose told him. "I guess we can try something like that when we get home."

When they reached their main camp the next day there was, of course, much comment about the fact that Antelope had come back with a lance sticking out of his body. The strongest man in the tribe, Bull, thought he could give the lance one good jerk and pull it out, but Antelope refused to allow Bull to try it, on the grounds that it would provide too good an opportunity for his soul to escape.

A saw was found, and duly sharpened; the lance ends were sawed off so close to Antelope's body that a few scraps of his skin were sawed off too. But such discomforts were minor. Instead of a floppy lance handle, Antelope now merely had a neat plug, could sleep on his back again, and even decided to change his name. His new name was Man with a Plug in His Belly. The women, to Old Moose's disgust, paid him more attention than ever.

34

"Dern 'em, they should die when they're sup-posed to!" he insisted.

"People won't always die when they're sup-posed to," Tom Fitzpatrick insisted. All those who had watched the young warrior ride away with his own lance sticking out of his chest were confused in their heads about what they had just witnessed. Kit Carson was terribly agitated — he had stayed in the lookout tower until the little band of warriors was out of sight, hoping to see the wounded man fall dead; but he didn't.

"Dern 'em, they *should* die when they're supposed to!" he insisted. "Right's right!"

"Now, Kit — just look at Hugh Glass," the Broken Hand argued. "I'd never seen a man that torn up, and neither had Jimmy Bridger. Hugh's chest was ripped open, most of his ribs were broken, and his scalp was nearly torn off. I thought he was dead and so did Jimmy, or we would never have left him, Sioux or no Sioux. But then, six months later, here he comes, as alive as I am."

"I 'spect you all know Tom Smith," Charbonneau remarked. "A horse fell on him and he busted his leg so bad that it couldn't be set, so Tom sawed it off himself. Not only that, he got up the next day and whittled himself a fine peg leg."

"One of Ashley's men had to have his guts sewed back in after that big fight with the Rees," Tom remembered. "Hugh Glass helped hold his guts in and Jedediah Smith did the sewing."

"I have seen a few sights in that line myself," Lord Berrybender remarked. Though Milly had done her best, his face still looked as if it had been nastily peppered.

"The Spaniards, you know, are cruel to their own peasants," Lord B. continued. "Stick 'em on sharpened tree stumps and leave them to die. Picked a fellow off that had been stuck on a stake for two days — the surgeon sewed him up and off he went. Never know what humans will stand until you've seen a bit of war."

Though Jim Snow listened to all this talk about combat wounds and mutilation, he did not contribute. Some men were tough, there was no denying that, but his failure to kill the young warrior still puzzled him. A bullet was a small thing — it might pass straight through and do little damage. But a lance? Yet the man had walked almost a mile, got on a mule, and rode away.

Pierre Boisdeffre was fretting that this miracle would embolden the Blackfeet, who were plenty bold anyway. The medicine men would use the incident to belittle the power of the whites. A hundred warriors might move against them tomorrow — he doubted that his little stockade would stop a hundred warriors.

"I expect it's time to start south," Jim said to Kit.

"I don't see why," Kit said, and then he got up and walked off. Everyone agreed that lately young Kit had been impossible to deal with.

"There's not a better guide in the West than our Kit," Tom said. "Only he takes bossing. What he can't do is boss himself."

Jim walked back to the nursery, which had been undisturbed by the brief attack. The mood in the nursery was calm, so calm that Jim felt awkward about going in. Monty had just nursed; he hung from a peg, waving his tiny hands. Tasmin was drowsing; she hardly yet had her strength back, which discouraged Jim's inclination to strike out on their own and let the Berrybender party follow Kit and Tom. With Tasmin still weak, it might be best to stay with the group.

"Can't I just trim your beard?" Tasmin asked, waking. Jim had the confined look he got when he was indoors.

The request annoyed Jim — she could immediately see it. Men were prickly about the least things, it seemed. Why would a snip or two cause him to draw away? Nothing made her feel as wifely as cutting Jim's hair, and yet he did his best to withhold the privilege.

"You and your snippin'," he said. "You need to get packed — you all do. We need to get out of here while the getting's good."

Tasmin refused to give up — she felt that she *must* put up a fight, else Jim would never let her do the things she wanted to do.

"Please, just a trim," she said. "I have very little to pack."

"If he won't let you cut his hair, I'll let you cut mine, Tasmin," Vicky said. She had been happy for a bit with her babe, but Lord Berrybender's brutal indifference, plus the absence of Drummond Stewart, had caused her to sink back into glum resignation. If she was to have only the love of her baby, why bother with three feet of hair?

Jim Snow turned and left, his beard unsnipped, which left Tasmin furiously annoyed. When Vicky made it clear that she meant what she had said, Tasmin grabbed some scissors and applied herself with such vigor that virtually the whole floor of the nursery — not a large room — was soon covered with Vicky's shorn locks. Coal and Little Onion watched in amazement — neither of them had ever seen so much hair come off one head.

As Tasmin clipped and cut, Buffum came in to watch, and then Cook and even Eliza.

251

Only Milly missed the cutting — as usual she was busy with Lord Berrybender, who was just getting fitted with a wooden leg, the work of the skillful Tom Fitzpatrick, who had been shaping it for several days.

"It looks a good fit, you'll soon be hopping about like a cricket," Millicent assured His Lordship, who did not welcome the comparison.

"Perhaps not quite like a cricket," he said. Helpful as she was, Millicent did not exactly have a way with words.

When Vicky Kennet first saw her new self in the mirror she could not hold in a shriek.

"I'm shorn like a nun — though I don't *feel* like a nun," she admitted.

"As usual, Tasmin has overdone it," Mary commented. "She has cut off far too much."

"Tasmin should have left you a bit more on top," Buffum ventured. "To me you look rather rabbity, I fear."

"Oh, I don't know," said Father Geoffrin, who had just wandered in. "In fact you look quite Joan of Arc–ish. I hope you won't be foolish enough to attempt martyrdom."

"Look at all this hair on the floor," Bobbety exclaimed. "It's as if a great yak has been sheared — or a musk ox, even."

"I might remind you skeptics that Venetia's hair will *grow*," Tasmin said. She was annoyed by the superior tone everyone was adopting.

From Coal's point of view, and Little Onion's, the great pile of shorn hair was the most exciting thing about the whole procedure. When Vicky indicated to them that they could *have* what had once been her great mane, the girls were almost overcome with excitement. In no time they had sacked up every hair — when Tasmin tried to find out what they meant to do with it the girls gave merry shrugs — they didn't know, really, but were firmly convinced that they had secured a treasure.

Then, almost at the same moment, to the surprise of all the onlookers, both Tasmin and Vicky began to cry.

"What in the world is it *now,* in this year of our Lord 1833?" Buffum wanted to know.

"It's . . . it's . . . ," Tasmin gasped — but then she stopped.

"It's . . . just . . . that life seems so wanting — I think I'll smash my cello," Venetia Kennet said.

35

" . . . and now he's chopping up the buggy."

Before Vicky Kennet could carry out this desperate action — one which would deprive them all of music for a very long time, as Tasmin, Buffum, Bobbety, Father Geoff, and even Mary pleadingly informed her — who should rush in but the large laundress, Millicent, sporting a large bruise on one cheek and blubbering loudly.

"Oh, please help me, Lady Tasmin," Milly pleaded. "First Lord Berrybender claimed that his peg leg was too short, and now he's chopping up the buggy."

"What?" Tasmin asked. "Has the old fool gone mad? We need that buggy."

"It's just that he's drunk and in a violent temper, I'm afraid," Milly cried. "When I tried to grab the axe from him he hit me quite a solid lick — not with the axe, of course, else I'd be dead."

"Being Papa's bawd is a rough job, just ask our Vicky," Mary said, with her mad grin.

They all rushed to the courtyard, where Milly's statements were soon confirmed. Lord Berrybender, swinging the axe wildly, had almost succeeded in reducing the fine London buggy to a pile of kindling.

Kit Carson and Tom Fitzpatrick stood nearby, solemnly watching the destruction. Of Jim Snow there was no sign.

"Very good, Father — I see you've been acting with your usual thoughtfulness," Tasmin said. "We've three infants in our company, thousands of miles of wilderness to negotiate, and you suddenly destroy our buggy — what's the sense in that?"

Lord B. ignored her remarks.

"I never liked that buggy," he informed them. "Felt damn good, chopping it up."

"I suppose this means you intend to cram us all in the wagon, then?" Tasmin inquired.

"Not at all — the wagon is for Millicent and me and my guns and shot," Lord B. replied. "No squalling brats invited — might scare the game. Besides, Milly and I will be wanting a little rest now and then — a little time out for human nature."

"Fornication, you mean — spare us these vague euphemisms," Tasmin said, in high indignation. "I do think you're the most selfish old bastard I've ever encountered. So Vicky and Coal and the rest of us will just have to walk, if we hope to get anywhere."

Lord Berrybender ignored her. He was staring at Venetia Kennet's shorn head.

"My God, Vicky, where's your hair?" he asked. "Did a red Indian scalp you?"

"No one scalped her — I cut it," Tasmin told him. "It's that much less she'll have to carry on our long walk."

"But I *liked* your hair," Lord B. said, with a look of distress. "You used to tickle me with it — it was one of our pleasant games."

Vicky didn't answer. The old brute had ruined her, ravished her, gotten her with child, and then abandoned her for a fat laundress. Now, no doubt, he meant to mock her for having cut her hair.

"Oh, I see — perhaps Tasmin was right to cut it," the old man said, hobbling over for a closer look. "I never noticed those pert ears — they were always covered up. Surprised you could even hear your own chords."

"I heard them quite well, thank you," Vicky said — she recognized all too well the rather husky tone that had come into His Lordship's voice. Husky compliments were sure to be followed by fondlings and gropings.

Milly recognized the lustful tone as well — though she stood only a yard from Lord Berrybender, it seemed he had quite forgotten her. Thanks to a haircut, he was intending to grab the prissy Vicky again. It would be back to the tubs for her.

"I'll be going now, Your Lordship — my little one needs me," Vicky said, turning quickly away.

"But wait, my girl!" he said. "Just wait till

I get my crutch — damn peg leg doesn't fit right, Mr. Fitzpatrick will have to whittle on it some more."

Vicky Kennet didn't wait, didn't turn, didn't slow.

"What's wrong with that girl? She might just have waited a moment," Lord Berrybender said, frowning. "Always liked Vicky — talented in more ways than one."

"She no longer wants you, Father — if she ever wanted you," Tasmin said coolly. "I think that's plain."

"Oh, nonsense — of course she wants me!" Lord B. exclaimed. "Many a fine tussle Vicky and I have had. Why wouldn't she want me, I'd like to know?"

"Because you're a disgusting, selfish, one-legged old brute," Tasmin told him. "I see you slapped Millicent — and no doubt you'll slap her again."

"Slap any woman I want to, I guess, starting with you, you whore of Satan!" His Lordship thundered. He advanced on Tasmin, hand upraised, but before he could strike, Tasmin grabbed the axe and held it high.

"Slap me and I'll cut off your arm, or whatever appendage I can reach!" she warned him. "Like to lose an arm, to balance off the leg?"

"Grab her, men, she's daft!" Lord B. said. "Childbirth has addled her!" He looked at

Kit and Tom, but neither man moved or spoke.

Toussaint Charbonneau sauntered slowly over, meaning to inspect the ruins of the buggy.

"It's a good thing old Claricia's gone," he remarked. "He was mighty fond of that buggy."

Just then Jim Snow stepped back into the stockade. He had been checking around a little, thinking it might be just like the Blackfeet to return and launch a sneak attack.

The old parrot, who sometimes liked to follow Jim around, flapped back too, and settled on the ruins of the buggy.

"There, sir — a timely arrival, I must say," Lord Berrybender said. "Do oblige me and take your wife in hand — saucy wench that she is, she seems to have found it necessary to threaten her own father with an axe."

"What fool chopped up the buggy?" Jim asked, glaring at Kit Carson.

"Not me," Kit said at once.

"You see how my nose is swollen?" Lord B. asked. "A hornet bit me — put me rather in a temper. I'm afraid I took it out on the buggy — inferior vehicle in any case. Never could get comfortable in it."

"Be careful with that axe," Jim said to Tasmin. It was a tool he knew her to be inexpert with, from having tried to teach her to chop firewood.

"I am being careful with it — do you see any blood, Jim?" she asked. "It is merely that Father intends to pester Vicky, and I won't have it. Vicky must not be agitated — it could well affect her milk."

Tasmin lowered the axe. Lord Berrybender looked sulky, but he made no move to follow Vicky.

Tasmin had hoped for a moment that Jim would take her side and pummel her father, but she soon saw that he meant to take no side. He strode over to Kit and Tom and asked them why they had stood by meekly while a perfectly good buggy was being chopped up.

"It's *his* buggy!" Kit pointed out, a little annoyed. In his view Jim Snow was far too hard to please.

"Most of us will be walking, it looks like," Jim said. "Let's try and get an early start."

36

Sticking to them close as a tick . . .

Jim could not sleep in the close, stuffy trading post, so Tasmin gathered up their son and a bit of bedding and walked with him about half a mile on the prairies for a night under the stars, which were as brilliant as they had been on her first evening in the West.

Sticking to them close as a tick was Little Onion. The girl, Tasmin realized, wasn't following them out of any impulse toward rivalry, or in order to usurp their privacy. She came because she thought it was her duty to stay near the baby, and, of course, to be available in case Jim Snow, her husband, had some chore he needed her to do. For a time Monty fretted and squirmed, alternately wanting the breast and then not wanting it. Weary, Tasmin let Little Onion take him — she walked him and soothed him until he was quiet, though from time to time throughout the short night, Monty woke and wailed briefly again.

"What's wrong with him? Indian babies don't cry like that," Jim insisted.

"Oh, Jimmy — of course they do," Tasmin said. "All babies cry sometimes. Monty's not used to sleeping out."

"He best get used to it — we'll be sleeping out till the snows come," Jim said.

"Do you wish you could just be rid of us — we're all such nuisances?" Tasmin asked. She knew it was the kind of question Jim didn't know how to answer, but she asked anyway. It was clear that the presence of two wives and a baby left him anything but happy. She knew she probably should keep quiet at such a time, but keeping quiet was not her way. She had mated with this man — surely it was not wrong to try and understand what he felt.

"I led you to this place — I guess it's my job to lead you out," Jim said. Why *would* Tasmin keep asking questions that had no good answers?

"That's what I feared," Tasmin said. "We're just a burden to you, all of us: Monty and I and Little Onion too. You don't want her any more than you want me."

"Less," Jim admitted. "I just married her because her sister asked me to . . . and now her sister's dead."

"That's hardly fair to Little Onion," Tasmin continued. "She's a very proper girl, and pretty in her way. She must find it very sad to have been given to a husband who doesn't want her."

261

"That's silly thinking," Jim answered. "They were going to give her to an old man who would have spent half his time beating her. I've never hit her once — she's better off with us."

Tasmin liked it that he said "us."

"Unlucky me," she said. "You've slapped me twice and punched me once. Did you ever hit her sister . . . the one who died?"

Jim could not remember that he had. Sun Girl had been an excellent wife — she rarely spoke and never provoked him.

"No, she knew how to behave," he said, being honest. "So does Little Onion, mostly."

"I see . . . and I quite clearly *don't* know how to behave," Tasmin said. "It's certainly odd that you accepted me as your wife, considering how worthless I must seem."

"I had to, so we could rut," Jim said simply. "Rutting's a big sin unless you're married."

"Well, at least you're frank," Tasmin said. "What about Little Onion — you just have to explain a few things to me. I've never been in a bigamous situation before."

"What?" he asked. "What kind of situation?"

"Bigamous — one of two wives," she replied. "When it's time to rut again will you be rutting with us both — or how will it work?"

"She's not much for rutting — too young," he assured her.

"Even so, she has a woman's heart and she's given it to our son if not to you," Tasmin pointed out. "If you and I do a great deal of rutting, as I suspect we might, and you do none with Little Onion, it's likely that she will soon be feeling left out. I know I would, if it were the other way around."

"We don't need to be talking about things like this," Jim said.

"You obviously don't, but I do," Tasmin said. "You left me alone for a long time when I was feeling very married to you. In your absence my married feeling went away, but now it's coming back. I feel married to you again. But there sits Little Onion, singing to our son, and she feels married to you too."

Jim made no response — he was staring into the dark distance.

"I suppose I just want to know that you have some kind of married feeling too," she went on. "That you still want me, in other words."

"It's a far place to aim for, Santa Fe," he said finally.

Tasmin sighed.

"All right, I give up," she said. "There's just no answers in you. I suppose it's just that I ask the wrong questions."

Then she got up, went over, sat down by Little Onion, and sang to Monty too.

263

37

The stars sent down a kind of fairy light.

In the night, while Jim, Little Onion, and Monty all slept, Tasmin awoke, stood up, and walked away a few steps, to relieve herself. The stars sent down a kind of fairy light. While she was squatting a skunk waddled by, passing Tasmin without alarm. She saw the white blaze of the skunk's tail move off into the grass.

For a time she had been too angry to sleep — angry at Jim for his refusal to address her concerns — they were concerns that seemed to be important for her future. But anger was followed by resignation: what was the use of even talking to the man? His intentions were not cruel, particularly, but his way of living had been so different from hers that they had little common experience from which to frame a discussion. The old patterns of English life — a life still being led by her own family — left many avenues for adjustment. Much was allowed, including frank discussion of what was or was not allowed. Conflicts there might be, but breakfast, lunch, tea, dinner followed inevitably.

264

Tasmin could not be sure that her parents, Lord and Lady Berrybender, had ever been especially close, yet they had produced fourteen children while leading lives that were, in the main, separate. They met at table, at cards, to procreate; conditions of life were very orderly. Despite Lord Berrybender's bluster, extremes of emotion were rarely attained.

But her mate, Jim Snow, knew nothing at all of social pattern — how could he? Survival seemed to be his principal goal — he was not even interested in making money, as the other mountain men were. On his terms he was successful: he had survived where many another man would have fallen. Only the day before, with her own eyes, she had seen him come within an inch of death from the Blackfoot arrows. More than that, she had seen him, in effect, kill a man — that the man hadn't died immediately was only due to some fluke of anatomy. Jim admitted that he had been lucky — surprise had made the warrior drop his lance, otherwise Jim might have been the one speared. The conflict, though brief, had involved life and death. Death in battle — a thing several of her noble ancestors faced — had been a likelihood for all of them. Only by the accident of the warrior's survival had a pitched battle been avoided; the defenders might have been overwhelmed, and she and her sisters taken into captivity or killed, with dire conse-quences for Monty, Coal's baby, and Vicky's.

Finished, Tasmin sat for a while in the rip-pling grass. Her anger at Jim subsided. With life or death in the balance, as it had been on many days of Jim's life, why would she expect him to worry about the kind of con-cerns she had expressed? Mating with Little Onion would be the last thing on his mind. Tasmin had been drawn to Jim in the first place because of the foppish English suitors she had rejected at home. They were men so positioned as to think only of their pleasure. Jim Snow was not indifferent to pleasure — Tasmin was wife enough to know that — but it was not unnatural that he should think mainly of danger, when there was such a lot of it around. What might happen conjugally if she and Little Onion and Monty were all in a tent together was a problem he had so far not even considered, and if he did focus his mind on it, he might be the one sur-prised the next time he faced a warrior with a spear.

Subdued by such considerations, Tasmin went back to where Jim rested on his blanket — Monty had begun to emit a few little mouse squeaks, meaning he was hungry, so Tasmin took him from Little Onion and sat down cross-legged and fed him. Her milk flowed easily, but her thoughts were not so easy. What of the little boy at her breast, a child they had made in reckless pleasure? What did she want him to be — an English gentleman, or a hardy frontiersman? This too was something she would be unlikely to get Jim to talk about. How could he? Excepting her own monstrously selfish father, he had never seen an English gentleman. The frontier had been his only school. He was anxious to read better, in order to comprehend more of the Bible, but how would he react if she suggested that Monty needed to make a beginning with Latin and Greek? What did she think about such an issue herself? She had always been an eager learner, and had resented having to more or less steal Greek lessons from her hapless brother's tutor. *She* wanted Latin and Greek, but did she want them for her son, a boy conceived on a blanket spread on the prairie grass, while buffalo roared in the distance and hawks soared high above? What *did* she want for Monty: the English life with its order and pattern, or the frontier life with its vast beauty and frequent danger? Of course, Monty had only just been born, there was time to consider many possibilities, but it would need to be thought about soon enough, and she was the one who would have to do the thinking. Jim Snow would be busy enough just keeping them alive.

Tasmin wished for Pomp — she could have talked it all through with him. After all,

Pomp knew both worlds. He had admired an Italian princess, dead on the Brenner Pass. He had been to plays and operas, and studied philosophy and science — his tutor, Pomp told her, had been a student of the great Kant himself, of whose profound speculations Tasmin had not the slightest notion. Pomp had been given by the generous Prince Paul of Württemberg, who adopted him, every benefit, everything Europe could offer — except, of course, noble birth; and yet he had come back and submitted himself to the spartan rigors of the American frontier. No one else of Tasmin's acquaintance had mastered both lives, both ways. Surely her sweet Pomp would give her good advice — so anxious was Tasmin to have it that she felt impatient for the morning, when, if there were no unexpected delays, they would start south, where Pomp and his patron might be found.

"Where'd you go?" Jim whispered, when Monty had been returned to Little Onion and Tasmin had returned to the blanket where he lay.

"Just to make water," she said.

"Lay back, while it's still dark," Jim said, still whispering.

Puzzled at first, Tasmin then realized that Jim didn't want Little Onion to hear him, though she would not have understood his words.

Obediently, since she felt she had taxed her husband enough for one night with her questioning, she lay down beside him and was startled, when, at once, his hand began stroking her, in the place that had recently made her a mother. Months had passed since Jim had caressed her so — Tasmin was startled — the last thing she had expected to receive from her husband that night was such a caress. For a moment she was nervous — almost resentful. How dare the man be so familiar! Nearby, Monty squeaked, and then quieted, as Little Onion walked him. Slowly, under the stroking of Jim's hand, Tasmin relaxed, forgot Little Onion, forgot the baby. Never passive, she turned and reached her hand inside Jim's leggings, so as to grasp her husband. And yet she was doubtful: Cook had advised her not to rush conjugal relations.

"You'll need just a bit of healing — a month I'd allow, if I were you," Cook had advised — the words had been meaningless at the time, when Tasmin had not even been sure she would ever see her husband again. They were not so meaningless now. Jim's hand worked, Tasmin sighed. Little Onion heard, but didn't care. She was happy to avoid men, when they were in that mood. The tiny male in her arms now was her dearest love, and he, in his squirmings, gave her plenty to do.

269

38

"You garlic fool, you should have kept it sharp."

"If the English don't leave today I think we should go back anyway," Aldo Claricia suggested. "I'm hungry — I need to eat. Boisdeffre would give us food."

"Surely they'll leave today," Pedro Yanez said. "Lord Berrybender might shoot us, if he sees us."

The two of them were holed up in a kind of excavation they had made for themselves, under the west bank of the Missouri River. Their excavation, a tiny cave, was hidden from prying eyes by a thicket of briars and berry bushes. They had been huddled there for four days, expecting, every minute, that the English party would depart. After all, the plains to the south were covered with game — surely Lord Berrybender would not ignore such good hunting.

Their own plans to follow the swiftly flowing Yellowstone south had stalled after only three days because of the lack of adequate knives. Though, when they left the hunting party, they had made off with the fine Belgian rifle that had belonged to Old

Gorska, the Polish hunter, and had plenty of powder and shot, they had been negligent in the matter of knives. When, on the second day out, Pedro had brought down a fat doe, they discovered that they had only one small knife between them — a pocketknife that Aldo used mainly for whittling sticks into toothpicks.

This pocketknife, though a fine instrument for making toothpicks, proved wholly inadequate when it came to slicking up a fat Western deer.

"You garlic fool, you should have kept it sharp," Pedro said testily; the comradeship they had proclaimed the night they left the company had quickly begun to fray. Almost everything Pedro did — or didn't do — irritated the sensitive Italian, and that applied in reverse to the testy Spaniard. The slightest contretemps led to heated quarrels. Here, at the very outset of their bold adventure, they were faced with a very formidable problem: a dead deer they couldn't get the hide off, though they were both starving.

"This knife was not meant to cut a deer," Aldo remonstrated — he was bitterly disappointed in the performance of his own knife.

"I don't care, go sharpen it on a rock," Pedro commanded. "This venison is going to waste."

Aldo tried, but the famous yellow rocks which gave the river its name proved poor grindstones. The little knife, despite much grinding, did not become sharper. Finally, driven mad with frustration, Aldo began to stab the carcass blindly, aiming at the belly, where the skin seemed a little less tough.

"Keep stabbing, you made a puncture," Pedro said. "Tripe is better than nothing."

Working in tandem, the two were soon able to pull out many yards of intestines, while the roasts, the steaks, the saddle — all the parts of the deer they had looked forward to eating — remained as inaccessible as ever. Desperately they sliced the gut into sections — even that taxed the potential of the little knife. They ate the gut, along with its greenish contents, while they sat on the ridge where the deer had fallen and contemplated their unenviable situation. They were just by the blue-green river — they could see it winding far, far across the plains.

"How far do you think it goes, Pedro?" Aldo asked.

"I don't know — a thousand miles, ten thousand, what does it matter?" Pedro said, overcome, for the moment, with the fatalism of his race. However far the river went, they would never get there.

"We will starve before we get to the end of it," he said, becoming lachrymose. "We will never get to the end of this river."

"There are many knives in Boisdeffre's trading post," Aldo reminded him. "We could go back and get some."

"No, it's in the wrong direction, and besides, the English are there," Pedro said, in his gloom.

"Direction? What difference does direction make, in this country?" Aldo exclaimed. "One direction is as good as another. Boisdeffre doesn't like the English any better than we do — at least he'll feed us."

Pedro soon grasped the wisdom of that suggestion. Here was a fat deer, well killed with one shot from the Belgian gun, and yet all they could eat of it was the guts.

So, talking of all the buffalo roasts they would eat once they got back to the post, the two turned north, followed the river, and then crossed and dug their little cave in the bank of the Missouri — from there they could watch the post without being seen.

Once in sight of the post their rage increased in keeping with their hunger. Why wouldn't the English leave? Lady Tasmin they saw twice, walking out with her husband and her infant, followed by the young Indian girl. Millicent, the fat laundress, made trips in and out, loading the wagon, which suggested that departure would soon occur. But when?

"Curs and bitches," Aldo raged. "This is a free country. The old bastard doesn't own us. Why can't we just go in and eat? Think of those beaver tails Boisdeffre cooks."

The Spaniard, though, was more cautious.

"Who knows what the laws are here?" he said. "We took the gun — the old fool might hang us."

"No," Aldo protested. "The gun was Gorska's. No one said His Lordship could have it. You could tell him Gorska willed it to you."

"Me? Why me? Why don't *you* say it, then they'll hang you," Pedro argued, his suspicion of the treacherous Italian coming to the fore.

On their fourth day in the hole, with the English party no closer to leaving for their hunt, both men tried to screw up their resolve and march into the trading post — yet they were still lingering when help suddenly appeared from an unexpected quarter. Who should come strolling along the riverbank with a butterfly net and a pouch filled with specimen bottles but the dumpy figure of Piet Van Wely, clay pipe in his mouth. And that was not all: accompanying Piet was Mary Berrybender, carrying what appeared to be a substantial picnic hamper.

Neither Aldo nor Pedro liked the finical Dutchman, who, for no better reason than that he knew the Latin names of plants, gave himself airs, refused to drink with them, seldom took snuff, and held aloof from all coarse badinage concerning the women on the boat, even though he was known to enjoy the caresses of the spindly Mary.

Nonetheless there Piet was, a fellow European. Surely he would be sympathetic to their need.

"If not, we'll beat them both and take the food and run," Aldo said with dignity. "Why should he get to feast with that English girl while we starve?"

"I hope they have sardines. . . . I could eat a hundred sardines . . . no, a thousand sardines," Pedro bragged, his mouth watering at the prospect.

Hastily they crawled up the bank, knocked the dirt off their clothes as best they could; a week in the wilderness, with no access to a laundress, had left them not exactly dressed for a parade.

But when they presented themselves in all their soiled dignity to Piet Van Wely and the young Miss Berrybender, their scruffy appearance caused scarcely any comment.

"Ho, fellows . . . so you're back, eh?" Piet said, looking far down the Missouri River.

"Back . . . very hungry too . . . I wonder if the young miss would perhaps spare us a bit of a loaf, or even a sausage?" Aldo asked.

"Of course I won't, you grubby beasts," Mary said. "Not a bite shall you have! Shame on you, you treacherous slaves! Deserting my good papa in his hour of need. You would both be bastinadoed if I had my way."

"She's a witch, let's cut her throat and take the sardines," Pedro whispered. Then, to his surprise, Piet Van Wely suddenly dashed off into the prairie grass, waving his butterfly net wildly at anything that moved: butterfly, grasshopper, moth, wasp, bee.

"Ha, Piet, you sluggard!" Mary yelled, with a sinister smile. "Now that the tiny prince comes, you at last bestir yourself. Hurry now, grab the grasses, the flowers, and any beetles that you see. Perhaps we can beat these rivals yet."

Greatly startled, Aldo Claricia looked around.

"What prince, Miss?" he asked, confused — Mary Berrybender deigned merely to point. Where there had been only the broad brown river, there was now a smudge, beneath which there was a speck that might be a boat.

"It's the steamer *Yellowstone*, more successful than our poor boat," Mary explained. "It carries, unless I'm mistaken, Prince Maximilian zu Wied-Neuwied, so celebrated for his researches in the dense Brazilian forests. Now he's caught us, and Piet is very likely undone, for the prince is a most determined explorer and will surely have brought with him many specialists: botanists, lepidopterists, entomologists, a painter, a mineralogist, and Lord knows how many others. Papa will be most vexed: first the lecherous Drummond Stewart quite turned the head of his mistress, Vicky Kennet, and now the little

276

prince of Wied will no doubt usurp us in many sound fields of knowledge, for Piet is but one man and the Germans will likely be many."

"If they are so many, why can't we just shoot them, these Germans?" Pedro Yanez suggested. "The fat beasts, what right have they to crowd us out here, we who have trekked through the snows?"

"Good for you, señor," Mary said. "A fine idea indeed, though of course there might be a bit of an outcry in the embassies. But we Berrybenders have never let a few outcries stop us. For that you'll get your picnic, señor! My good Piet has got to be about his collecting quickly — I doubt he will want to eat."

"We'll eat, he can chase!" Pedro said.

A moment later, mustache dripping, he was just finishing the first tin of sardines, while the more fastidious Italian, Aldo Claricia, was slicing himself a healthy hunk of sausage with his ridiculous little pocketknife.

39

" . . . I swing with the net, and the bruin looks up . . ."

Exactly how his large butterfly net managed to get round the head of a grizzly bear was something Piet Van Wely could never adequately explain, not even to himself.

"I am in the weeds, I reach out to scoop a big gray moth who is on a weed, I swing with the net, and the bruin looks up and gets his head stuck in the net. So I *run!*" he said.

The bear, after pawing at the confusing net for a moment, ran too — after the screaming botanist, who raced with all the speed his short legs could muster right toward the startled picnickers. Mary Berrybender, who could usually find no wrong with the plump Hollander, found much wrong in this instance: he was leading the loping grizzly right toward them!

"Fie! Fie! Piet!" she cried. "Can't you see we're picnicking? I must insist that you take your great bear elsewhere!"

"Kill him, Pedro, we'll be gulped!" Aldo said, but Pedro Yanez, as was his custom when in a state of great fear, grabbed the

278

Belgian rifle and fired both barrels straight into the air.

"You miss again!" Aldo said, dropping his sausage. Pedro likewise dropped his can of sardines. Then both men joined Piet Van Wely in flight. Somehow the fleeing Spaniard ran into the fleeing Italian, who tripped the fleeing Dutchman — all three went down in a heap, expecting at any moment to feel sharp teeth rend their flesh.

But the grizzly stopped, attracted, it seemed, by the smell of sardines. He ate up those Pedro had spilled, and then began to lick the can. Then, as the big beast lapped up the delicious oil, a shot rang out, from the direction of the river. A man in a somber black coat, his pant legs muddy from an abrupt leap into the shallows of the river, was hastily reloading his rifle, keeping one eye on the bear. He fired again, reloaded again, fired a third time. The first two shots the bear ignored, but the third provoked a rumble of annoyance, as he nosed among the ruins of the picnic.

"These big bruins, they are very reluctant to die," the rifleman said, nodding to the three men, who were just picking themselves up. To Mary Berrybender he made a deeper bow. She had been watching the contest silently.

Once more the man reloaded, watched the bear closely, stepped within twenty feet of him, and fired a shot directly into his brain.

The grizzly, a sardine can still in its paw, fell dead.

"These big boys only agree to die if you shoot them in the head — they are tougher than all the bears of Europe," the rifleman told them.

"Correct — that is why they are called *Ursus horribilis*," Mary agreed. "Very terrible beasts they are, and my good papa will be most vexed that you have killed one while he has not."

"Not one, young miss . . . six now," the hunter said, permitting himself a small smile. "Perhaps we ought not to mention it to His Lordship, though, or he might want to shoot *me!* And then where would you all be the next time a grizzly bear spoils your picnic?"

"Oh, I never lie to Papa, he is far too clever, Herr Dreidoppel," Mary said. "It *is* you, isn't it?"

The hunter made another small bow. "David Dreidoppel, at your service," he said, removing a small tape measure from a worn leather case.

"We heard about you in Saint Louis — they say you are the best taxidermist in Europe," Mary said. "Are you going to stuff this fine bear?"

"That is a decision for my prince," the hunter said. "I certainly am going to measure him, though — if one of these gentlemen will just help me stretch him out."

"I don't like him, he ate my sardines," Pedro complained, but before any of the others could offer an excuse Mary herself stepped forward and obligingly held the tip of the tape measure right against the dead grizzly's cold, wet nose.

"He is long, but not our longest," Herr Dreidoppel said, as he quickly rolled up his little tape. "Probably we won't stuff him, but that my prince decides."

"And did you once kill an anaconda thirty-four feet long?" Mary asked, excited.

"What a well-informed young miss you are — thirty-four feet seven and one half inches, that boy was — an anaconda of the Orinoco River," Herr Dreidoppel said. "How did you learn such a thing?"

"From the illustrated papers, of course," Mary told him. "Your beard was not so gray in the pictures they showed."

At this the somber hunter laughed aloud, rather to Piet Van Wely's annoyance — he was beginning to be rather jealous of the way the bearded man was bantering with his Mary, without whose protection his position in the Berrybender ménage would be a very shaky one indeed.

"It's wrestling with these big boys, these bruins and those snakes, that made me gray," the hunter admitted. "Ah — here comes my prince. He too is somewhat gray."

At first all any of them could see was a high, round black hat, of European make, making its way as if by magic along the tops of the high prairie grasses. But then, as they watched, a head emerged, wearing the hat, and a man of very modest height, dressed exactly as the hunter was, in a somber coat and muddy pants, appeared. One hand was stuck inside his coat, the other he held behind him.

He stopped, looked briefly at the dead bear, and bowed to Mary.

"I am the prince Max," he said in clipped tones. "I have something for His Lordship, your father, that I think he will very much like to have."

"Claret, I hope, Prince," Mary replied. "It's claret Papa misses most."

"Claret I have," the prince of Wied said.

40

. . . thick necks, eel eaters, fart bags . . .

Lord Albany Berrybender was seldom of a divided mind when it came to women or Germans. Women he mostly liked, if they were not reluctant in the matter of fornication and did not aspire to win at cards.

Germans he roundly detested: filthy Teutons, he called them, thick necks, eel eaters, fart bags, two-legged pigs. Should a German attempt to interfere with his plans in any way, terms of abuse would be heaped on him, accompanied, if necessary, by violent action. In the courts of the Georges, portly fools themselves, many thick-necked German courtiers had come to England — they were even seen in the best clubs. Lord B. had fought duels with a number of them, wounding three with his dueling pistols. He himself had yet to receive a wound or even a scratch. Once or twice, though, stolid princelings from one or another of the piddling German duchies had gained an advantage over him at the gaming tables, and once a German mare had beaten his fine filly Augusta in a race. The final indignity was that two of his greyhounds had been outrun by the fleet whippets of the Germans.

These last indignities came fresh to mind as His Lordship stood in Monsieur Boisdeffre's trading post, looking at the six large bearskins spread on the floor — a sight that astonished even Kit and Tom and Jim, none of whom had expected to see that many bearskins in one place. All had been killed, it seemed, by the cool and accurate marksmanship of the prince's hunter, Herr Dreidoppel.

Lord Berrybender's instinct had been to fly into a great rage and demand to know by what right a German prince had wandered out of the forests of Europe and invaded the rich hunting range which he supposed would be wholly his to plunder. Finding the annoying Scot Drummond Stewart already ensconced in this paradise of game was shock enough; *must* he now really tolerate German princes too — and one, moreover, whose hunter was clearly a very superior shot?

And yet, the fact was, this rather dumpy, unimposing prince had just made him a present of a dozen cases of rich red claret, the blessed elixir that he had so long been without. A noble who had had the forethought to bring such an admirable gift all the way from London could not simply be brushed off as a bad fellow, Teuton though he unmistakably was.

Still, the fact that Herr Dreidoppel had already shot six grizzlies — bears that, by rights, should have been his — put Lord Berrybender's tact to a severe test. The more he thought about the six lost bears, the more the great vein on his nose throbbed, pulsed, and finally turned red, as it only did when His Lordship suffered profound agitation. Lord B. rarely felt that he ought to be grateful; the need to balance gratitude with dismay was a very unaccustomed thing. Was he to overlook entirely the six bears that should have been his? He himself had yet to dispatch even one. On the other hand there was the claret, a bottle of which he had already quaffed, filling and refilling one of Boisdeffre's pewter goblets.

"Grateful, I must say, Prince," Lord B. finally managed. "Don't mind allowing that I was rather starved for the grape — you know your vintages, I see. Lucky you weren't victim to thieving *engagés,* as I was."

"Oh no, we Germans don't take such chances on our good boat *Yellowstone,*" the prince replied, in English that lacked nothing of correctness.

"The liquor was kept in a special room, and only I had the key," he went on. "Human nature is everywhere very bad, you know. It is best to remove temptation."

"Bad, yes, bad — human nature's a rotten thing, and particularly rotten if you have to deal with Mediterraneans," Lord B. said, glaring at Signor Claricia and Señor Yanez, whose excuse for their long absence — that they had gone off to relieve themselves out of sight of Milly and had become hopelessly lost — he knew to be an arrant lie.

Pierre Boisdeffre, Tom Fitzpatrick, Kit, and Jim all walked around the six bearskins, saying little but filled with amazement nonetheless. They looked at the skins, looked at one another, and shrugged. None of them, in all their years on the prairie, had ever heard of one man killing six grizzly bears. And yet the man responsible, an ordinary-looking fellow with an iron gray beard, stood quietly at the counter, leaning on his rifle and drinking a little of Boisdeffre's grog.

"That fellow must be the best shot in the world — what do you think, Jimmy?" Kit asked.

Jim Snow had been rather put out that the arrival of the prince had meant a delay in their departure, but, so far as shooting went, it was hard to disagree with Kit. It was obvious that the quiet fellow at the counter must possess unusual steadiness. Grizzlies had a habit of making even experienced hunters panic. He himself, having been much in bear country, had never killed one, though he had shot at several and had been chased twice for his pains. Once he had had to jump off a high riverbank, in order to escape a charge. A man who could down six grizzlies was no run-of-the-mill hunter.

"Look at his eyes," Kit whispered. "Icy blue. I bet that's his secret, good eyesight."

Looking once more at the bearskins, Lord Berrybender could not entirely suppress his sharp annoyance — why had *his* hunter, Gorska, been so incompetent, while the prince's hunter was a lavish success? His first thought had been to approach Herr Dreidoppel in private, perhaps attempt to hire the fellow — and yet there was a chilliness in the man's eyes that gave him pause. Claret or no claret, Lord Berrybender's vein was soon throbbing so violently that he could not suppress a complaint.

"I say, Prince," he began, "this hunter of yours has been helping himself rather freely when it comes to the bruins. I might have fancied killing one or two of these brawny fellows myself."

Prince Max remembered how coolly the old lord had greeted him, before the gift of the claret had caused him to change his tone. Now, it seemed, English ice was to be followed by English bullying. The one-legged old fool was trying to drive him out of the rich hunting grounds of the Yellowstone. Malice, cunning, brutality, chill: that was what one could always expect from the English.

The prince of Wied contented himself with the smallest of bows.

"We have counted thirty-two of these bears since leaving the Knife River," he said. "Your Lordship will soon find that there are many left — perhaps too many. As you journey up the Yellowstone I'm sure you will find all the bears you want.

"As for us," he went on, "we work only for science. I am, as you know, a zoologist. Herr Dreidoppel is not only a fine hunter, he is also the state taxidermist of Wied. We will not be bringing home a live zoo, as your friend Drummond Stewart hopes to do. But we will examine everything we kill. In fact, now we must go and open the stomach of the bear Herr Dreidoppel killed today, so that I can analyze his diet. We expect to find fish, berries, prairie dogs, even mice — imagine such a giant feeding on something so small. Would you like to come and watch the examination?"

"Oh hardly, Prince — don't care what the brutes eat," Lord B. said, signaling for Boisdeffre to uncork another bottle of the excellent claret.

Then a dark thought struck him. What if the small prince with the excellent hunter planned on traveling to the south, the direction he meant to travel and would have been traveling already had it not been for the distraction of his rabbly entourage?

"Not heading south, I hope, Prince," he said — better to speak plainly to the fellow.

"No room in the south. My good friend Drummond Stewart is, as you know, already there. Very active man, Drum — distinguished horseman and all that. Expect he's already wiped out the game down that way — it's crowding up a bit to the south, I can assure you."

The prince of Wied, well aware that he was being told where he couldn't go by a man who had no more rights in the country than he did, refrained from smiling.

"Oh, no, Your Lordship, we are proceeding west," he replied. "Fort Mackenzie is our goal. No zoologist would neglect the region of the Marias River, where there are said to be enormous herds. Besides, my painter, Herr Bodmer, wants to paint the white cliffs, which lie in a westerly direction.

"We have a fine keelboat to take us," he added, lest the old fool suppose that a proper German expedition would go off ill-equipped.

The notion that the dumpy little prince with the superlative hunter planned on traveling west, into the very heart of Blackfoot country, startled the three trappers a good deal. Six grizzly bears were one thing, but a challenge to the Blackfeet was bold indeed.

"Mackenzie? Marias River — you really mean to go *there*, sir?" Tom Fitzpatrick asked. "It's woolly doings in that country — Blackfoot country, you know. Woolly doings to the west."

"Yes, we hope to shoot the woollies, the big sheep of the mountains," the prince said modestly, although he knew perfectly well what the old trapper meant.

41

Six bearskins was big medicine.

Weedy Boy and the other Minatarees were becoming impatient. The three of them had come to the trading post to see if Boisdeffre would give them tobacco, and the trader did give them a little — he rarely refused them tobacco. But when they saw the six bearskins on the floor, Weedy Boy and the others wished they had not bothered coming to the post that day. Six bearskins was big medicine. When Boisdeffre told them that one man, a hunter with icy blue eyes, had killed all six of the bears, the three became even more agitated — the young warrior named Climbs Up was particularly upset. It was Climbs Up's opinion that whatever bears were near the fort would be wanting to do a lot of killing to revenge such a slaughter. The great bears would not be likely to discriminate, either. They would just kill whoever they met, which could as well be Minatarees rather than whites. Climbs Up, who was pessimistic at the best of times, thought that they ought at once to move their camp farther down the Missouri

River. The presence of bears bent on revenge was never welcome.

Weedy Boy was more or less in agreement with Climbs Up, for once, but he thought they ought to talk the whole matter over with Otter Woman before doing anything rash. The two wanted to hurry right back to their camp, but the woman who was with them, Squirrel, was looking at some beads and refused to be rushed, even though she could see the bearskins with her own eyes.

"Let's leave her — she'll be here all day looking at those beads," Climbs Up said.

But Weedy Boy didn't want to leave Squirrel. He was thinking of marrying Squirrel, even though she was rather moody. He told Climbs Up to wait a minute, which Climbs Up did reluctantly. Then, when Squirrel was finally ready to leave, who should show up but old Sharbo, who asked them if they would mind posing for a few minutes for a new likeness maker who had come on the big boat. This likeness maker was young — he wore a brown mustache, a brown cap, and smoked a pipe with a big bulge in it, like a pelican's belly. Sharbo said they could have the beads Squirrel wanted if they would just indulge the likeness maker for a few minutes. Weedy Boy and Climbs Up were disinclined to comply, but before they could leave, a short man appeared and began to hand out such excellent presents that they soon forgot the bears. Squirrel got her beads and a blue blanket, and Weedy Boy and Climbs Up got excellent hatchets with fine sturdy handles, as well as a couple of pipes like the one the likeness maker smoked. Such largesse was unexpected and did much to take their minds off the danger of bears. They went outside the stockade and arranged themselves as the likeness maker directed, with nothing behind them but blue sky and waving grass. Sharbo and the little present-giving man were in the likeness too, pretending to trade with the Minatarees, who of course had nothing to trade. Very quickly the likeness maker made a likeness of the group, which he freely showed them. Squirrel refused to look at the likeness — she thought such business could lead to bad things. In fact when the likeness maker approached with the likeness Squirrel took her presents and ran off, which was foolish, because the little present-giving man soon passed out some nice blue beads. The blue beads emerged from a magical pack that the little man wore over his shoulder. The new gift was really something special: Boisdeffre only had white beads and red beads; blue beads had not been seen by any of the Minatarees since they had left the camp of the Bad Eye in order to hunt upriver.

Weedy Boy took a string of the blue beads

to give to Squirrel — Climbs Up didn't think she deserved them because of her impatient behavior, but then Climbs Up was not the one interested in marrying her.

What interested Climbs Up even more than the blue beads was the dark marking stick the likeness maker used to do his likeness. The marking stick marked very dark.

"It wouldn't take long to put on war paint if we had that marking stick," Climbs Up pointed out. "Maybe we could steal it."

Weedy Boy tried to pretend he didn't even know Climbs Up — they had just been given some very fine presents, and now the greedy Climbs Up wanted to steal a marking stick. It was all too typical: Climbs Up had never been able to resist just grabbing anything that took his fancy. Now he wanted to insult the likeness maker by stealing his marking stick, which was nothing they really needed, since they rarely put on war paint, being too few and too weak to make war on any of the neighboring tribes. Much as Weedy Boy hated the arrogant Assiniboines he was not so foolish as to make war on them while his band only possessed two guns that would fire with any regularity.

"But the likeness maker is rich," Climbs Up pointed out. "He has many marking sticks. I only want to take one, to help with the war paint."

Weedy Boy pointed to the large boat the likeness maker had come in. It was anchored just below the place where the Yellowstone came into the Missouri.

"See that boat?" he asked. "It is the biggest boat in the world."

"So what?" Climbs Up said. "I don't want to steal the boat. A small canoe that doesn't leak is good enough for me when it comes to boats."

Weedy Boy was disgusted. It had always been hard to carry on a conversation with Climbs Up — he could never keep to any subject. Who would think of stealing a boat so large that it would take all the warriors from many bands just to row it across the river?

"I don't want to *steal* the boat," Weedy Boy protested. "I just want you to think of all the presents that could be on a boat that big. If we are patient and let the likeness maker do his work, and if we don't do anything bad like stealing a marking stick, then the little man with the magic pack might give us many *more* presents. Maybe if we are polite to him he will even give us a few guns. If we had several guns we could even go after those sneaking Assiniboines."

Such a fine possibility had not occurred to Climbs Up. He had to admit that what Weedy Boy said made sense. He still longed to snatch one of the nice marking sticks from the likeness maker, but he restrained himself, in hopes of getting, pretty soon, a fine gun that would make a buffalo or an Assiniboine dead with one shot. Such a gun would be worth waiting for.

42

Day after day he had gone out in bitter weather . . .

Karl Bodmer, the likeness maker, hurried to put the finishing touches on his hasty little charcoal sketch of his prince's meeting with the three Minatarees, one of whom, the girl, was now in full flight. Winter in the Mandan encampments, during which, despite the terrible cold, he had done much sketching, convinced him that only the most vain of the Indian warriors and chieftains really wanted to have their likenesses captured — and even the vain ones fidgeted too much, which is why the young Swiss artist devoted himself whenever possible to landscapes — the somber, pallid, and yet powerful landscapes of the wintry plains. Day after day he had gone out in bitter weather, attempting to solve, in the medium of watercolors mostly, why such a featureless land should yet be so powerful.

The two Minataree boys standing with his prince were clearly restless. Karl Bodmer focused on his sketch, looked at the group, drew; and then, to rest his eyes, glanced upward into the infinity of the great Western sky. The tones of the plains might be muted, a challenge to his sensitivity, but the skies were always wonderful — only this time, when he glanced up, instead of having his vision cleansed by the skies, he saw the very thing he most dreaded: a man with an easel strapped to his back, coming toward the group.

Then the man disappeared into a dip in the prairie. For a moment Karl thought he might have imagined him. A great white cloud the size of a galleon sailed over and floated on. Thinking, perhaps, that he had been mistaken, Karl looked again. The grass was waving, the sunlight was shining strong, and there came the man, with an easel strapped to his back.

Annoyed — indeed, furious — why *would* the fellow interfere when it was plain that he was not through sketching? — Karl Bodmer slapped his sketchbook shut. Teeth clenched on the stem of his fat pipe, he nodded once to his patient prince and strode off without a word toward the steamer *Yellowstone*, which was anchored not far away.

"Whoa, now! What's got into that fellow?" Charbonneau wondered. "Here comes George Catlin, he's *our* painter — he's got a big start on your man, Prince. George figures he's done three hundred Indians, so far."

Prince Max, imperturbable, watched the

skinny painter approach. He was annoyed that young Karl had behaved rudely, but then rudeness was apt to go with youth — even Swiss youth.

"Of course, Mr. Catlin," he said. "We heard much from Captain Clark about this eminent man. It will be my pleasure to greet him."

All winter, the prince reflected, young Karl had challenged the ice and cold that held them in the Mandan villages. Almost every day, in defiance of the bitter chill, he had gone into the bleak hills, or among the shivering villagers, seeking scenes to paint. But now, on a fine spring day, on a glorious plain, off he stalked, unwilling to meet a rival painter.

"I suppose our Karl was hoping to be the first one to paint these wild peoples," he said.

"Oh no, George has got a good jump on him here," Charbonneau replied. "On the other hand, you were lucky that the ice stopped you at the Mandans' — otherwise you'd have been chopped up, like George Aitken and the others we lost. And there's plenty of Indians George *ain't* painted. If you push on to the Marias River that young fellow will have the country all to himself — there's plenty of these wild boys over that way. Don't know if they'll sit still for a painter, though."

"I rely on presents," the prince admitted. "Good beads, good hatchets, maybe once in a while a musket to some great chief. If the presents are good they'll let Karl paint."

George Catlin saw a young man with what looked like a sketchbook stalking off toward the steamer — young Bodmer, he supposed. He was too weary at the moment to care whether he met the young fellow or not. He had heard that a large herd of buffalo were crossing the Missouri six miles or so below the trading post and had hurriedly tramped down that way to watch the enormous procession. He was not disappointed. Thousands of buffalo in a continual stream surged across the muddy river while he sketched and sketched. One wobbly calf, evidently just born, was swept downstream by the current and seen no more. George had hurried off without grabbing any vittles — he had tramped at least twelve miles on an empty stomach and was, as a consequence, very hungry. Nonetheless he stopped and greeted the small prince courteously.

"Why, hello — you're the prince, I suspect," he said. "Didn't mean to run that young fellow off."

"How do you do, Mr. Catlin," the prince said. "Our Karl is sometimes hasty."

"I've just been watching thousands of buffalo cross the river," Catlin told him. "What I want now is a bite to eat."

"We'll just stroll together, then," the prince said. He bowed to the two Minataree boys, who, seeing that no more presents were likely to come out of the magical bag, hurried off to find Otter Woman and tell her about the bears.

"Shall you go south with His Lordship, Mr. Catlin?" the prince asked. "Will you be the first to paint the beauties of the Yellowstone?"

"Not me, Prince," George said. "Much as I will miss some of the Berrybenders, I've a living to make, after all. I plan to go back downriver on that steamer, make a run at the Comanches perhaps, and then get along home."

"I see," the small prince said, hoping that the news would be enough to cheer up Karl Bodmer. Another day or two and his rival would be gone.

43

"A low thing, addition," Mary insisted.

Tasmin was first astonished, then amused, when it developed that there was one member of the Berrybender family who had not the slightest difficulty in getting Jim Snow to do what she wanted him to do. The lucky person, with the style of command that was needed to domesticate the sulky frontiersman, turned out to be their sister Ten, aged barely four years, the little girl who had cheerfully lived for some weeks amid the cabbages, training her mouse.

With Tasmin Jim was moody, with Lord Berrybender angry, with Mary suspicious, and with little Monty tentative — only rarely would he consent to hold his child, fearing, it seemed, that he might damage him, although Monty was already proving himself to be a sturdy customer.

Little Ten, a stout girl, possessed, to everyone's surprise, an early flair for mathematics — though Mary pedantically insisted that it was only a flair for addition.

"A low thing, addition," Mary insisted. "It's hardly Newton."

Ten began her rapid conquest of Jim Snow by refusing to call him Jimmy — his name, she insisted, was James.

"Mr. James Snow, are you ready to hear me do my numbers?" Ten asked in a loud tone.

"Ready as I'll ever be, I expect," Jim said, amused by the bold tyke. He was working with Signor Claricia to see whether the buggy Lord Berrybender had smashed could at least be fixed enough to make a workable cart.

"I shall begin with two plus two," Ten announced. She doubled and doubled and doubled, usually getting up at least into the thousands before Buffum or Mary or even Tasmin ran and clapped a hand over her mouth. If it was Mary who chose to interfere with Ten and her numbers, a sharp tussle was likely to ensue, there in the yard of the trading post, ignored by the various Indians and trappers who came and went.

Sometimes when the scuffles became too violent Jim would pick the small girl up and sit her on his shoulder. Ten's little gray mouse would sometimes perch on *her* shoulder, watching the proceedings inquisitively.

Usually Jim delivered his small admirer to Tasmin — on fine days Tasmin and Vicky and Coal all brought their babies out and allowed them to finger tufts of grass or test the textures of dirt.

"Do you know mathematics, Mr. James Snow?" Ten asked.

"No, but I know how to give you a better name, little girl," Jim replied. "If you're going to call me James, I'll just call you Kate."

"Very well then, Kate I'll be," the girl said. Then she grabbed Monty and thrust him high in the air a few times, an exercise his father would never have dared try. Monty burbled with excitement and then spat up on Kate's gray mouse, which chattered indignantly.

"Oh drat, now he's soiled my mouse," the newly christened Kate complained.

"It's unwise to bounce a baby up in the air just after he's nursed," Tasmin commented.

"I shall marry Mr. James Snow as soon as I grow up," Kate informed the little circle of mothers.

"But *I'm* married to him," Tasmin pointed out. "What about me, you brat?"

"I shall insist that you relinquish Mr. James Snow and go marry someone else," Kate told her. Then she went over and squatted near Jim, watching in silence as he worked on the cart.

"I believe you have a rival, Tasmin," Vicky said.

"Yes, and I mustn't underestimate her," Tasmin replied. "Little girls seem to be able to get their way with even the most recalcitrant men — even Papa sometimes feeds Kate the best morsels, if there's a goose to eat."

In fact, she was soon amazed at how rapidly Kate Berrybender managed to domesticate her husband, a task Tasmin herself had quite failed to accomplish. He whittled Kate small toys — a rabbit, a chicken — and made her a whistle from a reed, an instrument she insisted on playing loudly, despite Monty's distress.

"I do believe you like this little witch better than you like me, Jimmy," Tasmin said one evening, as they rested under a full moon. Not one hundred yards away, clearly visible in the moonlight, several deer were gamboling.

"I like Kate plenty, but she ain't my wife — you're my wife," Jim told her. His other wife, Little Onion, sat not far away, crooning a singsong tune to Monty. Kate was wandering around blowing her whistle. Jim didn't say it, but having the two young children with them made Tasmin considerably easier to be with. She was less apt to tax him with her queries. Her desire had come back, though — sometimes the two would walk well out onto the prairie to couple; otherwise Tasmin, still noisy in her pleasure, would wake the children. Little Onion, absorbed by her duties with Monty, seemed not to care a whit what they did.

Little Onion, keen of hearing, sometimes did pick up distant sounds of pleasure, but she felt no jealousy. She had Monty to care for, an easier thing than dealing with the lusts of men. Several times, before Jim married her, she had been ambushed and taken in heat by old warriors who smelled bad. The old ones had been excited by her youth. These encounters had been brief but unpleasant. Caring for a plump, jolly baby was more satisfying than what men did with her in the tent or on the grass. She was an obedient wife to Jim Snow and would have lain down with him had he required it, but she was glad she had Monty to deal with, and that Jim had Tasmin.

"She don't take her eyes off that baby," Jim commented, on the night of the full moon. "He'll be growing up thinking he's Ute. Do you think he knows you're his mother, and not Little Onion?"

"I expect Monty takes the practical view," Tasmin told him. "I'm where he gets his vittles — that's enough for now.

"Besides," she added, after giving the question some thought, "it's good that Monty has two mothers that he's thoroughly comfortable with."

"Why's that?"

"This is a dangerous place, that's why," Tasmin told him. "Life's unpredictable — one of us might get killed."

She took his hand and squeezed it tight.

"After all, *your* mother got killed," she said, taking a risk. She had never discussed his past with him.

Jim didn't answer.

"Two mothers are safer, and even three wouldn't hurt," Tasmin went on. "You wouldn't want our Monty to be hidden in a cactus patch, would you?"

"How'd you know that?" Jim asked, startled that Tasmin knew something he had labored to put out of his mind.

"Captain Aitken told me, poor soul," Tasmin replied. "He didn't tell me much — just that Mr. Drew found you."

Jim remained silent. Far away buffalo bulls were roaring in the night.

"Poor Captain Aitken wasn't lucky enough to have someone hide him in a cactus patch," Tasmin said. "I rather miss him."

Jim was thinking about the baby, and also about little Kate, who had so determinedly taken up with them. Tasmin was right about the dangers — she had, for once, shown good plain sense. What had happened to George Aitken — who wouldn't desert his boat — could happen to them. For Monty, and Miss Kennet's baby, and Coal's, extra mothers wouldn't hurt. He lay back and put his hand on Tasmin, happy, almost for the first time, in the thought that he had taken a sensible wife.

44

"My cart, bought and paid for . . ."

Lord Berrybender, furious rather than thorough, had not destroyed the buggy quite totally, as he had meant to. The cab he had thoroughly smashed, but the wheels had only lost a few spokes and the sturdy axle was undamaged. There was nothing to be done about the bonnet, but Jim and Kit went off and cut some logs, which Signor Claricia shaved and lathed until he had a smooth floor for a fairly commodious cart, a process Lord Berrybender watched in sour temper.

"That's not your cart, gentlemen," he warned. "Not your cart at all."

"Don't be so tiresome, Father," Tasmin threatened. "It's the *only* cart."

She did her best to act the diplomat in all proceedings involving Jim and her father; she knew that Jim was not likely to tolerate much guff from her father — her hope was to get them away on their journey south before serious violence could erupt.

"*My* cart, bought and paid for in Lincolnshire," Lord B. repeated. "Besides, even if it *was* yours, you have nothing to pull it with. There's only my good team, and I shall need them for the wagon."

"We'll use the mare," Jim told him.

"Which mare, sir?" Lord B. asked, surprised. "I know of no mare except my Augusta, and of course you can't mean her."

"That's the one — only her name's too long," Jim told him. "We'll just call her Gussie. She can pull a light cart like this one well enough, I guess."

Lord Berrybender was not disposed to let any man cow him — particularly not an American — but he did recall quite clearly the hard shove Jim had given him; he also remembered that Jim had threatened to cut his heart out. Such a degree of frontier irrationality must be dealt with gingerly, His Lordship felt, well aware that he had had little practice with gingerly dealings. He thought that his best bet might be to appeal to Tasmin, who certainly knew that a fine Thoroughbred mare, eligible to receive any stallion in England, could not be made to pull a cart. Nothing so ill-bred had ever happened to a Berrybender Thoroughbred; he felt sure his daughter would realize that and intercede, so as to spare the elegant Augusta such an indignity.

"Not right, Tassie . . . not right at all," he said, in rather a stammering manner. "Augusta's a mare of high lineage . . . Byerly

Turk, you know. Not suitable to have her pull a cart."

"Gussie's pulling the cart, Papa," Tasmin replied firmly. "There's three of us with infants to consider — no reason we should tramp a thousand miles, toting our infants over mountains and swamps, while you idle along in a wagon, shooting at everything that moves and tupping Millicent rather too frequently. Millicent, by the way, was quite a competent laundress before you corrupted her — now Buffum and Vicky and I have constantly to deal with mildewed garments that have not been properly aired, although there is an abundance of excellent air available, as you can well see. If you would just keep your big nasty, as Mama called it, in your breeches for a day or two, we might yet get our clothes done properly before we set off to trace the wild Yellowstone to its source."

Jim and Kit, who had been reinforcing the cart wheels, stopped and listened, as they generally did when Tasmin delivered one of her forceful speeches.

"How'd she ever learn to talk like that?" Kit wondered. Jim, a good deal awed by his wife's fluency, just shrugged.

"Shut your mouth, you impertinent harlot — how dare you be disrespectful of the organ that begat you?" His Lordship protested.

"Maybe it begat me and maybe it didn't," Tasmin warned him, coolly. "I intend to investigate that matter thoroughly, at the appropriate time."

"Beside the point, anyway," Lord Berrybender snipped, in no mood for a discussion of Tasmin's paternity, particularly not in front of a sizable company. He meant to keep to the point, and the point was his highbred mare.

"I won't allow it!" he added. "You and your ill-bred mate are not welcome to disgrace my filly."

Jim simply ignored the old man — let him rant and rave. They had given Joe Walker's mule to the Blackfeet, meaning that the pretty mare would have to be their cart horse.

Kate Berrybender, Jim's new champion, at once came to his defense. She marched over and planted her square little person directly in front of Lord B., whom she fixed with a firm, green-eyed glare.

"Take heed, Papa!" she declaimed. "Speak no ill of Mr. James Snow! Take heed! Do you hear me?"

"Not deaf, Puffin," Lord Berrybender said amiably, amused despite himself at the small creature's temerity.

"Where have you come out from, anyway?" he continued. "I thought we kept you in the pantry, amid the cabbages, potted meats, ham . . . some dim lair in the pantry. Why should your good papa need to take heed?"

"Mr. James Snow is my beloved," Kate informed him. "If you speak ill of him I will put a curse on you and it will be a bad curse, I assure you."

"Too late, Puffin — merely having children is a curse, and a bad curse," Lord B. remarked. "Ungrateful brats, every one of them, but Tasmin is the worst."

That a young child could speak to a parent as Kate had spoken to Lord Berrybender was evidence enough, in Kit Carson's view, that the English belonged to a different race.

"How does a curse work, now, Katie?" he asked.

"It turns you black and you become rot," Kate replied. "And you smell very bad and no one wants to take supper with you."

"There, Papa — be careful how you speak of my husband," Tasmin said. "Indeed if you're wise you'll be careful in general. We're about to start a dangerous trip — it must be evident that you can ill afford to lose much more of yourself."

Jim fetched the pretty mare, Gussie, and put her in harness for the first time in her life. The mare was perfectly docile, even nuzzling Jim Snow from time to time.

"I ought to shoot her — rather see her dead than watch this!" Lord B. said, flushing a deep red.

But the company, who had absorbed so many of Lord Berrybender's threats, paid no heed to this one. Mary Berrybender was chasing Kate, meaning to box her ears for having delivered such a melodramatic performance. Kate, shrieking wildly, proved unexpectedly fleet. Signor Claricia was nailing some rude sideboards onto the cart, so the babies wouldn't fall out. Venetia Kennet was tuning her cello, Cook was salting down some trout Tom Fitzpatrick had trapped in an ingenious seine, Father Geoffrin was reading Bobbety a particularly heretical passage of Voltaire, and Little Onion worked the skin of a lynx, brought in by an Assiniboine hunter — she had bargained for the skin with Boisdeffre, thinking it would make an excellent warm cap for Monty. Buffum, low in spirits, intoned a catechism, while Toussaint Charbonneau was talking with several Mandans who had wandered in after breakfast. Boisdeffre was in the process of receiving a gloomy report from some trappers who had just crossed from the Snake River, where, they said, the beaver were much diminished. Lord Berrybender felt quite left out. Everyone, after all, was doing something; no one was heeding his grumbles about the horse, or about the trials of paternity, or about his unfortunate son-in-law. Not only did he feel left out, he felt, on the whole, sad. Born to command, at the moment he commanded no one except a laundress. On his own children he made an ever-diminishing impression; on the rabble assembled in this remote trading post in the West he made no impression at all. He wasn't gone, he still breathed the air, and yet he was, if not entirely forgotten, disregarded — disregarded entirely. His late wife, Lady Constance, would never have disregarded him so. He found he rather missed Lady Constance — fortunately the feeling, though sharp, passed quickly. If Constance happened to disregard him — she had been, it must be said, very idle — a smack or two had been enough to bring her to attention. He thought he might just go seek out the cooperative Milly, who was herself perhaps not so meekly cooperative as she had been at first blush. Lately Milly had shown signs of acquiring airs — mistresses, however lowborn, frequently forgot themselves and took on airs — in Milly's case it was nothing that a smack or two wouldn't correct.

Feeling rather droopy, rather lorn, a man forgotten in his prime — and he felt sure he *was* in his prime — Lord B. went slowly inside. He turned at the door, but no one seemed to be aware of his departure — not a soul cared that he was leaving. Life seemed to be going on, but mainly in contradiction to his wishes. There stood his fine filly, Augusta, very evidently in harness but not

314

seeming to care much about her degradation. It all seemed rather lowering, distinctly lowering, so much so that he thought he had best hurry on and find Milly — get those skirts up over those ample thighs. Airs or no airs, his Milly would pay him some attention — rarely reluctant to attend him, his Milly — unlike everybody else.

Mary Berrybender, however, took note of her father's slow departure.

"I believe we have made our old papa sad," she observed. "He is getting quite ancient, you know, Tassie. We must try to be a little more thoughtful of him in the future."

"That's bosh and twaddle," Tasmin said emphatically. "Let him be thoughtful for a change. He's never been thoughtful once, that I can recall — not while I've been about, anyway. Here's his fine bouncing grandson, Montague, even now at my breast."

"Yes, sucking — always sucking . . . he's little more than a bag of milk, I fear," Mary replied.

"Shut up, we were talking about Papa," Tasmin reminded her. "Do you think he's bothered to look at Monty? He hasn't, not once."

"Mr. James Snow, are you ready to hear my numbers now?" Kate asked, beginning to add immediately, but she had only got to thirty-two plus thirty-two when her sister Mary rushed over and covered her mouth.

45

The prince of Wied and his company had departed in their keelboat . . .

"That German's got us beat by a mile, when it comes to getting up and getting off," Kit Carson reckoned, surveying the chaos of the Berrybender expedition as it attempted to assemble itself in the wagon yard of Pierre Boisdeffre's trading post.

"A mile? He's got us beat about twenty miles, I'd say," Jim replied. The prince of Wied and his company had departed in their keelboat well before dawn, Toussaint Charbonneau with them. The latter still had hopes of finding Blue Thunder, the third of his charges, whose people ranged not far from where the prince hoped to go. Coal and her baby he left with the Berrybenders; he meant to rejoin the party as soon as Blue Thunder had been accounted for.

"It's plain why that prince was so much faster than us," Jim stated. "There's no women in his bunch — that's why."

The Berrybender party, whatever it might lack, could not be said to lack women. Tasmin, Buffum, Mary, Vicky Kennet, Cook,

Eliza, Millicent, and even the tiny Kate were doing their best to cram their many necessities into one wagon and a cart. None of them were at all satisfied with the packing. Tasmin feared that Cook's jugged hares might somehow leak onto her precious stash of books. Millicent, meanwhile, was carefully packing the claret, under Lord Berrybender's exacting supervision.

"Crack a bottle and I'll crack your head," he informed Millicent sternly. "I like you fine, y'know, my dearie — but claret's claret."

Bobbety paced about in a state of high anxiety, the source of that being the wishy-washy behavior of Father Geoffrin, who had, even at that late date, not fully committed himself to the trek up the Yellowstone — a steamer bound for Saint Louis, after all, lay at hand.

"Oh please, Geoff — I'll be so wretched without you," Bobbety pleaded. "Besides, there's a great many natural wonders we might investigate: geysers and hot springs and who knows what. Tell him, Piet — you've been telling me about them for weeks."

"Oh, quite so, geysers and maybe dinosaur eggs," Piet said. "The eggs are very likely petrified, of course. And there may even be the lost sons of Madoc — who knows where those might be."

"And who cares, frankly?" Father Geoffrin said. "The Welsh, lost or found, do not entice me — and you can't make omelettes from petrified eggs, even if a dinosaur did lay them."

"I can't bear for you to leave me, Geoff," Bobbety begged.

"Well, I hadn't been planning to, but then I see that fine boat anchored there and I think: luxury, luxury. All I would have to do all day is read, and perhaps now and then scribble a quatrain."

"That's if the Indians don't catch you and mince you very fine," Tasmin told him.

"Yes, they might just mince you, Geoff," Bobbety seconded, thinking that for once his big sister might make a useful ally.

"But Mr. Catlin's going back on this boat and nobody's trying to stop *him!*" the small priest cried. "Why must I be the only one expected to tramp thousands of miles and get grass burrs in my vestments?"

"What are you talking about — George can't go back," Tasmin said, in shock. "George travels with me!"

She had long since come to take George Catlin's affection for granted; what nonsense that he would ever consider leaving them. There he stood, not fifty yards away, watching some small Indian children shoot tiny arrows at their skinny dogs.

"What's this, George — you're not leaving us, surely?" Tasmin asked, rushing over; but, in an instant, from the painter's sad expression, she realized that it was true and that he was leaving.

"Have to go, Tasmin, I fear," George said. "I'm a poor man, after all — have to take my daubings to market as soon as I can."

Tasmin, totally unprepared for this news, was at once overcome with feeling. She squeezed George Catlin in a desperate hug and gave him a kiss smeared with her tears, which were flowing freely.

George could but hold the weeping woman close — he himself was too moved to speak.

"Oh, George, how I'll miss you!" Tasmin cried. "I don't believe I meant a single one of all the wicked things I said to you on our trip — a devil gets into me somehow and I can't resist heaping abuse, even on you, who have been such a faithful friend."

Much touched, the painter managed a rather sorrowful smile.

"Oh, now . . . that was all just sport, Tasmin," he managed. "Just sport. Fine ladies can't seem to resist having a bit of a tease, with me. I'm sure it wasn't meant to wound."

"Shut up, of course it was meant to wound," Tasmin commanded. "It was beastly behavior, and you know it."

Kit Carson, observing this scene, was astonished — Tasmin was still crying.

"Why's she crying — I thought she despised that silly fool," Kit asked Jim, who just shrugged. What was there to say about a woman given to such loud moods? He was just backing Gussie into her traces, and was hoping that the babies, two of whom were squalling at the moment, wouldn't spook the filly.

"Besides, George, I can't understand it," Tasmin said. "Surely there will be Indians along the Yellowstone that you ought to paint. I promise I won't ever be mean to you again, if you'll just come with us."

It confused her that she felt such a deep pang of sorrow at the thought of parting from this skinny, awkward man — he was not young, his hair was thinning, his complexion splotchy, his teeth not the best — and yet she had watched him risk his life many times on the Missouri's banks, struggling to capture the likenesses of savages any one of whom were capable of killing him. She knew George had often been pained by her chilly rebuffs; she also knew that he was in love with her and had been in love with her almost from the moment they met. Was her husband, Jim Snow, in love with her? It hardly seemed so, although of late he had been an amiable, courteous, and fervently passionate male. Yet the fact was, love was reckoned differently on this raw frontier; the harsh practicalities that must constantly be dealt with left little time for the higher sentiments, the refinements of anguish or ecstasy that Father Geoff was always finding in the pages of Crébillon or Madame de Lafayette. These could hardly be indulged if one was fighting Indians or trying to scrape together adequate meals.

George Catlin, who was unmarried, and too old and too poor to enjoy especially good prospects in the matrimonial line, loved her — more than that, he was, in his skeptical and thoughtful way, a kindred spirit, the only one she could claim in this large, rabbly company. George had a brain, he had thoughts, he was smart — even if his little jests and mots rarely came off. That she would have to part with him in only a minute or two left her feeling greatly confused.

George Catlin patiently waited out Tasmin's little storm of feeling. He *did* love her, and in moments of foolish optimism had aspired to her — after all, there had been cases, even in staid Pennsylvania, where lovely women had bestowed their affections on rather unlovely men.

"Tell me again why you won't go with us, George," Tasmin asked. "I'm by no means convinced that your reasoning is sound."

"Poverty's a pretty sound reason, my dear," George said. "I'm poor — I need to sell some pictures. I have a sizable portfolio to hustle, and hustle it I must, while there's still much interest in the red men back East, where people have money. Might sell the whole thing to the nation, if I'm lucky."

"If you must leave me adrift in this wilderness, then I don't care for you to be lucky," Tasmin replied, not yet absolutely convinced that the cause was lost.

"We've heard that there's smallpox among the Choctaw," George said, attempting to give her a comforting pat, which only infuriated her more.

"Then, damn it, come with us — don't bother about the stricken Choctaw," she said.

"The point is that if smallpox comes up the river, there won't be any more Indians for me to paint — or for Herr Bodmer, either," he told her. "Sorry I didn't manage to meet the fellow — wouldn't have minded comparing techniques. Never too old to learn, you know, Tasmin — though I suppose it is possible to be too *young* to learn — probably Herr Bodmer didn't think he had anything to learn from an old dauber like me."

"Damn it, you're not saying anything I want to hear, George!" Tasmin retorted — then she caught herself and looked around apprehensively at her husband — if he had heard her curse he would surely come over and smack her. Fortunately the Sin Killer, in his domestic mode, was cleaning out one of the mare's hooves, and didn't hear.

"Will you ever finish that picture of Vicky

and me parading our fecundity on the virgin prairies?" she asked. "And if you do finish it, will I get to see it?"

"Oh, it's not abandoned," George assured her. "I'm still having a bit of difficulty with the perspective. I might bring it to England when it's done — I've been thinking of bringing some of my Indian pictures to England, in a while. I might be hawking old Blue Thunder and the others in Picadilly when you get home."

"*Will* I get home, do you think, George?" she asked. "I don't know that I shall. Jim talks of proceeding to Texas, which I judge is not too distant from Santa Fe."

"Texas? Now, there's a place brimming with Indians," George said. "I might go there myself — want to look at the Comanches and the Kiowa. Perhaps we'll yet bump into each other on the trail."

Tasmin suddenly felt foolish. Why was she arguing so, trying to keep this poor man from earning his living? She was rich — George wasn't. She gave him another hug and a slightly less smeary kiss.

"At least this leaves us two prospects for meeting again — Texas and Picadilly," she said. "I'll be hopeful, George."

"Texas or Picadilly," George said, with an awkward smile.

Tasmin hurried to the cart, yanked up a startled Monty, popped him into his pouch, strapped the pouch to her back, and strode off to the south, saying not a word to anyone. Behind her the others dawdled, packing and repacking. Pierre Boisdeffre was still trying to persuade Cook to accept a position with him, but he had made the mistake of attempting unwanted familiarities, a behavior Cook had no intention of accepting. Besides, it was hard to know when the company might again need her skills as a midwife.

Mary came striding out with Piet, both of them equipped with nets and bottles, but the mass of the company still dawdled.

Annoyed with this lagging, Tasmin turned and vented some of her irritation in a good loud yell.

"Say! You at the post! Ain't we leaving?" she yelled.

Then she resumed her march toward the purplish, distant mountains, and did not look back.

46

Tasmin marched off briskly . . .

Tasmin marched off briskly, but after a bit, her anger and confusion began to subside and she slowed down. Monty soon made hungry sounds. The plain was barren of anything to sit on, so Tasmin simply sat down in the long waving grass and gave him the breast. In the distance the Berrybender expedition could be seen leaving the post, widely strung out, as if each member of the company, vexed beyond endurance by the proximity of the others, had decided to seek his or her own path toward the mysterious south. Millicent drove the wagon, Kit Carson the cart. Jim Snow was nowhere to be seen, a fact which troubled Tasmin for a moment. She had not forgotten with what ease and rapidity Jim disappeared when he felt in the mood to go. But then, suddenly, there he was — the almost imperceptible swell of the prairie had concealed him for a bit. Better yet, he was alone, which was less and less the case now that Kate Berrybender had attached herself to him with the tenacity of a leech.

"I thought that sluggish bunch would never start," Tasmin said angrily. "I do hate dawdling."

"They're pokey packers," Jim agreed. "The Sioux could roll up fifty lodges and be up in the middle of Canada in less time than they took to get started."

He squatted beside her and urged a kiss on her, such a long kiss that it flustered her slightly. Lately it seemed that her angers awoke his lust — she had only to flare her nostrils like the mare and he would be at her. It seemed Jim had not known much of kissing before she taught him, but now he liked it and was frequently apt to surprise her. In this case his kiss was particularly reassuring: she had been cursing loudly over having to part with George Catlin. Jim might just as well have walked up and slapped her. He was welcome to her soft mouth, though at the same time she felt slightly embarrassed, with Monty nursing just below. Two males, it seemed, were feeding on her at once; which was all very well, except that a mite of some sort was attacking one of her armpits — she badly needed to scratch. Also, the company was coming closer — she could hear the steady creak of the wagon. Sitting in the tall, wavy grass, her baby nursing and her husband kissing insistently, Tasmin felt sweaty and muddled, half yielding, half resisting. Jim's kiss was no casual peck — he wanted her, if not instantly, then soon. But how were they to manage?

"Jimmy, the baby's not through," she said, withdrawing her mouth long enough to switch Monty to the other breast. "Besides, the expedition's coming."

"Let 'em pass," Jim said. "We're in a hollow. They won't see us."

That was true: the company, each member babbling about his or her own concerns, passed fifty yards to the west. Geoff had decided, after all, to stay with Bobbety — the two were chattering about Congreve.

"Let him guzzle all he wants to," Jim said. "Then I'm taking him to Little Onion."

"We mustn't rush him, now," Tasmin warned. "If he doesn't finish he'll get colic, and we don't want that." Though half pleased by her husband's desire, she was also half annoyed. Why must she have to manage these conflicting streams of need? Though she let herself be kissed, she was fully determined to allow Monty to finish; finally he belched and sighed sleepily before she surrendered him to Jim, who took him and at once ran off to hand him to Little Onion.

By the time Jim returned Tasmin was irritated.

"What *is* your hurry?" she asked. "You can have what you want, but you can't have it while the baby's nursing. I can't do everything at once. And besides that, this is a mighty scratchy place to copulate — couldn't you have at least brought a blanket?"

Jim looked around. The Yellowstone River was not far — there was sure to be a soft, shady spot along its banks. He had started to pull down his pants, but he pulled them back up and helped Tasmin to her feet.

Just such a soft, shady spot was soon found. Tasmin ceased hesitating, and, in time, the peaks of passion were scaled, though not quite mutually. Tasmin's ascent, eventually satisfying, required a bit of straining. It was not until her ardor was subsiding that she at last got to scratch the itchy mite bite in her armpit.

Later, the two of them bathed together in the cold green water, slipping now and then on the slick yellow stones from which the river got its name. They were as naked as they had been when they first glimpsed each other on the shallow Missouri's shore. Tasmin could not help noting that Jim looked just as he had looked then — it was *her* body that had registered change. Then, though not virginal, she had been a girl; now she was a woman and a mother, a change attested to by the fact that her breasts were still dribbling milk. Under the press of Jim's kisses she probably had rushed Monty a bit, after all — if it turned out to mean a colicky night it would be herself and Little Onion, not this man who had been in such a hurry to couple with her, who would deal with the colic. The fact that she liked being a wife and enjoyed her ardors did not entirely banish her annoyance at the general selfishness of men — little Monty not excepted! When he wanted the teat he wanted it immediately and was capable of violent protest if denied.

The slow-moving Berrybender expedition had gained perhaps two miles on them while they were coupling and washing up. The company was still spread out, straggling on across the plain.

"You're getting pretty forward about your lusts, Jimmy — kissing me like that when I've got our baby," she informed him. She had not, on this occasion, quite attained the dreamy state that sometimes followed their lovemaking. She felt, on the whole, rather grumpy. Though she harbored no physical attraction for George Catlin, she had, nevertheless, been gripped by a powerful affection at the moment of their parting. And then Jim Snow, like an insistent bee, had slipped in and buzzed and buzzed until he had succeeded in stealing George Catlin's honey. She had gone along with it, lavished her sweets on the bee — but now she felt annoyed.

Jim made no response to this mild complaint. Why wait to rut, if it was rutting you wanted? When he and Tasmin married she had been in such a hurry to couple that she had been annoyed with old Dan Drew for mumbling so over the service. Of course, she was right that the child needed to finish nursing, but, other than that, he couldn't quite make out why Tasmin now sounded annoyed.

"Just look at us, Jimmy," she said. "Please consider us in all our oddity. You're lost in my world and I'm lost in yours. I can barely make a fire, you can barely read a book. I know reams of history better than you ever will, and you know the world of nature better than all our scientists. We're very able copulators — but that seems to be the one skill we share. Without our ruts what would we be?"

Jim got the old, tired feeling he usually got when Tasmin began to complain. Though he had certainly enjoyed their coupling on the riverbank, he felt he might have done better, on this occasion, to just go drive the cart and let Kit Carson attempt to answer all his wife's questions — though of course Kit wouldn't know the answer to any of them, any more than himself.

"Nobody but you talks about things like this," he told Tasmin, though mildly, with no rancor.

Tasmin had been holding his hand, but now she snatched it away.

330

"Well, but I *do* talk this way and that's just your bad luck, Jimmy," she informed him. "I strongly suspect I shall always talk this way — I fear you're just going to have to put up with it."

They were just coming up on the stragglers of the spread-out expedition — in this case Vicky Kennet and Buffum Berrybender. Kit had stopped the cart for a moment so the two could pick wildflowers, of which a great profusion adorned the plain.

"Why, Tasmin — we thought you were lost," Vicky said. "I have a little gift for you, from George Catlin — he's such a nice fellow — he gave me one too."

She handed Tasmin a rolled-up sheet, which proved to be a lovely watercolor of herself and Vicky, both clearly with child, disporting themselves by a green river.

Tasmin saw that at the bottom of her painting George had written: "Texas or Picadilly — let's be hopeful! George."

"Oh, he was the dearest man — and we were both so mean to him, Vicky!" Tasmin said, tearing up again.

"I know," Vicky said. "Somehow it's hard to resist making decent men suffer — perhaps it's because there are so few to practice on. I fear we don't deserve such thoughtfulness."

"Well, we won't get it, either, now that Mr. George is gone," Buffum said. "He was even

331

decent to me, whom no one else even notices, and yet I too teased him cruelly."

"Perfidious females, all of us!" Tasmin cried — and then the three of them hugged one another and wept.

47

"How far is Scotland, now, Drum?"

Pomp was high on the shoulder of one of the
high peaks of the Wind River range when he
came upon the two little grizzly cubs. He was
tracking mountain sheep at the time — his
patron, Drummond Stewart, was particularly
anxious to take a pair of bighorn sheep back
to Scotland; and not just sheep alone.
Drummond Stewart hoped to bring back
breeding pairs of all the mammals of the
mountains and the plains, from the tiniest
chipmunk to the mighty grizzly bear, for the
great game park he contemplated on his
northern estate. His plan puzzled the trappers who had come south with him —
Eulalie Bonneville, the Sublette brothers, Joe
Walker — who could not figure out why an
apparently sensible man would want to haul
a bunch of wild animals such a distance.
Hugh Glass, who was the oldest of the trappers, and a man who had seen much in his
life, thought Drum Stewart's plan to be the
wildest piece of folly he had ever heard of.

"How far is Scotland, now, Drum?" Hugh
asked.

"Five thousand miles, I suppose," the Scotsman replied casually.

"Too far," Hugh concluded. "A buffalo could be born and grow up and get old and die and not travel *that* far. It's too far to think about."

"What are you, Drum? Some kind of dern Noah, gathering up critters two by two?" sophisticated Joe Walker asked.

"Why yes — I suppose I could be considered a kind of Noah," Drum said. "Only I won't need the flood. Anyway, I don't have to walk my pairs all the way to Scotland — but only to a place where we can catch a steamer, and didn't that Indian say there was a steamer nearby Pierre's trading post, even now?"

"That's what Skinny Foot says and he's a Ute," Bill Sublette told them. "Utes don't usually lie."

"Good news for us, if it's true," his brother said. "A boat big enough to take Drum's critters could also take our pelts — be easier than hauling them overland."

The flanks of the high peak where Pomp was tracking the sheep were never easy to ascend; thick bracken, fallen trees, tangled underbrush had to be fought through before he could reach the high sheep paths. Even then, once clear of the tangles of foliage, he might have to climb all the way to the snow line before spotting the tracks of the bighorns.

It was while struggling through a wicked tangle of brush that Pomp heard a rustling just in front of him. He could see nothing, but he kept his gun ready. It was in such a thicket that Hugh Glass had surprised the grizzly that had mauled him to within an inch of his life. On alert, Pomp stopped and waited. He could see nothing, but he had the strong feeling that he was being watched, whether by human or animal he couldn't be sure. Very cautiously he peered into the tangled bracken and was startled to see two brown furry faces staring back at him — the bear cubs were only three feet away. The little bears regarded Pomp solemnly; at first his chief concern was to spot the mother — in the whole West there was no animal so feared as the mother grizzly with cubs to protect.

For several minutes he waited, peering now and then at the cubs, whose solemn looks had not changed. There was no roar, no charge from the mother, but still Pomp waited. He remembered that his own mother, Sacagawea, had cautioned him about how sly the grizzlies were. He watched and listened; it was finally the buzzing of many flies that led him to the dead mother bear — she had been dead at least a day. Pomp looked, but could not determine what had killed her. Bears, like other creatures, sometimes just died, as his own mother had.

Catching the cubs — which would make a wonderful addition to Drummond Stewart's menagerie, proved no easy matter. Even though Pomp spoke soothingly to the little bears, they retreated deeper into the under-brush, where he could not follow. When he went around to the other side of the thicket, the cubs moved back to the side where they had been.

Pomp soon concluded that the best thing to do was wait. He had some venison with him — with their mother dead at least a day, no doubt the cubs were hungry. When he held it out to the cubs they merely stared at him with solemn caution.

Finally Pomp left the venison in the middle of a small clearing, and then hid himself close by. Though the little bears had no doubt been suckling still, he thought they might at least sniff at the meat. He waited more than an hour, hardly moving, and at last his patience was rewarded. Very cautiously the cubs edged out of their thicket and sniffed the meat. Then Pomp pounced — the little bears turned to flee but then floundered into each other and fell in a heap. Weak from hunger, they suddenly gave up the struggle, whining sadly when Pomp picked them up by their scruffs.

"Now don't be crying, bears — we'll soon have you fattened up," Pomp assured them. Having, by one stroke, captured the one species Drum Stewart had only faint hopes of securing, Pomp decided to give up on mountain sheep for the day and hurry to camp. He didn't want the bear cubs to die, as young animals sometimes would if weakened or discouraged.

Fortunately Billy Sublette had just returned from California, where he had purchased a dozen Spanish horses to help pack out whatever furs they took. Three of the horses were mares in foal.

When Pomp got to camp Jim Bridger was so delighted with the little bear cubs that he milked two mares himself. The two cubs, starving, at once lapped up the steaming milk and followed it with a big bowl of porridge that Joe Walker had whipped up, sweetened with a daub of wild honey. Both cubs whined piteously the first night, even though Pomp held them and stroked them; but on the second day, after more mare's milk and more porridge, plus much friendly attention from the trappers, the cubs accepted their role as camp mascots. After some sharp debate they were named Andy and Abby. By the third day they were thoroughly at home, getting into everything, laying waste the cooking supplies, and even eating a plug of tobacco that Joe Walker had left lying around, a feast that put them both in low spirits for a time. But they soon recovered and were as pesky as ever. The only trapper who didn't immediately lose his heart to the friendly cubs was old Hugh Glass, who at first refused to let them lick his face.

"Being kilt by a bear has rather put me off the species," Hugh declared. "These cubs will grow up pretty soon and eat one or two of us, if we're not lucky."

"Why, Hugh — how can you hold a grudge against our little Abby?" Jim Bridger asked.

"It wasn't you that was kilt, Jimmy," Hugh Glass replied; and yet, not more than three days later, he was spotted slipping choice bits of buffalo liver to Abby, who was soon trailing him like a puppy wherever he went. If Hugh slipped away for a day to hunt, Abby whined unhappily until he returned. They even had to chain her by one foot to keep her from plunging off after her friend Hugh.

"I wonder why she likes that old raunch so much," Jim Bridger asked — he was a little jealous.

"Hugh's half grizzly himself — that's why," Milt Sublette suggested.

"More than half, I'd say," Eulalie Bonneville declared. He had had some lively disputes with Hugh Glass over the years.

Andy, though friendly with everyone, attached himself mainly to Pomp, his rescuer, and Pomp was especially careful that no harm came to the cub, whose mother, like his own, had died.

48

He had been born in the wild, and then taken from it.

Excited by Pomp's capture of the two grizzly cubs — sure to be the noblest specimens in his great game park if only he could get them back to Scotland alive — Drummond Stewart tried again to get Pomp to agree to come back home with him and manage the park. None of the trappers was as good with animals as young Pomp. Already they had elk, deer, moose, antelope, and buffalo — all fawns and calves Pomp had taken — penned up in an ample box canyon, well watered and barricaded with logs. The other trappers seldom bothered with these young creatures, but Pomp went into the enclosure every day, his pockets stuffed with little cubes of sugar, which he dispensed to the spindly calves, none of whom showed any fear of the man. When the little bear cub Andy, Pomp's special pet, followed him into the enclosure, the young quadrupeds were skittish at first, but soon settled down and accepted the cub, who even romped a bit with the spindly buffalo calf.

"I'll never manage them without you, Pomp," Drum insisted. "I'll lose them all if you desert me."

"But I won't desert you, sir," Pomp assured him. "I'll stay with you until you are all safely on the boat in New Orleans — that was my promise."

"Well and good, but what will happen when I get them back to Scotland?" Drum Stewart asked. He was a man used to getting his way, by charm if possible, by bullying or by the expenditure of a great deal of hard cash if charm didn't work; but, in Pomp's case, none of the three worked. At a certain point in the discussion Pomp's mobile, handsome face and liquid eyes ceased to be mobile or liquid. He was never rude, he never shouted or cursed; but when implored to do something he had no intention of doing, his face became a mask, mild in aspect but glazed like porcelain. When that happened discussion proceeded no further.

Pomp respected Drummond Stewart, whose desire to bring the animals of the New World back to a park in the Old World — rather than merely slaughtering them, as Lord Berrybender did — seemed to him an ambitious thing. And yet, even as he devised traps and set lures, Pomp began to develop mixed feelings about the project. The innocence of the young animals touched him. Far from being too cautious, they were, in the main, too trusting, yielding their freedom too easily. Of course, he knew that both losses and gains were involved: the two appealing bear cubs would have soon died had he not found them. Cougars, wolves, or bears would have succeeded in dragging down many of the young quadrupeds. In capturing them he had saved them — and yet a feeling of disquiet wouldn't leave him. He saw the trusting creatures who learned to eat sugar out of his hand as being rather like himself. He had been born in the wild, and then taken from it. His parents had delivered him to Captain Clark in order that he might have schooling; a little later, kind Prince Paul of Württemberg had taken him to Europe in order that he have better schooling: he himself had been like a small animal in a game park, though a park with a gentle and amiable keeper.

Like the little bears or the spindly young elk, his life had been without the risks that would have been his every day if he had grown up with the Shoshone — his mother's people — or even the more settled Mandans or Rees. With those peoples he might have died any day, from attack, bad luck, arrows, weather, bears. He would have been free, but that might only have meant free to be dead if he had been careless, or merely unlucky.

Which was better: freedom with its risks, or the settled life with its comforts? It was not a question he could fully answer, but he did know that now he himself belonged to the wild. He did not intend to go back to Europe. When he returned from Stuttgart, when he stepped off the boat at Westport Landing and looked again at the great Western prairies, it seemed to him that those prairies had been there all along in his head, even when he hunted in the forests of Germany. At once Pomp rid himself of European clothes and went back to the Osage band he had been hunting with when Prince Paul found him. The Osage welcomed him — though many of the young braves who had been his friends were dead, victims of the wild way of life.

Very soon after coming back Pomp realized he was a man whose worlds were mixed. He spoke good Spanish, which meant that he had a value to anyone needing a guide for Santa Fe; he spoke fair French, which put him in demand with trappers who meant to trap the waterways of the north — and he quickly picked up a smattering of the tribal dialects of various Indian bands. Many customers of means — rich travelers like the Berrybenders — would have been happy to hire such a well-spoken and competent guide. Of many possibilities Pomp had chosen Drummond Stewart because the project seemed interesting. Merely helping rich people indulge themselves didn't interest him. But exploring little-known pockets of the

West *did* interest him, as did the chance to catch, rather than kill, animals. One of the few things Pomp could remember his mother telling him was that the animals were his brothers and he should treat them with the respect he would owe a brother. It was that duty that made him uneasy, as he walked through the box canyon, letting the young animals eat sugar out of his hand. Was it respecting his brothers to cage them, even if eventually they would roam free in a spacious Scottish park? Was it respecting them to move them from their homes, even if it allowed them longer lives? His kindly tutor, Herr Hanfstaengl, had tried to interest Pomp in philosophy, particularly the philosophy of Kant, of which Pomp grasped almost nothing. And yet, there on the slopes of the Wind River range, walking with his innocent brothers — elk, antelope, buffalo — Pomp wondered, even as Andy, the jealous little bear, tried to snatch cubes of sugar out of his hand before he could give them to the other animals — whether only some philosopher, some very wise man, could resolve the question he himself could merely formulate.

He knew that his parents had been trying to do their best by him, when they took him to Captain Clark to be schooled — his father had had little education and his mother none. Sacagawea had been of the wild — as purely of the wild as the bear cubs or the

343

little elk. The Hidatsa, to be sure, had stolen her from the Shoshone, but the Hidatsa had not taken the wild out of her, because they were wild themselves. Sometimes, walking amid the young animals, pestered by Andy, Pomp felt an ache inside — an ache so deep that he feared he would never be free of it. He had been removed from the wild, and had come back to it, and yet he had not come back to it wild — even some of the mountain men he camped with every night were closer to the wild state than he could ever be. The animal in Hugh Glass was barely subdued — nor was it subdued in Jim Snow. Those two at least, Hugh and Jim, were more like Indians than Europeans. It was a thing he envied them, since he himself was neither the one nor the other. He could fight, of course, if his life was threatened, and yet he didn't like to. Unlike Jim and Hugh, he had been tamed — yet in the West, where he was making his life, the tamed were of little consequence. The wilderness, the wild, only truly welcomed the wild. It seemed to Pomp that the best loyalty he could make his mother was to live where she had lived, on her plains, in her mountains. He didn't want to feed tame animals in some misty Scottish valley. There were times when he felt like kicking down the barricades and turning all the animals free — they were his brothers and they might prefer to stay wild.

Though he felt the impulse, he didn't kick down the barricades because he knew it was already too late. The captured creatures were not wild enough to survive; they would all be immediately eaten by keener creatures who had never been anything but wild.

Drummond Stewart, watching Pomp with the deer and elk and antelope, knew that in this case he had not won his man. Pomp Charbonneau would see him to New Orleans, as promised, but not a mile farther.

When he said as much to Eulalie Bonneville, the trapper at once agreed.

"Pomp will never go back, but you might tempt Jimmy Snow," Bonney said. "He's got that English wife."

"No thank you," Drum said. "Mr. Snow seems to me to be wilder than these animals. I doubt he'd take kindly to the kilt and the kirk."

Drum had often found himself thinking of Tasmin, though — the woman had from the first looked at him with scorn in her eyes. He didn't like Tasmin's attitude, but he was not disposed to challenge it — not yet, anyway. His thoughts more often turned to the long-legged beauty Venetia Kennet — their frolics had livened up the dullness of a northern winter. Her ardor had surprised him, indeed almost worn him out, but now that he had been absent from her for a few months, she had begun to swim through his thoughts again. He remembered her long legs, high breasts, avid mouth, untiring loins.

Lady Tasmin might look at him with scorn, if she wished. He thought he might just revisit the tall cellist, play a few new tunes between those long legs — for one thing, he liked her stamina. She had survived not only Albany Berrybender's rough treatment, but a northern winter too. Perhaps, if the two of them found that they still got on, he might even take Venetia Kennet to wife. It would outrage rigid home society, but then he had never been obedient to that home society's narrow rules. A man who aspired to be a proper Scot laird would not likely be camped by the Wind River, trapping animals that he would then have to transport for thousands of miles.

"It'll soon be high summer — I expect old Berrybender and his company will be showing up any day," Eulalie Bonneville said. "That tall girl with him had a considerable fondness for you, as I recall."

Dummond Stewart didn't answer. Bonney was as big a gossip as any woman — might as well cry a secret to the mountains as tell it to Bonney. Let the Berrybenders come — time enough then to see if the tall lass, Vicky Kennet, still favored his rod.

49

Blue Thunder had always flourished in winter — the cold sharpened his senses, made him feel keen. To a man brought up amid all the bounty of the northland, winter — so long as one was healthy — was a season to be welcomed.

Blue Thunder even enjoyed blizzards — when a good northern blizzard was blowing, at least there was some privacy to be had — and he liked privacy. In any band of warriors — even Piegan warriors — there were sure to be several chattering fools: just the kind of people Blue Thunder didn't welcome. Even if a man didn't happen to be at home in a well-banked lodge when a blizzard struck, anyone who knew the country could always find shelter under a creek bank, or in a thicket where firewood was plentiful. It was true that blizzards sometimes blew in rather quickly, but then Blue Thunder too was quick — the minute he sensed a lift in the wind, of the sort that made the snow fly, he chose his shelter and made his fire. Then, if there was time, he might catch a porcupine, a hare, or a couple of fat squirrels at least.

Blue Thunder had learned the ways of weather, and how to survive blizzards, from his wise old grandfather Black Toe, a cautious yet proficient man. Black Toe was by far the best snare maker in the whole of the Blackfoot nation. In all his life Black Toe had only been careless once — he had failed to look where he was going one morning and had been bitten on the toe by a small but venomous prairie rattler. Before that accident, which caused his toe to rot, he had been called Leaping Elk, a far more flattering name than the one he ended up with.

The injury to his toe in no way impaired Black Toe's skill as a snare maker. He carefully explained to his grandson that though it might be all very well for hunters to kill big animals — buffalo, moose, elk, even bear if they dared — the fact was that, to a man of sensitivity, the flesh of large animals was often stringy and tough. If there was nothing else to eat, of course, people had to make do; but for those with more delicate palates, who cared to pick and choose, the flesh of birds and small animals was almost always better. Old Black Toe liked geese, green-headed ducks, plump prairie chickens, quail, porcupine, hare, squirrels, curly green snakes, chipmunks, and tiny songbirds so small they could be eaten in one bite. Mice, too, could be eaten in one bite, but Black Toe had little fondness for mice, unless a bunch of them could be roasted together in their nests under a brush pile or somewhere. Of course, the fetus of any animal was apt to be tender — now and then he would roast part of an unborn fawn and leave the mother doe to be eaten by the tribe.

What Black Toe liked best was making snares, and not crude, all-purpose snares, of the sort a clumsy hunter might resort to, but intricate, delicate snares fashioned after long study of the habits and personalities of the various creatures that might be snared. Snares for hares could be made in a few minutes. Porcupines were so stupid and slow that it was not really necessary to snare them. Porcupines were best taken on the end of a lance and their needles carefully saved. Snares for waterbirds had to be carefully secured under the water, a tedious business, especially if it was winter and the water cold. Sometimes Black Toe preferred to net waterbirds, in order to avoid cold work in the water. Once, while setting a snare for geese, he had accidentally snared a small owl, a mistake that disturbed him so badly that he gave up snaring birds for some years. It was after he snared the owl that the snake bit him — the former Leaping Elk felt very lucky that his brush with the owl resulted in nothing worse than one lost toe.

Owls were the worst medicine of all, of course — confusion in one's behavior toward owls almost always meant that death would be coming soon — and yet Black Toe lived thirty years after his brush with the owl, plenty of time to instruct his grandson in the proper use of snares.

When Blue Thunder decided to leave the steamer and enjoy a nice walk home in the crisp winter weather, he took a sack of the white man's excellent axes, and a pouch full of good snares. To the expert snare maker the big boat had been a treasure house, with strings and ribbons and small ropes and other cordage available for the taking. Blue Thunder took plenty, and in fact spent the last week of his stay with the whites making a good assortment of snares. He meant to take his old grandfather's advice and live off small game and tender birds. He didn't really expect to have to defend himself on his walk — the great bears would be sleeping in their dens, and if he should run into some warrior who was in a mood to fight, he had his sack full of axes.

Walking away from the noisy boat into the quiet of the snowy country brought Blue Thunder immediate relief. Putting up with the loud Hairy Horn, and the even louder company of whites, had severely taxed his patience. Very likely Sharbo, the old interpreter whose care he was supposed to be in, would

try to catch up with him and attempt to persuade him to come back, but Blue Thunder
left at night, so as to get a good jump on the
old man. Since Sharbo would probably look
for him to go west, he angled north into
Canada. Almost at once a blizzard blew in, a
good thing from Blue Thunder's point of
view. In such weather Sharbo wouldn't
pursue him far. In a day the blizzard blew
out and the sun shone once more on the
plains.

Blue Thunder meant to take his time and
have a nice, leisurely trip back to the land
of the Piegans. One thing he had agreed
with Big White, the Mandan, about, was
that going back to one's people after a long
absence was a very uncertain thing.
Younger leaders would have had time to
emerge, chiefs and proud warriors who
would not be especially happy to see him
return. He had left three wives at home,
but any number of things could have happened to reduce that number in the years
that he had been gone. He might have a
child or two whom he had never seen —
but, on the other hand, he might return to
discover that he had neither new sons nor
old wives. None of his wives had possessed
much patience — they might have divorced
him by now and taken other husbands. Or
they might have died, been killed in raids,
been captured. He would have to wait to

find out all that until he got back to his old band.

In any case it was good to be once more in the spacious, beautiful northland, where the air was cold, and free of all the taints that air took on in the white man's cities, or on their boats. At his first camp he immediately snared two hares — enough for a meal. He saw a porcupine ambling by in the snow but he was not in the mood for oily porcupine meat, so he let the creature go.

In four weeks, moving slowly, enjoying his privacy, Blue Thunder arrived at the edge of his home country. Far away — perhaps fifty miles farther — he could see the faint outlines of some humpy mountains; much of his life had been lived in sight of those humpy little hills. Now he saw them most plainly at dusk, when the light was not so bright on the thin snow — the hills became reddish, then purple, as the light faded.

That night, although there was plenty of game around — the snow was crisscrossed with tracks — Blue Thunder made a fire but didn't kill or cook anything. He thought he might do better to begin a fast. When he left the boat Blue Thunder assumed that he would go find his old band and resume the life he had once led — a life of raiding and hunting, of trying to advise his people about where to camp, or see that they gave themselves good opportunities for hunting.

Now, though, that the hills of his boyhood and maturity were in sight, he felt uncertain. Usually a fast helped at such times of inner confusion. It cleared the head and the body and put a man in the mood to do some sharp thinking. But, on this occasion, fasting only made Blue Thunder feel more confused and uncertain. He had a feeling that going home might turn out badly. It made no sense that he should feel so pessimistic, and yet he did. Once he had been an effective and respected chief, which was why the president in Washington had asked him to come for a visit. But when he had agreed to accept the president's invitation he had no idea that he was setting out on a journey that would cover so much of the world. Sharbo had explained to him that Washington was far, far away, but everyone knew that Sharbo exaggerated. Discovering that, this time, Sharbo *hadn't* exaggerated came as a bad shock. Even after descending the one great river and ascending another for many days Washington had still been far away.

Now Blue Thunder was discovering what he should have been smart enough to figure out to begin with: that leaving one's destined country was not a wise thing to do. But he had gone — and now coming back was hard. Even if his people welcomed him and encouraged him to sit once more with the councils of the tribe, there was something even deeper that would need to be put right, if it could be.

People, of course, were restless — they were always coming and going — his whole band moved according to the needs of the hunt. But the land itself — the country itself — the land, the hills, the streams, the grasses — didn't go anywhere. It was always there, faithful to its children as long as they respected the earth, the animals, the seasons.

Intolerant of criticism, disdainful of most human opinion, Blue Thunder nonetheless felt that in this instance he had committed a disloyalty, not to his people, but to his place itself. He had been given certain responsibilities in relation to his place; he had been meant to live and die in uninterrupted contact with his own part of the earth, the prairies that surrounded those stumpy hills.

Many chiefs, of course, had been to see the president — Blue Thunder had foolishly let Sharbo persuade him that it was his duty to go also. He hadn't liked the whites, or their boats, or their cities, but what he had learned about them was sobering. For one thing, they were a huge tribe, as numerous as ants or lice, and, besides that, they possessed magic so strong that it was uncomfortable to be around.

One afternoon he and the Hairy Horn and Big White had been taken to a huge tent, where they had seen magic so powerful that it stunned all three of them. There was a man who swallowed fire. The same man could stick a great sword down his throat and yet not be cut. There were bears in the tent who danced to drums and whistles, and people who swung high in the air like birds, always catching themselves on short swinging branches. Most frightening of all, however, was a great beast out of time — it was called an elephant — a small brown man rode on its head and controlled it. The great beast had a nose many feet long that it could curl up if it wanted to lift its small rider down. Also, the beast had white tusks of great length. When the Hairy Horn saw it he wanted to leave at once. He thought it likely that the elephant would soon go berserk and trample all the people in the tent. Sharbo chuckled at their fears — he assured them that the great beast was really tame, and also very old — older than any living man.

Later, when the three chiefs were on their way back down the Ohio River, they had spent much time discussing the elephant. The Hairy Horn maintained that far to the west, in the hills sacred to the Sioux people, there were drawings on rocks which showed just such a beast. He had not seen them himself, but the medicine men knew they were there. His own brother, the Partezon, had seen the drawings, but of course the Partezon had not gone to Washington and so had not seen the living elephant. When the likeness maker Catlin heard about the drawings he became very excited and wanted to go there at once. Sharbo had had to point out to him that the Partezon was very hard on white people caught in the Sioux country, and even harder on anyone, white or Indian, caught in the Holy Hills. The likeness maker, being foolish in such matters, might have gone anyway had it not been for the approaching cold.

Now that he was almost home, Blue Thunder felt that all the knowledge he had gained on his journey — knowledge that some whites could swallow fire, others fly like birds — sat heavily on him. If he had stayed in his native country he would not have known of such things, or of the elephant, the beast from out of time itself. In his own country, in his lifetime, he would not even have had to deal with many whites — only a few trappers, probably, or, now and then, a daring traveler. His sons would have to deal with whites, but he himself would have been dead before whites came too close to the Piegans' range.

Until he went to Washington and saw the whites in their great ant heaps, he had supposed that they were merely a scattered tribe — any notion that they could ever mount a serious threat to the power of the Blackfeet would have seemed silly.

But now, nearing the end of his journey, Blue Thunder was forced to admit that all his calculations about the whites had been wrong. The whites were much stronger than he or anyone in his tribe had supposed; they were coming west much more quickly and in much greater numbers than anyone would have imagined possible, even three summers ago. What Blue Thunder now knew was that the power of the Blackfeet was as nothing to the power of these whites, men who could make boats that moved without being rowed. They could make guns that could kill buffalo at distances no arrow could travel; they could even tame the elephant, greatest of beasts.

The nearer Blue Thunder came to the valleys of home, the more heavily these thoughts oppressed him. What he knew was that the time of his people, the proud Blackfeet, was nearing its end. He didn't intend, though, to tell this to the people of his band — not even to the elders. This weight, this boulder of knowledge, was something best carried alone. There was no point in disturbing the old ones, whose lives would end before they had to witness too much change.

In three days more, traveling slowly, Blue Thunder saw the smoke of campfires ahead, with the stumpy mountains now not far away. Very likely the camp smoke was from the campfires of his own band. A little river, a clear, skinny stream, ran through this particular valley; his band often camped beside it.

Blue Thunder had no intention of making a big show when he arrived home. Human beings always came and went — it was rude to mark their reappearances with undue celebration. Blue Thunder intended just to walk in, greet an old friend or two, pay his respects to the elders, and go visit his wives, if he still had wives. When a man came back from a long journey it was better just to slip in quietly and not interrupt the important routines of tribal life.

Having decided on this simple plan, Blue Thunder felt a little better — he could see several lodges ahead, and some frames where women were working skins. Life was going on for these Piegans as it always had, with no thought being given to steamboats or elephants or men who swallowed fire.

It had been a long and complicated journey that he had made, but Blue Thunder gradually began to feel a little better. He had returned to where he belonged and could soon, he hoped, realign himself with the country he had deserted. He was west of the Yellowstone, a long way west, and with a little luck could enjoy some good years before the whites became a problem for his people.

As he walked toward the village he made no attempt to conceal himself — he expected that, at any moment, some of the young warriors would spot him and come racing out with lances ready, to determine if he was friend or foe. Indeed, he was a little surprised that the young braves had not yet spotted him — such carelessness on their part was a little imprudent.

But then he did see a horseman coming — but it was not a young warrior. The man coming toward him was old, wore a dirty cap of some kind, and rode an old, spavined, piebald horse, so ancient that it could barely stumble through the grass. To his horror Blue Thunder realized that the man coming toward him was his cousin Greasy Lake — the one person in the whole of the Western plains that he would have walked many miles out of his way to avoid. But there he was, Greasy Lake, appearing, as usual, just at the moment when he was least wanted. He was singing cheerfully, too, quite indifferent to the fact that the horse he rode was too old even to trot, or that the man he was coming to see had no desire to see him: for Greasy Lake had always been a man indestructible in his happiness, a man who wandered through massacres eating plums, serene and untouched, as better men were being hacked to death all around him. Some considered him a shaman or a prophet, others knew him merely to be a fool.

Why me? Why is he here? Almost home and he has to show up, Blue Thunder thought, well aware that the moment Greasy Lake was in earshot he would begin to mooch.

"You don't have a spare coat in your camp, do you?" Greasy asked. He had not seen Blue Thunder in seven or eight years. It had been chilly the night before, but here came his cousin, who had been to see the president, who might have given him a coat or two. Blue Thunder carried a good-sized sack over his shoulder; perhaps the sack had a coat or two in it, one that his cousin could easily spare.

"I don't have a coat, and if I did I'd give it to your horse, not you," Blue Thunder told him. "A horse that skinny needs a coat worse than you do — you should be ashamed of yourself for riding a horse that skinny."

"Oh, he'll fatten up in the spring," Greasy Lake replied. "In fact there's plenty of good grass under the snow but my horse is too lazy to dig for it."

Greasy Lake remembered that Blue Thunder was always quick to change the subject when it came time to be generous with his family. He was carrying a sizable sack — if the sack contained no coat perhaps it at least contained some good knives or a few green beads.

"What's in that sack?" he asked. Sometimes just asking point-blank was the best way to make a stingy person part with a gift or two.

"Axes," Blue Thunder said, continuing his slow advance on the village.

This was disappointing news from Greasy Lake's point of view. On the other hand an axe was better than nothing. He might find a woman willing to slip into the bushes with him if he gave her a good axe.

"I hope you'll give me one, then," he said. "All I have now is a wobbly hatchet with a loose handle. The head of my hatchet might fly off at any time."

"I'll give you an axe, all right," Blue Thunder told him, testily. "I'll split you wide open with one if you don't leave me alone."

In the end, though, he let Greasy Lake choose an axe — giving the old fool what he wanted was sometimes the best way to get rid of him. Naturally Greasy Lake took a long time making his choice — taking too long to choose was another of his irritating habits.

"These are white men's axes, they're all exactly the same," Blue Thunder told him, as Greasy Lake gave each axe a close going-over.

"No two things are ever quite the same," Greasy assured him. Like his horse he was piebald in color. Part of him was almost white, part brown, and part bronze.

Blue Thunder was hoping someone from the village would spot them and hurry out to rescue him, but no one did. The day of his homecoming seemed to be passing point-lessly, as his cousin examined six identical axes. In the village some women were stretching a buffalo hide over a frame. He thought he saw one of his wives in the distance, but she went strolling off to the river without once looking his way.

"This one is much the best, I'll take it, thank you," Greasy Lake said. The old horse's legs sagged when Greasy mounted, carrying his new axe.

"Do you live with these Piegans now?" Blue Thunder asked, wondering how long he would be expected to put up with the man.

"Oh no, I don't live anywhere, my horse and I prefer just to travel around," Greasy Lake told him. "When it warms up a little I am going down to the Green River — some trappers are having a powwow there, later in the summer. There'll be some rich traders there, I expect. If I'm lucky one of them might give me a good coat."

"That horse doesn't want to travel," Blue Thunder pointed out. "That horse would prefer to die."

Greasy Lake merely chuckled. The suggestion that his horse was played out just amused him. In any case Blue Thunder had never been a very good judge of horseflesh. The fact that his horse had a few ribs showing didn't mean anything.

"Didn't that horse have a funny name?"

Blue Thunder asked. It seemed to him Greasy Lake had ridden the same poor old horse all his life.

"His name is Galahad," Greasy Lake said. "It's hard to say until you get the hang of it."

"That's a terrible name," Blue Thunder complained. "Why give a horse a name that's so hard to say?"

"Oh, I didn't name him, that Englishman named Thompson named him — he had that little trading post up on the Kootenai, remember? I think you and some boys burned that trading post down."

"We did burn it down — but just because a white man gave a horse a bad name doesn't mean the animal has to have a bad name forever. You could have changed it."

Greasy Lake decided it was time to be going. He had a new axe, which might enable him to seduce a girl, an activity that would certainly be more enjoyable than talking to Blue Thunder — the man had never been easy to talk to. What was the point of arguing with somebody just because they didn't like your horse's name? In fact, Greasy Lake had little occasion ever to use the horse's name — the horse could be given all the directions he needed without the name ever being uttered.

"Do you know if any of my wives are alive?" Blue Thunder asked.

"I don't know a thing about your wives," Greasy Lake confessed. "I haven't been here long enough to get the gossip."

Then he whacked the old horse with the axe handle and went trotting off toward the camp.

Blue Thunder watched the odd pair go. Being whacked with an axe handle seemed to have put a little life in the skinny old horse. He trotted for perhaps fifty yards and then slowed to a walk, his legs sagging with every step. For a time Greasy Lake and his horse traveled at such a slow pace that it didn't seem as if they were moving at all — but eventually they reached the camp and disappeared.

Blue Thunder himself felt very tired — throughout his life, just talking to his cousin Greasy Lake had the effect of making him tired. His band's camp was right in front of him — a ten-minute walk would put him there — and yet a thing occurred which had often occurred when Blue Thunder talked to Greasy Lake: he lost track of the point of whatever he had been doing. His home village was right there, and yet, for a time, Blue Thunder could not remember why he had thought there was any point in going to it.

50

His welcome was modest and dignified . . .

Though it took a little while for Blue Thunder to recover from his talk with his cousin Greasy Lake, he eventually proceeded on home. His welcome was modest and dignified, as was appropriate. No one asked him a thing about his visit with the president, the cause of his long absence. To inquire about such a thing would have been presumptuous; and Blue Thunder himself made no mention of this great white man because to have done so would have seemed like bragging. An absence of comment about the honor he had been given seemed to be the best approach — it allowed Blue Thunder to settle gently back into the life of the tribe — to settle down slowly, as a great heron settled when it glided toward the surface of a pond where it might soon begin to catch many frogs.

In time Blue Thunder meant to catch a few frogs himself; that is, he meant to catch up on the gossip. A leader, after all, needed to know what was going on — and soon, much to his surprise, he discovered that he was expected to be the tribal leader once more. This was unusual — normally a challenger would have come along and attempted to lead the tribe, and, in fact, one had: a warrior named Cloud. But Cloud, being very hotheaded, had foolishly decided to fight some Shoshone on a day when it was rainy and muddy. Several warriors advised Cloud that this was not a good day to start a fight, since the Shoshone were better mounted than they were, but Cloud could not be made to see right reason. He rushed straight into battle, his horse slipped in the mud and fell, and Cloud was immediately hacked to death by the surprised Shoshone, who were astonished that any leader as badly mounted as Cloud would be so foolish as to fight them on a muddy, slippery day.

Cloud had been placed on his burial scaffold only a few hours before, leaving the tribe with several wise elders but no war chief to inspire the young braves. Blue Thunder was soon given to know that if he thought he still had the mettle of a war chief, then he was welcome to assume the task — he *did* assume it, once he had determined that there were no young rivals skulking around to become a source of trouble.

Fortunately all three of his wives were still alive — though a little subdued at first, his wives seemed glad enough to have him back, though his oldest wife, Quiet Calf, who had always been snippy with him, at once informed him that during his absence she had passed the age of mating — she no longer intended to be with him in the way of a wife with a man.

Blue Thunder knew better than to believe his sneaky old wife for a minute. No doubt she had no intention of being any use to *him* in the way of a wife with a man, but Quiet Calf had always been by far the most lustful of his three wives, and it seemed unlikely that her strong lusts had worn themselves out. Blue Thunder made no response to her big lie, but he resolved to watch her — very likely she had a boyfriend, and he meant to discover who it was. He had never allowed his wives to have boyfriends; it might be the way of the world but it was not his way, and it annoyed him that Quiet Calf would speak so deceptively to him on his first day back. If he happened to catch her with a lover he meant to beat her soundly with a good heavy piece of wood.

Except for this annoyance, which he had more or less expected, his homecoming went pleasantly enough. His wives killed two of the fattest dogs in the camp, in order to make a tasty stew. Blue Thunder sat in front of his lodge most of the day, watching the young warriors at sport: they were racing horses, wrestling, doing a little archery. Mainly they were showing off for the old chief who had returned and become the new chief. To Blue Thunder's critical eye these youngsters did not seem to be especially well trained, but what bothered him most was that there were so few of them — only about ten, not much of a fighting force. He mentioned this to old Limping Wolf, a friend who happened to stop by, and Limping Wolf agreed.

"The Piegans aren't making enough babies," Limping Wolf said, before limping off.

That would have to change, Blue Thunder thought. A band with only ten warriors could not make much of a show. Even the ridiculous Shoshone had many more young warriors than that, and the Sioux were said to have hundreds, probably an exaggeration but worrisome nonetheless.

Just as Blue Thunder was about to allow his wives to feed him the tasty stew, who should return but Greasy Lake. There had been no sign of him all day, which had lulled many people into supposing that the old pest was gone.

"I thought you left!" Blue Thunder said, a little rudely.

"Oh no, I was just down by the creek," Greasy Lake replied. As a guest it was necessary to give him the first bowl of stew. Codes of generosity *must* be observed, even if the guest was unwanted, a category Greasy Lake certainly fit into.

"I found a girl who needed a new axe,"

Greasy Lake went on. "I offered her that axe that you gave me and she agreed to copulate with me, so that's where I've been all day. She got a bargain — she's already chopping wood with that axe."

Greasy Lake ate so much of the stew that Blue Thunder's wives thought they might have to kill a third dog, but finally he got his belly full and wandered off somewhere to sleep. Quiet Calf was indignant at the way the old man had hogged the stew.

"Is he going to live with us?" she asked. "If he is, I'm moving out."

The remark merely confirmed Blue Thunder's suspicion that the old hussy had a boyfriend, but it had been a long day and he was not up to a big domestic blowup, after walking so far.

"He is my cousin, what can I do?" he replied.

Quiet Calf finally shut up — but as Blue Thunder was preparing for bed, Limping Wolf and Red Rabbit came by and voiced some doubts about having Greasy Lake in the camp at all.

"I just got home," Blue Thunder said. "Do I have to hear about this before I even sleep?" It had just come back to him that being a war chief was a never-ending job. People thought they were welcome to show up at all hours and have their complaints heard.

"I know he is your cousin but I think he brings bad luck," Red Rabbit explained. "Who knows what will happen to us if we let him stay?"

"He's just an old man whose skin happens to be different colors," Blue Thunder replied. What else could he say?

"He stayed with a bunch of Shoshone for one night and in the morning, when he left, some Assiniboines fell on the camp and killed every single Shoshone — except the women, of course. If he stays here those Assiniboines might fall on us."

"That doesn't prove anything except that Assiniboines are mean, and we already knew that," Limping Wolf objected.

"Does that mean you want him to stay?" Red Rabbit asked, annoyed by his friend's sudden softening where Greasy Lake was concerned.

"Well, he is a prophet and a shaman," Limping Wolf answered. "It's not a bad idea to have a prophet around."

"If he is such a good prophet, why didn't he tell those Shoshone that the Assiniboines were about to kill them?" Red Rabbit wanted to know.

"I don't think he liked the Shoshone," Limping Wolf conjectured. "They probably didn't feed him enough."

"What has he ever predicted, can you tell me?" Blue Thunder asked. He was more than a little annoyed at being kept up on his first night home.

"Well, forest fires," Limping Wolf offered. "He's predicted several forest fires."

"So what, forests are always catching on fire," Red Rabbit protested. "I can predict forest fires myself."

The two oldsters droned on, but Blue Thunder ceased to listen. He had his own solution to the problem of Greasy Lake. In the morning he would sneak off and see the girl who had the new axe; his plan was to advise her not to copulate with Greasy Lake anymore. If he had no one to copulate with Greasy Lake would soon go — he would look in other camps for women he might seduce.

Limping Wolf and Red Rabbit finally left and Blue Thunder prepared to turn in. His youngest wife, Wing, had been watching him with a certain look in her eye. Blue Thunder was considering indulging her in a bit of pleasure when a horrible thought occurred to him. What if Greasy Lake were Quiet Calf's new boyfriend? Such a thing would be irregular, but Greasy Lake had a big reputation with the women and irregular things did happen. Greasy Lake only followed rules or codes of conduct if they happened to work in his favor — such as arriving just in time to be served the first bowl of stew. In matters of carnal behavior he had always been quite shameless.

This thought disturbed Blue Thunder so much that he stretched out on his robes and did nothing about the look in Wing's black eyes, inaction which left Wing keenly disappointed. Had she waited chastely all these years — though opportunities abounded — just to hear this old man snore?

"Go to sleep," Blue Thunder told her. "This is what happens when Greasy Lake comes around. He tires everybody out."

"What makes you think I'm tired?" Wing said, but by then it was too late. Blue Thunder was sound asleep.

51

"Oh, woe betide! Oh doom!"

"Oh, woe betide! Oh doom!" Mary Berrybender gasped, racing back to the cart.

"What is it, imp?" Tasmin asked, but Mary was, for a time, too out of breath to answer.

"It's Cook — Papa shot her!" Mary gasped.

"Oh horror, not Cook!" Bobbety exclaimed. "What shall we do for vittles now?"

"In my opinion it was foolish of the prince of Wied to replenish His Lordship's claret," Father Geoffrin commented. "A bibulous nimrod is hardly likely to contribute to the health of the party."

"Piet is attending Cook," Mary said. "Perhaps the wound won't be fatal."

Cook had been inspecting some promising berry bushes, not fifty yards away. Tasmin and Buffum raced over and were relieved to see that she was sitting up — Piet Van Wely fanned her with his big floppy hat. Cook's face wore a look of mild surprise, and there was a spot of blood on her skirt.

"Merely a flesh wound — hit her in the fatty part of the thigh . . . it's not bleeding much," Piet said, to reassure them. He bent to show Tasmin the wound, but there was the crack of a rifle and a second bullet whacked into Piet, knocking him directly into the lap of the wounded Cook.

"Oh no! Now the old assassin's shot Piet!" Buffum cried. "Mary will be hugely distressed."

"Didn't hit me, hit my knapsack," Piet assured them. "However, he *might* hit me, if he is allowed to keep shooting."

"He won't be allowed — Jim's got him, and just in time," Tasmin said, as Jim Snow ran up to the wagon. He pulled her father off the wagon seat and shook him like a terrier might shake a rat. Tom Fitzpatrick and Kit Carson were close behind Jim, though their assistance was by then little needed. Lord Berrybender, after a severe shaking, was flung to the ground and left to consider his misdeeds. Tom and Kit, with the help of Señor Yanez, took all the guns out of the wagon, a precautionary action that caused Lord B., very red in the face, to struggle upright and begin a protest.

Monty giggled in his pouch as Tasmin hurried toward the wagon. Buffum and Piet were left to attend Cook, who was insisting that she ought to be allowed to pick berries.

"I'm sure they would be nice in a pie," she said, in a voice that had lost some of its accustomed force. It was no particular surprise to Cook that Lord Berrybender had shot her — relations between them had been chilly ever since she informed him that she might leave his service. Long experience with the senior Berrybenders had taught her that such inconstancy would not likely be forgotten, much less forgiven.

Mary fell in with Tasmin and the baby. When informed that her beloved Piet had been hit by a bullet, Mary looked grim.

"Let us puncture the old brute's eardrums and leave him wandering deaf on the heath," she suggested.

"Calm down, he only shot Piet in the knapsack," Tasmin told her.

"I shan't calm down, not at all!" Mary said. "We keep our bottles and entomological specimens in Piet's knapsack — it will be a costly loss to science if they are damaged. Valuable bugs might be lost."

"Hang science!" Tasmin replied. "I'm more concerned about Cook. There are plenty of bugs for you to capture, but there's only one Cook and she's now slightly wounded in the thigh."

Jim, Kit, Tom, and the two Mediterraneans stood near the wagon, beside a formidable stack of guns.

"That's the stuff, Jimmy — confiscate his guns before he kills us all," Tasmin remarked. "What excuse did he have this time?"

Jim was calming, but the red of anger was

not quite gone from his face, nor the flint from his eyes.

"He's dead drunk — it doesn't matter what he says," Jim told her.

"He claims he shot at a stag," Tom informed her. "But there's no stag — if there *had* been, Jimmy or I would have shot it ourselves."

Kit Carson made a fish face at Monty, winning a smile from him. Monty liked Kit but was less certain about his father, who never made fish faces.

"He shot Piet too, the old bastard," Mary declared. "Piet was struck in the knapsack, the repository of valuable scientific specimens."

"Did he, the damned scamp!" the old Broken Hand said to Mary — he had conceived a considerable fondness for the girl.

"Oh look, now he's beating Milly — come help me restrain him, Kit," Tasmin said, pointing.

Jim Snow looked as if he might go do the restraining himself, but before he could, Tasmin thrust Monty into his hands, an action that startled both child and father. Jim was getting a little better with Monty, and Monty a little more used to Jim, but fully harmonious relations had not yet developed. Tasmin thought it was high time — and past time — that they did. She thrust the two of them together whenever she could, hoping something would click.

"Let them puzzle it out — after all, they're related," she told Kit, as they strode off to the wagon. "Don't you think it's about time that they made friends?"

Kit hardly knew how to answer. He himself liked Monty, and Vicky Kennet's baby, little Talley, and Coal's wild mite, whom they called Little Charlie; but the notion of Jim Snow being friends with a baby wasn't easy to imagine.

"Jim, he keeps busy," he said, thinking his comment might strike a reasonable compromise.

It was, as usual, not the answer Tasmin wanted to hear.

"Why, yes — he hunts," Tasmin replied — for every day, as the company plodded southward over the long plain, Jim and the Broken Hand hunted far ahead; they hunted for the table, usually with success. It was necessary that they be far ahead, Jim told her, to be out of hearing of the fusillade Lord Berrybender fired off every day, to slight effect when it came to securing wild provender. Lord B. had not the patience for exact marksmanship — shooting a lot, in his view, was more likely to be effective than aiming well. Also, it was more fun. By hewing to this principle, he scared away more game than he killed. Even the stolid buffalo, which he had once knocked over like wooden ducks, were keeping well clear of the wagon, from which Lord Berrybender issued wild bursts of gun-fire aimed at very distant animals.

Tasmin knew Jim had to range ahead, but saw no reason why this fact should inhibit relations with his son. Evenings on the summer plains were long and soft; there was plenty of time, after Cook had worked her magic with spits and skillets and Dutch ovens, for Jim and Monty Snow to get acquainted.

"It doesn't take long for us Berrybenders to develop our likings," Tasmin said. "After all, Kit, I liked you the minute I met you. I do wish Jim and Monty would show more signs of liking each other."

"Well, Monty don't speak yet, and Jim ain't much of a talker himself," Kit replied.

"You can say that again," Tasmin replied moodily, but before Kit could say anything more they reached the wagon and had to grapple with the problem of what to do with her father, who was still petulantly attempting to box Millicent's ears.

"Father, if you don't stop that nonsense this minute I'm going to have my husband come and give you an even worse shaking than the one you just received," she began, grabbing his arm.

Lord B., wild with anger now, shook free of his daughter.

"No impertinence now!" he said, virtually

frothing with rage. "Have that young lout fetch my guns at once — there's a fine red stag about. I suppose I'm still free to shoot at stags."

"There's no stag, Father," Tasmin told him. "Our Bobbety mistook a horse for an elk, which is bad enough, but you've mistaken Cook for a stag, which is a great deal worse."

Before Lord Berrybender could reply, Milly jumped off the wagon seat and ran off, skirts flying and tears drying, to the cart, toward which Cook, assisted by Piet and Mary, was making slow progress.

"What's all this — why did Constance run off — don't like her running off . . . it was just a small little spat we were having," Lord B. said.

"Millicent, you mean, Father . . . It was Milly who ran off, not Constance," Tasmin replied.

The old lord, her father, looked at Tasmin with mild puzzlement. He was very drunk, his nose was peeling from repeated sunburns, his shirtfront was stained red from many drippings of claret, and his white hair was wild and tangled; but what startled Tasmin was his eyes: his look was not the look of a sane person.

"Who's Millicent?" he asked. "I'm afraid I don't know any Millicents."

"Millicent's our laundress — the large girl you were just slapping," Tasmin reminded him, looking quickly at Kit. She felt a sudden apprehension: something was afoot with her father, something beyond the brusque rudeness and habitual selfishness to which they were all long accustomed.

"I really can't fathom what you could be talking about, Tasmin," he said. "Your mother and I were just having a small quarrel — not an easy state, matrimony. Stubborn, both of us, your mother and I. Constance won't give way, and neither will I. Had many a fine row, over the years. Best just to leave Constance be. She'll calm down in a bit."

Tasmin looked at Kit again. Kit, who had always considered Lord Berrybender more or less crazy, just shrugged. What was there to say about such an old scamp?

"Father, that wasn't Lady Constance you were slapping," Tasmin told him, speaking calmly, even soothingly. Her fear was that some link was broken, the link that attached her erratic parent to his sanity. Usually Lord Berrybender's look was that of a selfish old brute, but better that, she thought, than the look of a madman. Perhaps if she spoke softly and addressed him gently she might be able to help him reclaim his wandering spirit.

That hope was very soon dashed.

"Look there, Tassie! It's the stag of Glamorgan — he's eluded me many a year," His Lordship said, pointing. "Can't think where I've left my rifle. Don't see the stag of Glamorgan every day."

Tasmin looked and saw only the Thorough-bred, Gussie, which Tim was leading to water.

"No, that's merely your mare, Augusta, Fa-ther," Tasmin informed him, still speaking quietly. "We are presently in America, fast by the Yellowstone River, you know. This is the American plain, not some Scottish glade. And our dear Lady Constance, your wife, my mother, lies buried far away, on a hill by the Missouri."

At this Lord Berrybender looked weary, and suddenly sat down, his back against the wagon wheel.

"It's very strange that you should say such things, Tassie," he told her. "Hard to think why you'd go on with such nonsense unless you've been into the brandy. Wouldn't sur-prise me if you *have* been into the brandy. I was often into it, when I was your age. Guz-zled down quite a quantity, I assure you."

He sighed.

"You know, I feel like taking a good nap," he said — a moment later, head tilted back, mouth open, he was snoring.

"God damn the luck, he's gone off! Crazy as a loon . . . and don't you be telling Jimmy I cursed," Tasmin declared to Kit.

"I won't, I won't," Kit promised.

52

Both stared into the distance, solemnly.

When Tasmin got back to the cart she found that Jim and Monty had established a stable if rather stiff peace. Both stared into the distance, solemnly.

"My goodness, couldn't you at least whistle him a tune or something?" Tasmin asked. "He's really not that hard to amuse."

"Never could whistle good," Jim admitted.

Vicky Kennet, on the other side of the wagon, was nursing her Talley, whose meal taking was interrupted briefly by screams from Cook, as His Lordship's bullet was extracted from her thigh. The successful surgeon, to everyone's surprise, was Father Geoffrin, who, after a minimum of probing, captured the bloody slug with his tweezers.

"Why, good for you, Geoff," Tasmin applauded. "It's the first useful thing you've done in six months."

"Oh, I was rather a keen student of anatomy once — attended several operations," Father Geoff said lightly. "I might have made a fair surgeon, I suppose, only I lacked application. Still do."

Cook, who had not thought it quite proper that a French Papist should become familiar with her naked limb, nonetheless thanked him sincerely and promised to remember him when next she made a pudding.

Millicent, for her part, could not seem to stop crying, though her copious tears earned her scant sympathy from the Berrybender party, since she had been quick enough to put on airs and boss them about since Lord B. had made her his mistress. Finally Tom Fitzpatrick, whose sympathies were broad, took the troubled laundress for a walk by the Yellowstone.

Tasmin did not at first reveal her suspicions about her father's sanity. Soon she got her baby to laugh and her husband to smile. When Tasmin was near, Jim became somewhat more playful with Monty, tickling his bare feet with a blade of grass or letting him grab at a brass button on his hunting shirt. Vicky Kennet went off to help Cook with the meal; no one wanted to trust the preparation of vittles to the clumsy Eliza. In the distance all could see Lord Berrybender, slumped against the wagon wheel, sound asleep.

Long after the evening meal was eaten and the sun lost beyond the distant hills, light seemed to cling to the long grassy prairies. Faint stars appeared, and the call of night birds was heard, though it was not yet fully dark. The sky deepened to rose and purple;

the white orb of the moon shone, as if to assist the lingering light.

Though nothing had been said directly about Lord Berrybender's sanity or insanity, a deep collective melancholy seemed to seize the Europeans, starting with Tasmin, who wondered if she would ever have the pleasure of showing off her fine son to old Nanny Craigie, who had raised all the Berrybenders and had been left behind to deal with the several children who had not been invited to travel.

Pedro Yanez, sitting not far away, feared that he would not live to taste again the oily sardines of Barcelona.

Aldo Claricia, his companion, felt that he would give much to eat just one luscious tomato from the fertile fields of Italy.

Venetia Kennet, rocking little Talley in her arms, thought that if she could have just one wish it would be to enjoy once more an opera at Covent Garden.

Father Geoffrin pined for a glimpse of the excellent milliners of Paris, while Bobbety missed most opportunities to attend lectures at the Royal Society — he feared he had not yet quite mastered the complex systems of Linnaeus.

Mary Berrybender, deprived of her helpful tutorials with the late Master Thaw, felt a wish to get back to her Greek, while her friend Piet Van Wely, sweaty from the day's heat, imagined an icy skate on the frozen canals of Holland.

Cook longed to be back in the great kitchen in Northamptonshire, where there was an abundance of ladles and pots, and of reliable kitchen maids as well. At home such a bumbler as Eliza would have been immediately sacked.

Buffum felt that the time had come for her to secure adequate drawing lessons, while her old lover Tim dreamt in the night of musky milkmaids, eager for his embraces.

The weepy Millicent's more modest hope was merely that Lord Berrybender would refrain from pinching her so cruelly.

In short they all of them, wanderers from the old country — Tasmin, Buffum, Bobbety, Mary, Vicky, Geoff, Piet, Pedro, Aldo, Cook, Eliza, Millicent, and Tim — were, for the first time on their long journey, in one mood: the homesick mood. Would those cherished pleasures and traditions, so longingly imagined, ever be theirs again? All were inclined to doubt it — had not the violent prairies already claimed Fraulein Pfretzskaner, stout Charlie Hodges, Old Gorska and his son, Gladwyn, Master Thaw, the somber Holger Sten, Lady Constance Berrybender, many *engagés*, and even the able Captain Aitken? Big White had fallen, it was said. Bobbety had only one eye, and Lord B. himself was much whittled down — Lord Berrybender, whose enthusiasm for the hunt had carried them across the Atlantic, down the serene Ohio, up the muddy Missouri, and now along the swift Yellowstone. Had he now drifted free of his senses, as Tasmin feared? And what would become of them all if, indeed, the master was mad? Only little Kate Berrybender, secure in her attachment to Mr. James Snow, had betrayed no interest in the question.

Even now the old lord was up, bellowing for Lady Constance, whose neck had been broken so long ago.

Jim and Kit and Tom Fitzpatrick had all seen bear tracks that day — in the long twilight Jim and Kit went off for a walk — it wouldn't do to have a grizzly shuffle in and snatch a baby. The old parrot, Prince Talleyrand, who had attached himself to the Broken Hand, wandered around the campfire, occasionally snapping up a scrap.

Tasmin could just dimly see, as twilight finally turned to full dusk, the tall figure of her father, stomping around the wagon on his peg leg, yelling dimly heard curses. He would not lower himself to visit the common campfire but insisted on Cook bringing his vittles, which Cook reluctantly did.

When Jim returned, having seen no bears, Lord Berrybender, though now well fed, was still roaring for his wife to present herself.

"He's gone off, you know, Jimmy — he's

insane," Tasmin told him.

"I expect he's just drunk," Jim replied.

All the claret was in the wagon, of course. Lord Berrybender guarded each bottle as jealously as an eagle might guard its eggs.

"There's more to it," Tasmin insisted. "Listen to me! He thinks Milly is my mother. He thinks Gussie is a Scottish stag. He's gone off, I tell you. I'm afraid Berrybenders have rather a tendency to do that. All of us might be considered rather eccentric, but some of us actually go mad."

"Happens here too," Jim assured her. "It's womenfolks mostly, it seems like. Old Maudey Cockerell, who helped raise me, was mostly cracked."

"What happened to her?" Tasmin asked.

"She wandered off in a blizzard and froze," Jim said.

"At home we've a castle where we're sent, when we go off," Tasmin informed him. "Fortunately we're rich. Castle Dismal, it's called — a great pile on the Scottish coast. Poor folks, of course, are just packed in Bedlam. My own beloved cousin Cimmie went off on her wedding day and had to be sent to Castle Dismal — it's stuffed with maiden aunts, second cousins once removed, batty uncles, dim younger sons, demented bastards, and the mildly deformed. I went there once to visit Cimmie. They're all waited on by servants not much less crazy than themselves. Cimmie insisted on being served fried mice on toast, and so she was. Nothing to do but listen to the wind wail over the North Sea. Papa's own brother, Elphinstone, went out and flung himself off the cliff. They hear his lonely spirit wailing in the storms, and there are a great many storms."

"That won't help us with your pa," Jim observed. "Too far away."

"Correct," Tasmin said. "Castle Dismal, I fear, is rather out of reach."

Venetia Kennet overheard the conversation — indeed, soon the whole camp was alerted to the fact of Lord B.'s derangement. When Cook took him his vittles he mistook her for Gladwyn and demanded that she serve the port.

"I wonder if he'd respond to a little Haydn," Vicky conjectured. "I might just try my cello. It used to calm him when I practiced my scales."

"Have a go, Vicky, if you dare," Tasmin said. "You alone have some chance of calming him, though I doubt it will be with your scales."

53

The heat had been blistering all morning...

The heat had been blistering all morning; the women, even Cook, had reduced their garb to the minimum that modesty required. Even the thinnest shifts were quickly sweated through. The babies were itchy and fretful — of shade there was none.

Little Onion was the first to hear the tremors. She was walking with Coal, who soon heard them too. They both began to run toward the wagon, Coal holding Little Charlie tight. Tasmin was driving the wagon that morning, thinking she might just be able to manage her father, who was now clearly crazed. But she began to feel uneasy, and so did the horses. The ground seemed to be vibrating, a thing she had never experienced before. At first she thought she might have a broken wheel. She had just got down to look when Jim and Kit came racing up.

"Run to the cart, go!" Jim commanded. "Tom will whip up that mare."

Then he and Kit began to fling things out of the wagon — everything portable went, including Lord Berrybender's claret.

Lord Berrybender, waking from a short nap, saw his precious claret being flung out and opened his mouth to protest, but then thought better of it. He felt they might be experiencing an earthquake — though how could an earthquake happen on such open prairie?

Tasmin stood for a moment, paralyzed — she felt in terrible danger, but could not identify the peril — although the ground was shaking.

"Run, I said — don't stand there!" Jim said, giving her a shove.

For the first time since her marriage Tasmin realized that her husband, too, looked scared. The Indians hadn't scared him, the blizzards hadn't scared him, bears didn't scare him, but now he was scared — a realization that put Tasmin to flight. If Jim was scared they must all flee. The cart was near — Tom Fitzpatrick was urging the women into it, telling them to hold tight to their babies. Pedro, Aldo, Tim, Bobbety, Geoff all made for the wagon.

"We might just make the hills — might just, if we fly," the Broken Hand said. Little Kate jumped out of the cart and dashed for the wagon — Jim hastily yanked her aboard.

Tom lashed Gussie, who at once broke into a run — Jim was driving the wagon, urging the horses on. Tasmin just glimpsed the terrified white faces of Bobbety and Father Geoffrin as they raced.

The swift Gussie soon outran the struggling wagon horses. The irregularities of the prairie caused the cart to bounce, as Tom had warned, but he didn't slacken his speed.

Then Tasmin smelled the dust and heard the rumble. To the west the whole horizon was dust — clouds of it rose high in the sky. It was a moment more before she saw the buffalo, throwing up the dust as they raced in a great stampede, right toward the two puny, speeding vehicles — thousands and thousands of buffalo, running as one beast and shaking the ground as they came. Tasmin clutched Monty tight, convinced that they were all surely doomed. The sight that had caused even her husband to blanch froze her with terror, though not for long. It took all her strength to cling to the bouncing cart while holding her child. Tasmin wished she had stayed with Jim — if they were all going to die, let it be together. The little hills they were racing toward seemed infinitely distant, the buffalo not nearly so far — she already felt choked by the smell of the dust.

Yet the old Broken Hand had not given up, and neither had Jim and Kit — Tasmin saw them flogging the wagon horses, now stretched into a full run.

Now and then the Broken Hand would glance at the buffalo and then at the hills that were to be their salvation, if they could only reach them. Tasmin remembered how grim Tom Fitzpatrick had looked when the Blackfeet were chasing him — yet he had won out then, with the help of her husband — perhaps if Gussie didn't fall or the cart break apart he would win out again.

Tasmin found that she could not take her eyes off the charging buffalo — their beastly concentration as they raced many thousands strong held her spellbound. She had no idea how far away the herd was — perhaps half a mile, at most — but she felt no hope. Against such a maelstrom of brute nature, who could possibly stand?

Then she saw several antelope, racing, as they were, for the hills — several antelope and six wolves. The beasts had made the same judgment as Jim and Tom and Kit.

"If we just don't hit a gully we might beat them!" Tom yelled, lashing Gussie afresh.

Once or twice they bounced high but they didn't hit a gully; the women clung grimly to the sideboards Jim had had Signor Claricia build.

Little Onion, with no baby to worry about, was by far the calmest person in the cart. She kept her eyes fixed on the charging buffalo — then she grabbed Tasmin's arm and pointed. Tasmin was at first puzzled — the buffalo were now very close — but what Little Onion drew her attention to was that the herd did have an edge, and along it the beasts were not so thickly packed. There were gaps in the wall of brown.

Then the Thoroughbred, Augusta, racing strongly, suddenly seemed to see the buffalo herself — for a moment her nostrils flared and she flung up her head in surprise, but, in a moment, as if having assessed the danger, her strides quickened, her legs became a blur of motion — everyone hung on, teeth gritted, and then Augusta zigzagged between a few straggling buffalo on the herd's edge and raced up the slope they had been making for.

"My God, what a horse — saved us all!" Tom said, as the mare, sides heaving, slowed and finally came to a stop.

"She saved *us,* but what about Jimmy and the rest?" Tasmin asked, looking back with apprehension — the wagon, considerably slower, was not yet to the slope or free of the pounding herd.

"Whip 'em up, Jimmy! You'll make it! Whip 'em up!" the Broken Hand yelled.

Jim and Kit *were* whipping them up and were just at the edge of the herd as the full tide of beasts swept by.

It was just as safety seemed at hand that catastrophe struck: a lone buffalo suddenly veered from the herd and ran straight into the struggling, straining cart horses. Tasmin watched with horror as the wagon bounced high and came down on top of the bewildered buffalo, whereupon the wooden vehicle simply burst apart. Everyone — Jim and Kit, her father, Millicent, Bobbety and Geoff, the Mediterraneans, Tim, even little Kate — flew out of the wagon in all directions.

"Now there's an odd bust-up for you," the Broken Hand commented. "They get past ten thousand buffalo and then one old cow's brought them to grief."

"I must help Jimmy!" Tasmin said, jumping out of the cart. "Do you think any of them could be alive, Tom, after such a crash?"

"Oh, certainly they'll be alive," Tom told her. "Might have to set a limb or two, a task Cook and I can handle, I suppose."

Dust had drifted so heavily on the prairie between the cart and the wagon that, for a moment, Tasmin had to stop. She coughed and choked — she could see nothing. But when a breeze thinned the dust a bit and she felt confident enough to stumble on toward the wreck, her heart leapt: there were Jim and Kit, working to try and cut the two horses loose from the busted wagon. The buffalo had evidently wandered on. Here and there the company could be seen, picking themselves up — all seemed pleased to be alive, and Jim was not slow in expressing his admiration for Gussie.

"I never saw a horse run that fast," he said. "She saved those babies, for sure."

"Why, she did *go*, didn't she, splendid old girl," Lord Berrybender remarked amiably.

"A tribute to her breeding, Byerly Turk, you know. Where's my Milly? Don't see *her* anywhere. I was rather in a fog, yesterday — hardly myself. Kept wondering where your mother was, Tasmin. Clean forgot she was dead."

"Well, Mother is dead, I fear, Papa," Tasmin told him.

Tasmin, Jim, and Kit exchanged looks, but said nothing. His Lordship seemed to be sane again — the great fright and the great race had brought him out of the fog.

"Great pity about the claret, though," Lord B. lamented. "Hope we run into that prince again — no doubt he'll have some to spare."

To the east the buffalo still ran, a brown river a mile wide, thousands and thousands.

"Why do they run like that, Jimmy?" Tasmin asked.

Jim just shrugged. "Something spooked them, I guess — might have been Indians," he told her.

"Or lightning," Kit suggested.

"Can we fix it?" Jim asked Aldo Claricia, who was poking around in a discouraged fashion in the ruins of the wagon.

"Gone . . . *finito!*" the Italian said. "We can only use it to make a fire."

"We don't have the guns, either — threw them out," Pedro Yanez reminded them.

"Well, we can go back and find the guns — maybe one or two of them ain't broke," the Broken Hand said.

"Best count up the people, first," Jim advised. "We need to be sure nobody's missing."

"I don't see young Miss Mary, or the Dutchman," Tom Fitzpatrick mentioned. "We didn't *leave* them, did we?"

Everyone looked around. There was no sign of Mary Berrybender, or of Piet Van Wely.

"They weren't in the cart," Vicky remembered.

"Oh dear, I think I saw them walking off a bit earlier, with their nets," Buffum said. "I'm not at all sure that they came back."

"You can't mean it! My dear brat lost — and she was doing so well with her Greek lessons, too," Lord Berrybender said. Then he sank down, sobbing, eyes wild again.

"Slap him, Milly, will you? You're a good touch," Tasmin said. "We don't want him slipping into the fog again, just now."

Milly carried out her commission with a will, peppering Lord Berrybender's cheeks with a succession of stinging slaps, until he waved her away.

"Not now, Milly — not now," he protested, thinking the pesky laundress was attempting to arouse him.

"I'm going back to see if I can find any guns that ain't broken," Jim said. "I lost my bow, too — if we don't find something that will shoot, then we're looking at starvation time."

Just then Prince Talleyrand, very dusty, landed on Tom Fitzpatrick's shoulder. When the buffalo came he had risen high in the air, but then so had the dust.

Tasmin insisted on hurrying off with Jim and Kit in the cart, determined to do her best to find Mary and Piet.

"You won't mind if I look for my sister, will you, Jimmy?" she asked.

"You can look," Jim said, "but if they got caught in that stampede there won't be much to bury."

The Belgian rifle and two other guns were recovered undamaged, as were a number of skillets and cook pots. All the clothes had been trampled to rags, and of Lord Berrybender's claret, only a few shards of glass remained. All the books had been thoroughly trampled — only a page or two, blown by the breeze, fluttered here and there in the grass. Tasmin gathered up every page she saw — there a page of Byron, here one of Mrs. Edgeworth's, there several pages of Father Geoffrin's beloved Marmontel.

"I'd rather read a page than read nothing," she said, tucking the pages into her bosom.

Jim and Kit, with Tasmin following hopefully in the cart, searched from one border to the other of the area of stampede — a thing easily done, since the buffalo had beaten away most of the grass — but not a trace of either Mary or Piet could be found.

"If they're alive at least they won't starve — Mary can sniff out tubers, you know," Tasmin reminded them.

"She can even talk to snakes — and some snakes are good eating," Jim pointed out.

Kit Carson had always been famed for his keen eyesight and his acute sense of smell, and yet he had never sniffed out a tuber, and was not entirely sure what one looked like. In love with Tasmin though he was, somehow just being with her made him feel that his own gifts were slightly inferior. Usually this made him mopey, but on this occasion he was too glad to be alive to mope.

Far to the east, the buffalo that had almost trampled them had run themselves out and were grazing quietly on the sunny plain.

"Kit saved us, as much as the mare," Jim pointed out. "The minute he seen the dust we knew we had to run."

They were in the cart — Kit was roaming around by the river, hoping to pick up clues as to what might have happened to Mary and Piet.

"Good for Kit — I'll try to control my urge to pick on him for a day or two," Tasmin said. "Right now I confess I'm rather atingle with the pleasure of being alive. Can't we celebrate?"

Jim looked at her curiously, not at once catching her meaning.

"It's how I felt after the hailstorm, shortly before we were married," Tasmin recalled. "I might have been dead, but instead I was alive and atingle! It calls for celebration."

When he started to answer, Tasmin stopped his mouth with a passionate kiss. Lately, due to the dust and the dirt, to Monty and the various frustrations of travel, their amours, from her point of view at least, had become rather sluggish, pleasures that occurred when she was half asleep, or else sweaty and rather more in need of a bath.

Now, though death had been close at hand, it had been defeated.

"We could have been mashed quite flat, but we're alive, Jimmy!" she continued.

Jim realized what she meant — what she wanted. Kit Carson was only one hundred yards away, scanning the riverbank.

"But Kit's right there," Jim said.

"Hang Kit! I'm so atingle I can't wait!" Tasmin said, giving him another long kiss. "Quick, quick — I'll help you get it out."

Jim barely had time to stop Gussie before Tasmin had it out.

54

Mary Berrybender whacked and whacked...

Mary Berrybender whacked and whacked with the thorny briars — her dear Piet's naked back and rump were quite streaked with blood: provident man that he was, Piet had noted the location of an excellent thicket of thorny briars the day before. The two of them had wandered off early, in order to hurry to the briar patch and select just the sharpest thorns so that Piet might enjoy a thorough scourging, a pleasure not always available on the trackless and, in some regions, thornless plains.

At first Mary had been reluctant to thoroughly cut Piet up with these thorny briars, but he had convinced her that such whippings were commonly practiced in his native Holland, both in public gymnasia and in the basements of many stately homes. Some of the wealthier Hollanders, Piet claimed, even employed a special servant to see that there was always a good supply of nettles, briars, or stout flexible switches cut from young trees. Sometimes the servant was even required to do the scourging, although that would normally be handled by the lady of the house — or, in some cases, by a cousin.

"Oh, yes, it's quite necessary for healthy circulation," Piet assured Mary, the first time he stripped down and persuaded her to lash him savagely.

"Keeps the blood flowing . . . keeps us warm during our cold winters," Piet said. "Harder, little one. No need to hold back."

Not wishing to disappoint, Mary soon learned to lay on vigorously and expertly with either briars or switches.

Evidently there was a sound biological basis for Piet's claim of improved circulation; by the time Mary had the blood flowing good, from a few sharp strikes to his rump, Piet would exhibit as perky an erection as could be expected from a man of admittedly modest dimensions. Often it was necessary for Mary to bloody Piet's whole back, from neck to thighs, before an effusion resulted — after which the two of them would bathe in the cold, swift Yellowstone; then Mary would carefully apply a little of Cook's useful salve to Piet's many scratches.

"A healthy life is the best life, little one," Piet would invariably remind her, after which he might nap for a bit, naked on a rock, while Mary, never idle when there were sci- entific investigations to pursue, would set off with her net in search of dragonflies, mantises, or even the lowly grasshopper.

There were, however, times when Piet's circulation was very slow to improve; by the time Mary noticed the great dust cloud thrown up by the stampeding buffalo, her arm was already quite tired from whipping, and many of the thorns had broken off during her scourge. They had nothing to fear from the buffalo themselves — the herd passed at least a mile to the south — but for some reason Piet's dimensions were very slow to expand, though his back and hinder parts were thoroughly bloody.

And then, most inconveniently, who should appear on the plain to the west of them but Monsieur Charbonneau, accompanied by a piebald man on an equally piebald but very slow horse.

"Here comes our long-lost interpreter — what shall we do, Piet? He might consider these healthy exercises somewhat unorthodox," Mary said.

"Damn Charbonneau, why *will* he appear at such inconvenient times?" Piet complained. "My circulation is very reluctant today — an excess of bile, I fear. Too much bile is sure to drag down one's constitution."

"On this occasion nothing seems to have come up," Mary admitted. "Wasn't it more effective when I merely fondled you under your smock?"

"Effective, yes . . . but is life to be merely

efficiency?" Piet asked, before dashing into the river to wash the blood off his back. Mary felt rather downcast — she hated for her Piet to suffer disappointment.

"I suppose I'm about of an age to copulate," she told him. "I'm as old as Coal, and she has had a brat."

Piet at once shook his head.

"Not the same," he replied. "I must have my rigors. Rigor! It's what has made the Dutch a mighty race."

"Even so, I think I'll ask Tasmin what's the best way to copulate — Tassie copulates all the time and perhaps could provide useful instruction," Mary told him as she proceeded to rub a good bit of Cook's salve on his scratched-up nether parts.

Much as he liked his little English dewdrop, Piet was horrified by this suggestion. Tampering with a Berrybender's virginity would very likely get him fired.

Besides, he liked to be whipped, and one of the few things the New World didn't lack was excellent brambles. A good scourging was far better for a fellow than any form of contact with the female pudendum — so dark, so dank, so hairy.

55

"Your friend rides a very slow horse . . ."

"Now there's a sight, Greasy," Charbonneau exclaimed, as the two of them came slowly down the slope toward the Yellowstone. "Why do you suppose our little English miss is whipping that Dutchman so?"

Greasy Lake, plodding along on his good horse Galahad, of course observed the whipping — the naked man's back was streaked with blood — but he could make no sense of such a proceeding. He had seen many men beat girls — old men almost always beat girls, if they happened to have one handy, as a wife or a slave. But, among his people, men who submitted to beatings by women — much less girls — quickly became laughing-stocks. Occasionally one would be laughed right out of camp.

In his many years of travel up and down the plains, Greasy Lake had seen so many strange happenings that he did not get upset if something a little out of the ordinary happened. Once he had found a live eagle, trapped in the horns of two dead elk. The elk had huge racks and must have locked

404

them in the course of a fight; then both starved to death. But an eagle certainly had no business getting himself caught between the horns of two elk. Greasy Lake had worked for more than a hour to free the bird, which was young; and then, instead of being grateful, the eagle had gashed his hand with its beak before it flew away. The rescue had occurred at a little creek that ran into the Beaverhead River. Greasy Lake immediately washed his wound in ice-cold water, but the gash became infected and his whole arm began to swell. The situation was serious enough that Greasy Lake sought out an old Shoshone woman who was good with herbal poultices. When she found out how he had got the wound she gave him a lecture about presuming to interfere in the problems of eagles.

"That eagle would have died if I hadn't saved it," Greasy Lake protested, but the old Shoshone woman continued to address him spitefully.

"What do you know — you aren't an eagle," she pointed out. "If you are going to go around letting eagles bite you, then quit wasting my time."

None of that explained why the English girl was whipping the Dutchman — it just meant that Greasy Lake had learned to take a calm attitude toward things that seemed a little bit unusual.

"Perhaps they made a sweat lodge," he suggested. "Sometimes the Sioux and even the Assiniboines hit themselves with branches when they come out of a sweat lodge."

Toussaint Charbonneau had been in sweat lodges, and knew that warriors sometimes whacked themselves afterward, but the Dutchman Mary Berrybender had just scratched up was no warrior. He was a man who studied centipedes and grasshoppers, weeds and seeds. Why would he need a whipping?

"That was a fine flogging you just gave our friend Piet," he remarked when he and Greasy Lake finally arrived at the river.

"*Bonjour* — yes indeed, monsieur," Mary said. "Piet finds it extremely hygienic — many Europeans enjoy a good spanking, I believe. I don't care for the practice myself, though it is said to relieve the menses."

"This is Greasy Lake," Charbonneau told her. "As you can see he slicks himself up with every kind of grease he can find — keeps off the skeeters, he claims."

Piet found it odd that the old Indian who accompanied Charbonneau was so splotchy in color. One of his cheeks was nearly white, the other bronze, his arms rather mottled. As a keen student of genetics, Piet would have liked to question the old man about his ancestry, but decided that it might be prudent to wait for a few days until friendly relations could be established.

"You're lucky you didn't get caught in that buffalo run," Charbonneau told them. "Where's the rest of the party?"

"South, I suppose," Mary said. "We lingered here because of these excellent briars."

Greasy Lake was not much interested in the Dutchman but the young woman was a more singular case. He had heard rumors among the Mandans that a sorceress was traveling with the English party, a young woman who befriended turtles and could converse with snakes. He had a notion this young woman was the sorceress. As a gesture of politeness, he tipped his cap to her.

"Your friend rides a very slow horse, monsieur," Mary observed, staring fixedly at Greasy Lake, who immediately began to feel regret that he had decided to accompany Sharbo to the Yellowstone. By so doing he had come to the place of a witch, and now he was stuck. In order to leave he would have to turn his back on the small English witch, and he did not think that would be wise. She might locate one of the Snake people and instruct him to bite Greasy Lake's organ while he slept; such a thing had happened to Big Muskrat, of the Crows. Big Muskrat had made an enemy of a powerful old witch, as a result of which a snake had wiggled into his blankets and bit his organ, which had turned black and stayed black for several years. Big Muskrat had never again been able to be of use to women.

"It might be wise to rejoin our party," Mary said. "Will you be coming with us, monsieur?"

"Oh yes," Charbonneau said. "I wonder if that little boy of mine can crawl around yet."

"Indeed he can," Mary said. "I'm afraid he crawled into a rather sharp cactus only yesterday."

As Sharbo, the witch, and the Dutchman proceeded south along the riverbank, Greasy Lake thought he might use the fact that his horse was so slow to good advantage — he might just gradually fade from sight behind them, without exciting the attention of the witch.

That plan failed because — to Greasy Lake's dismay — his horse, Galahad, suddenly acquired new energies. The old nag began to prance and even trot — instead of dropping back behind the three foot travelers, he was soon bouncing ahead of them. Galahad, who, to most observers, seemed little better than dead, began to behave like a colt again. This behavior on the part of a horse that was at least thirty years old strengthened Greasy Lake's conviction that he was dealing with a powerful witch.

But there was worse to come. Just beyond the dusty patch of prairie where the buffalo had had their run, Greasy Lake looked around and was startled to see, not far to the south, the Wandering Hill. This was a very bad shock indeed — it was the third time in his life that Greasy Lake had seen the Wandering Hill — and to see it even once usually meant death, for the small devils who lived in the hill were known to loose their deadly arrows at the slightest provocation.

Long ago, near the Little Sioux River, Greasy Lake had seen the Wandering Hill, just a small, conical mound with a single tree on top, and he had escaped the devils' deadly grass-blade arrows by crawling for more than an hour on his belly in the same tall weeds; years later, near the holy mountains of the Sioux, as he was building a burial scaffold for his second wife, he had seen the hill once more, this time many miles farther to the west. And now here the deadly hill was again, on the Yellowstone, and, what's more, his prancing horse was carrying him right toward it, a thing that would be sure to affront the short, large-headed devils who lived in it; they would hardly look tolerantly on a man who had been so forceful as to come near their hill three times in his life.

He stopped his horse at once, but Sharbo and the two others passed him and walked right toward it.

"Stop! It's the Wandering Hill — don't go near it," he cried, but only Sharbo understood him, and even he didn't stop.

"Why, I thought the Wandering Hill was supposed to be way down on the Cimarron, where Jedediah Smith got killed," Sharbo said. "Or was it by the Platte — I can't be sure."

"It wanders, that's why it's called the Wandering Hill!" Greasy Lake chided. How stupid could Sharbo be? The fact that the devils kept the hill moving was well understood by all the tribes of the plains and mountains. The presence of the Wandering Hill explained why ten thousand buffalo had suddenly taken it into their heads to stampede; for it was known to the tribes that the devils inside the hill could bring disorder in the natural world whenever they chose to. At their whim water holes suddenly dried up in a day, or dry rivers suddenly surged with floodwaters. The devils could shake the highest mountains, causing walls of snow to come sliding down. Sometimes small bands of native people who had carelessly camped too close to the mountains were buried alive when the devils sent snow walls plummeting down.

Once past the Wandering Hill the old nag Galahad suddenly lost his newfound energy and became, again, an old horse who could barely lift his feet. Greasy Lake well understood that the devils were toying with him now. The stampede of the buffalo had been merely a small demonstration of their power.

These large-headed devils, he knew, were very old. They had been in the hill even before the People had slid off the back of the great turtle who had borne them to their places on the prairie.

But it occurred to him that the small English witch might, for the moment, have a power of her own sufficient to hold the devils in check. It was not only large things that had power. The small rattlesnakes that abounded in the spring had venom much more powerful than that of the old fat snakes who lounged around their dens eating rats and ground squirrels. It was a tiny rattlesnake who had bitten Big Muskrat on his rod and turned it flaccid and black.

"You shouldn't have walked so close to the Wandering Hill," Greasy Lake scolded, when he and Sharbo finally left the small yellowish mound behind them. "Powerful devils live there! It's a wonder they didn't shoot you with their grass-blade arrows."

Toussaint Charbonneau was usually respectful when Indians talked to him about mystical matters and things that went beyond what could be learned through the senses; but in his view the notion of a wandering hill was nonsense. There were several small conical hills, here and there on the prairies, that just happened to have a single tree on top of them — none of them moved, of course, but it was possible to believe that they moved because they looked so much alike.

Nothing annoyed Greasy Lake more than to have some ill-informed white man try to explain away knowledge that the People had held for hundreds of summers. Hadn't his own grandfather seen the Wandering Hill, far to the south by a stream called the Brazos? If Sharbo wanted to remain ignorant of the deeper truths of existence, that was, of course, his right; but he would regret his ignorance someday, when next he came upon the Wandering Hill; perhaps next time he would have no small English witch to protect him. Then he would see how quickly the merciless devils filled him full of arrows made from poisonous grass.

"Explain it to me, Greasy," Charbonneau asked — he knew the old man was annoyed by his dismissive attitude. "How could a hill that was over by the Little Sioux get clean across the country to the Yellowstone?"

"It is easy for a hill to move," Greasy Lake explained. "All it takes is for the devils inside it to summon up a big wind. A hill is only so much dust — even in a bad storm, dust is always moving. In the land of winds it is easy to blow a small hill from one place to another. The spirits just take the dust from the hill on the Little Sioux and whirl it over this way. The hill dissolves and then forms again — who knows how far the dust will have gone?"

412

Greasy Lake stopped his lecture — Sharbo was not really listening to him. Travel was an odd thing, he reflected. The plains were a very large place. It was possible to climb a high hill and see many miles, from one mountain range to another, and the plains would seem to be perfectly empty, so empty that it should have been easy to travel great distances across them and see no one. But the truth was different — indeed it was seldom possible to travel even for a few days without running into other human beings, people like old Sharbo, whom he had not particularly wanted to meet. The plains that seemed so empty were actually crawling with people. Being alone on the prairies had never been easy, but now it had become impossible. Even the Wandering Hill was harder and harder to avoid — and that, in Greasy Lake's opinion, was a development that didn't bode well.

56

. . . talk of supernatural evil put Kit Carson off his feed . . .

"Here we are in the middle of a virgin wilderness, and yet some things never seem to change," Tasmin remarked, watching Little Onion rock Monty to sleep in her arms.

That day Jim had shown them several spurting geysers, after which all the women had a good bath in the deliciously warm, bubbly pools nearby.

"What things?" Jim asked. Watched by the ever-present Kate, he was just finishing the wrappings on a new bow — his old one had been broken by the stampeding buffalo.

"Your friend Kate won't go away — that's one thing that doesn't change," Tasmin replied. "It might just be, Kate, that now and again my husband and I might welcome a moment or two of privacy."

"I'm just working on this bow — I don't guess it hurts if she watches," Jim replied. "She might have to wrap one herself, sometime."

"That's highly unlikely, I'd say," Tasmin objected.

She considered Little Onion, who sat not far away with Monty. Had it not been for Little Onion's cleverness in devising an excellent travois from the wreckage of the wagon, all three babies would have had to be carried all the way across the valley of the Yellowstone. Thanks to the travois, the infants traveled in some comfort. Little Onion looked lovingly at the baby — her devotion to Monty was profound. And yet Tasmin thought she saw a sadness in the young woman's face.

"Get, brat!" Tasmin said to Kate, with such force that for once Kate obeyed — she was soon to be seen sitting on the knee of the Broken Hand, another of her favorites among the mountain men.

"Your other wife looks sad, Jimmy," Tasmin said. "I like our Little Onion very much and I don't wish her to be sad — I suppose it's because I get so much of you and she gets so little. Close to nothing, in fact. Glad as I am that it's me who gets the most, I do feel rather troubled for our Little Onion."

Jim continued his wrapping for a moment, and then looked up at Tasmin.

"She thinks I'm giving her back," he said to Tasmin, in low tones.

"But back where?"

"To her band," Jim said. "We'll probably meet them soon. Her people will think I'm returning her because she's barren."

"But you're *not* taking her back!" Tasmin declared. "She's a very fine girl, and our son's most loyal friend. She shan't be delivered up for some old man to abuse."

Jim said no more — he concentrated on his work. But Tasmin's agitation would not subside.

"She's no older than Mary, I wouldn't suppose," she said. "She has plenty of time to have babies — in fact no one's tried to give her one. How can she have them if no one mates with her?"

Jim said nothing. He regretted giving in to the pleadings of his deceased wife, Sun Girl, who was insistent that he marry her sister; and if he hadn't, Little Onion *would* undoubtedly have been sold to the violent old man who wanted her. Now he had come to like Little Onion himself. She was unfailingly helpful, quick to take the initiative when it came to any of the camp chores. And yet Tasmin was the wife of his heart — he was not sure how best to proceed with Little Onion. It was just one of the puzzling dilemmas that were apt to arise when a man ceased to travel alone, as Jim had for long preferred to do. He had had no way of predicting that he would ever meet a woman like Tasmin — yet it had happened: they mated, they had a child, and now he could not foresee a time when he could again travel alone. His great trip on Joe Walker's little mare, from the Knife River to the Green, might have been a last clean fling. Then, there had only been himself, the horse, the prairies, the snowfields, the winter sky. Life seemed simple again for a few weeks, although the forces that would destroy simplicity forever had already been set in motion.

Now, as they neared the place of the rendezvous with Drum Stewart and the other trappers, Jim was far from sure what to do next. He and Kit and Tom had had to hunt hard, just keeping the Berrybender expedition supplied with meat. They had done no trapping, had no furs to trade; they would have to rely on credit if they were to supply themselves for the winter ahead. They had three guns but not much powder; they had his bow, one cart, three horses, and a passel of people who had a tendency to quarrel with one another. At least Charbonneau was back — if they did run into Indians he could talk to them, in speech or in sign.

For some reason Charbonneau had brought with him old Greasy Lake, a wanderer of the plains whose origins now no one knew: most tribespeople shied away from the old man, either because they thought he brought bad luck or possibly just because his rambling prophecies were extremely boring to listen to. His horse was so old it could barely walk. No sooner had he and Charbonneau arrived than the old man began to talk about the Wandering Hill, a cone of earth that seemed now to be in one place, now another — Pomp Charbonneau knew the legend and had even spotted what he thought was the hill when they were hard by the Missouri; and Tom Fitzpatrick, usually skeptical, had been startled in the extreme to hear that the hill had moved once again.

"They say Jedediah Smith saw the Wandering Hill the day before the Kiowas killed him," Tom remarked.

Any talk of supernatural evil put Kit Carson off his feed at once. News that the deadly hill might be nearby stirred Kit to such an extent that he borrowed one of the wagon horses and hurried on down to the rendezvous, meaning to return with a few borrowed horses so that the party could make better time.

Tasmin soon saw that Jim did not want to talk about Little Onion. He never liked to talk about matters emotional — they were things not easily fixed. Jim's habit was to ignore such difficulties, to do nothing and hope that a solution would somehow turn up. It was this passivity in regard to awkward human situations that annoyed her most about him. One thing she could never be was passive. Jim Snow liked to slip by human problems, whereas she preferred to fling herself at them.

Unable to bear the melancholy look on Little Onion's face, Tasmin went over and hugged the girl and joined in humming, for a time, the little song that Onion was crooning to Monty. When Monty slept, and had been laid on the soft grass, Tasmin took Little Onion in her arms. She had never done such a thing before — Jim was startled to see it, and so was Little Onion, who kept quite still, like a captured fawn.

"We are not taking you back," Tasmin said.

She had learned a little sign; now she made the sign for sister. It seemed to Tasmin that she could feel this young woman's loneliness; it was there in the resistance of her body, and, of course, she had good reason to be fearful. Already she knew the hard ways of men — and they were in dangerous country. The future could always darken, and not only for their Little Onion. Tasmin wished she could explain to the girl that she was a loyal friend who would not desert her; yet she felt that she lacked the language to get the message across. Little Onion smiled, but in her eyes there was still a sadness.

That night, after an embrace, Tasmin couldn't sleep — she felt agitated rather than soothed. The mountain nights were already chill, so she took a blanket and walked down to a little grassy meadow where deer had been grazing at sunset. She felt she had failed to assuage Little Onion; now what she needed to do was take a sounding of her own emotions. How *would* she feel, for example, if Jim gave Little Onion a child and secured her place, as it were? Hadn't her own father produced thirty bastards? What if Little Onion produced a half brother or sister for Monty? Tasmin found that she could not predict what her feelings might be, should such occur. She knew that she herself would like more children — though perhaps no more children just now, when comforts were so scarce. In the security and order of their great manse in Northamptonshire, with Cook and Nanny Craigie in attendance, of course she would desire more children. But they were not at the moment in Northamptonshire. They were in wild, mountainous country, where great snow-tipped peaks seemed to stretch south forever. Her first delivery had been hard enough, but then she had at least been well sheltered during her lying-in. Now she was in a place where there were not even trading posts. What if she got pregnant again, which was not unlikely, due to Jim Snow's recent enthusiasm for their rutting? Where would they be when the child came — Santa Fe? Or in any town at all?

Moonlight shone on the great snowy peaks beyond the meadows. This wilderness of high mountains and green valleys was extraordinary — and yet, to Tasmin's eye, there was just too much of it. How much longer must they go tramping through it? Were there never to be clean sheets, frequent baths, and well-laid tables again? She remembered clearly the moment of exaltation she had felt that first morning on the Missouri; the feeling had carried her far without regret, and yet how much farther must it carry her? It was not so much England she missed as simply the minimal comforts of civilization: something as simple as a bed, a wash pitcher, or a new novel by Mr. Scott.

The little rill beyond the meadow where she went to bathe was so small that Tasmin could almost straddle it. The water was like moving ice — she dropped her shift and squatted in it, dipping her hands and splashing the chill water over her dusty, sweaty face and body. The air, with its mountain chill, soon had her covered with goose bumps — and yet the cold and the sense of being clean were delicious. Even in her most tomboyish years she had always liked to come home and get clean, an ideal that now, as wife, mother, and wilderness traveler, was often impossible to attain. Dust, sweat, blood, babies' drool, breast milk, the rich oozy seed of the male, and trail dust would likely be hers for some time to come. Only now and again, when she happened on a mineral pool or an icy stream, could she enjoy the fine feeling that came with having clean skin, fresh cheeks, puckered nipples, dripping legs.

When Tasmin stood up and reached for her shift she suddenly saw the great bear, standing only a few feet away, in the meadow through which she meant to pass as she walked back to camp. Too late she remembered that Jim had told her bears were likely to be on the prowl at night, particularly in places where there were many deer.

Now there a bear was — a large, dark shape, its coat shining silver in the moonlight. For a moment Tasmin froze, afraid to move; she held her dusty shift in front of her, longing to have her able husband by her side; but her husband, sated by their embrace, was sleeping soundly some distance away. She was alone with a grizzly bear, the most feared animal in the West.

Yet the bear was not attacking — it had not advanced even a foot. It merely watched her. Kit had told her that the great bears were very curious. Probably this one had never seen a young English lady at her ablutions before. The bear looked at Tasmin, Tasmin looked at the bear. She thought of yelling — and yet, once the first shock passed, she didn't feel like yelling — it might only provoke this great bruin, who could be on her long before anyone from the camp could arrive.

"Shoo, bear," she said in a tiny voice. "Shoo, now . . . shoo. Do go about your business elsewhere. I have a young child. I have to be going soon."

The bear merely watched.

"I suppose that wasn't a very respectful speech," Tasmin added.

Then she waited — and the bear waited too.

Tasmin had hoped to slip back into camp naked — she hated to have to slip the dirty shift over her clean body — in the morning she meant to huddle in their blankets while Little Onion washed a few clothes. But what should she do now that there was a bear? Would the bear care whether she was clothed or naked? Jim had told her that Indian women had to take serious precautions when their menses were flowing, lest bears be drawn to the blood. Tasmin had no immediate worry on that score — at the moment her menses weren't flowing.

Several minutes passed, with neither Tasmin nor the bruin advancing at all, though once the bear did turn its head. Little by little, Tasmin became less frightened. Somehow, perhaps wrongly, she had come to believe that her bruin meant her no harm. She might, to the bear, be no more than a novelty, her bathing a spectacle of a new sort, interesting enough to briefly interrupt whatever hunt had been in progress.

"All right, Sir Bruin, if you are a sir," Tasmin said. "My baby will be crying for me

soon. I fear I must end our charming inter-
view."

Yet she hesitated to move, hoping the bear
would move first.

It didn't, so gathering all her courage,
Tasmin walked straight across the meadow,
passing, as she did, within ten feet of the
bear, a proximity the bear found too startling
to be borne. With a snuff it turned tail,
splashed across the creek where she had just
bathed, and was gone.

In the morning, once news of the en-
counter spread, almost the whole camp company tramped down to the meadow to
examine the bear's footprints, two of which
were clearly visible in the mud by the little
creek.

Jim Snow was so flabbergasted that he
could scarcely speak — his wife, while he
slept, had walked right by a grizzly bear, and
yet been spared.

"Your bruin will do strange things," Tom
Fitzpatrick said. "I guess its belly was full —
that's why it let you go, Lady Tasmin."

"Why, its foot's bigger than mine — what a
huge brute it must have been," Lord
Berrybender declared. "I have few rivals in
the world when it comes to foot size, you
know."

"I think it liked me — that bear," Tasmin
said. "It was perfectly well behaved — in fact
I liked it too. Nothing wrong with a bruin if

the niceties are observed."

Just then came a whoop from the south. Kit and Billy Sublette, Pomp Charbonneau, and Drummond Stewart came loping up the slope, leading several horses.

"Good for them, I'm plumb tired of walking," Tom Fitzpatrick announced.

At the sight of Drummond Stewart, Vicky Kennet produced a deep blush, evident to Tasmin, though none of the men noticed.

"Why, your fine gallant returns," Tasmin remarked, smiling. "I suppose the last weeks have been rather a bore for you, Vicky — an absence of frolics takes its toll on us avid girls."

"Do hush, Tasmin — I'm just glad to see him," Vicky said.

57

Then, at the big rendezvous in the Valley of the Chickens . . .

"I'm telling you what I saw with my own eyes," Greasy Lake said loudly — he was filled with passion for his mission, an important mission upon which the safety of the People depended.

"Go on with you — you never bring anything but bad news," Walkura said. He was the greatest chief of the Utes — he and some of his warriors had once run off with more than a thousand horses in a raid into California; and now here was old Greasy Lake, upsetting his village with some wild talk about an English girl who could talk to a bear.

"I try to warn people when there is danger, that's all," Greasy Lake insisted. His feelings were hurt that Walkura was behaving so coolly to him, and acting so skeptically about the news he had ridden hard to bring. Of course, Walkura had always been a difficult person — though a great raider, of course. Greasy Lake would rather have taken the news to Blue Thunder, his cousin, but the camp of the Piegans was many days north and Walkura's camp only half a day's ride west.

"Not only that, there's more," Greasy Lake declared. "They don't just talk to one bear, they talk to three."

He had ridden on to the rendezvous with the other whites and seen the two bear cubs, which were as friendly with the trappers as two dogs would be. They didn't even try to eat the three babies, but merely licked them in their faces as a dog might.

Greasy Lake had had no intention of getting into a dispute about the Bear people when he followed the English girl to the creek that night — he followed her because he had always liked to watch naked women bathing themselves. The Englishwoman happened to be too tall and stringy for his taste — he liked short, compact women, young ones about fourteen or fifteen summers when possible. This particular Englishwoman was shapely enough, as such women went; it was interesting to watch her as she squatted naked in the stream. But of course Greasy Lake ceased to care how she looked the minute he saw the bear, a male grizzly, one of the largest he had ever seen. Yet the bear made no attempt to attack the woman, and when she told it to leave, in her firm voice, it trotted right off, a shocking thing to see.

Then, at the big rendezvous in the Valley of the Chickens — so called because of the abundance of prairie hens — there were the two bear cubs, being petted and made over by all the trappers. This obvious alliance between the white people and the Bear people was such a shock that he didn't even wait to secure the presents that he was sure William Ashley, the chief of the traders, would be happy to give him. Instead, he had rushed right over to the Ute encampment to warn the People, a warning Walkura received with unseemly rudeness, although several of his elders, old wise men who knew how extremely uncommon it was for any humans to successfully ally themselves with the Bear people, paid respectful attention and listened closely while Greasy Lake told his story.

"And listen, that is not all!" Greasy Lake insisted to his audience of elders. "There is a small witch there who can talk to snakes — according to the Sin Killer himself she is even friendly with the Turtle people."

"It sounds like a story somebody made up while they were drunk," Walkura replied. "White people playing with bears and little witches talking to snakes. What next?"

"It is a family of witches, I tell you," Greasy Lake went on. "The Piegan Blue Thunder traveled with them for many weeks. He says there are even whites who can swallow fire and not be burned."

"Now that's silly talk," Walkura said.

But then old No Teeth, himself a powerful medicine man — he had once made a mistake with a poisoned root, a mistake which caused his gums to turn black and all his teeth to fall out — remembered something important.

"If the Sin Killer is with them, that's really not good," No Teeth claimed. "The Sin Killer has eaten the lightning, remember. And now he's married to a witch who can talk to the Bear people — that's not good."

"Oh, that Piegan was probably lying," Na-Ta-Ha remarked. "The Piegans are all liars and Blue Thunder is the worst of them."

"How would you know — have you met him?" Greasy Lake asked. He was becoming more and more irritated at the stupidity and rudeness of these Utes. Of course, it was nothing new — no Ute had ever been particularly nice to him. Now he had ridden his horse hard to get to this village and warn the Utes of a big danger, and yet only one or two old men were bothering to take him seriously. No Teeth seemed to believe him, but No Teeth's reputation as a medicine man had fallen off in recent years. A medicine man foolish enough to consume a poisoned root could not expect to command much respect. Medicine men were supposed to know about such things.

Though Walkura and a few other strong

warriors were more or less indifferent to the news Greasy Lake brought, the young braves of the band were another matter. They were young and ready for any fight. There was nothing they would like better than to race over and kill all the trappers; perhaps they could even capture a few women, young women they could copulate with.

High Shoulders, the boldest of the young braves, the one Walkura expected to have the most trouble with, made so bold as to offer a comment, although young warriors were supposed to be quiet and respectful when their elders were holding a serious discussion.

"It sure sounds like a family of witches to me," High Shoulders said — "and besides, those trappers have no business being in our country anyway. I say we round up some warriors and go kill them all."

"Who asked you to say? You don't make decisions about war in this tribe," Walkura told him sharply.

The young brave's comment was particularly irritating because the part about the trappers being in Ute country without permission was true. These big rendezvous had been going on for several years — various chiefs had proposed attacking them but too many of the Ute women had got used to getting nice presents from William Ashley or Eulalie Bonneville or whoever had the best presents at any particular time. The presents, it was true, had begun to have a corrupting effect. Some Utes now claimed that they couldn't possibly catch a fish without the white man's fishhooks, an absurdity, since even the warriors making the claim had caught hundreds of fish on nice homemade bone fishhooks. Or, if not on bone fishhooks, in big reed fish traps.

The problem of the trappers and their big annual party was one Walkura had worried about in his mind for several years. It was true that the Utes ought to get together and kill all these trappers — they had trapped many of the streams and ponds so hard that it was not possible to find even a single beaver in some of them. All the furs they took ought to have been Ute furs, by right, and yet, in Walkura's experience the trappers were vigorous fighters — any force that moved against them had to be ready for serious fighting, with, very likely, considerable loss of life.

It was a lingering, troubling problem, and one Walkura had never quite got around to dealing with, and now here was that old pest, Greasy Lake, stirring up the young men and giving them dreams of battle.

"There is one more thing — I nearly forgot," Greasy Lake told them. "It's the worst thing of all."

"What does that mean — did one of those witches get ahold of your penis and pull it off?" Walkura asked, hoping to get a laugh. The young men were all getting in a war mode; a little comedy might cool them down.

"I don't go near witches — no one pulled my penis off," Greasy Lake countered indignantly. "What I was going to say before you interrupted me was that I saw the Wandering Hill."

His remark at once silenced the crowd. Old No Teeth was so startled that he let some tobacco fall out of his mouth. Na-Ta-Ha looked worried. Of course, medicine men knew better than anyone that a sighting of the Wandering Hill was no joke.

"Are you sure?" Walkura asked.

"Of course I'm sure," Greasy Lake told them. At last he had the tribe's attention.

"Where was it?" High Shoulders asked — he looked nervously around him, as if he expected to see the Wandering Hill sneaking up on the camp.

"Back on the big plain, two days north of the Shooting Water," Greasy Lake informed them. "And that's still not the worst."

"Go ahead — I know you're dying to tell us the worst!" Walkura remarked sarcastically — too sarcastically, in Greasy Lake's opinion. Sarcasm was well enough when some warriors were just joking around, but it was definitely something a leader ought to resist when real danger was being described.

Still, Greasy Lake did his best to hold his temper.

"The English witch walked right by it and the devils didn't kill her," Greasy Lake reported. "The little witch even climbed it partway, and yet the devils did nothing."

There was silence.

"To my mind that proves that all the English are witches — we ought to catch them and put them to death right away," Greasy Lake insisted.

"It would be easier if the Sin Killer and all the trappers weren't there to protect them," a third elder, old Skinny Foot, observed.

"The trappers stay drunk all day," Na-Ta-Ha observed.

"Drunk or not, those trappers are hard fighters," Walkura remarked. "Are you sure it was the Wandering Hill?"

"Of course — it even had that little tree on top," Greasy Lake told them.

Walkura hadn't paid much attention to Greasy Lake's talk of the Bear people and the English witches — that kind of information was often only a matter of opinion. Things could easily be exaggerated — in fact most of the bad news Greasy Lake spread around was exaggerated. All serious leaders knew how unreliable his information was likely to be.

But no one, not even Greasy Lake, would be so foolish as to lie about the Wandering

Hill. Only last year three Crow warriors were said to have fallen victim to the devils' deadly arrows. Greasy Lake, though irritating, was not an utter fool. It might be that there *was* a connection between the English witches and the Wandering Hill.

As a leader such a problem was one he couldn't entirely ignore, though that was a pity, because Walkura was feeling lazy. He had caught a new wife while on a recent raid to California, a fine girl of the Modoc tribe. She was a plump, jolly creature, and, once she got over the fact of capture, had become increasingly amorous. Walkura had planned to spend the rest of the summer doing a little fishing, a little hunting, and a lot of copulating. The last thing he had contemplated was the need to make a hasty war on the trappers, most of whom were formidable fighters. The presence of witches made matters even more complicated. The first thing he needed to do, Walkura decided, was to send a reliable man up to the big rendezvous, to see how many trappers were there and what kind of weaponry they had.

The young braves, of course, had no interest in a sober assessment of the situation with the trappers.

At once they set about sharpening all their weapons, honing axes and knives, fitting new strings to their bows, and firing off what few guns they had to be sure that they would still shoot. A few even began to paint themselves, though nobody had told them a battle was imminent.

After watching all this militant behavior for a few hours, Walkura — who was not young — began to be affected by what he was seeing. Watching the young men prance around with tomahawks and race here and there on their horses, he began to feel the tingle of war feelings himself. Was he not the greatest war chief of the Utes? Had he not taken thousands of horses from the Californians? Wasn't the big powwow of the trappers a brazen affront to Ute sovereignty? Little by little his mood shifted. Soon he began to gather up his own weapons, making sure they were as they should be. Was he not still the leader? How dare the young braves act as if they could just go make war anytime, whether he approved or not! Soon he had dispensed runners to other Ute bands nearby, telling them to gather up their battle gear and get ready for a good fight. He didn't bother to send a man to the rendezvous to check out Greasy Lake's reports, or ascertain the strength of the mountain men. As he got more and more steamed up, it seemed to him that the more mountain men there were, the better: however many there were, the mighty Ute warriors would soon make an end to them all. Then, once more, the ponds and streams would fill with beaver, whose furs would belong only to the Utes.

Walkura did not have to wait long for a response from the other bands, either. By the next afternoon warriors began to stream in, ready for a fine war against the trappers.

Seeing that his words had not gone unheeded, Greasy Lake caught his horse, who had been grazing on good summer grass, and slipped away. It was good that the Utes were finally going to act like men and kill the trappers. He hoped they killed the various English witches too, or at least took them captive, so they could be tortured properly, as witches should be. But he himself was a shaman, not a fighting man; his task was merely to understand the nature of the world, and the many things in it, from clouds to spiders. His policy had always been to stay as far as possible from the scenes of battles. Once men got to fighting they were apt to be careless — bullets or arrows might easily fly off in the wrong direction and kill whoever happened to be in their way. Greasy Lake wanted to avoid such dangers; he thought he might go south and meditate awhile beside the Platte River, on what his cousins the Sioux called the Holy Road. Along the Holy Road he might enjoy a quiet time, and do some thinking, without having to worry about arrows or bullets flying out of some big battle to wound him. News of whatever happened near the Green River, between the trappers and the Utes, would reach him soon enough. In the more and more crowded plains there would always be somebody to bring the news.

By the time he left the Utes, just at dusk, the encampment was already filling with warriors from other bands. The whites were going to be in for a hard tussle with these angry Utes, that was for sure.

That night, to be safe, Greasy Lake climbed up in a tree to sleep. He had come back east, meaning to slip quietly past the camp of the trappers, but then he bethought himself of the big grizzly bear that had been in that vicinity only the night before. That bear might still be near. The best thing to do was find a good stout tree and doze for a few hours high in its branches. A bear that large would probably not be able to climb high enough to get him.

In fact no bear came to trouble his slumbers, which were light in any case. He never slept deeply, or long — his life required alertness from him; deep sleep could make a man slow to respond.

Just as he was dozing off Greasy Lake thought he heard a flutter above him, which annoyed him somewhat. The bird most likely to be hunting at that time of night would be an owl — and if it was an owl he would have to change trees at once — owls were extremely bad medicine, and particularly bad if one happened to be a shaman. Owls were very jealous of shamans, because the shamans rivaled them in knowledge; as a consequence owls always did what they could to arrange shamans' deaths. There was some moonlight, just enough so that, when he wiggled around, he could clearly see the bird, only a foot above him; it was not an owl but only the white witches' talking bird. He himself had heard the bird speak two or three times — it mostly seemed to talk to the Broken Hand, and usually just cackled out a strange word or two, in a tongue the shaman could not understand. Greasy Lake was relieved that he wasn't dealing with a great horned owl, the most deadly owl of all — on the other hand he wasn't happy that the talking bird had followed him. It might be a sign that the witches didn't intend to let him get away. Greasy Lake thought he had a good solution to that problem: while the old parrot dozed, Greasy Lake reached up, grabbed him, and with one motion wrung his neck, making a speedy end to the witches' talking bird. If those English witches wanted to keep track of an experienced shaman such as himself, they would have to come up with something better than an old green bird who was slow to fly.

58

. . . she indifferently bared a breast . . .

The three little boys — Monty, Talley, and
Charlie — two of them new to the complex
art of crawling, and the third, Charlie, just
beginning to walk, were all of them struggling, each at his own pace, to reach the bear
cub Andy, who lolled on his belly, regarding
their approach without alarm, when, to the
blank astonishment of the grown-ups who
were idly watching — in this case Jim Snow,
Jim Bridger, Billy Sublette, and Eulalie
Bonneville — the blow was struck that was
to echo in mountain legend for many seasons. Tasmin Berrybender, a little unsteady
on her feet from having quaffed two glasses
of William Ashley's cool champagne but firm
of purpose nonetheless, walked up, made a
fist, and, without a word being said, drew
back her arm and struck her husband such a
solid and forceful punch in the eye that he
fell backward off the log where he had been
sitting.

The mountain men could only gape in
dismay, but the bear cub, Andy, not liking
what he saw, at once wandered off to seek

protection with Pomp Charbonneau, to the shocked disappointment of his three small pursuers.

Lord Albany Berrybender, several sheets to the wind himself, thanks to the generosity with which William Ashley dispensed his excellent champagne, merely chuckled at the sight, though William Ashley himself was as startled as the mountain men.

"Good Lord — she's knocked Jimmy over — I confess I never expected to see *that!*" Ashley remarked.

"Not wise to cross Tassie when she's in her cups," Lord B. remarked. "Apt to be bellicose when she drinks. Gets it from me, I fear. I've challenged many a man as a result of good champagne. Frankly didn't expect to meet with such excellent champagne this far out in the wild."

William Ashley, who had long since sold his interest in the Rocky Mountain Fur Company, but continued to come to the rendezvous just for love of the wild, had not expected the Berrybenders, either. He knew they were in the West but had supposed that Lord Berrybender would long since have had his fill of hunting and would sensibly have gone back down the river to Saint Louis. And yet, there they were, Lord Berrybender shorn of part of a leg, much of a foot, and three fingers of a hand — and there stood Lady Tasmin, a ruddy, well-browned Western

girl now, her fists doubled up, clearly prepared to do battle if her husband — by
common consent one of the most volatile of
the mountain men — chose to stand up and
fight.

Jim Bridger, Billy Sublette, and rotund
Eulalie Bonneville, though deeply puzzled,
were nonetheless well aware that they were in
the company of a very angry woman, a creature as much to be feared as any bear. Quietly they got up off the log and moved away.
It would be impolite to run, as Andy, the
bear cub, had done, and yet all of them were
rapidly making tracks.

Jim Snow was so startled that he merely
sat where he had fallen. That Tasmin was
very angry he had no doubt — but why?
They had finally straggled peacefully enough
into the big camp in the Valley of the
Chickens. Of course, Will Ashley had lots of
liquor handy: many of the boys only bothered
to show up at the rendezvous because of
Ashley's whiskey. The champagne Ashley kept
cool in a nearby stream was weak stuff compared to the raw spirits most of the trappers
drank. Hugh Glass in particular scorned
champagne, which he contended was no
more than sour water. Thirsty from her long
trip, Tasmin had quaffed a glass or two, as
did the others, but Jim did not immediately
connect the fact that Tasmin punched him to
Will Ashley's champagne. The morning had

been peaceful. Their son had been trying to pet the little bear cub, and then Tasmin had walked over, her face suddenly dark with fury, and knocked him off the log where he had been sitting with the boys. It was a wrong thing to do, of course — a wife shouldn't strike a husband; but there she was, her fists doubled up, quite prepared to punch him again. For the moment Jim was too shocked even to attempt to correct her — it occurred to him that she might somehow have lost her mind.

"That's for striking me last winter and knocking me out of our tent and causing me to scrape my leg quite painfully on the ice," Tasmin said, her blood up. She was fully prepared for a fierce fight. The minute Jim stood up she meant to slug him again. But Jim didn't stand up. Most of the camp was by now watching the conflict. All heads turned, all conversation ceased. Kit Carson looked especially worried.

"All right, then, coward," Tasmin told him. "But if you ever strike me again, I'll certainly do worse."

Then she whirled on the trappers, who were staring from what they had supposed was a safe distance.

"You are all invited to stop looking at me as if I've lost my sanity — I'm speaking to you, Mr. Bridger, and you, Mr. Bonneville. I have not lost my sanity, I was merely revenging an old injustice. Perhaps you too would like a punch."

Tasmin felt very much in the mood to throw something — she was filled with the same ugly and frustrated feelings that had once caused her to heave her father's hunting seat as far as she could throw it. In this instance the only thing she could see to throw was the jug of coarse whiskey which the trappers had been passing around. She at once picked it up and heaved it; by luck it smashed on a rock, which gave her a feeling of great satisfaction, though this feeling diminished once she saw that neither Jim Snow nor any of the trappers seemed inclined to fight. The sharp smell of whiskey stung her nostrils. Irritated beyond endurance by the mildness of these men who were supposed to be so fierce and wild, she walked up and gave Eulalie Bonneville a good hard punch in the mouth, then walked away, right past her son. Frustrated by the departure of the bear cub, and seeing his mother near, Monty reached out, hoping to be picked up, but his Tasmin strode right past him. She crossed the meadow and continued into a little glade, deep enough that she felt sure no one could see her; she then burst into a torrent of tears, but a brief torrent. The fit passed, her head began to clear, she felt happy to have finally got her own back with Jim, and she looked out with amusement at the scene she had created. Several of the mountain men were peering uneasily at the glade into which she had disappeared. But no one followed her, least of all her husband, which showed a serious lack of instinct vis-à-vis the female, she felt. She had stopped being mad but was yet filled with a feeling that an experienced seducer could have turned this to his amorous advantage. Her husband was not such a seducer — why could men not learn?

Tasmin resolved to stay right where she was. She did not mean to apologize, be meek, explain. She waited, deep in her glade, to see what the trappers, those terrors of the mountain, might do about her. Would her husband venture over? Since the moment when anger might have become lust had passed, Tasmin ceased to care. She suspected that the eventual mediator would be the mild, passionless Pomp Charbonneau, or, if not Pomp, perhaps it would be the rather prissy fur trader William Ashley.

Jim Snow finally stood up — he went over and began to talk to Pomp, whom Tasmin had come to regard more or less as her own possession. Then Pomp went over and chatted a bit with Ashley. Monty, meanwhile, began to fret. With no bear handy to play with, he remembered that he was hungry. Jim picked him up, failed to soothe him, and passed him off to Little Onion, who quieted him but, of course, could not give him suck.

Looking rather annoyed herself, Little Onion handed the baby to Pomp. Then he and Will Ashley together wandered over toward the glade where Tasmin watched. That the men felt the need to come in twos annoyed her again so that when they walked up with her hungry baby she indifferently bared a breast and delayed a moment or two before putting her child to the teat. This was mainly meant as a challenge to the affable Pomp, who had once told her that he was rarely troubled by lust, a stupid thing to say to a woman, even if true. Let him look at her breast and reflect on what lay below — that a man should decline to lust she considered an insult. Tasmin was of half a notion to see if she could change Pomp's mind on that score but for the moment, with Ashley there, she merely regarded the nervous ambassadors with all the hauteur she could muster.

"I guess you had your reasons for punching Jim," Pomp said — "but why'd you hit Bonney?"

"Because he's fat, I suppose," Tasmin said. "Besides, I needed a second victim to complete my attack on male complacency. It's your fault, really, Mr. Ashley, for providing the champagne."

Monty, by now, was guzzling heartily.

"When I drink champagne," Tasmin continued, "memories of old injustices — and there have been many — just seem to bubble up. Claret makes me amorous, but champagne makes me mean."

William Ashley managed a negligent shrug.

"Our esteemed captain, William Clark, has ever maintained that there is no wildness equal to the wildness in women," he said.

"How exquisitely philosophical," Tasmin replied coolly.

"Perhaps he said it about my mother — the two of them were close friends," Pomp remarked, hoping to change the subject, or mollify Tasmin somehow.

"I met Captain Clark," Tasmin reminded them. "He did not strike me as being a man who was free of lust."

"Oh hardly," William Ashley agreed. "No stranger to the battery of Venus, our Captain Clark, I can tell you that."

"How quaintly that sounds, how romantic," Tasmin replied. "The battery of Venus. My own first lover, Master Tobias Stiles, had little of the poet in him, I'm afraid. 'Cunt' was the term he preferred: blunt but adequate, like himself."

Both men retreated a step.

"Goodness, Tasmin," Pomp said, too deeply startled to hide a blush. "Goodness."

"Don't you chide me, Pomp," Tasmin remarked menacingly. The fires of her anger had been banked but were not extinguished.

"We Berrybenders *will* speak as we please," she continued. "I fear I've come rather to distrust the poetical when it comes to amorous matters. Plain speech and stout action are what's wanted — none of this battery of Venus folderol. You yourself, Pomp, would be a happier man if there were a bit more coarseness in you."

Pomp *was* shocked — he looked, to Tasmin's eye, virginal. Could it be that he had never even had a look at the article being discussed? It was the seat of life, of course, but rather likely to disappoint those who thought in terms of lovely locks, perfect breasts, and other goddesslike attributes, as imagined by the painters and the poets.

Then, in a moment, her mood turned, where Pomp Charbonneau was concerned. The thought that he might indeed be a virgin, might never have ventured into the wilderness between a woman's legs, made her feel protective of him suddenly. Shy Pomp, sweet Pomp — she wondered if she mightn't yet have to help him, guide him in.

"Do excuse me, Pomp, and you too, Mr. Ashley," she said. "I have a rough tongue — hope I haven't bruised your finer sensibilities. I keep forgetting that it is men who are tender souls. We women have our babies to make, and the brute necessities of the business may make us rather coarse."

She shifted Monty to the other breast, half of a mind to pour out more abuse — but the two men were careful to offer her no challenge, so, as an alternative, she went and sat in the sun with Coal and Vicky Kennet. The two bear cubs, seeing the prospect of attention, came over and licked the babies' faces, causing all three to sneeze.

Tasmin looked around for Jim, wondering when he might get around to taking up the difficult challenge of their marriage again. But Jim was shoeing horses, with the help of Joe Walker and Milt Sublette. He glanced her way once or twice but clearly didn't seem to feel that they had to have a reckoning, just then. In Tasmin's view, once she calmed down, that was just as well. Probably her punch took him so completely by surprise that his temper had failed to flare. Shock smothered it. When they could talk she meant to warn him that she could not be trusted when she drank champagne.

When Pomp next strolled by, Tasmin went over and took his arm, to show that no hard feelings remained.

"Don't you be telling on me, Pomp," she said quietly. "Don't be mentioning my coarse speech to Jimmy — he's rather a Puritan when it comes to such things."

"I won't," Pomp promised — in fact the unexpected scene with Tasmin had left him feeling somewhat sad.

"Anyway, you were right," he continued. "I'm the one who doesn't know anything about love."

There was a droop in his voice when he said this, an admittance of loneliness and inexperience that touched Tasmin's heart. She put a friendly arm around him.

"Now, Pomp — cheer up," she said. "You're young — no need to pine. I expect we just need to find you a girl."

Pomp smiled, but did not reply.

Jim Snow, punched in the eye by his wife, supposed that he would forever be a figure of fun among the mountain men. His wife had hit him and he had done nothing about it — of course, she had struck Eulalie Bonneville too, but Bonney was not married to her and bore no responsibility for her behavior.

Jim had hustled over quietly and begun to help out with the horseshoeing, expecting ridicule from the likes of Hugh Glass or old Zeke Williams, who had just arrived at the rendezvous, but, to his surprise, the fact that he was married to a woman of such pure fire produced the very opposite of the effect he had feared. Instead of falling, his stock rose.

"That's some fine gal, that wife of yours," Hugh Glass said. "Must be like living with a she-bear — wild and wilder."

"I suppose it makes Indian fighting seem like a picnic," Jim Bridger ventured. He felt lucky to have avoided being struck himself. Tasmin had favored him with an angry look just before she punched Eulalie.

Jim didn't reply — he worked. But it was

clear that the fact that he had gone so far as to father a child on such a woman made a big impression on the mountain men, a few of whom had been a bit skeptical of his abilities, previously. Several of them didn't think he was actually much of a Sin Killer, but Tasmin's utter fearlessness when she walked over and hit him at once banished all skepticism. A man who could hold his own with such a woman was indeed a man to be reckoned with. Jim shrugged off these awed remarks. He himself wasn't so sure that he *could* hold his own with Tasmin — but it was a welcome thing that so many of the boys thought he could.

In the afternoon an Indian wandered into camp and reported that there was a good flock of mountain sheep on the lower slope of a large hill just to the east: at once Jim and Pomp and Drum Stewart grabbed horses and guns — the bighorn sheep were the one species that had successfully eluded the restless Scot.

Tasmin was determined not to let Jim go without his at least acknowledging the fact that she had punched him in the eye.

"I suppose you're mad at me for having punched you," she said, as Jim was tightening his girth.

Jim had the look in his eye that men get when they have more important matters to attend to than anything that might possibly involve women — a maddening look.

"I guess I'll stay out of your way next time you're drunk," he told her. "I bet Bonney stays out of your way, too. He claims he's got a sore tooth."

Jim then raced off — once the hunters were gone, Tasmin went over and made a fine apology to Eulalie Bonneville.

"I'm so sorry I struck you, Mr. Bonneville," she said. "I fear I was very drunk."

"It is of no importance at all," Eulalie said. "I too often strike people when I'm drunk — particularly fat people."

Tasmin laughed. "How's that tooth?" she asked.

"Thank you for inquiring — the agony has somewhat abated," Eulalie said, with great formality. In fact he was terrified of well-spoken ladies such as Tasmin — his preference was for silent Indian girls who scarcely said a word a week.

The hunters did not reappear that evening — it had been late in the day when they left to go chase the sheep.

In the white foggy dawn Tasmin and Vicky Kennet sat by a low campfire, sipping coffee, their babies in their laps, when William Ashley wandered up, an unlit cigar in his mouth. He picked up a burning stick from the fire, lit the cigar, and took several deep puffs as he surveyed the layer of fog that enveloped the Valley of the Chickens.

"Ladies, what say we breakfast on a little champagne?" he suggested, just as Lord Berrybender appeared.

"I mustn't — it makes me mean," Tasmin told him.

"I'll drink hers, then, Ashley — and mine too," Lord B. said. "I'm rather past the dueling age, so I guess I can drink all the bubbly I want."

The trappers who had not gone on the hunt had drunk and caroused all night. Vicky Kennet and her old lover, Lord Berrybender, wandered down to a big campfire the mountain men had built, but Tasmin stayed with William Ashley — she was curious why a man who was said to be so wealthy would put himself at risk every year to journey to such a wild place.

"You're not a hunter, like my papa," Tasmin said to him. "Why do you come?"

William Ashley considered the question.

"Addiction, Lady Tasmin," he replied. "Some men can't stop drinking whiskey, some can't stop taking opium, and I can't stop seeking the wild. I like to be where I can smell it . . . imbibe it . . . the pure wild, if you will."

"But, sir, you've come so far," she reminded him. "Is there really such an insufficiency of wildness between Saint Louis and this remote place? And besides, if we're here — all the way from Northamptonshire — how pure can the wildness be?"

William Ashley smiled — he *did* like the way this English girl put things. One moment she might be calling a cunt a cunt, and the next referring coolly to such a concept as an insufficiency of wildness.

"That's an excellent point — you're here and your civilization will soon follow along," he said. "That's the sadness, Lady Tasmin — there's not much time between first man and last man, between wild and settled. Jed Smith and Zeke Williams and I were the first white men to see this pretty valley here. We saw beaver who had never had to fear the trap, and buffalo that had never heard the sound of a gun. That was scarcely twenty years ago, and yet the beaver are almost gone and the buffalo will go next. Then, if there turns out to be gold or silver or anything a merchant can sell in these hills, they'll tear the very mountains down and rip out whatever it is."

He looked, for a moment, sad.

"I come so I won't forget, ma'am," he said. "I want to remember the wonderful country as it was before it changed."

"Personally, I find it quite wild enough," Tasmin told him. "I can easily imagine a tribe of painted savages pouring out of those trees to kill us all, which would be *more* than wild enough for me."

"Oh no, Lady Tasmin — that sort of thing

won't happen," Ashley assured her. "We've been having our rendezvous here in this valley for eight years — the Utes and the other tribes have come to tolerate us pretty well. I have never been one to underestimate the need for presents, when you're treating with the native peoples. Everybody likes presents, you know. A wagonful of good presents, properly distributed, will take the fight out of most savages, given time."

Scarcely had he finished speaking than he heard the sound of thundering hooves and the scream and yip of war cries — along a ridge at the far eastern end of the valley, bent low over their horses, Jim and Pomp were racing for their lives, pursued by a wild horde of painted savages, such as Tasmin had just mentioned.

William Ashley, looking extremely startled, dropped his cigar — few of his statements had ever been contradicted so immediately.

"I can only think that you must have chosen the wrong presents, this year, Mr. Ashley," Tasmin said, with some indignation. "And now, worse luck, we're all going to be murdered, as a result."

454

59

. . . the deep grass of summer would cover him with its peace . . .

From Walkura's point of view the attack on the trappers could not have got off to a better start. The minute the big raiding party saw the three hunters and sent up their first war whoops, the tall hunter's horse bolted, carrying him right into the midst of the Utes. There was nothing the man could do to turn his panicked mount. The Utes were startled by this piece of luck, but not so startled as to miss such an easy chance to count coup. They immediately hacked the unhappy rider to pieces — it was what he got for choosing an unreliable horse. High Shoulders tried to scalp him and made a botch of it — he had never taken a scalp before — but already, with the battle just joined, several Ute hatchets were dripping blood, the best possible encouragement when one was going into battle.

"I wish it had been the Sin Killer," Na-Ta-Ha said, but of course that was only wishful thinking. The Sin Killer, and the hunter they called Six Tongues, because he could speak easily with many tribes, had a good jump on them. Both rode fleet mares, and were not going to be easily overtaken.

Still, with one easy kill under their belts, Walkura led the Utes in a wild charge into the Valley of the Chickens, confident that the day would be theirs and there would be many scalps to take home.

Unhappily this confidence only lasted until the charging warriors dropped off the ridge at the eastern end of the hunters' encampment and saw that the valley was covered with a thick white fog from one end to the other. Walkura had only seconds in which to make a decision. What to do? His warriors were in full charge — to halt now, after they had already made a kill, would very likely dampen enthusiasm for the battle ahead. If the Utes had to pull up and wait for the fog to clear, many of the warriors would probably lose interest in the fighting and go home. Some of them were so greedy that they might wipe off their war paint and claim innocence, in the hope that the generous Ashley would give them presents. After all, it was only because of an erratic horse that they had killed the white man — what were they supposed to do when a white man with a rifle rode into their midst?

"The witches made it foggy!" old No Teeth yelled — he had no business even being in the battle but had not been able to resist a chance to deal with the white witches.

Walkura ignored him and charged into the fog. He didn't need witches to explain a fog — the days were warm and the nights chill, and that explained the fog — which didn't make the problem any less disastrous to the Utes' battle plan, which involved taking the trappers by surprise and hoping they were too drunk to react quickly. In the night, getting himself ready for the fight, something had been nagging at Walkura's mind, something pertaining to the battle, but everyone in the camp was talking at once and the young warriors were placing bets on which mountain man they would kill — Walkura could never quite remember the factor he felt he might be failing to consider; but now, as his horse raced off the ridge right into a wall of thick white fog, he remembered what he had forgotten: the likelihood of early morning fog!

Only, now he was *in* the fog, and his warriors were in it too, still in full cry — and there was not a thing to be seen. It was as bad as going into battle in a white blizzard. Walkura didn't know what to do — the warriors were pressing on, right behind him; he now rather regretted that his vanity had prompted him to lead the charge. Now, if he wasn't lucky, he might be struck down by his own men; their blood was up, they would strike at anything they could see, and perhaps, once they got nervous, at things they *couldn't* see. Walkura was actually less worried about the danger of the mountain men, who were not likely to shoot their guns unless they could see a target. The Utes, with their dripping hatchets, were, for the moment, a worse threat.

Walkura cautiously pulled up his horse. He didn't want to race along and smack into a rock, and, as he remembered, there were several rocky outcroppings at the eastern end of the valley — it occurred to him that he might do well to veer to the north, where there was higher ground. He might get higher, above the fog, and gain at least some sense of where the combatants were as the battle proceeded.

Cautiously, Walkura turned north — the fine fury that had led him to charge into battle was quickly giving way to a feeling of glumness, even failure. What had he done now? He might have been home enjoying a bit of amorous activity with his Modoc girl, but, instead, he had let old Greasy Lake's wild talk of bears and witches and the Wandering Hill lead him into launching a foolish raid into the Valley of the Chickens. Those who questioned his leadership anyway — and there were always people who questioned a leader's decisions — would point out the obvious fact that he should have expected to find fog in such a valley in the early morning at that time of year. The fact that they had only launched the charge because they had jumped the three hunters would not matter to such people, who made a pastime of finding fault with his leadership. Even though they had killed a hunter, the naysayers would claim that this was no excuse for forgetting about the likelihood of fog — never mind the fact that once a bunch of Utes had killed a white man and were yelling their war cries and racing their horses, the last thing they would want to hear was that it was foggy up ahead.

Overhead, the sun was only a pale yellow ring — how Walkura wished it would gather strength and burn away this fog while there was still a chance of fighting. But the sun was weak yet, and everyone, whites and Utes alike, was groping around in a clinging mist, their weapons useless, their spirits sinking, as his were.

On one or two occasions Walkura thought he saw a shadow that might be a person — he had an arrow ready, but then realized, each time, that the shadow was only a tree. What amazed him was how totally this fog had managed to swallow his war party of nearly thirty warriors. They had all plunged into the fog and now there was not a trace of them — not a sound could be heard. For a moment Walkura thought he might locate a warrior or two by whistling like the prairie hens for which the valley was named; but he soon discarded that option. He had never been able to do birdcalls very well — if he flubbed his imitation he would only give his position away. What he had begun to wish for, as he inched his way north, was a means for just calling it all off and starting the day over. Only one life had been lost, and that had been an accident. There was no real need for this battle. The whites were irritating, of course, but at least they brought good presents. Why couldn't they just explain the accident, smoke a peace pipe, do a little trading, and perhaps have a few horse races once the fog lifted?

It was fun to plan a battle, rattle weapons, and dance and puff oneself up, but when something like this fog comes along and spoils everything, why try to pretend that there is still a chance for a glorious fight? If a warrior bumped into a trapper and they wanted to go at it, Walkura had no objection. But the big Ute assault had failed; the fog had just swallowed it up.

As Walkura picked his way carefully north, thinking these gloomy thoughts, the fog began to lighten a little. He thought he heard something like a bear, though not a full-grown bear. Then, for a moment, the fog broke in front of him and he saw not one but two young bears, cubs still, growling and rolling around with each other, having a playful tussle. When he realized that the bears were just cubs, his annoyance with Greasy Lake increased. Were these the Bear people the witches were supposed to be talking to?

Then Walkura saw one of the little witches, a girl just old enough to begin to be a woman, standing not far from the cubs, watching them roll around in play — he wondered if he ought to capture this girl — it wouldn't hurt to have two young wives, after all. But then the swift Six Tongues appeared out of the fog. He had a gun but didn't raise it — he seemed to want the girl to help him catch the cubs and carry them down into the safety of the fog.

Walkura at once loosed an arrow at Six Tongues — a good shot, too — but before his arrow even struck Six Tongues, Walkura suddenly tumbled off his horse. To his surprise, when he tried to rise, he saw that a limb had grown out of his chest. It took him several moments to focus his eyes and determine that the object protruding from his chest wasn't a limb, it was an arrow; and there stood the Sin Killer, ready to loose a second arrow from his bow. Walkura could not see Six Tongues, who must have wandered down into the fog. Walkura thought he had probably killed the man, but there was no way to be sure. What he *was* sure of was that the Sin Killer, a man some Utes scoffed

461

at as being no very good fighter, had just drawn his own heart's blood. Walkura felt mildly surprised: few white men could use the bow so well. He got to his knees and tried to grip the arrow hard and rip it from his breast; but quickly and quietly his grip loosened, his strength left him, his hands fell away; he slumped to his side and then lay back. He wondered if the Sin Killer would want to scalp him — but no one came, no scalp knife bit; the sky that should be growing lighter grew darker instead, grew as dark as deepest night. For a time, with the steady pulsing out of his blood, Walkura felt a sense of rise and fall, of soaring and dipping; beneath his palms he felt the grass, the good grass of summer, wet a little from the fog, the grass that fed buffalo and elk, antelope and doe — soon, Walkura knew, he would be one with all that had been, and the deep grass of summer would cover him with its peace; he did not feel sad, though he did regret, a little, that he had not had more time with that lively Modoc girl.

60

"I'll see that he wants to!" she said.

Na-Ta-Ha was not one to suppress his criticisms when he thought a raid had been handled badly; and few raids of recent years had resulted in such a complete botch as the raid Walkura had led on the trappers who were gathered with Ashley in the Valley of the Chickens. It was true that they had made an immediate kill, but that was the result of panic on the part of the hunter's horse — panic that brought the victim right into their midst.

Then, after that promising beginning, Walkura had insisted on plunging the warriors into a fog so blinding that they had to slow their horses to a walk, after which the whole war party picked its way timorously through the Valley of the Chickens, never making contact with a single trapper.

"I might have hit one trapper," High Shoulders said. "I think I ran over somebody just as we ran into that fog."

"You think, but you don't know," Na-Ta-Ha countered. "You probably just ran over a dog."

The Utes, who had ridden east to west through the valley, were on their way home. Nobody could expect warriors to fight in fog that thick — there was no reason to apologize for their retreat. Walkura had been in the lead when they all plunged into the fog, so everyone assumed he was somewhere up ahead.

"You watch — he'll be sitting there ready with a lot of excuses when we get home. He's an old man. He's been to the Valley of the Chickens before. He should have known there would be fog."

Most of the warriors, disappointed because there had been no chance to kill trappers or witches, agreed wholeheartedly with Na-Ta-Ha's criticisms.

But then Walkura's horse came galloping up from the rear, and Walkura wasn't on him, a fact that immediately contradicted Na-Ta-Ha's theory.

It was then that High Shoulders remembered that old No Teeth had been with them — they had all tried to make him stay at home but he defied them and had been racing along happily when they all dashed into the fog.

"I don't see No Teeth, either," High Shoulders said.

There was an uneasy pause — their war chief and their medicine man both seemed to be missing.

High Shoulders, with the boldness of youth, spat out a harsh opinion.

"We were chasing the Sin Killer, remember?" he reminded everyone. "The Sin Killer probably killed them both."

Na-Ta-Ha felt uncomfortable with that theory. What if the boy was right? What if he himself had just been criticizing a war chief who had died heroically, a victim of the deadly Sin Killer, the man who had driven a lance through a Piegan? If that turned out to be the case, Walkura's relatives, some of whom were in the war party, would never let him forget his wild criticisms. Na-Ta-Ha immediately changed his tack.

"We have to go back," he declared. "If those two are dead we have to recover their bodies — or else we'll be disgraced."

"And if we do go back we'll probably be killed ourselves, by the Sin Killer or Bridger or the Broken Hand," High Shoulders announced.

Bitter as the prospect was, the war party immediately turned back toward the Valley of the Chickens. They would be disgraced forever if they failed to see that the body of their great war chief, Walkura, was brought home and given proper burial.

When they reached the Valley of the Chickens the fog had long since burned off and the whites were themselves conducting a burial down by the river. A tall woman was playing an instrument that gave off very mournful music. The music was so sad-making that several of the warriors were close to tears, although they had no idea who was being buried.

When the whites noticed that the Utes had come back, Na-Ta-Ha hastily made the peace sign and old Sharbo, looking very sad, walked over to parley with them. He told them it was the old lord's son they were burying — he had been returning from the creek and had been fatally trampled in their wild charge.

"There — I knew I ran over somebody," High Shoulders observed.

Sharbo confirmed that both Walkura and No Teeth were dead. It seemed that Walkura had shot an arrow into Six Tongues, who was Sharbo's son. Six Tongues was not dead, but the arrow was near his heart and had not been removed, which was why Sharbo looked so worried.

"But if Walkura shot Six Tongues, who shot him?" one warrior wanted to know. Walkura had always been quick to discharge arrows — it was hard to imagine anyone beating him at that game.

"The Sin Killer," Sharbo said — his face was drawn and gray.

By the river the Englishwomen and a few of the mountain men were singing over the dead boy — their voices carried far. The

466

Utes did not consider it polite to linger any longer, or parley anymore — not while death songs were being sung. One Ute asked Sharbo if he thought that, after a day or two had passed, it might still be possible for them to do a little trading with Ashley. Sharbo said he didn't think Ashley would object — trading was the point of the rendezvous, after all. The Utes solemnly gathered up the two bodies and rode away with them. It was not clear what had happened to No Teeth, but he was known to be a reckless rider, more reckless than expert. Probably his horse had run into a tree, or pitched him off into some rocks. There was not a mark on him — he even seemed to be smiling. The cynical view was that he had overmatched himself when it came to the white witches. No Teeth was always bragging about how slowly and professionally he would put the white witches to death — and yet now it was No Teeth who was dead. No doubt the white witches had known the old shaman was coming and had used the fog to lay a clever — indeed, fatal — trap for him.

Tasmin sang dutifully over the grave of her unfortunate brother Bobbety Berrybender, whom she had so often ridiculed. He had been calmly pursuing his interest in freshwater *Mollusca* and had started to the camp for breakfast when he happened to walk right in front of thirty charging horses. Buffum

467

was nearly hysterical with grief, and Father Geoffrin not much better. How sad it was, Tasmin thought, to be dead on a day of such beauty, for, once the fog lifted, the valley was so lovely that merely looking at it produced a kind of ache. The fog that had doomed young Bobbety had saved the rest of them from attack — beauty and death thus closely bound together, as Tasmin supposed it often must be.

"He was ever my ally in family quarrels, Tassie . . . I shall be very lonely without him," Buffum sobbed.

The little priest, sad, small, and trembly, seemed shrunken with regret.

"I knew we ought to have taken that nice boat back down the river," Father Geoffrin said. "We could have gone straight to Paris and bought lots of clothes — and now we never shall."

Jim Snow had carried Pomp down the hill and laid him on blankets in William Ashley's wagon. Several of the mountain men looked at the arrow and shook their heads, so close to the heart was it. Hugh Glass was the only other trapper to have sustained an injury — he had stepped on a shard from the whiskey jug Tasmin had broken and cut his big toe to the bone.

As soon as the last hymns of requiem were sung over Bobbety, Tasmin rushed back to Pomp. She was torn by the knowledge of how cruel she had been to him, only the day before — he who had been so loyal through so much. As she rushed up the slope she was hoping that somehow Jim had pulled the arrow out, and that she might see Pomp smiling his diffident smile again. Instead she found Ashley, Jim, and the two bear cubs, both whining miserably, sure that something was wrong.

Pomp was still alive, but his breathing was shallow and irregular, his pulse anything but strong.

"What can we do, Jim?" she asked; but her resourceful husband for once had no answer.

"You might ask the priest," Jim told her. "He got that bullet out of Cook — maybe he could ease this arrow out."

Tasmin went to look for Father Geoffrin, who was still down at Bobbety's grave. The mountain men all sat around disconsolately, talking in low tones, drinking little. Joe Walker incautiously voiced the opinion that they might as well start digging a second grave — Tasmin at once whirled on him.

"No such thing, Mr. Walker," she said. "Pomp Charbonneau is going to live — I'm just hurrying off to talk to his surgeon now."

Father Geoffrin still sat by Bobbety's grave, sipping from a cup of brandy, which he at once offered to share with Tasmin. She took a searing swallow.

When Tasmin asked him if he would at

least try to cut the arrow out of Pomp, Father Geoff flexed his fingers thoughtfully.

"It's the arteries that worry me," he said. "If I nick one, our good Pomp will quietly bleed to death."

"Yes, but if you don't make the attempt, he will certainly die," Tasmin said. Just then old Charbonneau joined them, trailed by Pedro Yanez and Aldo Claricia, neither of them sober. Charbonneau seconded Tasmin's point.

"A Ute put that arrow in my boy, not you," he told the priest. "If my good son dies, it'll be the Ute's doing, not yours. I fear you're the only one among us who has the skill to save him."

Father Geoffrin looked thoughtful for a moment; then he handed the brandy to Tasmin.

"Very well, monsieur," he said. "I had better get to it while the light's good."

Charbonneau, dirty and disordered as ever, tears coursing down his cheeks, sat down wearily by Bobbety Berrybender's grave.

"Here I've been traveling thirty years in these wild places, and not a scratch on me," he said. "And now it's my young Pomp who gets an arrow in him."

"We were nearly killed by a great bear ourselves," Aldo remarked sadly.

Up the slope Tasmin could see a flurry of activity. Cook was heating water. Jim Snow and Kit Carson took the sides off the wagon, so it could be used as an operating table. Jim Bridger fetched more firewood. Father Geoffrin was painstakingly sharpening his knives and laying out his tweezers.

"If only Janey was here," Charbonneau remarked. "Janey could pull him through."

"Who?" Tasmin asked. She had never heard Pomp speak of a Janey. Could it be that he was not so virginal, after all?

"His mother, I mean," Charbonneau continued. "Captain Clark called her Janey — could never quite manage her Indian name."

"I'm going to be with him now," Tasmin said told him. "Will you be coming, monsieur?"

Charbonneau shook his head — he was staring, blank-faced, at the hills across the river. The two short Europeans lingered with him.

When Tasmin reached the arena of the operation, William Ashley was prancing around, looking officious and bossy.

"The danger will be when the arrow comes out," he was saying. "Very likely our Pomp's life will come with it."

"Get out of here and don't talk like that, you goddamn fop!" Tasmin yelled, suddenly furious. There was something she didn't like about Ashley — he seemed the kind of man who might wear scent.

Shocked, William Ashley backed away. Hugh Glass's mouth dropped open — he had been with Ashley on the day of his great defeat by the Arikaras, ten years earlier, but had never seen the man so dismayed — although, on the former occasion, men had been dropping dead all around him.

Tasmin looked around for her husband — as she always did, when she let slip an oath — but Jim was not there.

"Him and Kit went to stand guard," Eulalie Bonneville explained. "Drum Stewart's dead, you know — killed in the first minute, horse bolted, right into the Utes, Jim says."

"Jimmy will never trust the Utes again," Milt Sublette remarked.

The news of the Scot's death barely registered with Tasmin. She moved around by Pomp's head and kept her eyes fixed on him as Father Geoffrin began his work. Tasmin put her mouth close to Pomp's ear and whispered to him.

"I'm here, Pomp," she whispered. "I'm here to help you — don't die, don't you dare."

Very quickly, Father Geoffrin made two cuts and, to everyone's surprise, lifted out the arrow; but before anyone could speak he shook his head.

"Save the bravos," he said. "There's a tip I failed to get — the arrow must have hit a rib. If Cook will just let me have those long tweezers . . ."

472

Silently, Cook handed him the tweezers — the probe was longer this time. Tasmin kept her eyes on Pomp — she whispered again in his ear. She did not want him to get the notion that he was allowed to go.

Pomp, drifting in deep and starless darkness, heard Tasmin speak softly in his ear, saying she was here, she was here; but he couldn't answer. The easeful darkness held him in its lazy power; he floated downward, deeper and deeper into it, as the soaked leaf sinks slowly to the bottom of a pool, to a place deeper than light. Helpless as the leaf he sank and sank, until, instead of Tasmin's voice, he heard, "Jean Baptiste . . . Jean Baptiste!" Then the darkness gave way to the soft light of dream, and there was Sacagawea, his mother, sitting quietly in a field of waving grass, as she had so many times in his dreams. Though her dark eyes welcomed him, the look on her face was grave.

As always in his dreams of Sacagawea, Pomp wanted to rush to her, to be taken in her arms, as he had been as a child; but he could not move. The rules of the dream were severe — old sadness, old frustration pricked him, even though dreams of his mother were the best dreams of all.

As usual, when she visited him in dreams, Sacagawea began to talk in low tones of things that had happened long ago.

"When we were on our way back from the

great ocean I took you up to the top of those white cliffs that rise by the Missouri," she said. "I wanted you to see the great herds, grazing far from the world of men; but you were a young boy then, not even weaned, and I held your hand so you wouldn't step off the edge of life and go too soon to the Sky House, where we all have to go someday. Now that old Ute's arrow has brought you to the edge of life again, but the woman who whispers to you wants to pull you back, as I pulled you back when you were young."

Sacagawea was looking directly at him — Pomp wanted to ask her questions, and yet, as always in his dreams of his mother, he was gripped by a terrible muteness; he could ask no question, make no plea, though he knew that at any time the dream might fade and his mother be lost to him until he visited her in dreams again. With the fear that his dream was ending came a sadness so deep that Pomp did not want to wake up to life, and yet that was just what his mother was urging him to do — she wanted him to listen to Tasmin.

"I did not wean you until you had seen four summers," Sacagawea told him. "My milk was always strong — I filled you with it so that you could live long and enjoy the world of men, the world I showed you when we stood together on the white cliffs. Obey the woman who whispers — it is not time for

474

you to come to the Sky House yet . . ."

Then, with sad swiftness, his mother faded; where her face had been was Tasmin's face, leaning close to his. Pomp tried to smile, but couldn't, not yet. Even so, Tasmin's eyes shone with tears of relief.

At last Father Geoffrin, who had been probing very carefully, withdrew the long tweezers, which contained the tiny, bloody tip of a flint arrow.

"There . . . it's out — and he's not bleeding much," Father Geoffrin said. "I think our good Pomp can live now — if he wants to."

Tasmin had been watching Pomp's face closely. Her heart leapt when he opened his eyes.

"I'll see that he wants to!" she said, over-joyed that her friend had lived.

Father Geoffrin — priest, surgeon, and cynic — raised an eyebrow.

"I expect you will, madame," he said. "I expect you will."

LARRY McMURTRY, winner of the Pulitzer Prize for fiction (*Lonesome Dove*), among other awards, is the author of twenty-five novels, two collections of essays, three memoirs, and more than thirty screenplays, and the editor of an anthology of modern Western fiction. His reputation as a critically acclaimed and bestselling author is unequaled.

The employees of Thorndike Press hope you have enjoyed this Large Print book. All our Thorndike and Wheeler Large Print titles are designed for easy reading, and all our books are made to last. Other Thorndike Press Large Print books are available at your library, through selected bookstores, or directly from us.

For information about titles, please call:

(800) 223-1244

or visit our Web site at:

www.gale.com/thorndike
www.gale.com/wheeler

To share your comments, please write:

Publisher
Thorndike Press
295 Kennedy Memorial Drive
Waterville, ME   04901